HISTORICAL

Your romantic escape to the past.

How Not To Propose To A Duke
Louise Allen

The Marquess's Year To Wed
Paulia Belgado

MILLS & BOON

HOW NOT TO PROPOSE TO A DUKE
© 2024 by Melanie Hilton
Philippine Copyright 2024
Australian Copyright 2024
New Zealand Copyright 2024

First Published 2024
First Australian Paperback Edition 2024
ISBN 978 1 038 90776 9

THE MARQUESS'S YEAR TO WED
© 2024 by Paulia Belgado
Philippine Copyright 2024
Australian Copyright 2024
New Zealand Copyright 2024

First Published 2024
First Australian Paperback Edition 2024
ISBN 978 1 038 90776 9

MIX
Paper | Supporting
responsible forestry
FSC® C001695

Published by
Harlequin Mills & Boon
An imprint of Harlequin Enterprises (Australia) Pty Limited
(ABN 47 001 180 918), a subsidiary of HarperCollins
Publishers Australia Pty Limited
(ABN 36 009 913 517)
Level 19, 201 Elizabeth Street
SYDNEY NSW 2000 AUSTRALIA

Cover art used by arrangement with Harlequin Books S.A.. All rights reserved.

Printed and bound in Australia by McPherson's Printing Group

How Not To Propose To A Duke

Louise Allen

MILLS & BOON

Louise Allen has been immersing herself in history for as long as she can remember, finding that landscapes and places evoke powerful images of the past. Venice, Burgundy and the Greek islands are favorites. Louise lives on the Norfolk coast and spends her spare time gardening, researching family history or traveling. Please visit Louise's website, www.louiseallenregency.com, her blog, www.janeaustenslondon.com, or find her on Twitter @louiseregency and on Facebook.

Visit the Author Profile page
at millsandboon.com.au for more titles.

Author Note

Regency young ladies are supposed to wait modestly for gentlemen to propose to them. Regency dukes are strong, silent types not given to romantic daydreams... Or perhaps not. I wondered what would happen if my heroine decided that she would do the proposing. But, unfortunately for her, as she and I discovered, my hero is a true romantic who is looking for love, not just a very tempting dowry. There is liking there, even friendship, but not love. And then he realises that he really does need that dowry.

How is a romance going to flower with a start like that? I hope you enjoy finding out as much as I did, although here's a spoiler—it all ends in flowers in a riotous London May Day celebration.

DEDICATION

For AJH—the very best of pit crew

Chapter One

London—10th February, 1816

Just knock. And remember to breathe.

Miss Jessica Danby nodded, a sharp, decisive jerk of her head, and Alfred, her footman, trod up the remaining steps and gave a brisk tattoo with the heavy brass knocker.

Beside her Trotter, her maid, made a sound like a faint whimper. Jessica ignored it. Ignored, too, the ferocious Medusa head glaring at them as if in resentment at Alfred's finger-marks. She would not allow anything to shake her resolve.

Through the fine mesh of her veil she saw the door open to reveal the black-clad form of a butler.

'Miss Danby to call upon His Grace,' Alfred said and produced her calling card.

The butler blinked, just once. His eyes flickered from Alfred in immaculate livery to Jessica's veiled figure in its highly fashionable walking dress, then to Trotter beside her. Jessica defied even the most rigid dowager not to find Trotter a model of decorum and respectability.

'If you would care to step inside, madam. I will ascertain whether His Grace is receiving.'

He spoke with admirable calm, Jessica thought. The

most experienced butler would be forgiven for being disconcerted by the unannounced arrival of a respectable unmarried lady on a bachelor duke's doorstep at eleven in the morning.

She inclined her head in thanks and mounted the steps. *Remember to breathe. What can possibly go wrong? Everything.*

Alexander Francis Demeral, Seventh Duke of Malvern, slumped in the vast carved chair behind his desk and stared at the toes of his boots which were currently propped on the blotter.

They were very worn toes, because the boots were old, much repaired and comfortable, which was fortunate, because the latest in the line of the Pinchpenny Dukes had no more in the way of funds than his ancestors had.

King Charles II had created the obscure Viscount Demeral a duke as an apology of sorts for the short-lived regal *affaire* with Lady Demeral but, distracted by the calamitous events of the year 1660, had omitted to do anything about lands to support the honour. The plague and the Great Fire of London were enough to distract anyone and had proved a drain on the already constrained royal purse.

The King had, however, left a lasting legacy in the looks of the son born to Lady Demeral some months later. Even now, one hundred and fifty years on, the resemblance of the Duke to a young Charles Stuart was startling: the lean height, the black hair, the dark eyes under heavy lids and the assertive nose. All that was missing was the wig of tumbling black curls, the world-weary gaze and the procession of buxom mistresses.

Alex was contemplating his options for repairing the

houses of the tenants on his Hereford estate. It was not a pleasant topic. His choices seemed to boil down to two: sell yet another tranche of unentailed land—not that there was much of that left—or marry an heiress. The view of his boots was not providing any easy answers.

It was February, the Season was getting into its stride, marriage was the sensible option and this was the best possible time of year to find a bride. Marriage was also the prudent solution to his troubles as it would be the means of securing an heir, a necessity for a man whose nearest male relative was a somewhat vague rural dean. The Reverend Hector Demeral lived in genteel poverty with a brood of unruly sons, most of whom Alex predicted would end up on the gallows before much longer.

The problem was… The problem was entirely due to his own character, he admitted to himself after a short struggle. He was a romantic and he always had been. He wanted to fall in love. He *needed* to fall in love. There was a tradition that Demerals all married for love—after that one regal infidelity.

In that respect he was a true Demeral, growing up in a household where the two things that were never in short supply were love and affection. The problem with that was that Demeral men always seemed to fall for ladies as well-bred and impoverished as themselves, fathering yet another Pinchpenny Duke in the process.

Which meant that, in addition to finding his true love, she had to be a healthy, well-bred, intelligent young lady with a large endowment whose parents were willing to part with both daughter and dowry in return for the title.

He ought to have a clearer, stronger, sense of duty and break with tradition. He ought not to yearn for a relationship such as his parents and grandparents had enjoyed. It was, he acknowledged, a failing in himself. His peers would laugh themselves sick at the thought of a duke yearning for a love match.

He ought, in short, to be the last of the Pinchpenny Dukes and the first of the Comfortably Wealthy Dukes. The ones who made sensible marriages, expanded the estates, housed their tenants decently, repaired Demeral Castle and sired sons and daughters who would go forth and marry into the great families of the land, all of whom would bring honour, lands and influence with them. And yet... Something in him refused to give up hope that he would look across a crowded room—and there she would be. The One.

He had attended numerous balls, musicales, Venetian breakfasts and masquerades this Season already. Enough, surely, to have met most of the young ladies making their come-outs or embarking on a second or even third Season. There had been rich ones, beautiful ones, witty and amusing ones, along with many who possessed perfectly pleasant characters and countenances. But none of them had stirred anything within him that might be called love, or a desire to know them very much better.

Perhaps he had better sell the marsh grazing down near the Bristol Channel. A pity, because the sheep fed on the salt grass produced wonderful mutton. But the tenants' roofs were leaking, a new bore hole should be made for a well so it was not so far for them to collect fresh water and something must be done with the castle's east turret before it fell on the Great Hall. He would give it another month, he thought. And then—

'A Miss Danby to see you, Your Grace.'

Alex swung his booted feet down off the desk, sat up straight and stared at his butler, who appeared to have parted company with his senses. 'Who? I am not expecting any callers, let alone ladies.'

'Her card, Your Grace.' Pitwick offered a somewhat worn silver salver in the middle of which reposed a calling card, gilt edged and handsomely engraved on heavy stock.

Miss Danby
Adam Street

'Who the devil is Miss Danby?' Alex demanded. The address was good enough, one of the streets off the Strand around the Royal Adelphi Terrace, the handsome creation of the Adam brothers. Her neighbours would be wealthy and socially acceptable, if not of the highest *ton*.

'I regret to say I have no idea, Your Grace. She is accompanied by a liveried footman and her abigail appears to be a most respectable woman. Her attire is both of the mode and, I would judge, of high quality.'

'In other words, a lady. Not a...'

'A high-flyer, Your Grace?' Pitwick suggested with a discreet cough. 'Oh, no, most definitely not a person of that type. Quite a young lady, too, I would judge, although she is veiled.'

'You had best show her into the drawing room, Pitwick. Tea, do you think?'

'Yes, Your Grace. There is something reassuringly respectable about tea.'

There was much to be said for a butler with a sense of humour, Alex thought as he got to his feet and went to squint at his own reflection in the tarnished old mirror above the fireplace.

He straightened his neckcloth and ran one hand through his hair. He kept it cropped short, not so much to be in the fashion as to remove all possible resemblance to Charles Stuart's mass of black curls. It didn't make much difference—with his dark colouring and long nose he still looked like the young prince about to put on his wig.

As he crossed the hall he passed a man standing to attention, all six feet of him clad in dark blue livery heavily encrusted with silver lace. He was the very model of the perfect London footman, right down to his well-moulded calves in silk stockings. Beside him on one of the hard hall chairs sat a maid, again one who looked as though she had been selected from a catalogue of ideal servants. She stood as she saw him, eyes down, and bobbed a curtsy as he passed.

Interesting that she had not accompanied her mistress into the drawing room, he thought, warily leaving the door open by a good foot as he entered.

The figure standing gazing up at a portrait of his parents was of average height for a woman, her slenderness well displayed in a dark green walking dress. She turned at the sound of his tread and dropped into a curtsy. He registered curves and a youthful suppleness.

'Your Grace.'

'Miss Danby?'

'Thank you for receiving me, Your Grace.'

There was something vaguely familiar about her as she stood composedly regarding him. She had put back the heavy veil from her bonnet—he was relieved to see that she had at least the sense to arrive in decent anonymity—

and she returned his stare with a level, blue-eyed gaze. Honey-blonde hair, an oval face, freckles. An open, intelligent, expression without a hint of coquetry. A pleasant-looking young lady, if not a great beauty.

'Will you not be seated, Miss Danby? Tea is on its way.'

'Thank you.' She sank down gracefully on to the nearest chair and Alex took the one opposite, the low tea table between them.

'This is most unconventional, I realise that,' she said and for the first time he saw signs of agitation in her clasped hands and the slight shake in her voice. Her accent was educated and the tone would, he judged, be pleasant when she was not so tense.

'Perhaps if you were to tell me in what way I may be of service to you?' he suggested. Where was Pitwick and that confounded tea tray? And why hadn't he simply said he was not at home? Curiosity, he supposed. That could be dangerous—he was very aware of just how compromising this could be. It simply was not done for a man to be alone and unchaperoned with an unmarried lady of, at least, the gentry class.

'If you will allow me, I should tell you something of my circumstances,' she said, then fell silent as Pitwick entered, accompanied by James, one of the footmen, who was bearing the tea tray.

The butler gestured to the low table. 'There, James. Will you pour, Miss Danby, or shall I?'

'Thank you, I will,' she told him with a flash of a smile and proceeded to do so. Clearly she had received the typical upbringing of a lady. 'Sugar, Your Grace? Lemon or milk?'

Alex was conscious of his staff leaving, although the

slight draught on his nape reassured him that the door remained open.

'Lemon, thank you.' He took the cup, waiting until she had taken a sip from her own. 'You were about to tell me of your circumstances, I believe.'

'Yes. We have met before, You Grace. Twice you have honoured me with a dance, but, no, I do not expect you to recall me,' she added when he began to speak. 'London is full of young ladies, most of them far more memorable than I. But my father is Broughton Danby, an ironmaster. A very wealthy man. You will excuse the vulgarity of my mentioning the fact, but it is relevant to my purpose.'

'I have heard of Mr Danby, of course.' Who had not? Like a handful of other self-made industrialists who bestrode their worlds of iron and coal, steam, pottery and textiles, his name was familiar to any gentleman who took an interest in the economic affairs of the country.

'Papa is not in the best of health and has retired from the day-to-day running of the company which is now in the hands of my two brothers,' Miss Danby said. She set her cup and saucer down with a slight rattle. 'Papa and I have moved to London for a while. He wished me to make my come-out, to do the Season. To find a husband.' She drew a visibly deep breath.

'Again, I beg you to forgive my frankness, but my dowry is large. Exceedingly so. Papa wishes to ensure that I secure a husband of rank. Since the death of my mother it has become his passionate desire and the energy he is expending on that is all, I fear, that maintains his well-being now he no longer has the company to run.'

Alex, unable to think of anything to say other than platitudes, murmured that he was sorry to hear about Mr Danby's ill health. He was conscious of a distinct sense of alarm. Dowry? He should never have admitted her.

'Naturally, I wish to oblige Papa in all things,' this startling female continued composedly. 'I love him dearly and hope that I am a dutiful daughter. However, I find myself, on the one hand, courted by fortune hunters for whom I can feel no liking or admiration and, on the other, snubbed for my lack of breeding, for my association with industry.'

Miss Danby's deportment and accent were impeccable—no doubt the result of no expense being spared on her upbringing and schooling—and her taste in dress was without the slightest vulgarity, but of course that would not stop the whispers and sneers about Cits, about the 'stink of the factory chimneys'. The *ton* knew their *Peerage* and its pedigrees as well as they knew their own countenances in the mirror.

'I can imagine,' he said. Where the devil was this going?

'I feel I owe it to myself to marry someone with whom I could share affection and respect. So I decided to take more control, to take matters into my own hands.' Miss Danby sat up straighter and gave a brisk nod, as if to encourage herself. 'I decided to look around me and to attempt to judge the character of gentlemen and make my own choices. I noticed you, Your Grace. I saw you were courteous, that you took the trouble to ask wallflowers to dance and to converse with the elderly ladies. I never once saw you treat staff with discourtesy, nor overheard you speak crudely or with disrespect of anyone.'

She paused for another of those deep breaths and Alex swallowed hard. Surely she was not going to—

'And I heard that you are not a rich man—the rumours say that you are looking to the Marriage Mart to provide you with a well-dowered bride this Season. So I thought, I would… I would ask you. In case you had not realised that I would be suitable. To marry. Because I think I am,' she concluded all of a rush and closed her eyes, her face suffused with a blush.

Hell's teeth. I have just been proposed to.

Chapter Two

Alex put down his cup and saucer and realised he was braced to spring to his feet and escape.

'Miss Danby.' How the devil was he to turn her down? There were no precedents for such a situation as far as he was aware and all of his instincts were telling him that he was in a highly precarious position. How would she react to the rejection of her outrageous proposal? By making a scene and screaming that he had assaulted her? By rushing back to her father to say Alex had compromised her?

'Miss Danby, you honour me with your estimation of my character, but I must decline your most flattering suggestion. I have… I have hardly begun my search for a suitable duchess.' He took a steadying breath and decided that only honesty would do, even if she laughed in his face at the idea of him being such a romantic.

'I do not know whether there is, somewhere, the lady for whom I might cherish warmer feelings than merely liking. I will confess that it is my ardent hope that I will, that I will recognise her when I find her. To commit myself to a betrothal with someone I do not know and who, however observant, does not truly know me…that would seem to me to be imprudent. On both our parts. It could only lead to future unhappiness.'

He went over that speech in his head. Had it been tact-ful? Suitably kind yet definite? Miss Danby must have been racked with nerves, coming here. He had to let her down gently, but without leaving the slightest hope that he would change his mind. He thought he had done that and now he had to get her out of the house. Fast.

'Yes,' she replied after a moment and opened her eyes. 'I see. Of course. I quite understand. I had expected your reply to be in the negative,' she said, her voice tight with an emotion that she was rigidly controlling. 'But I felt I ought to try. In case you thought we might suit.' She stood up and Alex shot to his feet. 'Thank you for your consideration.'

'You may be assured of my discretion,' he said. Was it his imagination or could he feel the cold sweat rolling down his spine? 'You have come in your own carriage?'

At least, as her father was a commoner, it would not be emblazoned with a coat of arms on the door, he realised with relief.

'It is waiting around the corner,' she said as she lifted her veil and settled it to hide her face again as Alex tugged on the bell pull.

'Pitwick. Please show Miss…the lady out. Good day, ma'am.'

'Good day, Your Grace.' She dropped that neat little curtsy again and went out of the door the butler was now holding wide open.

Alex went to the window. By great good fortune Hill Street seemed clear of promenading fashionables, passing carriages containing Patronesses of Almack's or anyone likely to rush to the scandal sheets with the intelligence that a heavily veiled lady was leaving the Duke of Mal-vern's town house at a most unconventional hour. Given that the street ran between the fashionable haunts of Berkeley Square and South Audley Street this was a minor miracle and he duly gave thanks to whatever guardian angel watched over impoverished dukes.

Alex strode across the hall as the front door closed behind Miss Danby and her retinue and fell into the chair behind his desk with the sensations of a fox that had somehow eluded the hounds.

He should have refused to see her, of course. Whatever had he been thinking? He had been taken by surprise, he supposed, and then good manners made it impossible to simply insist that she leave the moment it became clear what her purpose was.

At least he hadn't been in two minds in the moments before he turned Miss Danby down. He had not been tempted to agree by the promise of her dowry. That would have been fatal, because he was certain any hesitation would have shown on his face somehow and she might have been emboldened to try persuasion. That could only have been deeply embarrassing for them both.

Only, now that he was alone and could think more clearly, Alex realised that he *was* tempted and it had only been the shock of being proposed to by a lady that had stopped him considering it. Danby was a very rich man and Alex could well imagine that he would stop at nothing, baulk at no expense, to maintain his daughter in true ducal style if she married him.

An ironmaster's fortune would secure what Alex already owned, enable him to purchase more land, create a great estate befitting a duke. It would repair the castle, provide the tenants with homes fit to live in. Perhaps even build a new model village with a school.

And Miss Danby, although no great beauty, was clearly intelligent, well-educated and the possessor of good taste—if not of the desirable maidenly virtues of modesty, discretion and reticence.

Such a match would cause titters and nudges, but then his ancestors had always been known as the Pinchpenny Dukes, so probably there would also be a great deal of admiration for him having caught such a prize. After all, dukes had married actresses before now. A respectable iron founder's daughter was a considerable social improvement on that.

But. But he would despise himself for it, he knew. He had accepted that he must marry a lady with a respectable dowry at the very least. And at the same time he had been determined to wed someone for whom he could feel the warmest emotions. Love. And he did not love Miss Jessica Danby. He had apparently danced with her without feeling the slightest glimmer of attraction and, on seeing her again, had noticed only a vague awareness of having met her before. Whereas she had learned of his title, had observed enough to feel confident of his character and had then made her proposal.

A prudent man would go out now, present himself before Mr Danby and request the honour of his daughter's hand and he would be accepted, he had no doubt of that. But Miss Danby would then know that he had cold-bloodedly assessed her likely fortune and had decided it outweighed the excuses he had made to her about warm feelings and affection. She would know him not only as motivated by the desire for wealth, which she accepted, but a hypocrite to boot. She would never be able to trust anything he said to her again.

He had burned his boats to a cinder because if he had only been resolute about abandoning his search for love and had been even vaguely aware of her dowry and that she found him tolerable, then he could have sought her out, established some relationship between them, assessed whether or not it might be a match both of them could commit to.

'Hell and damnation, you fool,' Alex said as the door opened.

'I beg your pardon, Your Grace.'

'Not you, Pitwick. Me. I should have done my research before launching myself on to the Marriage Mart and now I have lost what might be the biggest prize in it.' There was no point in trying to hide his circumstances from his butler, or his valet, come to that. They knew the financial situation as well as he did. And they probably knew as well as he did why he was being so stubborn about doing the right thing and ruthlessly finding an heiress. If only he could shrug off that conviction that somewhere there was his true love.

'Tsk,' Pitwick said, conveying in that one sound regret, sympathy and the assurance that he hadn't the faintest idea what his employer was talking about. He rather spoilt the effect by adding, 'And will you be launching yourself upon the choppy waters of the Marriage Mart again tonight, Your Grace?'

'I suppose I had better, Pitwick. Kindly tell Cook that I will be dining off the refreshments at Almack's this evening. That will save the cost of one dinner, at least.'

His butler looked sympathetic, as well he might. Lemonade and slightly dry seedcake was no meal for any man.

* * *

The earth had not opened up and conveniently swallowed her, embarrassment, blushes and all, Jessica thought grimly. Which meant that she had best grit her teeth and prepare for another excruciating evening at Almack's. It was a Wednesday, one of the nights the Assembly Rooms were open to those fortunate enough to possess the precious vouchers of admission.

'The blue silk gown, I think, Trotter,' she said. She had worn dark green that morning and instinct urged her to another colour, as though that would somehow shield her from the Duke's gaze.

The Duke had been all that was considerate, she thought for the hundredth time. He had been polite and thoughtful in producing a reason to turn her down that in no way reflected upon her. He could have refused to receive her—which would have been wise of him—or he could have recoiled from her unmaidenly proposal, snubbed her viciously for the source of her wealth and her humble antecedents. Instead he had been kind and tactful.

Which was why she had selected him in the first place, of course, she thought, sitting still while Trotter did something complicated with her hair. At least her judgement of his character had not been at fault.

'Are you well, Miss Jessica?' Trotter asked. 'You are a trifle pale, if I may say so.'

'Perfectly well, thank you, Trotter. I am merely a little tired.'

And, really, there was no need to fret about seeing the Duke again. He had danced with her twice before and had not even remembered her this morning. He would simply ignore her when he encountered her again and she could hardly blame him for that. 'The pearl and sapphire earrings, I think, with this gown.'

Jessica, accompanied by her chaperon, Lady Cassington, arrived at the Assembly Rooms in King Street at nine. At the start of the Season her father had engaged the services of her escort, a baronet's widow who was possessed of impeccable breeding, but very little funds, and who maintained the polite fiction that she was merely doing dear Miss Danby a favour by introducing her into polite society.

Almeria Cassington had proved to be an inspired choice because, as a cousin of Lady Cowper, one of the Patronesses, she had been able to persuade her amiable relative to grant Jessica one of the precious vouchers of admission to Almack's. It had required her to pay an afternoon call on the Countess, which had been terrifying, but the verdict was that she was a nicely behaved young lady who showed impeccable taste in her attire and conversation.

'One would never know about her background,' Lady Cowper had remarked, not quite quietly enough for Jessica to miss. 'She might do for poor Austin.'

Fortunately, Jessica had managed to contain herself until they were safely in the carriage. 'And who is "poor Austin" for whom I "might do"?'

'One of her godsons. No money and some very regrettable, er, habits. We can do much better for you, my dear Miss Danby. But I suspected that the prospect of your dowry would be enough to prise a voucher from her and I was correct.'

It was the first of numerous humiliations, some mere pinpricks, others that left her smarting, but Jessica had schooled herself to appear never to notice them. And Lady

Cassington was certainly assiduous in her promotion of Jessica's interests. She suspected that her chaperon had been promised a sizeable bounty if she secured a marriage proposal. It was probably on a sliding scale, knowing Papa, and would depend on how high up the aristocratic tree she could be boosted. A baronet or a baron would be a grave disappointment, they were both well aware.

Now, standing on the threshold of the Assembly Rooms, Jessica could see that the main chamber was filling fast. It might well hold more than five hundred before the end of supper at eleven o'clock when the doors were closed, regardless of who might arrive a minute late.

Jessica looked around for the group she thought of as her special friends, the group she had mentally labelled the Exotic Wallflowers.

There were the usual drab little group of everyday wall-flowers, of course: the desperately shy for whom this was a ritual torture and the plain girls without outgoing wit to make them sparkle, or helpfully large dowries to counterbalance their looks. The judgement of the fashionable elite was quite unforgiving to those who fell short of its standards.

Jessica's wallflowers had wit and spirit in plenty, but those were coupled with handicaps that separated them from the flock of other desirable young ladies who had the expected combination of prettiness, modestly simpering manners, excellent bloodlines and respectable dowries.

Her friends all appeared to be present in their usual alcove. Lady Anthea Mulrose, the bluest of bluestockings who had no time for any gentleman who was not interested in natural sciences, found the Classical authors fascinating and was *au fait* with the latest theories about the formation of the earth; Miss Belinda Newlyn, of genteel birth and modest endowments and who was pretty and witty, but walked with a severe limp; Lady Lucinda Herrick whose grandfather, an East India Company nabob, had married an Indian princess in the days before attitudes to those who were not Christian and European had hardened into intolerance and Miss Jane Beech, whose head of ginger hair was considered positively vulgar, as though she could do anything about it. Her pleasantly plain face was a mass of freckles and that combination, along with a very modest dowry, was enough to condemn her to oblivion.

Jessica liked them all in their own ways and had soon been absorbed into their little circle. They were rarely disturbed, except when a gentleman who had a better-developed sense of his duty, such as the Duke of Malvern, asked one of them for a dance, or a determined chaperon dragged along a reluctant young gentleman who was compelled to stand up with an equally unwilling partner. Or, of course, when a fortune hunter managed to track down Miss Danby.

She took a seat next to Miss Beech as Lady Cassington swept off on her endless search for an eligible partner for her.

'Did you manage to find a suitable paint box at Ackermann's?' she asked. Miss Beech was an accomplished water colourist and had decided to invest in better equipment than she had been using.

'Oh, yes. Thank you for recommending them. Their shop in the Strand is quite marvellous and I could have spent my entire quarter's allowance there.' She launched into a description of the range of choices she had been faced with. On her other side Miss Newlyn and Lady Lucinda were discussing the horrors of being fitted for Court dress—'I declare I look like a candle snuffer in those dreadful hoops!'—and Lady Anthea was, as usual, absorbed in a small pamphlet she had produced from her reticule.

Jessica became aware of the prickling sensation of being watched. Please, not the Duke, she thought, discreetly scanning the immediate area from behind the shelter of her fan.

A small group of young men were standing nearby, sniggering in the irritating manner of immature bores who think they are great wits. They were nudging each other and, Jessica realised, they were staring not at her, but at Jane Beech, as though egging each other on to do something daring.

She lowered her fan and gave them a discouraging frown, but they were intent on her companion. Three of them sauntered up.

'I say, it's Miss Beech, isn't it?' one of them said. They were very young, Jessica thought. Very young, very silly.

'Yes,' Jane said uneasily.

'We was wondering, don't you know, if you're keen on hunting.'

'No. Not at all.'

'Hah, told you so,' the youth said to his friends. 'You wouldn't be, of course,' he added, turning back, 'seeing as your mama was frightened by a fox when she was expecting! Hah, ha!'

Jane turned scarlet. Jessica opened her mouth to utter a savage set-down and a voice said calmly, 'Good evening, ladies. Miss Beech, my dance, I believe.'

Chapter Three

'My dance, I believe.'

It was the Duke of Malvern. Jane stared at him, blinking away the tears that had gathered visibly on her lashes. Jessica, who had half risen from her seat, sat down again with a bump and the Duke turned a cold look on the three young men.

'Are you by any chance annoying my partner?' he enquired. 'I find myself constantly amazed at the riff-raff that somehow manages to obtain vouchers for Almack's these days,' he added, turning back to the ladies. 'I must have a word with the Patronesses.'

Jane, without a word, took the hand that was extended to her and was led into the set that was forming nearest to them.

'That was the Duke of Malvern,' Lady Anthea said. 'What on earth is he doing? I know for a fact that dear Jane's card is quite without partners.'

'Coming to her rescue,' Jessica said, fanning herself. Really, she felt quite…quite breathless. That had been so smoothly done and with such authority. Across the dance floor she could just make out the backs of the three young men as they made for the door. They would not be sniggering now.

'But why would he trouble himself?' Anthea persisted. 'He doesn't know any of us. It was most gentlemanly of him, but so fast! I was about to give them a set-down myself, but I had hardly taken breath to do so.'

'I had a hairpin ready.' Lady Lucinda slid a jewelled spike back into her sleek black hair and turned to Belinda Newlyn, who was jotting something on the back of her blank dance card. 'What are you doing?'

'Writing a description. I intend to find out who they were,' she said tightly. 'I keep a little list of people I intend never to forgive. One day I will have my revenge.'

'The Duke must have been standing very near to us,' Jessica said, answering Anthea. 'Perhaps he had encountered those young men before, was expecting trouble and was keeping an eye on them.'

Or on me.

She had not been aware of him watching them, but then the room was very crowded. Through the whirling dancers she could see the Duke and Jane talking as they waited their turn to go down the line. Jane's furious blush had faded and she looked positively happy.

'Jane is a very good dancer,' Lady Lucinda observed as the pair sidestepped under the raised arms of the other couples in their set. 'But then she is musical and that no doubt helps.'

When the set had finally come to an end they expected Jane to return, breathless and in need of reassurance after her adventure, but all Jessica could see were occasional glimpses of red hair on the other side of the room.

'My goodness, he has introduced her to another partner,' gasped Belinda. 'Oh, do look, it is Mr Locksley.'

And, sure enough, Jane was making her curtsy to the only other person in the room whose hair was a match for hers. Mr Locksley, tall and bespectacled, was beaming at his new partner and Jane was smiling back up at him.

'And he is quite well off, I believe,' Lucinda remarked. 'A very nice estate in Warwickshire and his godmother is a cousin of the Bishop of Somerley.'

'It is only a dance,' Jessica protested. 'Not a betrothal.' But she could see other people were watching the couple and their smiles were kind, not mocking. Two redheads apparently cancelled each other out, or perhaps it was simply that Mr Locksley was well known and liked.

'How clever of the Duke,' Anthea said. 'And how thoughtful.'

'I believe him to be both,' Jessica said, a little stiffly. 'From what little I have seen of him,' she added before anyone could ask her how she knew.

'Well, in that case, perhaps he can find us all suitable partners,' Belinda said. 'He is doing far better than Jane's aunt has managed in a whole month. Now, if we can order up a university professor for Anthea, a horse-breeder for me, a connoisseur of the arts for Lucinda and a—what kind of a gentleman would you like, Jessica?'

A hard-up duke, please.

'Oh, the richest man in England,' she said with a laugh. 'Then he will not care about my dowry and is at liberty to fall madly in love with my elegant eyebrows and my exquisite earlobes.'

There was no sign of the Duke: clearly both her eyebrows and her earlobes had failed to make an impression.

* * *

Eventually Mr Locksley returned Jane to them and enquired if she would favour him with the supper dance.

To her friends' amazement Jane replied with tolerable composure, and much blushing, that she would be delighted and he bowed and left them.

'What was it like dancing with the Duke?' Lucinda demanded.

'Oh, I was ready to drop with embarrassment.' Jane fanned herself vigorously. 'But he was so kind and so matter of fact. He said it was a depressing fact about the immature men that they often could not recognise the true beauty of unusual things because of their lack of sophistication. Their insecurity, he said, made them clumsy and offensive. And I just gawped at him like a perfect airhead, because I couldn't believe that he meant my hair was beautiful, and he said that I should never be shy about accepting compliments about it.

'And then we just danced and chatted about ordinary things and I didn't fall over my feet once, as I'd feared because, really—a duke!' she said happily. 'And then he introduced me to Mr Locksley. And he was lovely, too.'

Jessica sat silently while the others demanded every detail about lovely Mr Locksley. Even Anthea put away her pamphlet.

Where *was* the Duke? She scanned the throng that was now hot, noisy and, if truth be told, becoming rather less than fragrant.

There, over in the far corner near the entrance to the refreshment room. There was no mistaking the dark head topping most of the men in the vicinity.

'Excuse me for a moment,' she said. The others, heads

together, acknowledged her departure with vague smiles before they returned to their analysis of Jane's sudden success.

Jessica skirted around the room, acknowledging a few greetings and ignoring several cuts from those who thought that daughters of industry had no place in Almack's Assembly Rooms.

The Duke was standing talking to a group of other gentlemen of about his own age. They were discussing racehorses, she thought, catching a few words as she passed slowly in front of them.

Long odds…soft going…too short in the back…

She caught the Duke's eye and, without stopping, inclined her head. *Thank you*, she mouthed silently and walked on.

That, she hoped, would be that. He had, perhaps, intervened because he felt uncomfortable about having refused her proposition. Whatever his motives, she had thanked him and there would be no need for their paths to cross again.

Jessica saw that she had walked around half of the ballroom, reaching the ladies' retiring room without noticing it. She might as well go in and make certain her hair was still in order and take a few moments in the relative cool and quiet.

When she emerged five minutes later a tall figure moved away from the wall and fell into step beside her.

'You wished to speak to me?' he asked.

'No! I mean, no, I merely wished to thank you for intervening just now, Your Grace. Those wretched young men were a moment away from having their ears boxed, being stabbed with a hairpin and beaten over the head with a pamphlet on the true age of the earth. It would have created a most unfortunate scene and probably lost us our vouchers. Not that any of us would be devastated by that.'

Almack's, a bulwark of respectability, was not provided with any little alcoves where couples could escape for a private conversation—or something more intimate—but the Duke steered her neatly into the shelter of a group of tall potted plants.

'There is no need to keep saying *Your Grace*, you know,' he said. 'Call me Demeral. Or *Duke*. Or *Malvern* if you feel uncomfortable with that in company.'

In company?

When am I likely to be having conversations with you in company? Jessica wondered.

But she managed to say, with a reasonable degree of composure, 'Thank you, Demeral.' She should go now. Return to her friends. But her curiosity got the better of her.

'Why *did* you intervene?' she asked before she could stop the question.

'Because I dislike bullies,' he said simply.

'I had not realised you were there.'

'I happened to be passing.'

'And there was no obligation to find Miss Beech another partner.'

'It was too tempting to see whether they got on together or clashed—literally or figuratively. But I happen to know that Locksley endured considerable bullying as a young man because of his colouring, so I felt certain that your friend was in sympathetic company.'

'So sympathetic that he is taking her in to supper.' Demeral smiled, clearly delighted that his stratagem had been successful and, off guard, she said, 'The rest of the Exotics joked that you should find us all our ideal partners.'

'The Exotics?'

'Oh, that is just my silly name for our little group. We are all wallflowers, but the reasons for that are somewhat unusual in each case.'

'Miss Beech's hair, your father's occupation. Yes, I see. Will you not take a chair, Miss Danby, and tell me about your other friends?'

She should return to the others and not risk being seen talking intimately with the Duke—with Demeral—behind the potted palms. If Lady Cassington saw her she would be reporting back to her father in great glee and he would be leaping to conclusions—conclusions that could only end in disappointment for him. On the other hand, she was not visible from the chaperons' corner and it seemed discourteous to hurry away when he had performed such a service for Jane.

Jessica sat down, perched on one of the uncomfortable little white and gilt chairs that seemed expressly designed to prevent one from lounging. 'Lady Anthea is highly intelligent and a bluestocking. She has a mind above all this—' she waved her hand in the direction of the dance floor '—and, although not exactly *against* marriage, despairs of finding a gentleman of equal intellect. She becomes very easily bored and they resent that.' From Demeral's expression she could tell he had some sympathy with the gentlemen in question. Certainly, keeping up with Anthea was a strain sometimes, even for her friends.

'Lady Lucinda's grandmother was an Indian princess. The fact that the East India Company positively encouraged their employees to make marriages with the local rulers at that time seems to carry no weight these days, now attitudes have changed so much. Apparently the fact that

Lucinda has inherited her grandmother's exquisite taste and deep interest in art is not enough to change the opinion of unpleasant people who whisper about "natives". And Miss Newlyn limps. It was the way she was born. She is a wonderful rider, however. You should see her when we go out together to Rotten Row. I must go back.'

She stood and Demeral rose with her.

'Now you know all about us.' She hesitated, then blurted out the question that had been puzzling her all day. 'Why did you not refuse to receive me this morning? Why are you being so…so *pleasant* when I must have been such a grave embarrassment to you?'

'I received you out of perfectly vulgar curiosity and the fact that I was half asleep, if you must know the truth. Then, once I had heard what you had to say, I admired your courage in going after what you wanted. And now I admire your loyalty to your friends.' He glanced around. 'Perhaps, for discretion, you should leave the cover of our little woodland first. I will wait a while.'

Jessica glanced back when she was halfway to her seat. There was no sign of the tall figure.

'Where have you been? It is time for supper and we are all faint with hunger,' Belinda said. 'Jane has already been claimed by Mr Locksley.'

'Then we will go and indulge ourselves in rather dry cake and insipid lemonade and pretend we are not watching them,' Jessica said and the four of them made their way around the edge of the dance floor to the refreshment room.

What a very strange day, Jessica thought as she sat at her dressing table once more, unhooking her earrings as Trotter removed all the pins from her hair and began to give it a firm one hundred strokes of the brush.

She had behaved like a complete hoyden and had somehow emerged with her reputation, if not her nerves, intact. She appeared to have gained the friendship of a duke, even if he was a most unusual one, and she very much feared that she had developed a mild *tendre* for the man, on top of the liking that had led her to make her outrageous proposal.

The sooner you forget that, my girl, the better it will be for you, she told herself, wincing slightly at the vigorous brushing.

Demeral had made it very clear that he was looking for a love match and that she was not what he was seeking in a wife.

She was going to have to make up her mind—tell Papa that she had met nobody so far that she could tolerate as a husband and give up this whole excruciating Season, or fix a smile on her lips, ignore the snubs and try to find a good man among the fortune hunters. *Another* good man.

'That was a big sigh, Miss Jessica.'

'It was rather a trying evening, Trotter. That is all it is.'

Chapter Four

Perhaps his decision to see Miss Danby yesterday morning had not been so wrong after all, Alex mused as he ate his breakfast the next morning.

She was sensible and tactful. She was also a loyal friend, as he had discovered last night. And one with a sense of humour. The Exotic Wallflowers, indeed! They had sounded an interesting, and intelligent, group of young women and he wondered whether one of them might be the right person for him. He had certainly disregarded them before, hardly aware of their presence.

He poured himself another cup of coffee and wondered how to get to know them better. In a formal social setting they were clearly ill at ease, clustering together for protection and company, but away from the ballrooms and drawing rooms they might be more relaxed and allow him to see the real women behind the careful smiles and calculated reserve.

Miss Danby had mentioned Rotten Row. Now that would be an excellent place to meet young ladies: very fashionable, but far more relaxed than an evening event. But it would not do to appear too obvious.

Carrying his coffee cup with him, Alex went through to his study and began to write notes. Safety in numbers.

* * *

Dusk came quickly at that time of year so, although the most fashionable time for riding and driving in Hyde Park was impossible in February, on a pleasant day the Row was still thronged in the early afternoon.

Alex kept his bay gelding to a walk as he made his way down through the park towards Rotten Row on its southern edge. Around him he had a group of friends: Major Percy Rowlands, riding his old grey cavalry charger, a survivor of Waterloo, Sir Harry Eynsham on his new chestnut mare that was proving something of a handful and Viscount Oakham, mounted on a handsome black gelding with perfect manners.

'That mare needs schooling, Eynsham,' Oakham remarked as the chestnut skittered nervily across the track. 'Pretty enough, but she'll have you off if she's spooked.'

'My brother-in-law bought her for my sister, the fool. He is no judge of horseflesh and she was besotted with this creature's looks,' the baronet said. 'No, there are no tigers behind that bush, you idiotic beast.' He halted the mare's sideways progress away from the threatening foliage. 'Susan can't manage her, so I bought her off him before she broke her neck, thought I'd see what I can do with her, but I think she needs work on a lunge rein in the paddock for a month or two before I bring her out in a crowd again.'

'Now that is what I call a handsome animal,' Oakham remarked, gesturing with his whip in the direction of the Row. 'And a rider who knows what she's doing.'

Alex did not recognise the rider of the dapple grey who was wearing a dark blue habit, a low-crowned hat and a veil, but he did know the driver of the phaeton she was riding beside.

Who was it that Miss Danby had said was an excellent rider? Miss Newlyn, that was it.

'A Miss Newlyn, I believe,' he said as they converged on the group.

Now they were closer he could see Lady Anthea Melrose sitting next to Miss Danby. She appeared to be reading a book, totally ignoring the crowds around her. Miss Newlyn, mounted on the fine long-tailed grey, was talking to a tall young woman on a bay mare and behind them were two riders deep in conversation too. Alex had no difficulty in recognising Locksley's red head as he doffed his hat to the occupants of a passing carriage. It must be Miss Beech beside him, her own fiery locks subdued in a snood with a hat and veil on top. That left the bay's rider as Lady Lucinda Herrick.

A full set of the Exotics.

Alex rode forward and raised his hat. Miss Danby reined in her pair and drew in to the side of the carriage drive. 'Good afternoon, Duke.'

'Ma'am. May I compliment you on your handling of that pair. Hanover bays, if I am not mistaken.'

'They are indeed. Aren't they fine? They would look even smarter drawing a high-perch phaeton, but I am afraid I have yet to convince my father that I would not overturn it.'

'I imagine there would be no danger of that,' he said, noting how calm she kept the high-bred pair and how steady her tan-gloved hands were on the reins. 'May I make known to you my friends, Miss Danby? Lord Oakham, Sir Harry Eynsham, Major Rowlands. Gentlemen, Miss Danby.'

'And I should introduce my companions,' she said as the gentlemen began raising their hats. 'Lady Anthea Melrose,

Lady Lucinda Herrick, Miss Newlyn and, behind us, Miss Beech. I am sure you all know Mr Locksley.'

There was a general exchange of bows and greetings. Even Lady Anthea tucked her book to the side of her seat and regarded them from under rather straight dark brows.

'Major Rowlands? Not the author of *Some Observations on the Inhabitants of the Pyrenees*?'

'Yes, ma'am.' Percy looked somewhat startled at the recognition. 'It is merely some jottings I made when I was serving in the Peninsula during the late hostilities and was prevailed upon to publish.'

'Rather more than jottings,' Lady Anthea said severely. 'You should not make light of intellectual endeavours. Now, I am interested in what you had to say about the difference between the folk customs of the Spanish and French sides of the mountain range. Do you consider them to be influenced by the differences in the climate and therefore the agricultural practices?'

To a man, his friends rode around to the other side of the phaeton, abandoning Percy to be interrogated, although, Alex saw, once he had recovered from his surprise, he seemed to be holding his own.

Miss Beech and Locksley rode up to join the group and Alex talked to Miss Danby about her bays while he covertly watched his friends and hers.

John Wilbraham, Viscount Oakham, had brought his gelding alongside the tall rider who, now he was closer, Alex recognised for certain as Lady Lucinda. She really was a very beautiful young woman with dark eyes and black hair that must be the legacy of her grandmother. Oakham appeared to be doing most of the talking and he wondered whether she was shy, reserved or braced for some insensitive remark about her heritage.

Miss Newlyn, on the other hand, was already laughing at something Harry had said and Percy was talking intently with Lady Anthea who showed every sign of thoroughly enjoying the argument.

'Whatever are you about, Demeral?' Miss Danby said with a severity that was at odds with the smile in her eyes. 'You descend on my little party of ladies with your battalion and have captured every one.'

So much for his bright idea of finding a bride for himself from among them: his friends were already showing their interest.

'Are you setting up as a matchmaker or simply carried away with enthusiasm after introducing Jane to Mr Locksley?' Miss Danby persisted.

'I deny it,' he said, mentally crossing his fingers. 'Locksley and your friend do appear to be getting along very well though, do they not?'

'Apparently he was on her doorstep at ten this morning with roses, sent them in with a request to know when he might call and was told to find her in the Park this afternoon. She does seem very taken with him, but whether it will endure closer acquaintance, I have no idea,' she said, keeping her voice low.

'He is of good character, or I would not have introduced them,' Alex answered as quietly. He decided that a white lie was called for. 'But as for the rest of them, it is mere coincidence that we happened to be riding out. Sir Harry appears as entranced by Miss Newlyn's grey as its rider. A fine animal.'

'Yes, I think I said she was an expert horsewoman. Her

family have a long tradition of breeding superb animals and that grey is possibly the best they have produced in many years. You would not think so to look at it, but it is a very spirited animal.'

'Then she is a most capable rider. As you are a whip, Miss Danby. Those bays are a strong pair that many ladies might hesitate to drive.'

'Why, thank you.'

He liked the way she accepted his compliment without false modesty or blushes.

'I wish Papa would allow me a perch phaeton, but he is convinced I would have an accident. He does not drive himself, so he finds it difficult to judge the dangers, I think.'

'How is his health? You mentioned the other day that it was not robust. He is not finding London too much for him, I trust?'

'He is rather improved, I think. I suspect the planning and the arrangements and the journey down and so forth were a strain—his heart is not strong—but now we are settled he seems much better. And he has been accepted into the Ironmongers' Guild which pleases him and gives him an occupation with their meetings and social gatherings.'

She smiled. 'It is not the same as the iron founders' association he belongs to at home, of course, but it stops him fretting about what my brothers Ethan and Joshua are doing with the business. He cannot accept they are thirty and twenty-seven now. They have been involved since they were hardly out of leading reins. It was impossible to keep them away from the forges as they grew up and now they are very confident in what they are about.'

'I know little about the guilds, I must confess,' Alex said.

Truth be told, he had little interest in them either, but he wanted to keep Miss Danby talking—his friends seemed to be enjoying their own conversations.

The bays moved uneasily as a noisy group of riders swept past them and Miss Danby collected them without fuss. 'The guilds maintain the standards of the craft and manage apprenticeships,' she explained. 'And there is a great deal of charitable work—widows and orphans, schools and so forth. And dining, of course. That is very important! I believe the Master has asked Papa to become involved in something to do with the charitable work—at breakfast time he said he wanted to ask my advice and it can hardly be about the fees charged for apprenticeships.' Her mouth curved into that warm smile again. 'It does him good to keep his mind active.'

Two carriages passed them and Miss Danby looked around. 'I think I should move along, before we cause an obstruction. It was pleasant to have the opportunity to converse again, Demeral.'

She brought the bays up to their bits and turned to her passenger. 'I believe we should continue on our way, Anthea.'

'We must? Oh, very well. Major Rowlands, here is my card. Please call, I feel there is a great deal to discuss about the links between modern religion in the Pyrenees and ancient pagan custom.'

Alex thought his friend looked slightly alarmed at the prospect, but he took the card and said, 'I look forward to it, Lady Anthea,' with a fair assumption of enthusiasm.

The phaeton moved off and with it the little group of three ladies and Mr Locksley who greeted the other men as he passed, but showed no sign of wanting to leave Miss Beech's side.

'An interesting collection of ladies,' Harry remarked. 'Originals! Wherever did you make their acquaintance, Demeral?'

'I hardly know them, but I have danced with Miss Danby on a couple of occasions.'

So she tells me.

How could he have forgotten her? She must have subdued all that intelligence and directness under a dull mask of propriety.

'Well, I am glad to have made Miss Newlyn's acquaintance. She tells me her father has some young colts that sound promising.'

'Happy to have been of help,' Alex said. 'And Percy found a fellow antiquarian, I think.'

'The poor fellow looks stunned,' Harry said cheerfully. 'I think Lady Anthea turned his brain inside out and gave it a good shaking.'

Jessica drove along the Row and then turned off on to one of the quieter grassy drives. Belinda and Lucinda promptly moved forward, one each side of the phaeton's seat, although Jane and her companion lagged behind.

'Was that meeting by arrangement, you sly thing?' Belinda asked. 'Fancy being able to produce a duke and three interesting gentlemen, just like that.'

'It was pure happenstance,' Jessica protested. 'I had made no rendezvous, I assure you.'

Although I had mentioned that we rode and drove in the Park. But surely he did not seek me out deliberately? And accompanied by three friends who had proved so compatible with my companions...

'Sir Harry appeared very impressed with Moonlight,'

she remarked to Belinda. 'How did you find Lord Oakham, Lucinda?'

'Interested in art—and he actually knows what he is talking about, instead of merely chatting about the latest fashionable show he has attended. I found him easy to talk to.'

That, from Lucinda, was high praise indeed.

'Perhaps we will encounter them again at Almack's or some of the events we are attending and you can continue your conversations,' Jessica said lightly. 'Shall we leave now? It is beginning to get quite chilly and the light will be going soon.'

Chapter Five

'What is all this I hear about a duke?' her father enquired at breakfast the next morning.

'Dukes?' Jessica took a hasty gulp of coffee. She was not feeling very awake after a late night at a stuffy, and not very entertaining, musicale.

'Lady Cassington tells me you have attracted the interest of the Duke of Malvern.'

Oh, dear. Quite the wrong way around.

'His Grace very kindly intervened when some rather obnoxious young men were making a nuisance of themselves at Almack's the other evening. Miss Beech was much embarrassed by them, but he handled the incident with great tact. Possibly Lady Cassington observed me thanking him.'

Her father's face fell. 'So you have no news for me?'

'I am afraid not, Papa,' Jessica said demurely. 'But we did meet him again in Hyde Park yesterday afternoon, riding with several of his friends. A viscount and a baronet among them.'

That cheered Papa up. Jessica felt a pang at deceiving him into thinking those two might be potential suitors, but at least their failure to propose wouldn't be as much of a disappointment as her not securing the interest of a duke.

'You were going to tell me about the Ironmongers' Guild activities, Papa,' she said, passing him the mustard.

'Ah, yes. They are good fellows. Not the same as iron *founders*, of course, but the best we can hope for down here in the south and they welcomed me with open arms, you know. Mind you,' he observed with a shrewd look, 'they probably know the advantages of being on the good side of a man with access to as much iron as I have.'

Jessica waited patiently while her father speculated on the opportunities for securing some advantageous contracts and then prompted, 'And this activity they asked you to manage? A charitable event, I assume.'

'May Day.' Her father appeared to think that was all that needed to be said and addressed himself to the sirloin steak on his plate.

Jessica finished her omelette before saying, 'May Day? But we are not in the country.'

'Apparently it is as much a festivity in the City as it is at home. No maypoles, I believe, but processions and wreaths and music.' He passed her his coffee cup to be refilled. 'And we need milkmaids.'

'Milkmaids? Whatever for? But that should not be a problem, surely? There are milk cows in Green Park and I believe I saw some in Lincoln's Inn Fields. There must be dozens of milkmaids around when you think of the demand for fresh milk in London.'

'They are all engaged. This is the first time the Ironmongers have participated and the other guilds have been using the same girls for years.'

'What else might be a problem?' Jessica was prepared to believe that her father knew everything there was to know about iron, but a more unlikely person to be organising a May Day festivity she could not imagine.

'We need lads.'

'The Guild can find many apprentices, I imagine.'

'And maidens.'

Would the apprentices be safe with the maidens? Or vice versa? How literally were they expected to interpret 'maiden'?

'Is it the kind of festivity that respectable young ladies might take part in? Perhaps you could enquire.' The daughters of the Guild members might do, provided it was not too much of a romp. 'What else?'

'Horse-drawn floats, garland makers, musicians. Chimney sweeps.' He frowned. 'Or perhaps I am mistaken about that. It seems improbable.'

It was beginning to sound like a formidable list, even without the sweeps. 'Never mind, we have more than two months to assemble all of those elements,' she said encouragingly. 'Do we need the cows to go with the milkmaids?'

'Fortunately, no.'

'I think we need more information, Papa. Timing and how long the procession route is to be and a map of where it will go and how many of the different kind of participants we will need. And what they are expected to do.' She pondered it over her next cup of coffee and realised that she could go to the newspaper offices and ask to see their accounts of the previous year's parades. The newspapers were all located to the east, in Fleet Street, as far as she could recall.

Papa would probably consider that area a den of iniquity. She knew that ladies did not walk about the City without a male escort and even then only with a very good reason, such as visiting her lawyer or banker to sign documents.

'May I involve my friends in this? I am certain they would find it interesting, discovering all about the festivities.'

'As you wish. I must confess, I would be glad of the assistance. It seems far more of a female endeavour to my mind.'

After breakfast Jessica went to her desk and made a list of the things her father had remembered would be required and then one of things to do. Then she wrote notes to her friends. Would they be interested in helping her?

Footmen were dispatched to deliver the notes and Jessica sat and thought about milkmaids. If London's milkmaids were already spoken for, where would one find others?

On great estates, of course. A duke must employ a number of milkmaids and his friends would also need them. Perhaps there were enough near London to supply a suitable number.

The first thing she must do was to visit the newspapers and see the reports, because, for the life of her, she could not imagine how the congested, dirty, utterly urban streets of the City of London could be transformed into a celebration of the arrival of May.

Jessica went upstairs, telling Henry, the first footman she encountered, to be ready to accompany her in half an hour and to order the carriage. She rang for her maid when she reached her bedchamber.

'I hope we are not calling on any more gentlemen, Miss Jessica,' Trotter said severely when she was asked to find a simple walking dress and a bonnet with a veil.

'We are not. Instead we are visiting newspaper offices and I am reliably informed they are not the place to find *gentlemen*. Quite the contrary.' Trotter did not appear to find that amusing, but Jessica kept talking. 'I am looking for reports of last year's May Day festivities as I am helping Papa with the Guild's efforts this year, so you may be easy in your mind.'

'Easy in my mind? With you gallivanting about the City? You know quite well, Miss, ladies don't visit the City, any more than they go calling on gentlemen.'

'Absolutely no gallivanting will be involved, Trotter. And no dukes. I can assure you. No dukes at all.'

It was not far to Fleet Street from Adam Street. Along the Strand, past Somerset House and they were there. The problem was, Jessica discovered as she sat in the carriage turning the pages of the *Directory* she had borrowed from Papa's study, the offices were certainly in the Fleet Street area, but not they were not all lined up neatly on the street itself. She was going to have to be more adventurous in her travels.

She selected two that she had heard of as reliable—*The Times*, which was in Printing House Square, just south of Ludgate Hill, and the *Morning Herald*, in Catherine Street, off the Strand. She had just passed that turning, she realised.

'Pull the check string, please, Trotter.'

The carriage drew up at the kerb amid much shouted abuse from passing carters and hackney coach drivers and Henry jumped down for instructions.

'Printing House Square off New Bridge Street first and then we will return to Catherine Street off the Strand if necessary.'

'Very good, Miss Jessica.'

They set off again to renewed shouts and catcalls. Trotter jerked up the window strap, her cheeks red.

Printing House Square proved to be difficult to find. Jessica traced their path as best she could on the map in front of the *Directory*. Down New Bridge Street, into Earl Street, immediately up Water Lane—and then into Playhouse Yard to turn around, because George the coachman had missed the narrow turning into Printing House Lane.

Jessica was beginning to feel a trifle flustered by the time Henry opened the carriage door and let down the steps for her, but she adjusted her veil and, flanked by Trotter and Henry, walked into the offices as confidently as she could.

It was noisy, dusty and seemed full of people, many of them shouting. A man looked up from a desk flanked by rows of pigeon holes. 'Yes? Advertisement, is it?'

'No, I wanted—'

'Only ladies with veils, it's usually an advertisement of some kind.' The slight leer on his face made Jessica feel exceedingly naive. What on earth could he mean?

'No, I do not wish to place an advertisement. I wish to see the reports in this paper of last year's May Day celebrations,' she said firmly.

'That's a new one. Patrick!'

A skinny youth trotted up in response to the summons.

'Take this lady to see Mr Baggley, then get your lazy ar—' Henry cleared his throat loudly and the man glanced at Jessica. 'Your lazy *self* back here.'

Mr Baggley proved to be an elderly and very dusty gentleman with a bald head balanced by vast side-whiskers. He presided over what Jessica assumed must be the newspaper's archives and, to her relief, not only knew where to find what he wanted, but gave her a seat at a relatively clean table to sit and take notes.

'I think I have all I need,' she said with some relief when she had thanked Mr Baggley and emerged from the depths of the building. 'We do not need to go to Catherine Street, George,' she told the coachman. 'But it occurs to me that while I am here, we could call at Rundell, Bridge & Rundell to collect the necklace they were repairing for me. Papa took it to them two weeks ago, so it might be ready by now. When we get there, Henry, please go in and enquire.'

'Thirty-Two Ludgate Hill, Miss Jessica,' the coachman said, nodding. 'I know the place. I reckon if I go down that lane there and cut through the back we'll be virtually on the doorstep.'

To her surprise they emerged on to Ludgate Hill without any further problem. George drew in to the kerb and Henry jumped down to push a brake shoe under a rear wheel against the slope of the road. It was even more crowded and chaotic than the Strand and Trotter put her hands over her ears at some of the language as a stagecoach made its way past coming from the Belle Sauvage Inn further down towards the valley of the River Fleet, the horses labouring as they took the steep incline up to St Paul's Cathedral.

Jessica looked out of the window, enjoying the colourful scene and trying to ignore the language. She caught the eye of a small boy who clutched his hoop and fidgeted with boredom, while his parents stood looking in the jeweller's window. The woman was pointing something out and the man was shaking his head. As Rundell, Bridge &

Rundell held the Royal warrant, the display in the window was especially lavish and glittering and priced accordingly, no doubt.

Henry was being a very long time and it was not only the small boy who was growing impatient. Jessica opened the door, ignored Trotter's protest, stepped down to the pavement and went to look in the window, too.

As she did so the lad gave the hoop an experimental twirl, got a sharp word from his father, pouted and then, as soon as the man's attention was back on the window, did it again. This time it spun out of his hand and went bowling across the pavement past Jessica, bounded into the air when it hit the kerb and then rolled into the road, its owner scampering after it.

'No! Look out!' Jessica cried.

A carriage wheel crushed the hoop, the boy stopped dead in the middle of the road and burst into tears and the blast of a horn signalled the approach of another coach, this one forcing its way down the hill.

Jessica ran, dodging a cart, a horseman and a tilbury, caught hold of the child by the arm and whirled around, looking for a safe way out to the opposite pavement. There wasn't one. The stagecoach driver reined in hard, the horses skidding on the cobbles as the wheelers went down on their haunches as they'd been trained in an effort to brake the coach on the hill.

It was too late, they'd be under those hooves in seconds. Jessica braced herself to jump under the heavy dray in front of her. If she could just avoid the wheels—

Alex folded the bank draft and slipped it into his breast pocket. The quite hideous diamond and emerald parure had fetched considerably more than he had expected when he took it in to the jewellers. He had found it quite by chance in the back of an elaborate chest of drawers that had stood in his grandmother's long-unused dressing room. How long it had been there he had no idea, but it was completely out of fashion now. Perhaps one of her rumoured lovers had given it to her decades before her death and she had hidden it away from her husband's suspicious eye—it certainly was not on the inventory of entailed family gems, which meant he might dispose of it with a clear conscience.

He could tell that the manager had been interested, despite pointing out how dirty it was and how out of the mode. Alex had shrugged and said he would take it elsewhere. No doubt, he said, it would be a simple job to clean and the stones could be recut and reset, at which point they began some serious bargaining.

Now he felt positively light-hearted as he opened the shop doorway. He would take the draft to his bank while he was in the City—his banker would be almost as pleased to see it as he had been. It wouldn't solve many of his problems, but he would be able to get the new well dug and that was desperately needed by the villagers.

The tinkle of the shop bell as he closed the door and emerged on to the pavement was lost in the noise of Ludgate Hill. Then the quality of the racket struck him— shouting, the screams of passengers on top of the stage-coach that was coming to a sliding halt, the shriek from the window of the carriage standing just up the hill from where he stood.

'*Miss Jessica!*'

Chapter Six

❦

There in the middle of the traffic, frantically clutching a small child to her, was Jessica Danby. Her only hope of escape was to dive under a slow-moving wagon and Alex saw her realise it at the same moment he did.

Alex was already running before he completed the thought. He crashed into her, wrapped his arms around both of them and leapt for the wagon, rolling under it and then digging in everything—heels, elbows, his one free hand—to keep them there safe from its great wheels.

They were in a little bubble of silence in the middle of a torrent of sound. Alex found he had stopped breathing. And then the child began to cry and he heard Jessica murmuring something soothing. They were all alive then.

The wagon had stopped, people were reaching for them. Cautiously Alex untangled himself from the others and looked down. 'Are you all right?' he asked urgently.

'Arthur! Arthur!'

The child scrambled free and scooted under the wagon into the arms of the woman kneeling on the pavement, regardless of the dust and worse that coated the stone.

'The boy seems to be,' Jessica said, her voice shaky. 'And I do not think that I have broken anything.'

'Let's get out from here.' Alex slid out and reached for

her, realising as he did so that the index finger on his left hand was at a strange angle. And, now he saw it, it hurt like the devil.

Jessica took one look at his hand and scrambled out unaided, only to be fallen upon by the child's mother who burst into tears. Behind her, her husband, little Arthur in his arms, was repeating over and over, 'Thank you, thank you.'

'I suggest you take your son to see your physician as soon as possible,' Alex said, getting to his feet and helping Jessica untangle herself from the grateful woman. 'Miss Danby, is that your carriage over there?' As her maid was clinging to the half-open door sobbing in relief, it seemed a reasonable assumption.

'Yes, indeed. I will drive you to a physician.' They crossed the street with little trouble as most of the traffic had come to a halt now, drivers and riders gawping at the scene. 'Now, Trotter, stop that noise at once, I am quite all right. George, please drive us to—could you tell us the direction of your physician, Demeral?'

'Thank you.' He told George the address and climbed into the carriage after Jessica. *Miss Danby,* he reminded himself as he sat, carefully holding his left hand away from his body. The shock of the last few moments was the only excuse for thinking of her by her first name. That and the lingering memory of her, soft and vulnerable, crushed between the hard road and his body. 'But should we not go first to your own physician?'

'I do not have one. Papa has engaged the services of a Dr Frazier, but I do not place much hope of him doing anything but bleeding me, and giving me something for my "nerves". All ladies suffer from nerves, apparently. I do not feel that a tonic would be helpful.'

'Not for bruises, no,' Alex agreed. 'In that case you might like to ask my doctor's wife, Mrs Chandler, to tend to you. Robert Chandler was an army surgeon and his wife followed the drum with him, even assisting him on the battlefield. You may be sure she will miss no injury that needs attention.'

He watched her as she sat back against the squabs and closed her eyes. Her bonnet was a crushed and dirty wreck on the seat beside Trotter, her hair was coming loose, her face was filthy and she must be aching all over from a mass of bruises. But she was not weeping, not complaining, not even impatient with her maid who was trying to thrust a smelling bottle under her nose and fan her with a handkerchief.

A rare young woman, Miss Danby. He found himself having to resist the urge to reach over and touch her cheek, as much to reassure himself as her. Life was so very fragile.

'What happened?' he asked.

'The family were looking in the jeweller's window. The child was bored and wanted to play with his hoop,' she said without opening her eyes. 'It is matchwood now, I fear.'

The carriage came to a halt and the footman opened the door. 'Should we go and tell Mr Danby what has occurred, Miss Jessica?' He was looking anxious and well he might be, Alex thought. The ironmaster would expect the strapping footmen he employed to keep his daughter safe from as much as a jostle on the pavement, let alone a close encounter with the iron-shod hooves of a stagecoach team and the foot-wide wheels of a heavy dray.

'No, it is perfectly all right, Henry. And it was not your fault. After all, I sent you into the shop. You cannot be in two places at once.'

The young man looked a little relieved at that and helped her down, closely followed by the agitated maid, then ran up the steps to knock. The front door opened and Alex followed them, trying not to wince as he moved.

It took a few minutes for Jessica to properly realise where she was. The drama on Ludgate Hill had shaken her more than she had realised and her body was beginning to feel every point where she had hit the road. And every point where Demeral had lain over her.

She was aware of him talking to another man, one with a deep, reassuring voice, of being seated on a hard hall chair and then of women's voices, of a firm but gentle hand under her arm and of being helped to climb a flight of stairs.

'Where—?'

'I am Anna Chandler and this is my maid, Morris, and this must be your own maid, I assume. Now let us take off these clothes and loosen your stays and we can see if you have done any damage. That's right, do not try to help, just let us work and then you can lie down and everything will feel much better...' The voice faded away and so did the blurred image of the room.

The faint cannot have lasted many minutes, Jessica thought as she began to make sense of what was happening around her. She was lying on something soft and the pressure of stays and lacing had gone. When she opened her eyes she saw she was dressed only in her shift with a sheet over her and an unknown woman had folded it back so that she could examine her right leg.

'Ah, good, you are back with us, Miss Danby. Please can you wriggle your toes for me? Excellent. And bend your knee up. And down again. Turn the foot to the side. Does this hurt? And this?'

The examination went on methodically, one limb after another. Then her chest, her shoulders and neck, her head. She was rolled over, prodded some more and then rolled back.

'There is a lot of bruising and it will be very painful as it works out. I can give you a salve for it and I would recommend hot baths at least twice a day. Take willow bark tea for the pain; I would prefer it if you did not take anything stronger and certainly not any quack medicines.'

Jessica wriggled up a little against the pillows. 'Mrs Chandler? Is that correct? Are you a doctor?'

'No.' Her smile was rueful. 'But I have learned battlefield medicine and surgery by both assisting with it and performing it. You appear to have been ridden over by a troop of cavalry, so your injuries are quite familiar to me, Miss Danby.'

'It was almost a stagecoach, but the Duke landed on top of me and rolled me to safety.' As her head cleared she remembered how he had looked: tough, dirty, pale under the grime and with an injury to his hand that he was ignoring. 'How badly is he hurt?'

'A dislocated finger, I suspect, rather than a break, and probably a fine collection of bruises, although perhaps less than you, as he landed on top of you.' She turned from the basin where she had been washing her hands and picked up a towel. 'But do not worry about Alex, he is hardier than the average society gentleman.'

'You know him well, Mrs Chandler?' Jessica managed to sit up a little further, very curious now.

'Anna, please. Yes, Alex is an old friend. We all grew

up together. He lived at the castle, my father was the vicar and Robert was the doctor's son. We played as children, he and Robert shared the same tutor and I would slide in to the schoolroom and listen and learn. I grew up thinking I would marry Alex—that was my firm intention from the age of five—but then when Robert came back from his studies and said he was going into the army as a surgeon I realised who it was I truly loved.'

'You have lived an adventurous life.'

'It was.' She smiled faintly. 'And hard. But only five years of it were with the Army. Robert always intended to set up his practice in London.'

She was about Demeral's age, Jessica thought, past her mid-twenties but not yet thirty. Anna was tall, brisk and handsome rather than pretty, with dark hair coiled at the nape of her neck.

'Do you wish you could practice medicine or surgery in your own right?' she asked, curious about another woman with such skills.

'Yes, of course. Perhaps one day women can be admitted to the medical schools and be accepted as physicians. As it is, I have my own practice of sorts—many women come to see me, even if their fathers or husbands receive a bill for my services in Robert's name. Now...' she tossed the towel aside '... I suggest we get you dressed, without your stays, and you return home. Alex tells me that your father is likely to become agitated if you are away for a long time.'

It was painful, but eventually Jessica was dressed again, her clothes brushed and sponged by Trotter and Anna Chandler's maid. Not all the buttons would do up without the stays tightly compressing her waist, but she was decently covered, at least.

'Tell me,' she said, when the other women had left the room and Anna was helping her with her shoes, 'what was Demeral like as a boy?'

Anna chuckled. 'A little devil. We all were, I suppose. But he was the worst. He was always getting into scrapes, always inventing new games or adventures. He has a wonderful imagination. If he had his way, he would have been a knight, or an explorer.'

'That sounds as though he was a romantic.'

'Very. Or do you mean as a young man in relation to women? Oh, most definitely that. It was how I managed to run away with Robert. Alex saw we were in love and helped us in every way he could—he lent us money, even though he had little himself, he pretended he had seen me in the town when I was three hours down the turnpike road in the opposite direction heading for London, then he led everyone on a wild goose chase suggesting that I must be lost in the hills. He said that one day he would fall in love, too, and he hoped that then someone would help him.'

So, it had not been an excuse to spare her feelings when she had made that impossible proposal. Alex Demeral really was looking for his true love and she was not that woman. He had made that quite clear.

'Keep it strapped up for a day or two until the swelling goes down and then exercise it gently.' Robert Chandler tied off the bandage bracing Alex's little finger to the one next to it. 'A brave young woman, that Miss Danby,' he added casually.

Alex was not deceived. 'An original, and a very wealthy

one,' he said, equally casually. 'The daughter of Danby the ironmaster.'

Robert whistled as he began to pack away his instruments. 'Her papa will be very grateful for your rescue, then. Unless you were her escort, in which case he'll probably have something in mind for you involving blast furnaces, or heavy hammers, for allowing her to stray into danger.'

'I had no idea that she was in the area. I came out of Rundell, Bridge & Rundell and there she was in the middle of Ludgate Hill with this child in her arms and a stagecoach bearing down on her.'

'So you were the hero of the hour.'

'No, that was Miss Danby. The child would have been killed if it were not for her. All I did was arrive late on the scene and push them under a passing wagon.'

'But you were acquainted with her before this?' Robert leaned against his desk and began slowly re-rolling what was left of the bandage.

'What is this? An interrogation? I had met her two or three times at social events and once in Hyde Park.'

'And the size of her dowry has not convinced you that you have fallen in love?' Robert was having trouble suppressing a grin, curse him.

'No, it has not,' Alex said, trying to look mildly amused and not at all defensive. That was the trouble with old friends, they knew you too well. Damn it, he liked Jessica Danby and he admired her courage, but he was quite easy in his mind regarding his feelings for her.

'How is the practice shaping up?' he asked, firmly changing the subject. 'Are you building a good list of patients?'

'I am and so is Anna. Quite a number of ladies who have

met her as chaperon when consulting me have switched their allegiance to her. We have to be careful—it would cause me a lot of trouble if she was accused of trying to practice as a doctor. But we are certainly very comfortable now.'

'That is good.' Alex tried not to feel jealous of his friend's happiness. Robert had a wife whom he loved, a career that was fulfilling and one which apparently maintained him in some comfort.

He would find the same for himself, he told himself firmly. The wife for him must be out there somewhere. They would meet and fall for each other. He had the title, she would have the wealth and together they would make the estate prosper and raise a brood of happy, healthy children.

He gave a firm nod, encouraging himself, and then felt a fool as he saw the amused expression on Jessica's face. She was standing in the doorway, probably wondering what on earth he was grimacing about.

What was it about this young woman that made him feel so self-conscious?

Chapter Seven

'I did not hear you come in, Miss Danby. You look much recovered,' Alex added truthfully. The dirt had gone, she had regained some colour and, thankfully, she had incurred no damage to her face. He tried not to think of the bruises she had suffered on the rest of her body. In fact, he tried not to imagine her body at all, although he couldn't help but notice that her curves were rather more natural than before, which meant Anna had removed her stays. He was definitely not going to think about that. His body reminded him about how she had felt beneath him and he tried to flex the injured finger until the pain drove those thoughts out of his head.

'I am, thanks to Anna's skill,' she said, smiling at him as he held open the consulting room door for her. 'How is your hand? Is it very painful? I hope you did not break any bones.'

'A dislocated finger, that is all.' He held up his bandaged hand to show her. 'It will be perfectly all right in a few days.'

'I am so glad. Now, may I offer you a place in my carriage? If you give my driver your direction, we can easily make any detour necessary.' She drew on her dirt-streaked gloves as she spoke, perfectly composed.

Why the devil was he feeling quite the opposite? Delayed shock, or, more likely, his imagination conjuring up the image of pale curves disfigured by the black and purple marks of cobblestones.

'Thank you but, no. I was on my way to my bankers and I should return there. It is in quite the opposite direction, so I will take a hackney.' Now he was talking too much. He turned back to his friends. 'Thank you for this, Robert.' He held up his bandaged hand and then turned to kiss Anna on the cheek. 'You must both come to dinner very soon.'

He escaped into the hall and took his hat and gloves from the maid who was waiting patiently with them, then went briskly out and down the steps, stuffing his now shredded gloves in his pocket and hailing a passing hackney as he went. Once again after an encounter with Jessica Danby he had the sensation of having escaped. But from what?

Alex pulled the bank draft out of his pocket and read it again. At least there was no mystery about that, only thoroughly good news.

'May I settle my account now?' Jessica asked as the door closed behind the Duke. 'Only I would prefer not to worry my father with the realisation that I had to seek medical attention.'

'There is nothing to settle,' Anna said. 'Not for a friend of Alex's.' She gave Jessica a quizzical look. 'You *are* a friend of his, are you not?'

'I believe so,' Jessica said coolly. 'I have much to thank him for. And thank you so much, Mrs Chandler. Mr Chandler. Trotter, it is time we returned home, please go and summon George.'

'He's just outside, Miss Danby,' Trotter said, tight-lipped.

Miss Danby, not Miss Jessica. Now what was the matter with her? It soon became clear when they were seated in the carriage.

'You have no bonnet, Miss Jessica. What are people going to think?'

'What people?'

'Whoever sees you arriving home, of course. No lady goes out without a hat.'

'I did not go out without it,' Jessica pointed out. 'But I can hardly put on the dirty, crushed object that it has become. And if anyone sees me between the carriage and my front door in such a shocking state of undress, they may think what they like. Now, do not go alarming Papa with exaggerated tales of what took place on Ludgate Hill. And there is absolutely no need to mention it to any of the staff either. Henry and George will not, I am certain.'

'Because they would be in trouble for not looking after you better, Miss Jessica, that's why,' Trotter said smugly.

'They are no more to blame than you are. You did not try to stop me getting out of the carriage,' Jessica said, rather unfairly, and saw that sink in. 'It is best for all of us if we do not worry my father with this.'

Jessica had spent two days endeavouring to move about as little as possible when her father was present. The bruises had made themselves painfully apparent and she had been hard put to it not to hobble and wince.

By the third day she was feeling better. There was no word from the Duke, for which, of course, she was very grateful, so she caught up with her correspondence and completed a chart from her notes at the newspaper office.

'Here you are, Papa,' she said, carrying it into his study

after luncheon. 'I have listed all the parts of the various Guild parades last year—the number of floats, what they portrayed, all the different groups of people involved, how they collected money and so forth.

'I believe the first thing is for you to establish what theme, if any, the Guild wishes to represent and what the budget is. Then we can make firmer plans. And several of my friends say they would be interested in helping me.'

'Excellent, my dear. What a support you are to me.' He scanned her notes and nodded. 'Yes, I will be off to the Guild this afternoon and find out about all these points.'

He got to his feet and enveloped her in an affectionate hug that almost had her yelping with pain—it seemed the bruises were not as improved as she had thought. Perhaps she would not attend the ball this evening and plead a head-ache. Squeaking with discomfort every time she raised her arms would not be the behaviour expected of a young lady.

It took a week before the worst of the aches and pains subsided. Jessica had resumed her social activities sooner than she really wanted so as not to worry her father and she could not help be glad when he announced at luncheon that he was going out. But the prospect of an uninterrupted afternoon of rest with the latest three-volume novel from the circulating library was shattered—no sooner had the front door closed behind her father than there was the sharp rap of the knocker.

'Miss Beech has called, Miss Jessica. Are you receiving?' the butler enquired.

'Yes, certainly. Have tea sent in, please, Markham.' Although whether Jane would want it so soon after luncheon was doubtful.

What Jane did need, however, was a supply of handkerchiefs. The tears she was holding in check burst free the moment the door closed behind Markham.

'Whatever is the matter?' Jessica sat her on the sofa and put her arm around the shaking shoulders.

'It's Sydney,' Jane sobbed into her handkerchief.

'Sydney? Who is he? Oh, Mr Locksley, I suppose. What has happened? He is not ill, is he?'

Or dead... This degree of distress...

'He came to ask Papa for my hand in marriage,' Jane said.

'But that is excellent news.' Jessica reached into her sewing basket and found the handkerchief she had been hemming. 'Here, take this and try to speak more calmly, I can hardly understand you. Mr Beech did not refuse him, did he?'

Jane managed a snuffle, a nod and a gulp. 'Yes, he did. He was *horrible*.'

'What on earth has your father against the match? Mr Locksley has land and very eligible connections, has he not?'

That produced even more sobs, but eventually Jessica managed to get her friend calm enough to declare, 'Sydney wants to enter Parliament.'

'But that is good, surely? I thought that your father was deeply involved in politics and is thinking of standing for Parliament himself.'

'But Sydney is a *Whig*.'

'Oh. I understand the problem now.' Mr Beech was a Tory of the old school and Jessica had once had the misfortune to have to listen to him declaiming about the evils of the Whig party for a full half-hour. To him Whigs were disloyal to the Crown, would bring down the country by giving votes to the residents of the industrial towns—who were little more than rabble who would bring in revolution and the guillotine given half a chance—and attack the Church of England by extending rights to non-conformists.

'Sydney must have told him his plans to stand for election, because the next thing I knew—I was waiting in the little parlour—was that Papa was shouting for the footmen to throw Sydney out and declaring that he would see me a lifelong spinster rather than marry a Whig. I ran down the backstairs and out of the door into the yard and managed to catch Sydney before he could hail a hackney and we went to talk in the garden of the square.'

Jane blew her nose and took a gulp of her cooling tea. 'Sydney says he can never renounce his principles, although he would give up his Parliamentary ambitions for me. But that would be no better, Papa would still object to him now he knows his allegiance. And besides, how could I stand in the way of Sydney's ambitions? I could never forgive myself.'

'What does Mr Locksley propose doing?'

'He says we must wait until I am of age because we can marry then without Papa's permission. But that is two years!'

'Not so very long,' Jessica soothed.

'Papa knows this gentleman, Sir Willoughby Grafton, who is a political ally of his and he thinks he would be the ideal match for me. But Sir Willoughby is almost forty and takes snuff and has a damp handshake and I hate the way he looks at me. Papa says he will have me despite my hair,' she concluded miserably.

'Then you must just keep saying *no*.' Jessica was brisk.

'This is not the Middle Ages…your father cannot force you to the altar.'

'That is what Sydney says.' Jane dried her eyes and sat up straighter. 'But I am such a mouse, I know I am. I cannot bear anyone shouting at me. If only I had the courage to *do* something.'

'What are Mr Locksley's intensions for this evening, do you know? Perhaps if he is at a gathering that I am attending I can have a word with him, see if we can come up with a plan to change your father's mind.'

'He is going to his club this evening, he said. I was too upset to ask him about every day this week, but I know he is going to a masquerade at the Pantheon with a party of friends in three days' time because he told me yesterday. I wanted to go, too, but he said it was quite unsuitable for a young lady. Apparently it is attended by anyone who can afford the price of a ticket and some quite…er…loose, women will be there. I said in that case I was surprised he would go to such a place, but he says some of his friends who are supporting his candidacy will be in the party and he does not wish to offend them.'

'So what does Mr Locksley propose you do now?'

'He said we should meet in the Park tomorrow, but I think it will rain and Papa will find it very strange if I want to go out in that. And I began to cry and then Sydney became cross and said I was not helping by being over-emotional. So I told him he was being a beast and to go away because I never wanted to see him again.'

'Then you shall come for a drive with me in a closed carriage tomorrow and we will tell your father we are going shopping. An outing will do you good and I am sure Mr Locksley will apologise very soon and you can have a sensible, calm discussion about what is best to do. Now, don't you think you had best go home now and show Mr Beech a calm face? We do not want him guessing you are planning to disobey him, do we?'

'I need to do *something*…anything. Talking will do no good,' Jane said mutinously, but she left with a kiss for Jessica, a vague promise about shopping and a murmur of thanks for her support.

The encounter had left Jessica feeling decidedly unsettled. She spent the rest of the day brooding over what she could do to help Jane and not coming to any sensible conclusions, other than to try to strengthen her resolve to wait for two years. Later she would be attending a party at the home of Lady Archibald, who had secured the services of a leading soprano to give a recital during the course of the evening. Perhaps her other friends would be there, too, and they could put their heads together and come up with some ideas on how to help Jane, or at least lift her spirits.

It had given her an uneasy feeling to hear Jane speak so wildly. Jessica shook her head at her own fancies: Jane herself had said she was too much of a mouse to do anything. Even so, it was difficult to settle to Walter Scott's *Guy Mannering*, the hero's convoluted adventures doing nothing more than confuse her thoughts further.

Three days later Jessica had begun to relax and decide that her friend was not going to do anything foolish. Then, at half past nine, as Trotter was fastening her evening cloak for a soirée, Henry tapped on the door.

'What is it, Trotter?' Jessica asked impatiently. She was already late because between them they had dropped her jewellery box and everything had spilt out, some of the earrings vanishing under the bed and the dresser and having to be searched for on hands and knees.

Trotter came back with a decidedly sour expression on her face. 'That red-headed friend of yours has done something rash by the sound of it and her maid is downstairs asking to speak to you. I wouldn't get involved with it if I were you, Miss Jessica. You can do without other people's scandals.'

So her forebodings that afternoon were not so foolish after all. 'Henry, please bring her up,' Jessica called, ignoring Trotter's tut of disapproval.

Jane's abigail was much younger than Trotter and very agitated. Her bonnet was askew on her head and her coat buttoned wrongly. 'Oh, Miss Danby, thank you for seeing me, only I don't know what to do for the best, I don't truly. I'm scared to go to the master, but what if Miss Jane's in danger?'

'Take a deep breath, calm down and tell me what your name is.'

'I'm Rigby, Miss.'

'Now, what has happened?'

'Miss Jane has gone to the masquerade, all by herself,' the girl gabbled, wringing her hands together.

'The masquerade at the Pantheon?'

'Yes, Miss, that's the one. And she shouldn't go there, I'm sure. I've heard they are dreadful romps, not fit for any decent lady.'

'When did she leave, Rigby? Was she by herself?'

'About nine it was, Miss. I think she must have had an invitation she hadn't told me about, because she's been in such a strange mood all day. I thought she was staying in for the evening, but then she rang for me and told me to find her an evening dress and a domino and a mask. I asked her what time the carriage was ordered for and she said a friend was collecting her. But when she went out she hailed a hackney carriage and Peter—that's our footman—said she asked for the Pantheon. But that's not at all respectable, is it?'

'I should say not indeed,' Trotter said. 'A den of iniquity. Ruined she'll be. Ruined.'

Chapter Eight

'Trotter, be quiet and let me think,' Jessica said, holding up a hand to stem the flow. Jane must have decided to rebel against her father and show Locksley that she was an independent woman—always assuming she had applied any rational thought at all to the matter and had not been simply acting out of frustration and pique.

The best outcome would be that Jane found Sydney Locksley at once, that her mask and the hood of the domino concealed her identity and he was able to get her home and back into the house undetected.

What was far more likely was that she would become lost in the throng at the masquerade and would be recognised or, even worse, was assaulted. Or both.

'We have to get her away from there,' she said out loud.

'*We*, Miss Jessica? I hope you are not thinking that you or I are going to involve ourselves with this fiasco,' Trotter stated flatly.

Jessica could not delude herself that she was capable of finding and removing Jane by herself, or even with Trotter. Without help she would be as vulnerable as her friend. There was only one person that she could think of who could help her, although whether he would put himself in such a compromising position she had no way of telling.

'Trotter, I need the simplest of my evening gowns, the black domino and a mask.' The maid opened her mouth, refusal written plain on her face. 'Unless you want me to tell Papa that you wish to return home to Shropshire? If that is the case, then Rigby can help me dress. I am going to write to the Duke and ask for his help. I will be quite safe with him.'

As she turned to her little writing desk she saw the sudden calculation cross Trotter's face. If Jessica was compromised with the Duke, then that would be a very satisfactory outcome in Trotter's opinion—and in her father's, too. The maid began to shake out a gown with considerable enthusiasm.

Jessica scribbled a hurried note, not disguising how serious she thought the situation was and ending.

I know you have no reason to assist me but, for the sake of a young lady too innocent to realise what danger she is in, I beg you to come. J.D.

'Trotter, find Henry.'

She sealed the note, wrote the Duke's name and address on the wrapper and thrust it into the footman's hand. 'Henry, deliver this as fast as you can. If the Duke is not at home, find where he has gone and follow him. It is very urgent. If he agrees to return with you, do not bring him into the house. Ask him to remain in the carriage and come and fetch me.'

'Yes, Miss Jessica.' He turned and she heard his shoes clattering down the back stairs.

Now all she could do was change her clothes, wait and hope.

* * *

'I found the Duke at home, Miss Jessica,' Henry announced half an hour later, breathless after running back up the stairs again. 'He says of course he will help and he's waiting in his carriage outside. Oh, and he says to bring a maid with you.'

'So I should hope,' Trotter said with a sniff. 'I'll get my bonnet.'

'I think it had better be you, Rigby, if you are willing.' Jessica was already wearing the concealing domino over her gown, with no jewellery at all. She picked up the plain black silk mask that would conceal the upper half of her face.

'Oh, thank you, Miss Danby. I'd be easier in my mind if I was doing something and that's a fact.'

'Come along then, Rigby. Trotter, if anyone asks for me, simply reply that I was engaged to go to Lady Dreyscourt's entertainment, which is the complete truth.'

'Yes, Miss Danby.' It was clearly going to take a lot to soothe Trotter's ruffled feathers tomorrow, but for now Jessica had other things to think about.

Henry hurried to open the door of the carriage standing outside, its side panels covered, presumably to hide the ducal crest. Demeral was inside and half rose as they entered. He, too, was masked and wearing a domino, its hood thrown back.

'Miss Danby, good evening. This is not Trotter, I think?' He rapped on the roof and the carriage moved away immediately.

'No, this is Rigby, Miss Beech's abigail.'

Rigby, clearly finding the entire evening almost too much, gave a faint squeak of agreement.

'What was your mistress wearing, Rigby?' Demeral asked.

The girl gulped, but managed to speak clearly. 'A white silk evening gown—quite a plain one, because of the domino, sir. I mean, Your Grace. And a dark red domino and a half-mask with the face of a cat—white with black whiskers.'

'At least it is not another black domino,' Demeral said. 'That is something. Miss Beech's hair is very distinctive. Did she attempt to disguise that?'

'No, Your Grace. It was quite a simple arrangement though. I don't think much of it would show when the hood was up.'

'Then all we have to do is find her in a throng of several hundred people, most of whom will be drunk and all of whom will be bent on having a wildly good time which will not include respecting women. Rigby, you had best stay in the carriage. My driver and groom will be with you the whole time. Miss Danby, you and I will brave the masquerade.' He looked at her, no amusement in his expression at all. 'Do not, even for a moment, leave my side.'

'I will take hold of your domino and not let go,' Jessica said earnestly. 'I promise you.'

The eastern end of Oxford Street was not somewhere Jessica would usually have reason to visit and certainly not at night. She looked out of the carriage window and confessed to herself that, even if she had been foolhardy enough to come in pursuit of Jane by herself, she would have turned tail and fled when she saw the scene outside.

They were on the opposite side of the street to the Pantheon and she was surprised their driver had managed to get so close. The road leading west out of London was a busy highway at the best of times, but now it was chaos, with throngs of revellers on their way to the theatres, the inns and the more dubious pleasures of Soho, mingling with those who were arriving at the Pantheon and the crowds who had gathered to watch the spectacle.

The frontage of the building, with a portico and four Classical pillars, was clearly designed to look imposing, but the effect was somewhat spoilt by the position, crammed between narrow houses and shops on either side and opening directly on to the pavement. The milling crowd in front, most of whom were clearly not of the *haut ton,* did not help in raising the tone either.

Hawkers with baskets of pastries and oranges slung around their necks wove though the throng and others with barrows added their cries to the racket. Someone appeared to be selling meat for dogs, of all things.

'Are those…er…courtesans?' she asked as a flock of bejewelled women passed them. Their gowns appeared designed to reveal, or hint at, considerably more than they covered. In fact, Jessica thought they all looked as though they had come out forgetting at least one layer. Their hairstyles were wildly extravagant and their voices shrill with laughter.

'I think you are giving them a status in their profession that is more elevated than the reality,' Demeral said drily. 'A courtesan will be in the keeping of a gentleman with her own apartment and maid. Those girls will be going home to an entirely different kind of establishment, or to some squalid room. Not that I should be telling you any of that. Rigby, you stay here. Keep the blinds down, do not open the door except to me or the driver and groom.

'Come, Miss Danby. On with your mask. The sooner we find your friend, the better. And do not let go of me for a second.' Demeral adjusted his mask, a simple band of black silk with eyeholes, raised his hood and lifted her down to the pavement. He put his arm through a slit in the side of his domino and she did the same, tucking her hand firmly under his elbow. It felt strange to be so close to a man, to feel the warmth of him against her side, to grip the muscles that flexed slightly under her hand. Strange and rather exciting.

They crossed the street and Demeral forged a path to the door, paid for admission and led her inside. The noise was tremendous, echoing around the space which resembled nothing more to her eyes than a theatre without the seating. Music was being played loudly from the stage at the far end, dancers in every kind of fancy dress were energetically cavorting in the main body of the hall and the tiers of boxes lining the walls each seemed to be the venue for a private party of the wildest sort, with participants leaning over at dangerous angles, wine bottles being waved and—goodness! Jessica hastily averted her eyes from the nearest ground-level box where a man appeared to be undressing his fair companion.

'I thought there was a dome,' Jessica said, looking ceiling-wards in the hope things were less embarrassing higher up.

'There was, that is why the original building was called the Pantheon, like the original in Rome. But that version burned down. Now, we will start searching at this level and work our way up to the boxes if we have to. Look out for Locksley's hair, he'll have no reason to disguise it. He'll be easier to find than one girl in a dark red domino.'

* * *

It was a slow business and Jessica was beginning to panic, convinced they would never find Jane. There seemed to be an improbable number of red-headed men present and Jessica clung to Demeral as they criss-crossed the floor, getting close enough to study each one they saw.

Fortunately, despite Demeral's prediction, dark red dominos were not as common as red-headed men, it seemed, and most of the women present were not troubling with them at all, relying on their masks to conceal their identities. Or perhaps not… Jessica's attention was caught by a group of laughing young women, none of whom was wearing more of a mask than a tiny arrangement of feathers and lace. It was simply an aid to flirtation, she realised.

A large man, worse the wear for drink, jostled them and Demeral pushed him away with his free hand.

'This is getting rough. If we do not find her in a few minutes, I am going to take you back to the carriage.'

'Over there—look, another red-headed man.'

He was sitting on the low padded edge of one of the boxes at ground-floor level. There were little doors to allow the occupants to step out, but all along the row men were simply climbing over on to the dance floor and swinging their partners across, too. Demeral pushed a path to the box and the man looked around. It was Sydney Locksley. His mask had gone and he was gingerly touching a red mark across one cheek.

'Found you at last, Locksley.' The Duke pushed back his hood.

'Who the devil are you?' Locksley narrowed his eyes, wincing. 'Demeral?' He shook off the hand of one of the scantily clad girls who was pawing at his coat for attention. 'Let go of me, you've done enough damage already tonight.'

Jessica could see the entire box now. There were three other young gentlemen and two pretty girls draped across their laps and a table with bottles and glasses.

'Where is...?' She dropped her voice and whispered, 'Jane?'

'I don't know.' Locksley seemed dazed.

'Pull yourself together,' Demeral snapped. 'I don't care how drunk you are and I don't care what I have to do to sober you up. I want to know where the young lady is and I want to know now.'

'I tell you, I don't know. We'd settled in the box and were joined by these...ladies. There were four of them, but I told them to go away, that wasn't what we were here for. One left—she flounced off—but one sat on my knee, and then Jane appeared. I have no idea how she found me. She called me all kinds of names and before I could explain we hadn't invited the girls she slapped my face and it caught me off balance. The chair tipped, I fell off and hit my head. Knocked me out for a moment, I think. When I came round she had gone.'

He looked around, blinking as though he expected to see Jane still standing there. Jessica realised he must still be befuddled from the blow to his head.

'How long ago was this?' Demeral demanded.

One of the other men shrugged. 'Ten minutes? Less, perhaps.'

'We have to find her,' Jessica said to them. 'You go that way and you, that.' She pointed towards two corners of the room. 'We will search this way. That dark red domino with a cat mask must be an unusual combination.'

They hesitated, clearly unused to being told what to do by young women, but Demeral jerked his head and they climbed over the edge of the box and disappeared into the crowd. Jessica let herself into the box, climbed on to a chair and then on to the table, uncaring that she was showing her ankles or that several young bucks turned and stared.

'Get down from there.' Demeral raised his hands to lift her.

'No, I can see better up here.' She turned slowly, the little table rocking beneath her. Demeral took hold and steadied it. 'Look, over there under that big chandelier—a dark red hood. Oh, and something is happening.'

Chapter Nine

'Locksley, you stay here and get your wits back. Jane may return.' Demeral grasped Jessica around the waist and lifted her off the table and over the edge of the box. At that level there was no glimpse of the red domino, but he headed confidently into the crowd, forcing his way through. Jessica clung to his cloak.

Even above the noise all around them they heard the shrill voice as they came closer. 'No, I will not take off my mask! Let me go, I want to leave, you horrible man!'

Three young men, their clothing respectable rather than costly and fashionable, had surrounded the red-cloaked figure and were making playful snatches at her cat mask while one held her arm. Whether it was Jane or not, this young woman needed help, Jessica thought as she took a firm grip on the strings of her reticule. It was a fashionable one, stiffened with card to hold its geometrical shape and sharp angles.

'Let her go this minute,' she said, poking her finger into the ribs of the nearest man.

He turned with a snarl and she hit him with the reticule, squarely on the nose. He retreated, howling. Demeral had the arm of the man holding the girl.

'The lady told you to let her go,' he said.

He was answered with a few short words of abuse that broke off in a gasp of pain. 'You've broken my bloody arm!'

'Excellent. Do your friends want to see what else I can break?' Demeral enquired of the man's remaining companion.

He took one look at his friends—one clutching his arm, the other with a handkerchief clamped to his bloody nose—and retreated back into the crowd.

The young woman gave a cry of 'Jessica!' and reached out for her.

'Jane, are you hurt?' Jessica demanded, pulling her friend close. The whiskers of the pretty cat mask were bent and below it there were tear tracks on Jane's cheeks. Her hair was coming down and her domino had been pulled crooked.

'No, not really, though my arm is bruised, I think. This is a horrible place. *Horrible*. I want to go home.'

'And so you shall. We will just go and collect Mr Locksley first.'

'I am never going to speak to him again! He is a libertine.'

'No, he is not,' Demeral said calmly as he started to guide them both back towards the box. 'Those women will go from box to box, uninvited, hoping to have drinks bought for them and to be paid for their company. They are devilish difficult to get rid of. There he is and he appears to have recovered from your assault. You knocked him out, you know.'

'Good. I hope it hurt,' Jane said, but she did not sound as though she meant it. When Locksley vaulted over the barrier and took her in his arms she went into the embrace with a sob and hugged him tightly. There was no sign of his companions,

'Have you got a carriage?' Demeral asked as the two men started towards the entrance, Jessica and Jane sheltered between them.

'No, we came in a hackney.'

'We have Miss Beech's woman in mine. I suggest you take it and escort her home in that. If the worst happens and you are discovered trying to get her inside, then at least you'll have been in a respectable carriage with the maid. We will find a hackney.'

But when they stepped back from the kerb as Demeral's carriage set off, containing a weeping Jane and a very grateful Locksley, there wasn't a hackney in sight.

'There never is when you want one,' Demeral said. 'At least it isn't raining. If we walk west a little, towards Mayfair, we should find one.'

'We could walk all the way,' Jessica said. 'It cannot be more than a mile, can it? And I put on very sensible shoes because I had no idea what we would have to do.'

'You put on sensible shoes.' Demeral said flatly, then looked down at her and grinned. 'Has anyone ever told you that you are a very remarkable woman, Miss Danby?'

'No,' she said, suddenly feeling very cheerful and full of energy. 'Shall we go? And call me Jessica, please. We can't be formal if we are having an adventure.'

'Jessica, then. And I am Alex and if we begin our adventure by going that way, eastwards, for a couple of turnings we will find Wardour Street. That will take us down to Leicester Square. Then we will cut across the bottom of that and work our way down to the Strand. Let me know if you become tired and I will find a hackney.'

'Very well.' She slipped her hand into the crook of his elbow and they walked briskly away from the crowds around the Pantheon, passed two streets on the right and then took the third, heading south.

'This is Soho. It is not an area a respectable lady would ever dream of going, so keep you mask on and, if there is any trouble, get behind me.'

'But it all seems very busy, and well lit,' Jessica said, looking around with interest. It was not at all what she might imagine a notorious district to look like. There were small houses, probably divided up into apartments, she thought. There were shops, too, each only a few feet wide, their doors open to spill light into the street and business going on briskly inside. She saw one had the three golden balls that signified a pawnbroker hanging crookedly from its frontage. That was doing particularly good trade.

The smell of meat pies and ale wafted from several places and on one corner a man was playing the fiddle, his black and white dog carrying a battered cap around the onlookers. Someone tossed in a small coin and the dog put down the cap, barked a thank you and picked it up again to general laughter. A woman, middle aged, buxom and wearing what looked like several layers of tattered skirts, took the arm of a man and swung him into a dance. Someone was passing around a stoneware flagon and both men and women were taking swigs from it.

'Gin,' Alex said.

Jessica did not feel at all intimidated by what she had seen so far, even if this was one of London's more louche areas, but that was probably because she was on the arm of a man who had already demonstrated that he was very effective in dealing with trouble. She felt a little frisson of excitement, although whether it was at the thought of the possible dangers or the closeness of the Duke, she was not sure. *Alex*. She was very aware again of those muscles under her hand.

'It all feels good natured,' she ventured. 'Although perhaps that will not last long if everyone is drinking gin like that.'

'Yes, we are fortunate it is this early.' He sounded relaxed, but she could sense his alertness, the slight shift of balance, the turn of his head, at each movement in the shadows, each unexpected sound. 'In the small hours I wouldn't dream of bringing you down here.'

'Are you armed?' It was a very long street, not wide and with many side turnings and dark entrances. She suppressed a gasp as two figures staggered out of one alleyway, singing and passing a bottle between them, and then vanished into another. Their tuneless song echoed back, distorted by echoes.

'A pocket pistol and a knife,' he admitted. 'And I have no hesitation in fighting in a most ungentlemanly manner if that is required. But it will not be, never fear.'

'I don't. I feel quite safe.'

With you.

A young woman came out of the shadows and smiled at Alex. 'You can do better than that with me, luv. Or she can join in if she likes. I'm not fussy.' Her dress looked fine in the poor light, then Jessica saw the hem was ragged and the woman was not young beneath the paint, her smile gap-toothed.

'I do not share,' Jessica said firmly, returning a smile just as false. Her imagination reeled. What on earth was she proposing? 'So sorry.'

Alex chuckled and guided her on, giving the street walker a wide berth.

'Don't laugh. The poor soul,' she chided as they passed on down Wardour Street. 'Imagine having to make your living in such a way.'

'And there are many of her sisters out on the streets. It doesn't take much for a woman to fall from safe respectability into that kind of life,' Alex said. 'At least it isn't raining or bitterly cold tonight.'

They walked in silence for a few steps then, Jessica said, 'Alex suits you. Why did your parents choose it, do you think? Alexander the Great? The Czar? It means warrior, I believe.'

'I am named for one of my godfathers. The richer of the two,' he added drily. 'Not that the flattery did much good. He left me a pocket watch, a collection of very dry volumes from his library and fifty pounds. And Jessica? Were your parents Shakespeare enthusiasts?'

'I am certain they were not. But Mama read somewhere that it means gift in Hebrew and she and Papa had wanted a daughter, so that is what they called me when I finally arrived after two large, noisy sons.'

'Are they still large and noisy?'

'Goodness, yes. They fill a room just by entering it. So much energy and self-assurance and such loud voices. I am finding London quite restful in comparison,' she said with some feeling. 'Do you have siblings?'

'I had a brother and sister. Twins. But they never thrived and died very young.'

He must have spent a lonely childhood, she thought, unless his parents took pains to prevent that—perhaps he'd had good friends. Ethan and Joshua were exhausting, but they were good brothers and she had never felt alone or isolated as the only girl. But she did not know the Duke—*Alex*, she reminded herself—well enough to ask about his child-hood. She suspected he would resent probing questions.

'This does not seem quite real, does it?' she said instead.

'What doesn't?' Despite her hood she was aware of him turning his head to look down at her.

'Walking through the streets of London after dark. Catching glimpses of other people's lives. It is magical, somehow.'

That provoked a snort of amusement. 'Magical? Drunks and drabs and the stench wafting from dark, dangerous alleyways?'

'I mean out of this world. Out of my world, anyway. I feel…free.'

'And you do not feel free normally?' he asked, sounding puzzled.

'Try being a woman for a while and you would not ask that,' she said tartly. 'Especially being a respectable, un-married lady. You may never be alone, you may never act on impulse. Every action, every word must be guarded, be correct, or you are labelled fast and ill bred. Perhaps being a widow is best for a woman. A rich widow, of course.'

'To be a widow you would have to be a wife first,' Alex pointed out.

'I know.' She gave an exaggerated sigh. 'Depressing, isn't it?'

'You, Miss Danby, are an original, I think.'

'I know what that means,' Jessica retorted. 'Indefinably odd, but everyone is too polite to say *eccentric*.'

'It is *not* what I mean,' Alex said, no longer sounding amused. 'You are a refreshing change from young ladies who have been schooled to hide whatever wits or original-ity they have, who have been trained to throw themselves squeaking in alarm into the arms of the nearest gentleman at the slightest provocation—a mouse, a loud noise—and who must never, ever disagree with a man.'

That was a compliment indeed and it made Jessica feel uncomfortably flustered. 'The impulse to throw oneself into the arms of a man because of spiders, mice or any other trivial alarm is soon shaken out of any girl with brothers,' she said. 'And Papa said that as I would have money then I must learn to look after it, so perhaps some of the lessons I shared with my brothers would surprise you. Then, when Mama died five years ago, I had to start learning how to manage the household. It would have been chaotic if I had pretended to have less wits than hair.'

'I imagine it would have been. We have just passed Lisle Street, so we will be in Leicester Square very soon. You are not tired?'

'No, not at all. Have you been to Mr Barker's Panorama?' Jessica asked, deciding it was time to move away from personal revelations. It was dangerous to become too friendly with this man, she told herself. He was the perfect gentleman, of course, but her unruly feelings were already a little bruised. 'It is just along here, I think. I hear it is exceedingly interesting.'

'I confess I have not.' He sounded rather short. Perhaps he thought she was angling for an invitation, which was embarrassing. 'Now, which would be the best way to Adam Street, I wonder? I think we will cut across the bottom of the Square towards Chandos Street and then down Bedford Street to the Strand. That keeps to the wider streets, but avoids you walking along the Strand for any distance.'

'I am hardly likely to be recognised, am I?' Jessica pointed out. 'But I suppose, so close to home, it would be sensible. If we go into Salisbury Street, just past Adam Street, then we can get to the back entrance of the house. I do have a key.'

'Sensible woman,' Alex said, sounding less distant again. Perhaps he was feeling the responsibility of allowing her whim to walk through the dark streets.

It was not so much fun now, she realised. The magic had gone out of the evening as the lights of the Strand grew closer. Now it was a question of negotiating the broad, busy thoroughfare, of worrying about getting into the house unseen.

'I hope Jane has returned home safely and that she has made it up with Mr Locksley,' she ventured as they made it safely to the southern side of the Strand and Alex tossed a coin to the crossing sweeper. 'And I do hope it will force them into some kind of decision about their future. They have to make a plan, not simply mope about.'

'You are a great believer in plans, are you not, Jessica? Down here, you say? Yes, I see. Which is the back gate to your house?'

'That one.' Had that remark about plans been a jibe over her scheme to propose marriage to him? 'I do try to form strategies, yes. I have been brought up to be businesslike. Sometimes they do not work out as I had intended, I suppose,' she added, trying to sound cool and not defensive.

'Jessica.' Alex stopped, just outside the tall gate leading into their small back garden.

'Yes?' She looked up at him. He was very close, a dark shadow in his black domino. The silence seemed to stretch on, full of a strange tension, and to break it she slid her hand from under his arm.

'No.' He caught her hand, held it, then lifted it to his lips.

Chapter Ten

'No, do not be offended. I was not criticising you,' Alex said and dropped a light kiss on her knuckles.

Jessica was wearing gloves, of course, but the tissue-thin kid of evening gloves was no barrier against the warmth of lips, even in such a fleeting brush.

'There is no need to apologise,' she said and found her voice husky.

He released her hand. 'Where is your key?'

'Here.' She found it in her now somewhat battered reticule. Alex unlocked the gate and eased it open. 'What about the back door?'

'I have that, too.'

They walked quietly across the back garden, fitfully illuminated by a lamp that had been left burning in a first-floor window. A cat shot out of the shadows with an angry hiss, sending Jessica rocking back on her heels.

Alex caught her, steadied her and she turned in the circle of his arms, some instinct making her lift her hands to his shoulders, one of them sliding across to the back of his neck.

He bent his head, his lips so close she could feel his breath, taste the faintest hint of the brandy he must have been drinking when her note reached him. 'Jessica?'

The magic had returned to the night and with it a strangeness, the sensation of being out of her world, of leaving convention and common sense behind. She went up on tiptoe and their lips met, a fleeting touch, the merest sensation of warm flesh meeting an answering heat, then she was back firmly on both feet and Alex was a step away.

You fool, what have you done?

'That was a thank-you and a goodnight kiss combined,' Jessica managed to whisper with the lightest of laughs that she hoped did not sound as forced as it felt. He would never know how it had affected her, would he? 'You really have saved the day for Jane.'

'I hope so. Now, back inside, quickly, before anyone hears us.'

There—Alex did not sound shocked to the core that some idiotically impulsive female had just kissed him. It was probably simply her own lack of sophistication and experience that made that small touch seem such a significant thing. He probably kissed women goodnight on a regular basis.

'No, you must leave first so I can lock the gate behind you.'

He nodded and went out, a silent shadow among the alleyway's deeper shade. She thought he raised his hand in farewell as the gate closed behind him, but she could not be certain.

Jessica turned the key, then returned to the back door. It opened with the faintest of creaks as she crept inside, closed and locked it. The bolts at top and bottom had been barely opened—Trotter must have slipped down and done that after Markham, their butler, had made his rounds before retiring—so she slid those home, wincing at the scrape of metal through the hasps.

There was the dull glow from the banked-down range to guide her across the kitchen floor, then the dark of the passageway to negotiate before she found the foot of the servants' stairs where there was a perceptible lightening of the darkness. When she reached the first landing the light grew stronger and she found the lantern had had been left on the sill of the narrow window. She blew it out, then turned to open the door which led on to the first floor. Now she only had to creep past Papa's bedchamber and she was safe.

There, I have done it.

Trotter, dozing in the armchair in front of the fire, sat up with a jerk. 'Miss Jessica. I've been that worried,' she whispered.

'No need. We found Miss Beech and she will be home by now, although whether she has got in safely without being discovered, I have no idea.'

'That young lady deserves a good spanking, if you ask me, Miss Jessica,' Trotter muttered, but her fingers were busy with the fastenings of Jessica's gown and she added, almost grudgingly, 'You're a good friend, I'll say that.'

As the lock snicked closed Alex backed across the narrow alleyway so he could see the faint light in the upstairs window. If that vanished and no others were lit, then Jessica would have made it to her bedchamber undetected.

He told himself to stop thinking about bedchambers, but that fleeting, innocent, kiss had been powerfully arousing. Jessica meant nothing by it, of course. She was naturally warm and friendly, they had just shared an adventure that had been highly unconventional, slightly dangerous and, as Jessica had said, magical. A mere brush of the lips at the end of that meant nothing.

All his feelings proved, he decided, was that he was missing intimate female contact. It had not felt right, somehow, to set up a mistress at the same time as courting a wife, so in the New Year he had parted on good terms with the goldsmith's widow in the nearby town who had welcomed the *company*, as she put it, but by no means expected any permanent arrangement.

The light at the window flickered and was gone. He would wait another few minutes, just to make certain there wasn't a sudden uproar signalling her discovery, although what good he could do if that occurred, he couldn't imagine. The presence of a man would only make things worse.

Or would it? As he turned to make his way back to the Strand it occurred to Alex that if they had been discovered in the garden they would have been thoroughly compromised and then he would have had to marry Jessica. He would have secured his wealthy wife and Mr Danby would have captured his noble son-in-law.

Was that a twinge of regret he was feeling? Alex gave himself a sharp mental shake. He liked Jessica, he admired her and he found her stimulating company, but he was not in love with her. And she, although apparently liking him well enough at the start to suggest marriage, clearly considered him now in the light of a friend. From what he had observed, young ladies in love with a gentleman were incapable of behaving in an open, relaxed and friendly way around him. They blushed, they were shy, or they hung breathless on his every word. There was giggling. Much giggling. He had never heard Jessica giggle.

Laugh, yes, She had an attractive range of laughs from a throaty little chuckle to a clear, musical, peal.

What he needed was a drink. Alex turned and made his way towards the Coal Hole Tavern, haunt of actors and the location of the Wolf Club drinking society, founded by actor-manager Edmund Kean, for the benefit of, as he said, gentlemen whose wives would not let them sing in the bath.

The story always made Alex smile and he was in the mood for rowdy, cheerful and uncomplicated company. Women were, most definitely, not uncomplicated.

Jessica woke the next morning with a mixture of sensations. There was a general feeling of uneasiness, a flicker of panic and a warm glow of something indefinable. She blinked herself awake in the chilly February light and sat up to sip her cup of hot chocolate while Trotter supervised the maid who was setting the fire.

The panic was anxiety about Jane, she decided, the warm glow was satisfaction over having found her last night and hopefully settled the rift with Sydney Locksley. The uneasiness she explored, tentatively, much as one probed an aching tooth with the tip of the tongue.

Last night she had kissed Alex. Kissed the Duke of Malvern. He had not kissed her—except her hand—*she* had been the one to take the liberty.

Now what would he think of her? That she was wanton? Or perhaps that she was still trying to lure him into marriage? Or perhaps he would realise the truth, that she had been giddy with excitement after their adventure and had acted without thought or intention.

That was the best she could hope for, although she had no idea now what had possessed her, there in the dark. She finished the chocolate and found she was smiling. It might have been immodest and reckless, but she had enjoyed it.

Such memories from a fleeting moment of contact. Warmth, that faint hint of brandy, a taste she could not quite describe, but supposed must have simply been Alex, the sensation of his lips, soft and yet firm, and the slight prickle of masculine hair.

What now? It would not be discreet to send Alex a note to thank him for last night and besides, she had probably already done more thanking than she should have done. On the other hand, she had to find out whether Jane had reached her own bed safely or she would perish from curiosity. She would go after breakfast, far too early for a normal social call, but nothing out of the ordinary between young ladies and their friends.

At breakfast her father looked up from the pile of post he had been reading as she entered and she thought how much improved his health seemed to be. Perhaps it was the realisation that leaving her brothers in charge of the business had not resulted in the immediate collapse of the company, she mused with an inward smile.

'Good morning, Papa.'

'Good morning, my dear. And how was your party last night?'

'I am afraid it made absolutely no impression upon me at all,' she confessed truthfully, pouring him another cup of coffee before sitting down and thanking the footman for the pot of tea he placed beside her. 'Is there anything I can help you with today, Papa? I had thought of visiting Jane Beech this morning, but it should not take me long.'

'No, nothing, my dear. I am going to the Ironmongers'

Guild to attempt to shake some answers out of them about this May Day affair. I could not find anyone with much idea when I called the other day. It seems to me that they decided to take part because most of the other guilds do and then did nothing about planning it. They have no concept how they wish to represent the guild. It is no way to go about a business,' he said with a sorrowful shake of his head.

'I expect they all run their individual businesses very efficiently,' Jessica said, undecided over which jam to choose for her toast. 'But put them together and they lose focus. Because you are not an ironmonger yourself, you will be able to take a dispassionate view. I am sure you will guide them firmly, Papa.'

He preened slightly at her praise, his chest seeming to swell under the green brocade of his waistcoat. 'You may well be right, my dear. I shall be firm, but tactful. I have to thank them for taking an ironmaster from Shropshire into their company, after all.'

Jessica arrived at Jane's doorstep in Conduit Street on the stroke of ten. 'Good day, Fitton,' she greeted the butler. 'Is Miss Jane at home?'

'Good morning, Miss Danby. Miss Jane is in her sitting room. I will show you up.'

'Please don't trouble, Fitton, I know my way.' She ran up to the first floor where Jane had a small room with her writing desk and some comfortable chairs where she could entertain friends without disturbing her parents. Mrs Beech, who possessed the reputation of enjoying exquisitely sensitive nerves, much preferred to keep her drawing room free to entertain her own acquaintances.

The door had hardly closed behind the butler when Jane leapt up and ran to embrace Jessica. 'Oh, you've come! Thank you, I was going to send a note, but it is so difficult to think what I could safely write.'

'Tell me what happened,' Jessica said, disentangling herself and sitting down. 'You got back safely, obviously,' she added, keeping her voice low. It was a mistake to assume that servants never listened at doors, even in the best-run households.

'Rigby was wonderful—she had thought to bring the back door key with her and she had asked one of the other maids, who thought Rigby was slipping out to go courting, to open the bolts for her after Fitton had locked up. I have given her a very nice present of money, because if she had not warned you, I do not know what would have happened.'

'What on earth possessed you?' Jessica asked bluntly. She had a very good idea of what would have happened, even if Jane had not.

'I thought Sydney had simply given up and didn't care enough about me. Which was so unfair, because he was unhappy, too, which is why he went out with his friends. I thought I would be dashing and decisive and do something—and then when I got there, it was horrible and those girls who were with them were so pretty… And poor Sydney, I hit him and he banged his head. I don't know why he has forgiven me.'

'He loves you.'

Jessica's woebegone face broke into a smile. 'Oh, yes, he must do. He was so sweet in the carriage coming back. He said that we should elope because he could not think of any way to change my father's opinion, but I said, no, because it would blight Sydney's chances if there was a scandal.'

'I am not so sure about that,' Jessica said thoughtfully. 'As a young man Lord Eldon, the Lord Chancellor, eloped. I remember reading about it. His sweetheart climbed down a ladder from a window in her house in Newcastle in the dead of night and they were married over the Border. I'm sure I read that both his father and hers forgave them after a while and you can hardly say that *his* chances were blighted! He was made a baron and has been Lord Chancellor for simply years.'

Jane stared at her. 'The Lord Chancellor eloped? My goodness, how wonderful. Perhaps I am wrong to worry about Sydney's career. After all, it is not as though Papa is a well-known public figure and, although he may have many friends and have influence among the Tories, his opinion will not hold any sway with the Whigs.'

'That's the spirit,' Jessica encouraged. 'If you are certain that Locksley is the one for you, then you will have to do something drastic or face the future with someone who is second best. Has he any money?'

'He has a doting godmother who gives him an allowance and he has been offered a post as secretary to Lord Wantage.' She frowned in thought. 'He needs to make certain both his godmother and Lord Wantage would not disapprove, but if they will support him then we would have enough to live on modestly, even if Papa cuts me off without a penny.'

'There, you have a plan. Now all you have to do is talk to your Sydney and he has to consult his patrons. Now I had better go, because I need to help Papa with this May Day planning for the Guild and he is visiting them today to press for some decisions.' It was an excuse because her father would not return for some time, but she wanted to encourage Jane to do some hard thinking for herself.

They kissed cheeks and Jessica, mentally crossing all her fingers for the couple, collected Trotter from where she had been waiting in the hallway and emerged on to Conduit Street. They had walked because the day was dry with a little weak sunshine breaking through the clouds, but now, as the wind freshened, she was glad of the warm pelisse she was wearing.

'Where now, Miss Jessica?'

'Home, I think, Trotter,' she said, wondering why the maid was staring over her shoulder with a decidedly odd expression on her face.

'Good day, Miss Danby.'

It was the Duke, driving a high-perch phaeton drawn by a fine pair of matched bays.

'Would you care to take a turn around the Park?'

Chapter Eleven

'Drive with you?' Jessica said, then collected her scattered wits and bobbed a slight curtsy. 'I mean, good morning, Demeral. Thank you, but I am not certain—'

I am not certain of what I am not certain! she thought, almost ready to laugh at herself for being in such a fluster.

And over what? An innocuous invitation from a gentleman to drive in an open carriage.

'As you see, I have my groom up behind, so we would be perfectly respectable, although I regret there is no room for Trotter to accompany you.' Alex was keeping a perfectly straight face, although she strongly suspected from the twinkle in his eyes that he, too, was amused by her confusion.

'Thank you, Demeral, I should be delighted. Trotter, His Grace will return me home, so there is no need for you to wait.' She opened her reticule. 'Here is the fare if you would prefer to take a hackney carriage.'

'Thank you, I'm sure, Miss Danby.' Trotter had her sucking lemons' expression back. 'What shall I tell Mr Danby should he enquire as to your whereabouts?'

'That I am driving with a friend in the park, of course. Papa is a busy man, Trotter. There is no need to disturb him with tittle-tattle about my doings.'

'No, Miss Danby. You will be back in time for luncheon?'

'Of course. Thank you.' That was to the groom who had jumped down from his perch to assist her up to the high seat that balanced precariously over the front axle of the carriage. 'Goodness, what a long way up! I am already changing my mind about asking Papa for such a carriage.'

'This one will be on the market soon,' Alex said with a grimace as the groom ran round to climb up behind. 'Both the carriage and the bays. They are an extravagance to maintain. I won them at cards last year, but I should content myself with my curricle and greys.'

That was frank speaking, Jessica thought. Most gentlemen would avoid any suggestion that they could not afford their blood horses or their sporting vehicles and would cheerfully run up large debts if that was what it took to maintain them. She liked it in Alex that he would tell her so candidly; it argued that he had little false pride and also that he trusted her as a friend.

'A curricle must be equally stimulating to drive,' she suggested. It was also rather more dashing than a phaeton in her opinion, if not as showy for parading about in the park.

'That is true. Do you have a taste for speed, Jes—' He broke off and she was suddenly conscious of the groom behind them. 'Miss Danby?'

'I fear so. At home in Shropshire I have a gig and I am always in trouble with Papa for dashing about the countryside. But I would not dare attempt anything more than a sedate trot in London. It would be considered fast for a lady to do so, would it not?'

'I fear so, but if you go out to Richmond Park, for example, you could enjoy more freedom. Would your father object if you were to drive me there with your own groom in attendance?'

Jessica shot him a startled glance. 'No, he would not object in the slightest.' She dropped her voice. 'But he would leap to a quite incorrect conclusion if we were to do so. In any case, I think you should be driving other young ladies about, in search of your kindred spirit, not spend your time with me, a mere friend.'

The bays checked as though Alex's hands had tightened involuntarily on the reins, but he answered her lightly enough, 'Never *mere*, Miss Danby. Tell me, have you news of our mutual friends and their adventures?'

'She arrived safely home, I am glad to say. I have spoken to her and suggested that concerns about his career if they take drastic action might be pessimistic. I told her about Lord Eldon and his youthful elopement and that seems to have stiffened my friend's resolve to take action, or, at least to discuss tactics calmly with the gentleman.'

'Excellent. Let me know if I can assist. I am sure I can lay my hands on a rope ladder if required.'

That made Jessica laugh. 'I really cannot imagine anything as foolish as leaving a house that way—although that is how Lord Eldon managed it, I understand, and from a window at the front of the house on quite a busy street by Newcastle's riverside. Perhaps it was an ordinary ladder, though. Just think, with a rope one it would be swaying about, the lady clinging on for dear life and probably squeaking in terror. And down below the gentleman trying to keep his horses quiet and reassure his love at the same time. If that was not enough to wake the household, nothing would.

'No, if I were to elope I would do it in the morning, announcing that I was going to my dressmaker for a lengthy fitting and then planning on taking luncheon with a friend and spending the afternoon shopping. I would have smuggled out the necessities for the journey over several days and I would take enough money with me for things I had forgotten—tooth powder, for example. You cannot expect gentlemen to remember such things. As a result there would be no drama and no one taking alarm at my absence for hours.'

'Very practical, but not very romantic. You leave little scope for the lover to display his courage in confrontations with footmen or in frantic races for the Border,' Alex said as they turned through the reservoir gate into Green Park. It sounded as though he was trying not to laugh. 'Tell me, would you care to take the reins once we are past the reservoir? The rides towards the Queen's House look quiet to me.'

'I would, thank you,' she said eagerly, watching as Alex eased the bays past the more crowded area around the long reservoir, always a favourite area for nursemaids to allow their small charges to scream with excitement as they chased the unfortunate ducks, or threw them crusts of bread. There were several ladies walking small dogs on leashes, most of which stopped to yap shrilly at the passing phaeton. The bays, well-schooled, loftily ignored them, although Jessica felt herself tense each time.

'There now, a nice quiet track ahead of us,' Alex said once they were well past the water. He handed her the reins and then the whip. 'The angle will seem strange at first, being higher and further forward than you are used to. Relax your wrist and hold them just here. That's right.'

The bays stood obediently while Jessica's heartbeat

speeded up strangely. Two pairs of gloved hands meeting, that was all it was, she told herself severely. And she should be concentrating on the instructions Alex was giving her, not on how close he was.

'I think I have got it,' she said, hoping the slight squeak in her voice could be mistaken for nerves over driving the swaying carriage.

'Then off we go,' Alex said sitting back.

Help, she thought, resisting the urge to thrust the reins back into his hands, then relaxed her grip, made an encouraging clicking sound to the pair and let out a breath as they walked placidly forward.

'It is easier than I had feared,' she confessed after a few minutes of sedate walking. 'But I do not think I want to trot yet.'

'Take your time,' Alex said comfortably. 'Neither the bays nor I are in any haste.'

'But surely you were going somewhere when we met?'

'I was on my way to visit the other party in last night's excitements,' he explained. 'But my mind is now at rest, although I suppose I had better call at some point today and offer my support for whatever scheme he has come up with. I will pass on your views on rope ladders and discourage him from any attempts at escape in the small hours.'

That made Jessica laugh and relax her hands and the bays broke into a trot. She resisted the urge to rein them in and let them continue, pretending she had intended the increase in speed all along.

Alex, who seemed as relaxed as his horses about her driving, glanced towards another grass ride converging with theirs. 'That's Percy Rowlands driving his curricle. I wonder who—can that be your friend Lady Anthea?'

Jessica risked a look. 'It is and without a book in her hands, which is a minor miracle. They seem to be deep in conversation. You don't think—surely not?'

'To be frank, my mind is having problems with the thought of the two of them driving together, let alone anything more…personal. Do you want to stop and talk when we reach them?'

'No, not really,' Jessica confessed, reining in the bays to a walk. 'They seem very engrossed in each other.' Besides, she did not welcome an intrusion into her companionable drive with Alex.

'Then let us stop here and take a stroll through that grove of trees. The ground looks dry enough.' He twisted around on his seat. 'Will, when we stop, take the reins and bring them around to meet us on the other side of that clump.'

'Yes, Your Grace.'

Jessica brought the bays to a halt and tried to feel confident when Alex jumped down leaving her alone in the vehicle. But it was only for a moment before the groom climbed up to take the reins from her and then Alex was reaching for her.

For a giddy moment she was in the air, his hands firm around her waist, and then she was on the ground. 'Thank you.'

Alex did not move, his hands still holding her lightly, and she found she did not want to stir either, because she was looking into his dark eyes and reading things there that made her catch her breath. Then the carriage moved slightly as the bays fidgeted and the moment, whatever it had been, had gone.

Imagination, Jessica told herself. Dark eyes like Alex's always seem soulful. But she could still feel the warmth of his fingers at her waist, the sensation of exhilaration as she was held in mid-air and the confidence that she was safe with this man holding her. All dangerous thoughts. She set off briskly towards the trees along a path trodden through the grass.

'We are very fortunate with the weather for the time of year,' she observed with the firm resolve of keeping the conversation strictly impersonal. It was bad enough to feel as she did about the man, without entertaining ideas about the way he looked at her. Or allowing him to see how he affected her.

'We are indeed.' Alex caught up with her. 'Would you like to discuss the King's health or the latest exhibition at the Society of Watercolourists? We could compare our thoughts on the latest novels, perhaps?'

That surprised an unladylike snort of laughter from her. 'I was attempting the conventional conversation expected of a young lady walking in the park with a gentleman.'

'But you are not conventional, Jessica,' he pointed out. 'So why should—? Oh, Lord. Now they've stopped. Quick, stand behind this tree.'

'Why?' Jessica demanded, flustered at being unceremoniously bundled into cover. 'And it isn't a tree, it's a prickly bush. A *very* prickly holly bush, in fact.' She glanced up from freeing her skirts from the spiky leaves. 'My goodness!'

Major Percy had brought his horse to a stop and, apparently feeling they were adequately screened by trees, had taken Lady Anthea firmly in his arms and was kissing her. And Anthea, far from boxing his ears as Jessica would have expected, was returning the embrace with considerable fervour.

'Whatever has come over them?' she whispered.

'I would have thought that was obvious and I do not know why you are whispering. I cannot imagine that they would hear us if we were accompanied by the band of the Household Cavalry,' Alex said, somewhat tartly.

'Don't you approve? Of them as a couple, I mean, not of them kissing in a public park.'

'I have no right to approve or disapprove, but Percy is an intelligent fellow. If he has decided to fall for a ferocious bluestocking, then I imagine he will somehow make it work. She is not likely to be trifling with his affections, is she?'

'I should not think that Anthea has ever trifled with anything in her life, let alone a man's affections,' Jessica said, making herself stare at the glossy green leaves of the holly bush and not at the couple in the curricle or the man next to her. What if he were infected by his friend's mood and wanted to kiss her? That would be...

'That is two of my acquaintance now,' Alex said, jolting her thoughts away from improper musings.

'What do you mean?'

'Falling in love at first sight—Locksley and Miss Beech share a couple of dances and two weeks later are contemplating elopement. Percy encounters Lady Anthea and, if he is not planning marriage now, then he is not the gentleman I always took him for. It seems that I am not the only man foolish enough to be a romantic.'

'You believe that is the only way to find true love—to be struck by the emotion on first acquaintance? You do not think it can develop more slowly as people get to know each other, discover each other's true character?'

'That is friendship,' Alex said. 'It could grow into love

of a sort, I suppose. But it is not as I imagine true, deep, romantic love to be. That is a case of finding one's soul-mate, not simply a congenial partner.' He half turned and looked down at her quizzically. 'Do you think that makes me unmanly, talking of romantic love, seeking for it?'

'Not at all. It makes you the kind of romantic hero that Sir Walter Scott writes about. You have high ideals and only the right lady will meet them.'

And that is not me, obviously.

'They have driven off now, thank goodness,' Alex said.

'Yes, that is a relief.' Jessica rather wished she had a fan to hand, she really was becoming rather heated despite the cool breeze. 'Shall we walk on?'

Chapter Twelve

Alex fell in beside her and they strolled together under the bare branches of the elms until they were clear of the copse. In the distance they could see William, the groom, driving the phaeton at walking pace away from them, which was a relief. There seemed to be too many thoughts jostling for attention in her head to be able to concentrate on driving a valuable pair.

Jane and Anthea, two of the Exotic Wallflowers, young ladies who had no expectation of making happy marriages, if of any marriage at all—and there they were, apparently head over heels in love with two perfectly eligible and pleasant gentlemen. Who might be next? Not her, of course. The only gentleman she felt the slightest inclination to marry was strolling next to her and showing no signs of regarding her as anything except a friend.

A congenial companion, she thought, wrinkling her nose.

Perhaps if she were to dress up in flowing robes and don a pointed headdress with veils it might arouse some knightly passion in his breast, but Jessica rather doubted it. Alex expected to walk into some crowded room, look across it and have his eyes alight upon a lady who would look back directly at him, alerted to his presence by some mysterious element in the air. Their gazes would interlock as they experienced a mutual jolt of powerful recognition as killing as a lightning strike. She sighed.

'What is wrong?'

'Sometimes I think that it is women who are the sensible sex, grounded in reality, and men are the fanciful ones, holding on to dreams and illusions.'

'And becoming romantics?' he said. 'You may well be right. Men are certainly the hypocritical ones. We pretend to believe that women are frail and simple and need protecting and sheltering, when all along that suits us very well. My mother was certainly the one in that marriage who ensured that we did not slip from being merely the Pinchpenny Dukes to becoming the penniless ones.'

'How long ago did you lose your parents?' she asked.

'Four years past. It was an epidemic of the influenza. The entire village seemed to be infected and we lost perhaps a dozen souls altogether. I had it, too, but not badly, which was a good thing—there was a great deal to be managed once I had recovered.'

'And you must have been young for such a huge responsibility,' Jessica said. No wonder Alex clung to his romantic dreams as some sort of relief from what must be, for a conscientious man, the enormous responsibility of estates and tenants. It would be a weight of obligation that would never leave him.

She did not make the mistake of thinking that his feelings made him any less strong and determined than men with a more cynical or ruthless temperament. Never once on that strange night-time walk had she felt anything but safe and protected. The only danger she had been in was from her own emotions.

'I was twenty-two,' he said. 'Old enough. It was hardly as though the state of the estates came as any surprise. My father had done his best, but he had become depressed and, I think, had somehow given up. I will not do that. The tenants deserve better, the land does, too.'

'And the family name, I suppose,' she said.

The family name?

Alex gave a short laugh. 'You would think that, for a self-confessed romantic, I might find something attractive about how we became dukes, but I have to say that the elevation of the family owes everything to the amatory skills of my ancestress and nothing to any merits of the Demerals. There are no acts of chivalry or valour, no gallant knights or battles fought in our history, despite what I dreamed of as a boy. The only consolation is that we never had wealth in the first place, so it has not been frittered away, or lost in gambling. All my predecessors appear to have done their best.'

They were so close as they walked along a narrow path cut through the grass that he felt Jessica's shrug beside him. 'There is no virtue in relying upon the deeds of one's ancestors,' she said. 'You have a good name, Alex, one you made for yourself. I have never heard anyone speak sneeringly of the Pinchpenny Duke, even if they might use the nickname.

'I have no patience with members of the *ton* who appear to think that their title is everything, that they have merit and entitlements above others simply by an accident of birth and they need do nothing to earn the respect of the world except simply exist.'

'And yet you proposed to a duke,' he said and this time

Jessica stiffened so that the sleeve that had brushed his was drawn away, leaving him oddly bereft of the slight contact.

'I proposed to a gentleman who appeared to have the makings of a tolerable husband, as I must have one, it seems,' she said. 'My father's dearest wish is for an aristocratic son-in-law. If he had desired that I marry a red-headed man with political ambitions, perhaps I would have sought out Mr Locksley and embarrassed *him* with my boldness.'

Damn.

'Now I have offended you. I had no intention of doing so and I apologise for my clumsiness. I spoke without thought.' He realised that he sounded as stiff as she. 'And you did not embarrass me.'

'Now that is an untruth,' Jessica said. 'You know perfectly well you were furious with yourself for not denying me in the first place.'

He did not contradict her. Refusing to admit Miss Danby would have been absolutely the correct thing to have done. 'I admit, I should have done just that. But I was half awake when Pitwick announced you. I was brooding on economies, if you must know.'

And what had Pitwick been about, even enquiring if he would receive an unaccompanied lady? Any other butler would have politely informed her that the Duke was not at home. Yet Pitwick was a very experienced upper servant...

'You know, that was strange,' he said, thinking aloud, 'Pitwick ought to have refused you and yet he did not. He looked at your card and... Confound it, the man knew who your father was! Now my servants are matchmaking for me. Presumably in the hope of an increase in wages,' he added bitterly.

'Oh, goodness. He must be furious that you acted in such an honest and gentlemanly fashion.' Jessica was laughing now, all the irritation of their tiff completely gone.

'Old family retainers are the worst,' she said confidingly. 'Our butler at home, Chesterfield, looks as though butter wouldn't melt in his mouth, he seems so chilly, but he is always nudging us in the direction he thinks we ought to go. *"Oh, Mr Danby, sir, I'll send that new coat back to the tailor's, shall I? I know you are too kind-hearted to let your valet know he advised you ill on that colour."* And, of course, he knows Papa chose it himself. Or, *"Miss Jessica, I wouldn't be attending the Wilkinsons' picnic, if I were you. I hear they obtain their lobsters from a* very *dubious source"*—said with the clear implication that the entire family is second-rate. In truth, Markham runs the household and our lives. I doubt we have a single secret from him.'

Alex opened his mouth to say that a trusted retainer in a family was different to a bachelor duke's butler and closed it again. He must pay more attention to Pitkin in future; the man was more devious than he had imagined and he did not appreciate being managed. But at least the *froideur* that had developed between Jessica and himself had thawed.

Jessica was still looking up at him, a little smile on her face as she watched him absorb her words.

'Be careful, the ground is rather rutted here.'

'Where?' She turned her head sharply, but too late. 'Oh!'

As Jessica tripped he reached out and caught her arm, spinning her around. She flailed for balance with her free arm, ending up flattened against his chest.And the breath left his lungs.

Jessica clung to his lapel with her free hand and Alex put his arm around her.

Just to steady her, he told himself.

But the tightness in his chest did not ease and he found himself staring down at the brim of her blue velvet hat with the intensity of a man seeing a great work of art for the very first time.

His breath came back with a gasp. What the devil had just happened? He realised that he was aroused and had the fleeting thought that it was fortunate he was wearing comfortable old breeches and not fashionably skin-tight inexpressibles. But physical desire was not all that was making his heart race and keeping Jessica's hand wrapped tight in his.

Then it dawned on him that she was making faint sounds of distress and released his hold as though her fingers were hot iron. 'I am sorry, I hurt you.'

'No, no, you didn't. You stopped me falling.' She reached for his arm and steadied herself, sending his pulse racing again. 'I turned my ankle in a rut. So foolish. I should have been looking where I was going.'

And so should I. I have just walked into something I do not understand.

But Jessica was hurt. This was no time to stand around grappling with his feelings. 'Do not put any weight on that foot. William has turned and is driving back towards us. I'll soon have you in the carriage.'

He took off his hat, waved it and saw the groom urge the pair into a brisk trot. 'We'll have you home in no time at all.'

'I am certain it is not a serious strain, please do not worry.' Jessica spoke as though she was trying to reassure him and Alex wondered if he was sounding strange to her ears. What the devil was wrong with him?

'Even so, you should have your doctor look at it for you. I will take a message once I have taken you to Adam Street.'

'I would rather see your friend Mrs Chandler. I am sure she will strap it up for me without any nonsense about bleeding me, or nasty-tasting doses of medicine.'

'Very well, but then I will take you straight home,' Alex said firmly as the groom drew the bays to a halt beside them. 'William, get down and hold them steady, Miss Danby has suffered a slight injury.' At least he had not mentioned anything as improper as a lady's ankle, he thought with a returning flicker of humour.

A high-perch phaeton was not the easiest vehicle to lift a lady into, but he took Jessica by the waist and lifted her until she could put her sound foot on to the step and then twist to lower herself to the seat. She did not appear to be in any great pain and managed it without a grimace, which was reassuring.

'Should I remove your half-boot, do you think?' he asked, sincerely hoping the answer would be, *No.* The thought of such a personal touch was unsettling. Lifting her had been bad enough. Jessica accepted him as a friend now; she would be appalled if he let her glimpse this new physical attraction he was feeling for her. That was all it was, surely?

'I do not think so. I cannot feel it swelling. In fact, I feel something of a fraud now. Perhaps I should simply go home and rest it for a while.'

'And then find it is worse than you thought? You have a busy social round, you cannot afford to be limping around the dance floor.'

She laughed a little at that, sending a strange tingle down his spine. 'I am certainly finding myself with more partners now. The effect of a dance with a duke on a wallflower's desirability is clear. I find myself actually enjoying balls now and I never thought I would say that of ones in London.'

It struck him that he knew nothing of Jessica's life before she had come to London. 'You enjoyed a varied social scene at home?' he asked as he took the reins and brought the pair up to the bit.

'There is no lack of society, even if it is not exactly Society with a capital S as the *ton* in London would recognise. Shrewsbury is our nearest large town, but Wolverhampton has more assembly rooms. Bridgnorth is also pleasant, if rather quieter.' After a pause she added, so softly he hardly heard her, 'I would have been quite content to remain there.'

'But your father has ambitions for you.'

'Yes,' she agreed, rather coolly, he thought. 'And also, it seemed a good idea to have Papa away from the business while my brothers found their feet running it. He truly wants them to succeed, but he finds it very hard to let go of the reins.'

'So did you reluctantly leave any beaux behind you in Shropshire?' Alex asked, with the sensation of prodding an injury to see if it was as bad as he thought—irresistible, even though he knew it would be painful.

'One or two.' Yes, Jessica was definitely cool now, although she answered him readily enough. 'But reluctantly? No. I think some distance is always wise. Familiarity can blind one to characteristics one would find…tiresome in marriage.'

Alex reminded himself that Jessica had been equally dispassionate in assessing his character before she proposed to him. She took the question of marriage very seriously, but she also seemed to regard it in the same way as her father might approach a business proposition. How very different from the other young ladies launched on to the marriage mart, schooled only to think of attracting the 'right' gentleman with their looks and their pretty manner and their complete lack of any characteristic that was unconventional or threatening to male sensibilities.

Jessica saw people very clearly, even those she loved, like her own father. It was an uncomfortable realisation for a man who did not want his own thoughts probed too deeply just now.

Chapter Thirteen

'And any proposals, if I might venture to ask?' Alex recognised that reckless need to probe again.

'Six,' Jessica said with composure. 'One ridiculous, one all too obviously mercenary and four that were—' She made a rocking gesture with one hand. 'Four that aroused no emotions in me whatsoever. Papa says I am now expending too much thought on the plans for May Day festivities and not enough on finding a husband.'

'And how are the plans for the Guild's procession progressing?'

'Surprisingly well. Having established that the world will not end if the milkmaids are not the genuine article, I find that many friends have young female servants who would love to dress up and take part. Our coachman is finding float-makers and hirers of dray horses so we can have them committed early, even though the Guild members are dithering about what exactly they want depicted on the floats.'

'So what else is needed?'

'Flower garlands, musicians and whatever the themes of the floats require, but I am feeling much more optimistic about it all now.' She sounded warm and relaxed and Alex felt himself relax, too, now the coolness had gone from her voice. He should take care not to probe into her personal affairs again. They were, after all, none of his concern, unless someone upset her when, as a friend, he would deal with them. As a friend.

He realised that they were at the Chandlers' front door and he must have driven there without any recollection of the journey. William jumped down to knock.

'Your friends are going to think me ridiculously accident-prone,' Jessica said as the groom returned to hold the horses and Alex could climb down to help her descend.

'You are somewhat prone to accidents,' Anna Chandler said as soon as they were alone.

'I was just thinking you would conclude that I am very clumsy,' Jessica confessed. 'And I am feeling something of a fraud now. My ankle gave me a very painful twinge when I turned it, but now it barely aches. Demeral would not hear of taking me directly home without it being examined, however.'

'A stubborn man, especially when he is looking after someone,' Anna said. 'Can you remove your half-boot yourself or shall I help you?'

'No, I can manage, thank you.' She eased off the shoe, relieved to see no swelling. 'Demeral has a strong protective instinct, I think.'

'Certainly, with anyone or anything he feels responsible for,' Anna agreed. 'Now, just put your foot on the stool. I do not think we need to have your stocking off.' She bent over Jessica's foot, peering closely, then took hold of it and began to move it gently back and forth. 'Say if it hurts.'

'That is fine. Ow, just there.'

'Wriggle your toes, please. Many landowners who are short of money would raise their tenants' rents, but not

Alex. Instead he tries to improve their living conditions, which is admirable, but means his are not much better, for all that he lives in a castle.'

'Is it a real castle?' That would be enough to give any impressionable boy romantic daydreams.

'Yes, a real medieval one, not a sham built in the last century. It is quite small and in very poor repair, but it has all the right features—battlements and turrets, arrow slits and a drawbridge, plus a rather green and smelly moat, I'm afraid.'

Anna settled back on her heels. 'I do not think you have done more than give it a slight twist. I will strap it up just to support it, but you can take the bandage off tomorrow. Try to use that foot as normal.'

'Thank you. And this time I really do insist on you charging me for my treatment.' She took a card from her reticule. 'Please send the accounting to this address. I will tell my father that Dr Chandler was recommended to me by a friend and I will confess to turning my ankle. Then, in future, if I do need a doctor, Papa will not think it strange if I consult you—in the guise of your husband, of course.'

'Very well.' Anna stood up and took the card. 'Perhaps it would be best if we send you home in our carriage.' She hesitated, half turned to the door. 'Do be careful of Alex, won't you?'

'But I feel perfectly safe with him,' Jessica protested.

'It was not your safety I was concerned for,' Anna said wryly and opened the door. 'Ah, Alex. I am sending Miss Danby home in our carriage. Morris, tell John Coachman we need it at once.'

Jessica walked in to the drawing room and found to her relief that her strained ankle hardly ached at all. Perhaps it was Anna Chandler's skill, or perhaps it had not been such a wrench after all. Perhaps, she thought uncomfortably, she had made a fuss about it to distract both her and Alex from the surprise of finding themselves in each other's arms again.

It had made her feel positively shivery at the time and still did in recollection. And Alex had seemed somehow arrested as he held her, as though his attention had been caught. Probably by a smudge on her nose, or him wondering why she was so very clumsy, Jessica thought gloomily.

'Ah, there you are, my dear.' Her father lowered his newspaper and looked up from the depths of his armchair. It made her jump, she had been so absorbed in her thoughts.

'Papa.' She stooped to kiss the top of his balding head. 'I went to visit a friend and then walked in the park. And then I turned my ankle. Fortunately I remembered a recommendation from a friend for their doctor, Dr Chandler, so I went there. His wife looked after me admirably and I am told it is just a slight strain and will be well tomorrow.'

He nodded, clearly with something else on his mind, which surprised her. Usually he was inclined to fuss if she was unwell. 'I am glad to hear it is not serious, my dear, and that you have had a recommendation that proved so useful. I have had a very interesting visit while you were out, Jessica.'

'That's nice,' she said vaguely, dropping bonnet and reticule on to a side table and beginning to draw off her gloves.

'From the Earl of Branscombe, no less.'

'Who? Oh, yes, I recall him now. I danced with him a night or so ago, I think. Just the one dance.' Tall, dark and handsome. Very pleasant, not overly talkative. Quite restful, in fact. Jessica unbuttoned her pelisse and wriggled out of its tight sleeves.

'He came to ask my permission to pay court to you.' Her father was beaming now. 'Of course, he is not a duke or a marquis, but an earl's not to be sneezed at, now, is he?'

'No, absolutely not,' Jessica agreed. She had dropped her coat and knew now that she was making too much of a business of picking it up, folding it and laying it neatly over a chair back. 'Did he say why?'

Other than a desire for my dowry, of course.

'He said he greatly admired your charming character, your poise and your amiable nature. Apparently you befriended a young relative of his who was feeling very shy at Lady Ambleside's musicale the other evening and he was much struck by that. He observed how much kindness is to be valued in the wife of a nobleman who has to consider not only the welfare of his tenants and dependents, but also the upbringing of his children.'

Well, she must award Branscombe points for coming up with some personalised compliments and managing not to mention her dowry while he was about it. The thought of him did not set her heart aflutter, however.

Jessica sat down, assumed her best dutiful daughter expression and enquired, 'And what did you say to Lord Branscombe, Papa?'

'That I had no objection—mind you, I will have him investigated, never you fear—but that it is entirely up to you who you accept, my dear.'

'Thank you, Papa.' Jessica regarded the toes of her slightly grass-stained half-boots and tried to work out just how she felt.

It was a proposal from a nobleman likely to meet Papa's

stiff criteria for lineage and character, a handsome man who seemed intelligent and pleasant, even if he was a trifle stiff and reticent. A man showing a degree of thoughtfulness in presenting himself to her father and, she suspected, a rather conventional man as well.

Did that add up to the makings of a good husband? Probably. But did it make him the right husband for her?

He is not Alex Demeral.

But what if she had never met the Duke? Then Lord Branscombe would have seemed a very suitable match and she would have been interested in knowing him better, discovering if he would make the kind of husband she had decided was for her. Intelligent, considerate, a man with depth of character.

But now she had met Alex and every gentleman she encountered from now on was going to be measured against him, she admitted to herself. And that was setting the bar high.

'I would like to become better acquainted with the Earl,' she said firmly, as much to herself as to her father. After all, she had no desire to end her days a spinster. Papa would become anxious if she did not show signs of being serious about matrimony very soon and that was bad for his health. Daydreaming about a pair of fathomless dark eyes and a pair of broad shoulders was not going to get her anything but heartache.

'Excellent. He mentioned that he would be at Lady Outram's ball next week and I believe you are attending that. There is no need to mention that you know of his call on me, of course. Meanwhile I will have the usual checks made. I want to make certain there are no skeletons in his cupboards.'

By the time Papa's London lawyers and his men of business had finished there would be little they did not know about the Earl of Branscombe, from his debts to his choice of tea and probably the name of his first pony and his first mistress. Certainly any skeletons would be taken out, dusted down and thoroughly inspected. Not that any of that would be for her eyes, of course. Either Papa would approve or he would not. But she knew where he kept the keys to his desk and she would read the report, too: after all, she would be the one who had to live with the man.

It ought to be exciting, the prospect of a personable new suitor. Jessica fixed a smile on her lips and stood up. 'I shall take special care in choosing my gown for the ball, Papa.'

His look of pleasure went some way to lightening her mood. Bless him, he wanted only the best for her.

Over the next week the society columns in the news sheets heralded the arrival in town of several families joining the Season. They were the ones whose country seats were furthest from London, even some from Scotland, and they had wisely avoided an early journey, fraught with the increased risk of snow and heavy rain.

Alex scanned the columns before he looked at the post that had arrived after luncheon. Perhaps there was a young lady newly arrived from the West Country or the Borders who would be the one for him. For some reason the thought did not lighten his spirits as it usually did. He must be getting jaded with London life. He certainly missed Longstone where Demeral Castle sat in a wide bend in the river, brooding over the surrounding lands as it had done for centuries.

But if it were to brood for another few hundred years

he needed to return to it with money. He tossed the papers aside and went to shuffle through the pile of invitations on his desk. The Outrams' ball that evening would be one of the biggest squeezes of the Season and he should not miss that.

Would Jessica be there? He had restrained himself from calling to ask about her foot, knowing it would only excite her father unfairly. Perhaps she would not be dancing if the sprain was still painful, but even if she was there only to sit out, he would enjoy the pleasure of relaxed conversation with someone who seemed to find the same things interesting or amusing.

Yes, he would attend the Outram ball and perhaps a miracle would occur and he would find the One. And if it did not, then perhaps he and Jessica would have the interest of watching their friends' romances flourish.

Lady Outram had the reputation of one of the best hostesses in town and the house just off Grosvenor Square was ablaze with light, inside and out, when Alex arrived at eleven.

Crowds lined the pavements to stare at the stream of fashionables making their way along the red carpet that had been run from the front door, down the steps and across the pavement. Burly footmen in livery kept the onlookers back and supervised the flow of carriages which crawled along at a snail's pace before they reached the carpet.

It would never do to be seen actually *walking*, even if one lived two houses down, Alex though with a grin as he jumped down from his humble hackney carriage well back in the queue and made his way past to fall in behind the Dowager Marchioness of Witherby as she shepherd her three granddaughters ahead of her to the steps.

She had the reputation for being insufferably stiff-rumped but she condescended to talk to him as they ascended the stairs to the receiving line. He was, after all, a duke.

One step, pause, wait with one's nose a few inches from the spine of the person in front. Another step...

Alex looked around while maintaining his end of the dialogue, nodding to acquaintances, bowing to ladies. No sign of Jessica, but there was Lady Anthea and Lady Lucinda with Percy Rowlands between them as escort.

'Indeed,' he agreed, listening to Lady Witherby with half an ear. 'We have been fortunate with the weather so far this month.'

'Girls, do not fidget,' she admonished her charges, releasing him again to scan the guests.

Then he saw Jessica just a few steps ahead and to the right. She, too, was looking around her and, after a moment, saw him.

She inclined her head formally, making the small ostrich feathers set in her hair bob and flutter, but the smile she sent him made his heart give that strange little kick again.

Alex was still puzzling over it when he reached the landing and began to move along the receiving line, shaking hands, greeting his host and hostess before he could escape into the ballroom and look for Jessica again. She would be sitting down, surely?

He had arrived as partners were walking on to the dance floor for the new set and there was Jessica, saucy plumes nodding over her smooth coiffure, her hand in that of the Earl of Branscombe as he led her out and not a hint of hesitation in her walk.

Chapter Fourteen

It was foolish of Jessica to be exerting herself, Alex thought. He must keep an eye on her and insist she sit out for several sets to rest. He was certain Anna had not expected her to go throwing herself into vigorous country dances after only a few days' rest. Even as he thought it he recognised that as merely a distraction for a flash of jealousy.

It was too late to find a partner for this set, so he strolled around the room, chatting to acquaintances until he found Lady Lucinda in conversation with a rather earnest young woman wearing pince-nez on the end of her nose.

'Lady Lucinda, ma'am.' He bowed; they curtsied.

'Your Grace, allow me to name Miss Worthing. Miss Worthing, the Duke of Malvern. Miss Worthing is a keen student of the Italian Masters and we were just discussing the exhibition at Somerset House. Are you interested in art, Your Grace?'

'Appreciative, but woefully ignorant, I fear. Might I solicit a dance, ladies?'

Miss Worthing, it seemed, did not dance. 'I came this evening in the hope of viewing the Outrams' gallery,' she confessed.

Lady Lucinda granted him the next set and he moved on, his gaze roaming over the dancers. There was Lady

Anthea, talking earnestly to Percy as they processed down the line of dancers. And just behind them, Jessica, laughing at something Branscombe had said to her.

She did not seem to be in any discomfort, which was good. And she appeared to be enjoying herself which was, of course, excellent. There were new faces among the guests, many of them families he was acquainted with, but who must have recently arrived in London to launch their daughters into society.

Alex stopped to exchange greetings with several, asked for dances and was met with smiles and blushes and acceptances. All very pleasant young ladies, he was sure, but there was no spark. He found himself curiously distanced from what was going on around him.

Should I give this up, go back home and sell some land? he found himself thinking.

Then he realised the last dance of the set had come to an end and went in search of Lady Lucinda.

Four sets later as he was talking to an acquaintance about selling his phaeton and pair, he noticed that Branscombe was leading Jessica out again. Two sets, when there were so many partners to choose from this evening? It was not outside the bounds of convention, of course, but it made him wonder. Branscombe was a decent fellow. Rather a cold fish, Alex had always thought, but there was no reason to be concerned if he was paying his attentions to Jessica. None in the world.

Lord Branscombe was a very pleasant partner, Jessica decided. He danced well and maintained a flow of intelligent conversation.

His manner was somewhat formal and she had to suppress a smile when he said that he felt it would draw untoward attention if he asked her to dance a third time, but would she allow him to escort her in to supper?

Yes, she agreed, that would be very agreeable. It meant, of course, that she would have to make her excuses if anyone asked her for the supper dance, but as her ankle was beginning to ache a little that could be done with a truthful explanation.

She mentioned the sprain to Lady Cassington, who tutted, but suggested that she sat out all three sets before supper in order to rest it.

Jessica agreed and made her way to some vacant seats beside an array of potted palms where her chaperon could join her when she had finished talking to the Dowager Lady Troughton who was in full flow about her rheumatics, her unsatisfactory nephew and the horrors of finding a decent cook. Jessica felt there was little of value she could contribute.

She took her seat, turned down two offers to dance immediately, but sent the gentlemen away happy with the promise of resuming the floor after supper.

Alex was present; she had seen him several times, on and off the floor, but he had not approached her for a dance. She wondered why. Had he heard of Lord Branscombe's interest or was he assuming she would not want to dance with her sore ankle?

There he was, dancing rather slowly with a very young lady Jessica had not seen before and who was clearly concentrating fiercely on her steps. Alex caught her eye and they exchanged smiles, amused on hers, somewhat rueful on his.

They passed on and Jessica shifted on her seat, conscious of a draught behind her. The great room was becoming hot, but not yet so warm that it was pleasant to have cooler air stirring the hair on the back of her neck. She turned and saw it was coming from a jib door, almost concealed in the panelling, that was just ajar.

There were no footmen nearby so Jessica got up and went to push it closed.

'Let me go now, please,' someone said from the room beyond. It was a woman and she sounded young and uneasy. 'I want to go back.'

A male voice answered, the tone low and with an edge to it that Jessica did not like. She hesitated, her fingers resting on the door handle. She had no wish to walk in on a tryst, but on the other hand, if an inexperienced debutante was in an uncomfortable situation, then she could not simply ignore it.

She pushed the door half open and stepped inside. 'Oh, do forgive me, I did not realise this room was occupied.' Yes, something was very wrong here.

A girl she did not recognise—very young, very pretty— was pulling away from a man who had hold of her wrist. She was in tears.

He turned, an unpleasant look on his face. 'Well, it *is* occupied, so you can take yourself off, Miss Iron Smelter.'

She might not know the girl, but she knew who this was. Sir Matthew Hobson had an unpleasant reputation with women and she been forced to dodge when he had tried to push her into a corner in a deserted corridor at the theatre several weeks previously. The memory of the brush of his groping hands still made her shudder.

'I do not think so, not without this lady. Do you wish to leave, my dear?'

'Oh, yes, please.' The girl tugged against his hold.

'Then let her go this instant or I shall fetch some footmen and have you removed.'

'I do not think so.' He mimicked her voice unpleasantly. 'Miss Fawcett is my fiancée, or she will be before this night is out. Think of the scandal if she is discovered here alone with me.'

'But she is not alone with you, is she? I am here. You do not wish to marry this person, do you, Miss Fawcett?'

'No, of course not. I was hot and I wanted to sit down after we had danced and he said it would be cool in here and then… Then he…' Miss Fawcett burst into loud sobs.

Jessica took the two steps to bring her to them. 'Let her go.'

Sir Matthew pushed her away, his hand landing on her breast. It was not by accident, she was sure.

Jessica slapped him, hard. It stung, but it felt good. The girl screamed and began to struggle wildly. A chair fell over against an ornamental plant stand which fell with a crash. Jessica stabbed at his hand with her folded fan and then suddenly there was someone beside her.

She was aware of movement, decisive and powerful, and Sir Matthew reeled backwards to land sprawled over the plant stand. Jessica dodged aside and caught hold of Miss Fawcett, turning her away into the shelter of her arms. Over her shoulder she saw Alex rubbing his knuckles and looming over the fallen man.

Alex. Thank goodness.

The door opened again and there was Lord Branscombe.

'Miss Danby? Are you all right? I was coming over to speak to you and I heard a scream.'

'Let me past, sir! Jessica? What is going on?' Lady Cassington swept past the Earl and closed the door behind her. 'Keep your voices down, all of you. Do you want a scandal?'

The room was now decidedly overcrowded with Sir Matthew still on the floor, two large, angry men looming over him, a sobbing debutante, Jessica and now an indignant chaperon.

'Everything is under control,' Alex said without looking around.

Lord Branscombe stepped over the man on the floor and, for a moment, Jessica thought he was reaching for her. Then he said, 'Miss Fawcett! I had not realised your family had arrived in London. Good friends and neighbours of mine, you know,' he added to Jessica as Miss Fawcett threw herself on his chest.

'Oh, George, thank heavens. That horrible man—and then this lady tried to help and he pushed her and then this gentleman came in and hit him. Take me to Mama, please, George.'

'Here, wipe your eyes and blow your nose before you go out.' Jessica handed her a handkerchief, then pushed them both towards the door. 'By the sound of it people are going through to supper, you should be able to find Mrs Fawcett without attracting too much attention.'

They went out, both thanking her distractedly. Jessica shut the door after them and leaned against it. 'What are we going to do with him?'

'We must leave immediately,' Lady Cassington declared, loftily ignoring both her question and Sir Matthew who was trying to disentangle himself from the plant stand. 'I can only hope nobody saw you slip in here in that furtive way as I did, Miss Danby.'

'I was not being furtive,' she said indignantly. 'I was closing the door because of a draught and then I heard Miss Fawcett. She was clearly in distress. I could hardly walk away, now could I?'

She turned to Alex. 'What shall we do with him?'

'I am waiting until he stands up so I can hit him again,' Alex said. 'Did he touch you?'

She could almost feel the impression of one large hand on her left breast, but Jessica had no desire to provoke Alex into killing the man, which, from the look on his face, he very much wanted to.

'He pushed me. He was holding Miss Fawcett, poor girl. I slapped him.'

'Good.'

Hobson made no move to get up, so Alex leant down and hauled him to his feet, holding him upright with one hand clenched in his shirtfront.

'If I ever find you within half a mile of this lady, or of the one you have just so grievously insulted, I will take a horsewhip to you. I would call a gentleman out, but you clearly have no claim to the rank.'

Sir Matthew made vague gobbling noises.

'He is turning very red,' Lady Cassington said. She was quivering with indignation, the bugle beads embroidered around the hem and bodice of her gown shimmering in response. 'I suggest we leave him to make his way out, Your Grace. Your warning, in addition to the fact that I shall inform every chaperon and the Patronesses of his behaviour, will ensure he has little opportunity for this kind of outrage again.'

Jessica saw a door in the far wall and went to investigate. It opened on to some kind of service corridor. Alex let go of Hobson and pushed him that direction. 'Out.'

As the door closed behind him Lady Cassington sank down on the sofa. 'Well! It appears we have much to thank you for, Your Grace.'

'How did you realise what was happening?' Jessica asked, finding that she, too, needed to sit down.

'I happened to notice where you were sitting and then I saw you go to that door, which seemed strange. When you did not come out again I was concerned.' Alex appeared more focused on his bloodied knuckles which he dabbed with a handkerchief. He put it back in his pocket and looked across at Jessica and she realised that he was very aware of her indeed. 'I heard a scream as I got near. I thought it was you.'

'And as I was leaving the Dowager to join you I encountered Lord Branscombe who was seeking you to take you in to supper,' Lady Cassington explained. 'We heard sounds from this room and the rest you know.'

'Well,' Jessica said, striving for a lighter note, 'I appear to have lost my supper partner. I rather think that the Earl has realised that he had feelings for his neighbour Miss Fawcett that he had not been aware of. They appear to be reciprocated.'

'He was certainly struck, was he not?' Lady Cassington said. 'I have seen it before. A man grows up with a neighbour and never notices her, never sees she is now a young woman. Then she comes out, all grown up, and he has a revelation.'

Alex muttered something that sounded like, 'Not just neighbours.' He tugged his cuffs into order. 'I will leave you, unless there is anything else I can do, ladies? It might be more discreet if you wait a few moments.' With an abrupt bow he was gone.

'I do think he might have taken us in for super,' Lady Cassington said. 'Men can be so thoughtless. No doubt he does not wish to appear with broken knuckles. You appear to have lost your suitor, my dear.'

'Papa has told you about Lord Branscombe?'

'He has.' Her chaperon sighed. 'I did have hopes of Malvern as well but, for all his gallantry just now, he could not remove himself fast enough, could he?'

'He has never spoken to Papa about me,' Jessica said carefully. She was still feeling somewhat breathless, not so much from the encounter with the odious Sir Matthew, she suspected, more from witnessing the ruthlessly effective manner Alex had dealt with the man.

My hero. Oh, dear, this is not going to help me put him out of my mind.

'Let us take ourselves in to supper, Lady Cassington. I have to admit that I will feel very much better after a glass of champagne.'

Chapter Fifteen

Alex stood to one side of the dance floor watching the room. Branscombe was deep in conversation with Miss Fawcett and a lady he imagined must be her mother. By the look of it the young lady was rapidly recovering herself after her ordeal, helped, he had no doubt, by Branscombe's reassuring presence.

The man had been knocked into as much of a heap as Hobson, at least mentally, Alex thought with a wry smile. There would be a marriage agreed before very much longer.

As for himself, his hand throbbed and the anger he had felt flood through him when he had seen Hobson with Jessica was still churning unpleasantly, but the real facer was the revelation that scene had brought.

The possessiveness had hit him like an opponent's fist. *Mine,* he had thought through the red anger when he saw Jessica struggling with the man. Mine.

When had that happened? How had it happened? He had gone from regarding her as a friend, as an unconventional, intelligent companion, to wanting her as his. It was not physical allure, he thought, trying to get his feelings into some kind of order. Yes, he found her attractive and arousing, but not to the point where he thought her perfection, or could not sleep for thinking erotic thoughts of her.

He hadn't fallen in love. Again, he felt quite rational about this, not ecstatic, not dizzy with romance. This was not at all what he had expected and yet... Was this the revelation he had been waiting for and he had now found the bride he had told himself it was his duty to marry?

He liked Jessica a great deal. He admired her, thought her intelligent, honest, attractive and courageous. He had just discovered that he felt protective towards her. She was someone he could rely upon to work with him to make a marriage a success, raise children, care for the estate and its people.

Marriage. It was time to accept that he had a chance of real happiness and could rescue his estates, if he could only grasp it. The sense of relief was almost tangible, as though he had laid down a heavy burden he had been carrying for years.

Tomorrow he was going to call on the house in Adam Street and ask the iron founder for his daughter's hand in marriage.

But would Jessica accept him after all the things he had said to her when they had first met? She would think him a hypocrite and somehow he must overcome that.

Alex pushed away from the wall against which he had been leaning and made for the double doors. Miss Fawcett was in good hands, Jessica and Lady Cassington had passed him by on their way to the supper room without seeing him and Sir Matthew showed no sign of returning. He could safely go home and find the right words.

He would not need them for Danby, he was sure, but what was he going to say to Jessica to convince her of his sincerity?

* * *

'The Duke of Malvern!' Trotter, all pretence of being the superior lady's maid abandoned, rushed into Jessica's little sitting room.

Jessica dropped her pen, splattering a list of *Things To Be Done For May Day* with black ink. 'What? Where? Trotter, please calm down.'

'He called just now, Miss Jessica. Handed his card to Alfred and asked for Mr Danby, cool as you like.'

'He asked for Papa?' Surely he had not come to… No. Impossible.

Her father was in no very good mood, having received over breakfast a very formal note from Lord Branscombe withdrawing his request to pay his attentions to Miss Danby on the grounds that he did not feel it fair to her, given that he had realised his affections were engaged elsewhere.

Jessica had received a rather less stilted note, warm in its thanks for her help the previous evening, expressing the hope that she had not been too distressed by the incident and admitting very openly that he had realised that his heart was with Miss Fawcett. He apologised, with more humour than she had previously detected in him, for being so blind to his own emotions.

'He's fortunate not to receive a suit for breach of promise,' her father had huffed angrily over his sirloin steak.

'He made no promises, no proposals, Papa,' Jessica said soothingly. 'He was quite open about wishing to explore whether we were mutually compatible. I thought that very sensible—it would have been quite dreadful if he had proposed and then discovered that his heart was engaged elsewhere.'

Her father growled something about modern manners and nonsense about love. 'All this foolishness about romanticism and sensibility. Grown men not embarrassed to be moved to tears over some sunset or picturesque ruin. The awful majesty of the ocean and mountains, for goodness sake! Stuff and nonsense, I call it.'

'Papa, you know perfectly well that you and Mama made a love match,' Jessica had said with a smile and he had stopped grumbling and smiled sheepishly.

She told him what had occurred at the ball, judging it was better that he heard it from her rather than perhaps pick up some gossip if someone had seen something amiss.

'Good for you, my girl,' he'd said. She was not surprised: he had always been very frank about the dangers that some men posed and the actions a woman could take to defend herself. A pity the daughters of the *haut ton* were not so frankly advised.

'Swine like that should never be allowed near respectable ladies. I am glad the Duke came to your rescue.' He had looked at her hopefully and she had smiled.

'He happened to be passing and heard Miss Fawcett cry out,' she had explained, disappointing him again.

Now what could Alex be doing calling at two in the afternoon? Perhaps, she thought, blotting her ruined page, he had come to set Papa's mind at rest over the scene last night.

She should wait up here, of course, and Papa would tell her about it in due course. Or she could go downstairs into the breakfast room which adjoined Papa's study and apply her ear to the panelling. She knew it was thin, because her father had complained about the staff clattering dishes when clearing after the morning meal. 'Slipshod work,' he had said, rapping the wall with his knuckles. 'Simply battens with panelling nailed over.'

'Thank you, Trotter,' she said now calmly. 'Perhaps he has come to ask me to drive out. Please go and make sure a suitable walking dress is ready.'

She counted to ten when the maid had gone, then slipped out and ran, silent in her light shoes, down the stairs. She tiptoed past the study with its murmur of deep male voices muffled by the heavy door and gained the empty breakfast room.

The voices were much more audible now and, when she pressed her ear against the wall, they were startlingly clear.

'...think any more trouble from Hobson,' Alex said. 'I am glad to hear Miss Danby has recovered from the unpleasant experience. She showed great spirit.'

'She's no shrinking violet, my girl. I taught her how to deal with menaces of that kind. But I must thank you,' Papa said.

Alex replied with something inaudible, then said clearly, 'I have come to request your permission to ask Miss Danby for her hand in marriage, sir.'

Jessica sat down abruptly on the chair next to her.

He is proposing? After what he had said about falling in love? He has said nothing to me.

Jessica leaned close to the wall again.

'...have to say I am delighted to agree.'

That was Papa.

Of *course* he was. A duke was the summit of his ambition for her. She was suddenly very angry.

Both men got to their feet when she swept in to the study after a perfunctory tap on the door. 'Papa— Oh, forgive me, I did not realise you had company,' she said, hardly troubling to make that sound credible.

Her father would probably not notice at that moment if she had appeared with a peacock on her head, let alone sense her mood. Alex, however, raised one dark brow, looking more than ever like his cynical royal ancestor.

'Perhaps you could take the Duke through to the drawing room,' her father said, beaming. 'I believe you have much to talk about.'

'Yes, Papa, if you say so. Please come this way, Your Grace.'

'You were eavesdropping,' Alex said the moment the door was closed behind them.

'Yes, I was.' Jessica took several agitated paces down the length of the Chinese carpet. 'And I am now wondering just what has changed in the last month. You are not going to tell me that you looked at me last night, the scales fell from your eyes and you recognised your one true love, are you? Because I can tell you now, I will not believe a word of it.'

'No,' Alex said bluntly. 'I am not going to tell you that.'

'I see.' That took the wind out of her sails a little, but she rallied. 'So you have now had the opportunity to meet all the available young ladies, found none of them was the one and decided that my dowry made up for the lack of romance after all?'

'No,' he said, equally flatly. 'Not that either.'

His firmness took some of the heat from her anger and she stared at him, confused and strangely hurt.

'Please sit down, Jessica. Let me explain.' Alex did not sound as though he was going to move even if she started throwing the ornaments at his head, so she sat, hands folded in her lap, in a semblance of ladylike calm.

She thought he would pace up and down as Papa or her brothers did when they wishing to make a point, but instead Alex dragged a stool away from the wall, put it in front of her and sat down facing her, eye to eye.

'I know what I said and I believed it. I still do believe that there is such a thing as an instant attraction, a meeting of souls. But I have come to think there are other ways in which a happy marriage can be founded. There is friendship, mutual respect and liking. An attraction.' He must have seen her blush. 'We share those things, I believe. Am I wrong about that?'

'No,' Jessica admitted. 'I agree we have all those feelings. But you will always be wondering where your soulmate is, looking at every woman you meet. *Is it you? Or you?* And what if you meet her?'

'It is a risk that every marriage faces, surely?' he asked. 'That is where honour and loyalty come in. And trust.'

'Trust is important to me,' she confessed. 'Perhaps it is because I come from a background of commerce where so much relies upon accepting the word of the person you are dealing with. Where a handshake and a promise are as good as a legal contract.'

Alex sat back a little. 'That was how you saw this from the beginning, was it not? A business transaction, a merger of two firms? Your dowry for my title. You trusted me when you came to my house with your proposal.'

'I did not know then that I was dealing with a romantic,' she said. 'I thought I was proposing an exchange of assets between people who would deal fairly with each other.'

I did not know then how much I would come to yearn for

you. I did not know how much it would hurt if you looked elsewhere for something you needed in a marriage.

'Are you now saying that your feelings for me make the question of my dowry irrelevant?' she asked, steadying her voice with an effort. That was the crucial question: a great deal depended on how Alex answered it.

'No. No, I cannot in all honesty say so, because I cannot afford to make a marriage without that,' he admitted.

Thank goodness, he had not lied, not prevaricated. He was being honest with her.

'So, why have you changed your mind now?'

'Because now I know you. Now you have come to mean something to me. When I saw Hobson manhandling you I experienced more than the anger I would feel at seeing a man assault any woman. I felt that it was an attack on someone personal, someone who mattered to me. I knew then that I had to ask you to marry me.'

Her pulse thudded and she felt a little dizzy. Jessica wanted to say *yes*, to snatch at this offer. 'You have made this more difficult,' she confessed. 'Before, it was clear-cut and straightforward. You say I matter to you. And I feel the same way. You are more than my friend, you matter to me, too. It may not be love, but now there are feelings involved this becomes a greater risk, for both of us.'

Alex reached out and took her hands in his. Now she did not know whose pulse it was that beat so strongly. His dark eyes were full of understanding. 'I know. Trust me.'

There was something else that she thought she knew the answer to, but could not be certain. 'Marriage is more than an exchange of vows. There's—' She broke off, blushing.

'I think I understand. May I kiss you?' Alex said. He held out his hands to her.

There were no words she could find, her tongue seemed incapable of moving. Jessica fell into his embrace, felt his arms around her. Safe. Then his lips found hers and all thoughts of safety vanished. This was not safe. This was dangerous, wild, a joining with another being that felt earthy and elemental. This was not something for two well-dressed people in an elegant drawing room with satin-covered sofas and Wedgwood vases. This was something that belonged under the open sky with bare skin against bare skin.

There was heat and moisture and the taste of a man and her tongue that had refused to speak was twining with his in a way that felt quite wonderfully wicked.

Then the heat and the touch of him left her and Jessica blinked up from the depths of the sofa cushions to find Alex kneeling beside her.

'I think, after that, we need have no concerns about any lack of mutual desire,' he said, his voice hoarse.

'Yes,' Jessica agreed, amazed to discover that she could speak. She sat up, tugged her gown into some kind of order and pushed back a lock of hair that had fallen into her eyes. *Alex.* She reached out and clung to his hands as though she stood on the edge of a chasm and he would help her across. She closed her eyes for a second, then opened them and leapt. 'Yes. Yes, I do. I will marry you.'

'I swear you will not regret this, Jessica.'

'I think we should go and tell your father—'

'The devil!' The roar of fury from outside the door silenced Alex and brought Jessica to her feet.

'Papa?' She scrambled from the sofa, flung open the door and found her parent, red in the face, standing in the hallway and brandishing a letter in one hand. Both footmen came running and skidded to a halt at the sight of them.

Chapter Sixteen

'The stupid idiot!' her father spluttered. 'The fool. He'll be the ruin of me.'

'Come and sit down, Papa. You will make yourself ill.' Jessica tried to steer him into the drawing room, certain he was about to have a seizure at any moment. 'Alfred, fetch water. Henry, go to Dr Chandler at once. His Grace will give you the direction.'

Behind her she heard Alex say, 'Take my carriage, the driver knows the address. Tell the doctor that I think it urgent.'

Between them they managed to get her furious father seated. Jessica loosened his neckcloth and unbuttoned his waistcoat. 'Sit back, Papa. Put your feet up.' She added some brandy to the glass of water Alfred brought. 'Sip this slowly.'

When he finally did as she said she took the letter from his hand and read it.

'It's from my elder brother Ethan. He is writing to inform Papa that he is on the point of concluding an agreement with Bracegirdle and Sons—they are iron founders, too—to jointly buy the Fosdyke Works. And to seal the deal he is intending to marry Jane Bracegirdle.'

Her father sat up and slammed the glass down on a side

table, sending brandy and water sloshing over the finely polished surface. 'The Fosdyke Works are no use to us, but they will give Bracegirdle access to that watercourse he wants to divert to his foundry. And Jane Bracegirdle hasn't the brains of a peahen. She's not the wife a man of business needs. Bracegirdle must be beside himself, thinking he's got behind my back on this.'

'If your son has already offered for Miss Bracegirdle, it could be a problem,' Alex said.

'No,' Jessica said. 'At least he hasn't done that. He is writing to obtain Papa's blessing first. I can only hope he hasn't led her to believe a proposal is inevitable. But if he has entered into an agreement over the works...'

'He cannot. I did not give him control over enough funds.' Her father was slightly less puce in the face now and, to her relief his breathing seemed easier. 'He wants me to direct Earnshaw's Bank to release the money. The young fool seems to think he has managed a coup.'

'What does Joshua say?' Jessica scanned to the end of the letter. 'Oh, he opposes it, which Ethan says shows his lack of vision.'

'Good lad,' her father muttered. 'Good lad. I must return, fast as may be before Ethan lands us in a mess of broken promises and lawsuits. I should never have taken my eye off the business. Never.'

'Well, Papa, you will be glad to hear that some good has come of our trip to London,' Jessica said brightly, in an effort to distract him from his woes.

'Very much so,' Alex said. 'Sir, I am happy to tell you that Jessica has honoured me by accepting my proposal of marriage.'

To her alarm her father greeted this news by slumping back against the sofa cushions, eyes closed.

'Papa!' Was that the final shock that had been too much for him?

She reached for his wrist and then sank back in relief as his eyes snapped open again and he sat up, beaming. 'Wonderful. I am delighted, my dear. Everything your dear mama and I would have wanted for you.' He got to his feet with a grunt of effort and held out his hand to Alex, who shook it.

'Thank you, sir.'

'Well, don't hang about. Send your lawyer around at once and I'll get mine in. Then you must sort out the special licence as soon as possible. You had best get around to the Faculty Office if we're to have a wedding tomorrow. I can only hope the Archbishop is in residence at Lambeth Palace.'

'Tomorrow?'

'Of course, if I am to see you wed and get up to Long Welling as soon as may be. I'll send a letter off to Ethan now, express, and one to Joshua, too. Tell them to do nothing, agree nothing—sign nothing—until I get there.' He strode towards the door. 'Alfred!'

'Sir, I do not see how you expect us to be in a position to marry tomorrow,' Alex protested.

'You certainly won't be if you dally around here, lad. Er, Your Grace.'

Alex turned to her. 'Jessica, is this what you want?' he asked over the sound of her father's study door banging and the footsteps of Alfred hurrying along the hall.

The front door opened and Alfred came in, Robert Chandler, medical bag in hand, on his heels.

'In there.' Alex pointed at the study door. 'But I think the danger is past.'

Jessica found herself standing in the drawing room feeling as though she was on the edge of a precipice with seconds to decide whether to jump forward or backwards.

Should she marry Alex tomorrow? Or step back, say it was too soon, that she needed time. This gave her no room for second thoughts, but was that such a bad thing?

'Yes,' Jessica said. 'If it can be done, I will marry you tomorrow. Papa wants me settled and he will not be easy until I am, especially with this upset at home, and he has made up his mind you are the very best choice for me. There's the title and then he will have had you investigated—I am sorry,' she added as Alex's brows drew together in a dark line. 'He will have done that to every single nobleman in London between the ages of twenty and fifty, I'm sure.

'I will feel easier about him,' she confessed. 'He worries so much, for all that bluff exterior. I want him to have this positive thing, this marriage he desires so much for me. He will be calmer when it comes to dealing with matters at home. And, I confess, I have no yearning for some great society wedding.'

'Nor I,' Alex agreed. 'Mr Danby is a man who likes to tie up the ends and to draw a line under one matter before he tackles another, I perceive.' To her relief he did not seem too put out by her father's demands now. 'I do not know whether we can manage this for tomorrow, but I will try. It might help that the Archbishop is a cousin of sorts. I had best be off.' He bent and pressed a kiss on her cheek, then a fleeting brush of his lips on hers and he was gone.

Jessica sat down on the nearest chair with a bump, her fingers pressed to her lips. What had she done? She was going to marry Alex, perhaps tomorrow, certainly the day after. None of this seemed real.

The sound of the front door closing and the sight of both footmen out on the pavement hailing hackneys brought her to herself. Tomorrow she might be the Duchess of Malvern and she had not a single thing that might be described as bride clothes. Well, he would have to take her as she was and she could shop afterwards.

Jessica took two long steadying breaths then jumped to her feet and made for the stairs.

'Trotter, I am marrying the Duke tomorrow,' she announced as the maid came in to the bedchamber in reply to her ring.

'Lawks.' Mouth open, Trotter sat down on the end of the bed and stared at her. 'The Duke? Tomorrow? Does your father know?'

'Of course he knows, Trotter. Now, there is no time for shopping, so we must find the best gown we can for the wedding. I have no idea where we are going afterwards—His Grace's town house or the castle in Herefordshire, or somewhere else entirely, so you must pack bearing that in mind.'

'Castle,' Trotter repeated faintly.

'*Gown*, Trotter.'

'Oh, yes, Miss Jessica. The new rose pink, don't you think? Thank goodness we had the silk slippers dyed to match. And your mama's pearls and the little silver and pearl tiara for your hair—that will set off the silver embroidery on the hem and at the neck of the gown. And then a travelling outfit... My goodness, we will need all your trunks down from the attic.'

'That will have to wait until the footmen have come back. Papa sent them on errands. Oh, and then I will need one of them to deliver invitations to my friends. But I cannot write those until His Grace returns with news of the licence.'

She flopped down on the bed beside Trotter who, suddenly realising that she was not only sitting in her mistress's presence, but on her bed, stood up and bustled to the wardrobe, covering her embarrassment by pulling out hatboxes.

'I do not know whether I am on my head or my heels,' Jessica confessed. 'People spend months preparing for weddings.'

'If you ask me, Miss Jessica, this might not be such a bad way of doing things.' Trotter sounded more herself now. 'Saves a lot of time and worry, now I come to think on it. And what's a big society wedding for? Just give all those people who've turned up their noses a good meal and the opportunity to gossip about you,' she added with a sniff. 'And if you love him, you want to be with him, not waiting about buying stuff.'

For Trotter that was an amazing descent into sentimentality, but Jessica hardly noticed.

Do I love *him?* she wondered.

It was an uncomfortable idea. Loving someone meant you could be hurt by them and this was a man who confessed he thought his true soulmate was out there somewhere in the world.

She liked Alex, desired him, trusted him, but love was another step. A step too far. That was not what she had been looking for when she had begun to assess the eligible bachelors. Falling in love seemed too much of a lottery to be relied upon, she had told herself. True, her parents had loved each other, but she had seen so many marriages where cool indifference, or even polite toleration, seemed the overriding emotion.

Far safer to look for liking and compatibility and respect—those were qualities that lasted.

'Someone's at the door,' Trotter said, cocking her head at the sound of the knocker.

'That will be Papa's lawyers, I expect.'

It was, as she discovered by hanging over the banisters in a most unladylike manner. They were followed soon after by another two gentlemen in sombre black who looked much the same: Alex's representatives. The legal affairs were being looked after, now she just had to wait and see what luck he had had with the clerical matters.

It had seemed a long wait. The lawyers emerged from her father's study after two hours and were shown into the breakfast room where refreshments were brought to them while, presumably, they dotted I's and crossed T's. Papa, she knew, would have already drafted her settlement with his legal advisors, but the ducal pair had to agree and their proposals must also be scrutinised. It felt uncomfortably like a business merger was being arranged.

But that is what you wanted, she reminded herself.

Jessica fidgeted about the house from bedchamber to dressing room to her own sitting room and then back to the bedchamber where she fingered the hem of the pink and silver gown. Was she making the biggest mistake of her life or were those first instincts, that she could be happy with the Duke, that she trusted him, correct?

Finally, at six o'clock, Alex returned carrying a flat box. 'I have it and I persuaded a clergyman who was at the Faculty Office to come and preside. You and I, Miss Danby, are getting married in the morning.'

He laid the box on the table and opened the top to reveal a large document written on parchment with a big red seal at its foot. Jessica read the heading.

Charles Manners-Sutton By Divine Providence, Archbishop of Canterbury...

There were their names in flowing script. They were apparently 'well-beloved' of the Archbishop, which felt alarmingly personal, and it seemed that they could marry anywhere, at any time, provided the ceremony was conducted by a minister of the church.

'Well done,' she said faintly. 'Was it very difficult?'

'It would have been impossible if I was merely Mr Demeral, or even the Viscount Demeral. Dukes, however, are another matter.' He took her hand and drew her close, not quite touching. His fingers were chill from the outside air and she could smell damp wool from his greatcoat and the faint tang of citrus, perhaps his soap.

'It doesn't have to be tomorrow, Jessica. There is no date on this. This will reassure your father if you need to take more time. After all, I am asking you to trust me with your heart and your whole being. You must be certain.'

Was he looking for a way out, hoping perhaps, after all, that she would think twice about this? Jessica gave herself a mental shake. He had proposed, she had accepted. Either she went through with this now—or never.

'I trust you, with everything I have and I am,' she said and it felt like a vow. One that should be sealed with a kiss. She put her hands on his shoulders and he drew her closer.

'I am cold and damp,' Alex warned.

'And I am warm.'

His lips were chill, but his mouth was hot and she could feel the heat of his body because he held her so close. There was an urgency, an intimacy that she had not sensed before from him and, she realised with a shock, from her. This was something different from her awareness that he was an attractive man and she was drawn to him. This was something far more primitive, more physical.

As his mouth moved slowly over hers, drawing her tongue in to meet his, his hands held her, close and possessive.

Tomorrow I will be in his bed, she thought as she sank into the embrace.

Somewhere, at the back of her mind, she was surprised at her own lack of apprehension.

'I think it will be all right, don't you?' Alex said and she came to herself to find her cheek pressed against his chest. She could feel the reassuring beat of his heart.

She tried again. 'Yes. Yes, it will.'

Chapter Seventeen

'Here comes your papa, if I am not mistaken,' Alex said. 'Shall we sit chastely on the sofa and discuss tomorrow?'

Her mind was so full of imaginings of the night that would follow their wedding that it took Jessica a moment to realise what Alex was discussing. 'Yes, of course. We will be married here, I assume, but then what? I did not know what to tell Trotter to pack.'

'I have requested the clergyman—the Reverend Dixon—to attend at eleven. Then we can have a substantial luncheon and set out for Herefordshire in the early afternoon. I suggest we stop for the night at the Angel in Oxford, a six-hour journey, provided the weather holds. There has been no chance to reserve rooms, of course, but Oxford has many decent inns if we cannot be housed at that one.'

Jessica was agreeing to this—really, she had no alternative suggestions, even if she had been unhappy—when her father came in followed by two of the lawyers.

One for each side, she thought with a twinge of amusement.

'You have the licence? Excellent.' Papa listened to Alex repeating what he had just said to her, then handed him a sheaf of papers. 'All agreed and awaiting your approval.'

'Thank you. Excuse me, my dear.'

It was the first time he had used any form of endearment to her and Jessica found it rather disconcerting. 'Yes, of course.'

Alex settled down to read, his lawyer standing beside him and occasionally leaning over to point something out and murmur a few words.

Jessica took the opportunity to ask, low-voiced, what Dr Chandler had said.

'Told me not to drink so much port, eat smaller meals and not let my sons throw me into a rage,' he said with a snort. 'I could have told him that. At least he did not quack me with some expensive potion.'

Jessica patted his hand soothingly and he subsided with a grunt into the nearest chair.

After some time Alex stood up. 'Very satisfactory, provided you are satisfied, sir.'

'I am.' Her father snapped his fingers and Henry put an inkstand and pens on the table. They signed, shook hands and the lawyers took themselves off with the document, promising copies within days.

'I want to invite my particular friends,' Jessica said. 'I will write now.'

'And I will invite mine, which should please some of yours,' Alex said with a grin. 'Is there anything I can do to assist further, sir? I intend asking five guests, if that is agreeable.'

'And five for me, Papa. I think we should include Lady Cassington. So that is ten, plus us, plus you. Oh, thirteen.'

'Ominous,' Alex agreed. 'I shall invite Locksley, thus pleasing Miss Beech and evening the numbers. And now I must go. There is a great deal to arrange.'

He took Jessica's right hand and raised it to his lips.

'But I must not leave without doing this.' From his pocket he took a small leather box and handed it to her. 'By tradition this was presented to my ancestress by King Charles II. Rather a risqué origin for a betrothal ring, but it has served as such for every Demeral bride since then. Does it please you?'

Jessica opened the lid and stared at the domed ruby glowing on its velvet nest, surrounded by diamonds. It was an old-fashioned setting, but no less lovely for that and something deep in the red heart of the stone seemed to call to her.

'It pleases me very much. It has a personality, if that is not too fanciful a thing to say about a jewel.'

'It is not, but I suspect that it needs a wearer of equal distinction to see that,' Alex said as he took the ring from its case and slid it on to her finger. 'A good fit, I think.'

'A perfect fit.'

His hand tightened on hers and she looked up, met his steady, dark gaze. Yes, this was a fit and not only the gold band of the ruby on her finger, but this match with the man who had just given it to her.

Even her father, not a man of great sensitivity about emotions, seemed to sense something. He cleared his throat and turned away.

'And now there are letters to write and a wedding breakfast to order,' she said brightly, not certain she knew how to cope with all this. It was too soon, too unsettling. 'And there will be fifteen, now I think about it—we must invite the clergyman, must we not? Oh, and packing. So much packing!'

'Only take what you need for the first week,' Alex said, standing up and pocketing the empty ring box. 'The rest can come by carrier and we will not be entertaining or going out immediately. Pack plenty of warm clothes. Castles might seem romantic, but they are cold places.' She nodded. 'I will be here before eleven tomorrow. *À bientôt,* Jessica.'

And then he was gone. Jessica stared at the closed door for half a minute and then reached for the bell. 'Wedding breakfast, invitations, packing for both of us. Papa, I do not know whether I am on my head or my heels.'

'You will manage, my dear. My daughter, the Duchess. Now here's Henry—send my valet to my room, lad, and Miss Jessica's woman to here, and get down the trunks and tell Alfred to stand by to deliver messages. And send up Cook.'

Alex strode in through his front door. 'Pitwick, I am getting married in the morning. Tell James to be ready to take messages and then he's to pack my things. I need a valet, Pitwick, but I'll have to take him for now.'

'And you require a secretary, Your Grace. And several more staff in all departments.' Nothing, it seemed, shook the butler's composure. 'May I offer my respectful felicitations on behalf of the household? And ask who is the lady in question?'

'Miss Danby,' Alex said over his shoulder on his way to the study.

'Ah,' was all the butler said, but there was a wealth of relief and satisfaction in the soft sound. Then he hastened down the hall after Alex. 'Several letters have arrived from Longstone this morning, Your Grace.'

'I've no time for them now. I will read them on the journey. I'll be able to deal with whatever they are about in three days' time in any case.'

Alex scrawled notes of invitation to his close friends and sent the footman off with them with orders to call at the florist on his way back and have flowers dispatched to Adam Street. Then he swept the correspondence from the desk into a valise, added the various papers and ledgers that always travelled with him and put it in the hallway with the portable writing slope.

From below stairs he could hear Pitwick setting the remainder of the staff to work. Pitwick would follow them with the heavy luggage. Cook and the scullery maid would stay behind and keep the house secure.

'Pitwick!'

'Your Grace?' The butler, his black apron tied on over his dark suit and striped waistcoat, appeared through the baize door.

'We need to hire a carriage for you and all the trunks.'

'That is all in hand, Your Grace. I will take charge of your dressing case and the silver.'

'Thank you. You think of everything, Pitwick.' There was not much silver remaining and what there was travelled with him, so at least he could set a respectable dining table when he was entertaining.

'I endeavour to, Your Grace. I will supervise James with your packing when he returns. I have ventured to set out a decanter of the ninety-five port in the drawing room: I thought the occasion merited it.'

It took a glass of the dark red liquid before Alex could stop making mental lists and relax. He had done it. He had found a wealthy bride and had saved the estates. Now all the people who were his responsibility would be well

housed and gainfully employed. The castle would be res-
cued from dereliction. He could hope to father children
and provide them with security and education. The line of
the Dukes of Malvern would continue, but the Pinchpenny
Dukes could be consigned to history.

And in return for all this he simply had to be a decent
husband. A faithful, concerned husband who would ensure Jessica's happiness and allow her to enjoy the status
the title would give her. Used to the rank all his life, he
could not but think he had the best of the bargain and that
increased his responsibility to his new wife.

He had promised himself a love match and he had
compromised. Now he swore to himself that, whatever
happened, Jessica would never have cause to regret her
decision. They might not be in love, but he had asked her
to trust him and, for him as a man of honour, that was as
binding as a declaration could be.

He had arrived too early. Nerves, he supposed, although
he felt oddly calm. Alex was politely shown in to Mr Danby's study with the unspoken comment that bridegrooms
were of little importance and were expected to stay well
out of the way.

The sound of guests laughing and talking in the drawing room, and the chink of tea cups in saucers, penetrated
the closed study door every time someone went in or out
of the other rooms and servants were scurrying back and
forth along the hallway. There was no sign of his future
father-in-law and, naturally, none of Jessica.

He looked at the clock on the mantelshelf. Ten-fifteen.
He should have brought a newspaper to occupy him until
Robert Chandler, his best man, arrived. But he did have

the valise with his correspondence, because that also had the special licence in it. He dug into the depths, came up with that morning's post and the unread letters from the day before and began to sort through them.

There were three in handwriting he recognised: his steward's. That must be the two that Pitwick had mentioned the day before and another that had been delivered that morning. What the devil was concerning Paulson so much that he had set pen to paper three times in two days? Usually he was as sparing with the written word as he was terse with the spoken.

Alex cracked the seal on the most recent one.

Old Mrs Jenkins died last night. The Williams child is still very poorly and little hope is held for him. The others, whose injuries are not so severe, seem likely to recover.

The words seemed to swim in front of his eyes. Deaths? Injuries? What the devil was this?

I have housed the twelve homeless families and those injured in the castle. We are working first on making the less damaged homes weathertight. I hope this meets with your approval and that I will hear from you soon, Your Grace. The expense is considerable, but I felt you would agree it.

Alex dropped the letter back into the valise and opened the others, a hard lump of dread in his gut as he read. A fire had started in the thatch of Widow Jenkins's cottage in the small hours. Neighbours thought she must have overturned a candle or lantern in her attic room. By the time it was discovered, the fire had spread and taken hold and hers, and twelve other cottages, had been destroyed or rendered uninhabitable. Injuries ranged from burns to broken limbs as people had jumped to safety and all were coughing badly. The unseasonably dry spell that had made the thatch and kindling stacks more vulnerable to fire had now been succeeded by torrential rain. Paulson had brought all the homeless families into the castle for shelter.

The pages crumpled in his hands as he sat staring at them. Old Mrs Jenkins, an infallible source of jam tarts for a small boy. Michael and Jenny Bond's new baby. More than half the little hamlet destroyed. Somehow he had to rebuild an entire community.

And then it hit him. Now he could. Now he could create a new village, build a school. Now he was a rich man, or he would be by the time he reached home.

But he had to be married first. He could hardly ruin Jessica's day by informing her that he would be taking her, not on a honeymoon, but to the scene of tragedy and devastation. He would have to break it to her on the journey.

Tomorrow, he told himself.

By then he would have plans made. Rapidly he scribbled a note to Paulson.

Spend what you have to. Spare no expense. Will be with you in two days with my Duchess.

Alex sealed it with a wafer and had just written the address and scrawled his name and title to ensure free delivery when a footman showed in Robert, his best man, and the Reverend Dixon. He handed the man the letter and told him to despatch it urgently, then, with what seemed like a physical effort, smiled at the new arrivals and put some warmth into his voice as he greeted them.

Somehow he had to get through this and reach home and he had to do it without causing Jessica any distress. He had thought all his troubles were over. He should have known better: Fate was not going to loosen her hold on the Penniless Dukes that easily.

Chapter Eighteen

'I wish your dear mama was here to see you now.' Her father unashamedly wiped a tear from his eye before settling Jessica's hand on his arm.

'So do I. But I have you, the best of fathers.' She gave the superfine suiting a comforting squeeze. 'You do like him, do you not, Papa? It isn't just the title?'

'If he were a rogue, he'd not get my blessing, duke or not,' her father said. 'Yes, I like him. He's honest and all the reports I've had are that he's a worker, a man with a sense of his responsibilities for those dependent on him. That's more than I expected from a lofty nob like him.'

They began to walk along the passageway leading to the head of the stairs, then he stopped. 'I've not tied the money up too tight. I trust him and it does a man no good not to be master of his own money. But I've set you up a nice little allowance as well, all of your own. There are all the details packed away in your luggage. I don't want him spending it all on that castle of his and you wanting for pretty dresses.'

'Thank you, Papa,' Jessica said and kissed his cheek.

'And very fine you look, too,' her father said as they began walking again. 'You'll make His Grace's jaw drop, see if you don't.'

Jessica hoped so. The gown was certainly charming,

Trotter had worked marvels with her hair and she had daringly allowed the merest touch of lamp black on her lashes and powder on her cheeks after the maid had pinched them ruthlessly to bring their colour up.

But did she look like a fit bride for a duke? At least this was no great society wedding with accounts of everyone's outfits in the Court pages of the newssheets and rows of critical matrons assessing everything from the length of her hem to the colour of her bouquet.

And she had Alex to thank for that. Hothouse roses of every shade had arrived that morning with a note.

I thought perhaps you would not have time to order these.

From them she and Trotter had created an arrangement of varying shades of pink with asparagus fern and silver ribbon. As she held it the great ruby glowed like a heart amid the pink petals. Looking down at it now carried her over the last few nervous steps to the head of the stairs.

Down they went and Alfred, who had been standing in the hall, darted in to the drawing room. Immediately there was the sound of the piano and of chairs being moved as people rose to their feet. It isn't even twenty people, she thought, concentrating on keeping her chin up and her shoulders back.

Trotter hurried down behind her. 'Veil, Miss Jessica.' The maid arranged the Valenciennes lace to cover her face and she breathed in the scent of lavender and dried rose petals that it had lain folded among since her own mother's wedding day. It brushed against her cheek like a kiss from long ago and she swallowed hard against the tears.

But now they were through the door and there was a clergyman in black cassock and white bands, standing at the table that had been draped in white with flowers and candlesticks as an altar. And there was the stocky figure of Dr Chandler, solid in well-tailored black with a cheerful red waistcoat.

And next to him... She made her eyes focus through the intricate mesh of the veil. There was the man who, very soon, would be her husband. Alex seemed very pale and very serious. Perhaps he was as nervous as she was. That was a strangely reassuring thought.

The rest of the room came clearer. Belinda seated at the pianoforte, her friends and Alex's mingled among the seating and not divided into bride and groom's sides. Lady Cassington half turned, beaming. Anna Chandler nodded encouragingly as she passed and then, in only a few steps, she was standing beside Alex.

Was his heart beating as fast as hers? Was his mind as suddenly and completely clear of doubts as hers was?

This was the man she wanted to marry. Not to satisfy Papa's ambitions, not to secure a place in society, but because she wanted very much to be his wife.

The Reverend Dixon was speaking and she realised that the service had begun. Nothing more important was ever going to happen to her, she must be aware of every moment.

'Who giveth this woman?' Papa lifted her hand and offered it to Alex and then stepped back, taking her old life with him.

There was no hesitation in Alex's voice as he took his vows, only an exciting urgency as though he could not wait to make her his.

Jessica had expected to be nervous, but when it was her turn she found the words came easily to her tongue and she could speak her vows clearly.

And finally, 'I pronounce them man and wife together...'

Alex put back her veil, lifted her hand with its new plain gold band next to the smouldering ruby and kissed her fingers. He still looked pale and serious, but there was a smile in his eyes for her.

'Is all well, Your Grace?' he asked her.

'All is very well, Your Grace,' she replied and laughed out loud with sheer happiness.

'Then let us go and greet our guests.' Alex placed her hand on his arm and walked down between the rows of seats and their friends stood and clustered around them, not waiting for the formality of a receiving line to offer kisses and handshakes and the warmth of their congratulations.

It seemed to Jessica, admittedly through a happy haze, that Alex was eager to draw everyone into the dining room. It must be because he wanted them to set off as soon as possible, to be alone with her.

For the first time the thought of that made her feel shy. This was real now, even though it had all the makings of a dream. She was the Duchess of Malvern—at least ten people had already greeted her by her title, the staff were saying *Your Grace* with every sentence.

Doctor Chandler rose to make a toast once the party was seated. 'To my old friend Alex Demeral and to my new friend, his wife: long life, happiness and every blessing.'

The Reverend Dixon said grace and there she was, Alex on her right hand, her father on her left, presiding for the first time as a hostess and married lady.

'This is the most elegant gathering you are likely to experience for some time, I fear,' Alex said as he raised his glass to tap against hers. 'Not only is local society in the immediate area somewhat limited, but our reception rooms are sadly lacking.' He sounded concerned about her reaction.

'We will have all the fun of renovating and then we can hold house parties and bring society to us,' she said. The idea of restoring a castle back to life and making it fit for a family in a new century was very appealing.

'Yes. That might take some time,' he said, rather flatly.

Had she blundered? Been tactless about the fact that it would be her dowry that would be paying for the renovations?

'I have concerns about the tenants and the estate,' Alex said. 'Those must take priority.'

'Yes, of course.' So it was not so much the money, she guessed, it was the fact that she had not comprehended the importance of his role as landowner and his responsibilities to the people who depended on the estate for their livelihood. 'You are going to have to teach me my duties in regard to the tenants,' she said. 'And the other villagers, too, I suppose. My family has never owned land as such, so I have a great deal to learn.'

'I imagine industrial employees have a different relationship with their employers.'

'It varies a great deal,' Jessica said carefully. It was certainly nothing like the feudal connection she sensed that landowners felt. Her father was considered soft by many of the neighbouring industrialists for providing a doctor for his workers and making sure they had time on Sundays to attend church and chapel. There was schooling of a sort for the children who were employed as well, but even so, she doubted her father knew the names of his workers below the rank of foreman, whereas she would wager her allowance for a year that Alex knew every one of his tenants and the local villagers by name.

But she had guests to attend to now and the problems of agricultural workers were for the future. The breakfast was becoming noisy with chatter and laughter. The Reverend was deep in conversation with Lady Cassington and her friends and Alex's were still showing the attraction for each other that she had seen from the start. How many more weddings were to be expected in the near future? She looked around the table, plotting where to throw her bouquet to best effect.

The last of the desserts had been reduced to crumbs and scrapes of cream. 'I think we should leave soon,' Alex said.

'Yes, of course, I will go and change at once.'

All the female guests came with her, descending on her bedchamber like a flock of gaily coloured birds while Trotter had her out of the pink silk and into her newest carriage dress with a smart bonnet, trimmed in blue velvet, and a matching blue redingote.

'That will keep you snug however draughty the carriage,' Trotter announced, standing well back to survey the results.

The others flocked out to assemble in the hall, but Anna Chandler remained behind. 'You love him, don't you?'

'I do not know,' Jessica confessed. 'I think I could, very easily. I do not know whether I dare let myself.' Even saying it gave her a little ache in her heart.

'It is a risk,' Anna agreed. 'But I think you have the courage.' And then she was gone, too, and there was nothing for it but to make her way down the stairs, leaving her girlhood behind, stepping into the unknown future.

She was passed from person to person, kissed by every-one—except the Reverend Dixon—and found herself out on the pavement with Alex waiting by the open carriage door. A second vehicle for the luggage, Trotter and one of Alex's footmen who was acting as his valet, stood behind.

There was nothing left to do but wave to the assembled staff, kiss Papa and pretend they were not both weeping, and toss her bouquet over her shoulder.

It found its mark, as she had intended, in Lady Anthea's hands. She blushed and glanced at Major Rowlands and said something about, 'Such nonsense', but her cheeks were a very pretty shade of pink and his ears had turned red.

Jessica was not conscious of climbing the step into the carriage or of sitting down, but there she was and Alex was next to her, leaning over to drop the window strap so she could lean out and wave.

When they turned the corner into the Strand he closed it again and handed her a handkerchief. 'It is quite clean. James is taking his duties as temporary valet very seriously.'

'Thank you.' She dried her eyes and folded the linen square neatly. 'I am not crying because I am sad, you understand. Just...' She waved a hand vaguely.

'It is a very big step,' Alex agreed. 'And a very abrupt one.'

'Yes, I am sorry about that. It has meant you have had no time to hire a valet or do any of the things I am sure you wanted to do in London before you left.'

'As it happens—' He broke off abruptly, then said, 'As it happens, I am not sorry to be returning to Herefordshire at this time.'

After that they settled down to watching the passing scene from the window. It proved less awkward than Jessica had feared—she had been rather dreading making conversation for almost twenty hours. They had never seemed to have any shortage of things to talk about before, but now she felt almost shy. Perhaps it was the thought of the wedding night ahead.

Now they could find plenty of interest to comment on and, when the light began to fail, Alex suggested that she remove her bonnet, gloves and coat and wrap a travelling rug around her legs.

'I have a basket of cakes and some lemonade. Have something to eat and drink—I noticed you did not manage a great deal at the breakfast.'

To her surprise Jessica found she was both hungry and thirsty and the refreshments were welcome, although she felt slight surprise and, if she was honest with herself, disappointment that Alex had shown no signs of amorousness. Clearly, as a gentleman, he would not attempt full lovemaking in a moving carriage in broad daylight, but perhaps a kiss...

Alex packed away the picnic basket and moved to the seat facing her. 'Try to sleep,' he suggested. 'It has been a long and tiring day.' He tucked her up warmly under the blanket when she stretched out on the seat and folded another blanket under her head.

Jessica closed her eyes and felt the brush of his lips on her cheek, the weight of his hand on her hair for a moment, then heard the sounds of him settling in the corner opposite her feet. He was clearly being considerate of her weariness and that accounted for his restraint.

There was the sharp click of a steel striking flint, a glow against her closed lids and the faint odour of warm oil. He had lit one of the lamps that were fitted against the bulkhead of the coach. There was a rustle of paper. It was curiously comforting and domestic, despite the jolting of the coach. Even that was not so bad. The road to Oxford must be one much travelled by the Mail as well as the stagecoaches, and the Royal Mail let very little stand in the way of their schedules, certainly not potholed roads.

She would just doze a little, then she would be bright and alert when they arrived at the Angel Inn, ready for her wedding night. Jessica found she was looking forward to it now, the apprehension and shyness had somehow disappeared.

The carriage slowed, stopped, there was the bustle of horses being changed, but she ignored it and slipped down into sleep.

Chapter Nineteen

She was in a garden, a large, wild, overgrown garden full of roses and ferns, tangles of brambles and clumps of nettles. Someone was blowing a horn, summoning her. A herald at the castle gate? A sentry on the battlements?

Jessica gathered up her trailing skirts and began to run towards the sound, but the thorns caught at the veils trailing from her wimple and tree roots tried to trip her. And then she came out into the open and found herself on the banks of a moat. The water was sparkling and swans were swimming and across it was a castle, white and perfect with turrets and banners. If she could only get there in time—

The horn blew again and she jerked awake out of her dream into faint light. She was stretched out on a bench of some kind that was moving and the room was swaying.

Of course—the carriage. And this was the nineteenth century, not the Middle Ages. That horn was the groom blowing for a toll gate to open or for a change of horses. She had fallen deeply asleep. Jessica sat up rubbing her eyes. Strange that she should feel so stiff after such a short nap, but it was not yet full dark.

It was difficult to see properly because the lamp had gone out, but she could make out the still figure of Alex in the corner diagonally across from her.

'You are awake,' he said.

'Yes.' She yawned and rubbed her eyes. 'Goodness, what a deep sleep. I was dreaming about a castle and a moat with swans and someone blowing a trumpet—but it was the horn, of course. Are we nearly at Oxford?'

'We passed Oxford long since.'

'We drove through the night? We haven't stopped?' No wonder she felt stiff and hungry and in need of a nice inn and its facilities.

'You were completely sunk in sleep. Exhausted. I thought it best to simply keep going.' Alex did not sound like his usual amiable self and he was staring out of the window.

Jessica bit back the retort that he might at least have discussed it with her, then decided that starting an argument when half awake, on the first day of their married life, was not a good idea.

It was daylight now, a misty March morning with a distinctly damp chill in the air. Jessica sat as the carriage slowed, turned, lurched over a hump-backed bridge. She glimpsed water foaming over rocks below. Then she glanced up and saw the castle. Her castle.

Three towers built of a reddish stone, slate roofs, a curtain wall linking the towers, punctuated with what must be arrow slits. No flag flew to welcome its master home and she could see no sign of the moat.

'I should have woken, you, warned you. I kept putting off waking you,' Alex said, his voice choked with some emotion she had never heard before. 'I am sorry.'

Then Alex threw open the door and jumped down, not waiting for the coach to stop. When it did, after a few more yards, Jessica leaned further out, completely confused by his words. Perhaps she was still only half awake.

She was not certain what she had expected to see. A pleasant village with friendly inhabitants coming out to greet their lord, she had hoped. Rather tumbledown, of course—Alex had spoken feelingly about the need for repairs and improvements and this was not the prosperous countryside surrounding London, after all—but a community. Children and old people, ducks on the pond and perhaps a goat on the green. A little church, an ale house, no doubt.

It was the smell that hit her first, before what she was looking at made any sense. There was the unmistakeable stench of burning, of wet ashes, the foul smell from still-smouldering old thatch. Then she saw the shells of cottages, most with the roofs completely gone, some with tumbled gable ends, others with their stone and plaster blackened by tongues of smoke. Charred timbers were everywhere, some sticking up like the skeleton of a long-beached whale, others jumbled on the ground.

The short tower of the church was visible behind, halfway to the castle. A cottage near the river bank was intact, but the bush hanging over its door—the sign of an ale house—was charred. There were no children, no animals, to be seen.

Men and women were working in the trampled mud that surrounded each pathetic wreck. Jessica clutched at the doorframe as she tried to count. Ten at least, perhaps more. Half of this little settlement gone. Even she could tell there was no hope of repairing these. Those poor people.

Alex was striding across the battered grass—the green she had imagined with playing children and a goat. He called out and the workers turned and flocked to him. She saw him put his arms around two weeping women, the men clustered close and from the direction of the church a clergyman hurried down, his hands held out, in greeting, blessing or in supplication, she could not tell.

When had this happened? Faint wisps of smoke still rose from some of the buildings, but she knew that thatch and wood could smoulder for days, she had seen it when one of the casting sheds at the works had burned down, taking a neighbouring thatched hovel with it.

Alex had known about this. He had made no exclamation of horror or surprise, but had been tensed to leap from the carriage the moment they arrived. No wonder he had been sleepless and drawn on the journey. He must have known before the wedding, even—there had been no messages delivered for him once he had reached the house.

The groom climbed down to unfold the step for her and she descended on unsteady legs. This was a crisis and there were far more important things to think about than her own anxieties. But she had to know.

Alex had gone to look at one of the cottages with a small group of people, so she walked across the green to where the vicar stood. He was drawn and unshaven and his cassock, which was filthy around the hem, had been buttoned incorrectly.

'Vicar?'

He turned to look at her uncomprehendingly. 'Madam?'

'I am the Duke's wife. We were married yesterday. Can you tell me when this happened, please?'

'Your Grace? When? Three days past, in the night. His Grace's steward wrote—'

'Yes, of course. His Grace did not want to worry me with details, but I need to be sure I understand everything.'

He nodded as though that made sense. 'Forgive me,

Your Grace. I am Harold Goodson, the Vicar here. I should welcome you to Longstone, but it hardly seems...'

'Please, do not concern yourself with me. Was anyone hurt?'

'Several people—burns, of course. Some were hit by falling beams and most inhaled smoke. We lost Widow Jenkins and the Bonds' baby died this morning.'

'A baby? Oh, *no*.' The scene in front of her seemed to tilt and sway so that she held on to the side of the coach. 'The poor parents. I can't imagine...' Mr Goodson took a step forward, concern on his face. She took a deep breath. She must not distract him with her distress, he had an entire village to comfort. And so, she realised, had she. 'Where is everyone? These cottages must be uninhabitable.'

'In the castle, Your Grace. There was nowhere else for them to go. The church is too small.'

'Your Grace!' That was Trotter, stumbling across the grass, batting away James's attempts to help her. 'What has happened?'

'As you can see,' Jessica said with a snap, 'most of the village has burned down. We must go up to the castle: there are people who need help. James, go to His Grace, see what he wants you and the others to do.' She managed a smile for the Vicar, then hurried back to the carriages.

The two vehicles bumped up the track, across a draw-bridge—there was a moat, of sorts as Anna had described—and through an arch. The sound of the carriage wheels echoed and bounced off stone in the deep shadow and then they were through and into an internal courtyard.

It might have been a scene from the Middle Ages. Children played in corners, women stood around the well, wait-ing their turn as a man drew up bucket after bucket of water for them to carry inside. Plough horses were tethered against one wall and sheep and goats bleated from a pen.

'Your Grace?'

'Wait. Wait a moment.' Jessica sat and fought for composure. Alex had known about this when he proposed to her and he had offered because he desperately needed the money. Yes, this was a crisis and, yes, these people needed help urgently—but why had he not been honest with her? She had agreed to marry because she trusted him and, it seemed, she had been wrong.

Had he thought she would refuse? But she had known all along that he needed money, had known it when she had made him that audacious offer. Why had he not come to her and told her what had happened, told her that she had been right, that they could make a good marriage and that he had been too optimistic in thinking he could find romantic love.

Instead he had said nothing about that critical need for money. Why not? Because he did not believe she would accept him, she supposed. He had been very fortunate that the crisis at home meant that Papa insisted on a hasty wedding. But then, simply letting it be known that they were betrothed would have meant that lines of credit would suddenly open up for the Pinchpenny Duke. He could have waited months, if that had been what she had asked.

She supposed he had wanted to make sure. Sure of his bride, sure of her fortune.

Chapter Twenty

Jessica's bitter thoughts had not taken long. A man was hurrying across the courtyard towards them, chickens and ducks scattering before him. He opened the door, his expression one of profound relief. 'Your Grace!' When he saw her it changed to a look that would have been comical, if only she had been in the mood to appreciate it.

'The Duke and I married before we left London,' she said. 'I am the Duchess. And you are?'

'Paulson, Your Grace. Steward here. The Duke is with you?'

'He is down in the village. If someone can show my woman where my rooms are and take up our luggage, then perhaps you can show me the arrangements here for these unfortunate people.'

'Certainly, Your Grace. Chris! Billy!'

Two young men hurried forward, were given instructions and, hoisting the first of the luggage on to their shoulders, led Trotter away through the great double doors into the depths of the castle.

'This way, Your Grace. I will summon the housekeeper and arrange for refreshments for you.'

'I have just breakfasted, thank you, and I am sure she has many urgent matters to attend to. And I think that *ma'am*

will do, Mr Paulson. This is no situation for formalities.'
She took off her bonnet and coat and tossed them into the
carriage.

'No, indeed. Now, if you will allow me, I will show
where we have housed the displaced families. Oh, do mind
your footing, ma'am. The geese make such a mess.'

An hour later Jessica sat at the kitchen table, drinking
tea in company with a weary steward and a somewhat
flustered housekeeper.

'If we'd only known to expect you, Your Grace... His
Grace's letter said something about a duchess, but we could
make no sense of it and thought he must have written the
wrong thing in haste. And your suite hasn't been aired out
and the bed isn't made up.'

'The wedding was brought forward because my father
had to return home to deal with an urgent matter. As for
the room, if you can spare a housemaid, Mrs Black, then
she and my maid Trotter can make up the bed and do whatever else is necessary.'

There had been no sign of Trotter, which meant that either she had found a maid herself and was dealing with the
room or she had thrown up her hands in horror and was
even now composing a letter of resignation.

'My rooms are not a priority. I am full of admiration
for the way in which you have managed to accommodate
the families.'

A range of ground-floor rooms had been cleared of the
stored lumber, barrels and stacks of kindling they had been
used for, swept and scrubbed and furnished with whatever furniture the families had managed to save, supple-
mented by a motley collection of items taken from around

the castle. All the families had two rooms each, the single men were sharing and the elderly and frail were in guest bedchambers.

'And we've dug a row of latrine pits, if you'll excuse me mentioning the matter, ma'am,' Mr Paulson said.

'But it's feeding them, Your Grace,' Mrs Black said. She was a thin woman with greying hair and frown lines which spoke of habitual worrying. 'It's not that they're fussy—they're used to good plain food, all of them, but most have lost what stores they had and there's only a dozen of us here, so Cook hasn't that much laid by.'

The cook, Mrs Brightwell, nodded agreement and went on stirring what smelled to Jessica like a vat of porridge.

'Make a list of what you need. Not just food. Mattresses, bedding, clothes—whatever is lacking—and then send staff into the nearest large town and buy it all.'

'Ma'am?' They stared at her.

'Money will not be a problem.' Jessica opened her reticule where she had stowed the roll of banknotes her father had given her just before she left.

'It might take a while to set up the bank accounts and so forth,' he had said vaguely.

She hadn't counted it, but now she put it on the table and the notes curled across the scrubbed pine. Paulson, Mrs Black and Cook stared.

'Yes, Mrs Black, money will no longer be a problem,' said Alex from the doorway. He was still drawn, but the pallor had left him and he looked alert and grimly determined.

Jessica looked across the table and their gazes locked. She held the look for a moment, then glanced down at the money and back up. Now was not the time or the place for recriminations or explanations, but if her husband thought she was accepting the situation passively, he was much mistaken.

The staff who had been reticent about accepting the invitation to sit with Jessica at the kitchen table were far more at their ease with Alex, she realised.

They all leapt to their feet, of course, and there were respectful greetings of 'Your Grace' from all of them, but their smiles spoke of affection and relief, not servility.

'Thank you for all your work,' he said. 'Everything that could be done has and with real thought to what the displaced families need. I have spoken to the Vicar and the funerals will be tomorrow morning. Mrs Jenkins first and then the child.'

Jessica wondered whether she should go to the bereaved parents. She felt that she should and yet they did not know her—they might feel they had to somehow be on their best behaviour with her, which was the last thing they needed at this time. Perhaps she should go after the funeral.

'The place is in a right mess, Your Grace,' Mrs Black said. 'We haven't touched the family rooms since this happened, none of the fires have been lit for days up there and everywhere smells of the smoke from the village.'

'That does not matter,' Alex said.

'Indeed it does not,' Jessica added, cutting across what he was going to say next. She was mistress of this household now and instinct told her to take a firm grip now or she would find it harder later. 'Looking after the displaced people and the staff who are all working so hard must take priority. His Grace and I both have our personal servants with us—between the four of us we can make our beds and light our fires. Perhaps we can all have some breakfast now, then we can make lists and plans.' She had an instinct that if they did not have a second breakfast now it might be evening before they ate again.

'Of course, ma'am. You'll be more comfortable in the small drawing room, I'll be bound, and you can send your people down here, we will look after them.'

Jessica interpreted that as the staff feeling more comfortable if she and Alex removed themselves and she did not argue. She needed to speak to her husband alone. Soon.

He led the way up the back stairs and into the hall, or rather the Great Hall—the capital letters were quite audible. It was vast, with a table to match in the middle, fireplaces that could roast an ox, and probably had in the past, and a vaulted ceiling vanishing into cobwebbed gloom.

They met Trotter and James halfway across the stone-flagged floor.

'We've made up the beds, Your Grace,' Trotter said. 'And lit fires in both bedchambers and put the bedding to air. It all needs a good dusting, but it is comfortable enough. I have unpacked what I think you will need for today and tonight, Your Grace, and the girl showed us our accommodation.'

'Is it suitable, Trotter?' Jessica was conscious of Alex beside her, but she was not concerned with his reaction to her doubts. Trotter was a London-trained upper servant. She was entitled to a good bedchamber and was quite within her rights to take herself back to London if she did not have one.

'Perfectly, Your Grace, thank you.'

'Ma'am will do, Trotter,' Jessica said, not for the first time. 'If you go down to the kitchen they will make you your breakfast.'

That was one thing she had learnt about housekeeping very early—make sure the staff were comfortable. Jessica followed Alex through into a room that, to put it politely, seemed to have been lived in. It was a quarter of the size of the Great Hall and it was filled with a hotchpotch of furniture, some very ancient, some relatively modern. All of it looked well-worn but comfortable. This was no formal reception room, this was a room where you could kick off your shoes and curl up on a sofa to read a book, although most of the sofas appeared to have welcomed dogs as well as humans.

Alex closed the door behind him and faced her. 'You want to know why I did not warn you about the fire,' he said bluntly.

'Yes, I do.' Jessica sat down cautiously on the edge of the sofa that looked least likely to swallow her up in its mounds of cushions and sagging webbing. She folded her hands neatly in her lap, took a deep breath and told herself to say calm. She would not allow him to see how hurt she was feeling.

'I could think of no way to tell you, under the circumstances.'

'Circumstances?' Her resolution to stay in control vanished in a burst of anger. Jessica found she was on her feet, confronting him.

'You proposed to me because now you need my money and that overrides your romantic desire to seek your true love and everything you said to me about friendship and trust is so much flummery. If nothing else, surely I deserve your honesty? Could you not have said that your circumstances had changed for the worst and that you now find my practical proposal for a marriage of mutual convenience is acceptable if I am still of the same mind? At least that would have been honest. Instead,' she concluded on a sob she could not quite control, 'you lied to me by omission, let me believe that we might have...have something that had a meaning, that was built on trust.'

Her words rocked Alex back on his heels as though she had hit him. 'You are telling me that you thought that I proposed to you knowing this?' He swept his hand towards the window where she could see thin trails of smoke rising upwards.

'Yes. Of course. I know your steward wrote to you at once.'

'Of course,' he echoed. 'You think you cannot trust me now? It seems I never could believe in your professions of faith in me.' His face was set in anger, his voice bitter. 'I did not know about the fire until an hour before the wedding ceremony. I had not opened my post the day before because I was too distracted with thoughts of all we had to plan, to do.'

Alex turned from her, rested his hands on the windowsill and stared out. 'I had not opened it the day before that because I was nerving myself to propose to you. I do not have a secretary—it cannot have escaped your notice that I could not afford one.'

Jessica sat down again. The fire of her anger had left her feeling sick. 'Yet on the journey, you knew. You did not tell me. You let me think we would break the journey, yet you drove on. You could have explained—did you think I would refuse to come?'

'If I had, then I would have been right. You refused to believe in me when you descended from the carriage this morning,' he said over his shoulder.

'I was tired, half awake and taken utterly by surprise. What did you expect?'

'Trust—the quality you seem to set so much store by,' he said, turning to face her. 'If you can allow yourself to believe that I did not know until I opened my letters while I waited in your father's study, then perhaps you can believe that I was shocked, desperately anxious—and faced with telling my new bride that, far from spending the first weeks of her marriage in peace and tranquillity she would be pitchforked into tragedy and chaos. I judged it best to wait until you were rested before telling you. Clearly, I was wrong.'

Was this *her* fault? Is that what Alex was saying? That she should have believed in him and not judged without giving him the chance to explain?

She was angry and hurt and had been feeling a fool for believing in the honesty of his proposal. Jessica picked her way through her emotions.

'I assumed, when Mr Paulson told me when he had written, that you would have seen the letter when you proposed to me. If you tell me that was not the case, then, of course, I accept your word and I apologise.'

She meant the apology, but at the same time, she deeply resented it. The world was full of deceived wives who blindly put their faith in husbands who betrayed them, cheated them, deceived them. She had always thought herself too clever to be taken in by such a man and now she was being asked to apologise for perfectly natural suspicions. A lady was expected to meekly accept whatever her husband decreed, but she was not surrendering without some semblance of fight.

'Even so, I still think that you should have told me on the journey before I went to sleep,' she said as calmly as she could. 'You showed no faith in my willingness to put this disaster above my personal comfort and convenience.'

Silence. They stared at each other, Alex stony-faced, Jessica biting her lip. Then he said, 'That is true. I also apologise. I suppose we are having our first married argument.'

'Technically, I believe we are not actually married,' she countered.

'Because the union has not been consummated?' Strangely, this appeared to amuse Alex, or at least he seemed to relax a little. One dark eyebrow quirked. 'Am I to conclude that this is unlikely to occur?'

'No, of course not.' Jessica, who had spoken without really thinking, felt decidedly flustered. 'I mean... Oh, I do not know what I mean! I am upset, I am appalled by what we have found here, I feel sick that our trust in each other seems to have such shaky foundations, I am very well aware that to the villagers I am a complete stranger and one who does not understand their lives or their world. And I suppose I am feeling all the emotions of any inexperienced woman at the prospect of the wedding bed, and— Are you laughing at me? Because if you are, I am never going to speak to you again, Alex Demeral.'

'No, I am not.' He came across the room, knelt in front of her with head bent and took her unresisting hands in his cold ones. 'I am bone weary. Like you, I am appalled at those shaky foundations. I know these people, but I fear that whatever I can do for them might not be enough. I am feeling all the emotions of a man facing the prospect of lying with a virgin and dreading getting that wrong. And if you wish to laugh at me, you may.'

Chapter Twenty-One

Alex felt the touch of Jessica's hand on his hair, fleeting, tentative. They had made such a mull of this between them, he wondered if it was possible to find their way back to solid ground again.

Then Jessica's touch became a caress and he looked up and found she was smiling at him. It was a cautious smile, but it held hope and affection. She swayed forward, he leaned in to meet her and he felt that smile against his own lips and answered it.

It felt as though a boulder had been lifted from his chest. When he put his arms around her she slid from the sofa and curled against him with a soft sigh.

With an effort he kept the kiss gentle, slow. It was not what he wanted and, he suspected, if he had obeyed his instincts and made love to his wife there on the floor, she would have made no protest. But this was too important to get right and he broke the kiss and lifted her back on to the seat.

'Later,' he promised and this time her answering smile held certainty.

'Yes, we must think what is most important to do now.'

He sat down a little way from her and she asked, 'Where is the nearest town?'

'Hereford.'

'Then I suggest I go in with one of the carriages with a driver and groom from here who know their way around. I will ask Cook for a list and we will buy food and medical supplies. Plenty of both and blankets. The other things are important, but if people are well fed, warm and their hurts are taken care of, then I think they will feel more positive. Perhaps after the funerals I could visit each family and find out what they need to be comfortable in their temporary accommodation and then we can have another expedition with wagons to bring things like mattresses back.'

'Yes, I agree. I will make certain we have enough fuel in to keep everybody warm.'

'I will go as soon as we have eaten,' Jessica said. 'Can you find a driver and groom who know the town and a footman to help me? There are footmen, aren't there?' she asked.

'Two. One rather doddery. You take Sim.'

Alex was beginning to become concerned when dusk began to gather and Jessica had still not returned. He went up on to the battlements, warily skirting the more crumbling sections, looked out and sighed with relief as he saw the carriage making its way slowly along the potholed road.

Had she managed to get credit? he wondered. The local shopkeepers understandably wanted cash in hand from the castle—they knew the financial position as well as he did. But there had been that roll of banknotes, of course. It was still hard to accept that money was no longer a problem.

As the carriage drew up in the courtyard he came down the worn old steps. Jessica climbed out, saw him and gave him a triumphant grin.

'We are loaded! I defy you to find a space to squeeze in another potato.'

Even as she spoke, people began to emerge from the building to carry the stores in. Cook came to stand on the steps and beam at the procession and Mrs Black seized the package that Jessica gave her.

'Salves and bandages and willow bark powder. I explained to the apothecary what sort of injuries there are and he says this should all help,' Jessica explained.

'There was no trouble with paying?' Alex asked, leading her aside.

'No, I went to the bank first and gave them the letter of credit and introduction from Papa's bank. I paid in cash in the shops, but I told them where I was banking. I have no doubt they'll all be making enquiries and we will not have difficulty setting up accounts now.'

Alex watched the purchases being unloaded, conscious of an odd feeling of surprise. It took him a moment to identify it: he was not feeling the discomfort he knew some men would experience at having their wives pay for all this. It had not occurred to him before because he knew his duty was plain—what he had struggled with was trying to find both a woman to love and a wealthy one.

Now, he accepted, he had made a fair exchange. Jessica would not have married him if she had not wanted to. Despite what she said about pleasing her father, she was too intelligent and too independent to condemn herself to a miserable marriage. Nor was she a woman whose head was turned by the prospect of becoming a duchess and who would have married him whatever his character.

And a fair exchange is no robbery, ran the old saying— provided it *was* fair. And that was where his duty lay, to ensure that Jessica became fully his Duchess in every sense and was happy. He had never been responsible for another person's happiness before; it felt a daunting responsibility.

Dinner was excellent, even if the wine glasses were cloudy with age and the china plain and the crests on the cutlery worn by years of polishing.

They ate at one end of the great table as close to a fireplace as possible. Even with both fires lit, the Hall seemed to suck heat upwards and replace it with insidious little draughts around their ankles.

Jessica wondered how to tactfully discover what improvements would be acceptable and then decided as Alex passed her bread rolls that it was better just to ask.

'You said that the castle needs structural work,' she said, watching Alex. He seemed to be savouring the vegetable soup and a well-fed man was usually an amiable one in her experience. 'What about the interior?'

'The interior has hardly been touched for two hundred years and it needs dragging into the nineteenth century,' he said. 'It will not be easy. I suspect the draughts will be a lot worse when all the cobwebs and starlings' nests are removed.'

'One would not want to harm all the original features, though,' she said, ladling out more soup for both of them. It had been a long, tiring day and the hot food seemed to be doing them both good. 'How old is it?'

'The centre is the keep which was built in about 1390, then it was added to until Henry VII made it clear he did not appreciate local lords maintaining highly fortified castles. It has been gently mouldering ever since then—'

He broke off as the elderly footman whose name Jessica had not yet learned came in with a roast, followed by Sim with platters of vegetables. 'Pork? That smells magnificent. My compliments to Cook.'

Dinner, then, was a success, which was a good start, Jessica decided. Not that she had anything to do with the cooking of it, but she thought that she had bought well.

Now, as she scraped the last delicious traces of posset from the dish, she realised that there was not a great deal to do except think about what happened next. Should she retire to the drawing room and sit alone while Alex drank port, then joined her for conversation before she rang for the tea tray to be brought in and then...?

No. Better to get it over with, although she was not at all sure whether the butterflies in her stomach were entirely agitated by dread. Some, at least, were excited anticipation.

'It has been a long day,' she said. 'I think I will retire now. If, of course, I can find my way to my bedchamber.'

'Allow me to escort you.' Alex was on his feet before the footman could step forward to pull back her chair.

Jessica swallowed. 'Oh. Thank you.' This was not what she had anticipated. 'But I would not want to keep you from your port.'

'I doubt there is a drinkable bottle in the place,' he said ruefully. 'Brendon, see to it that hot water is sent up to Her Grace's chamber.'

Another name to remember. Jessica focused on that and then on following the twists and turns that led her from the head of the massive oak staircase along corridors, through a door and up a short flight of curving steps.

'You have your own turret and it is one of those still securely attached to the main building, I promise.'

It was not as much a turret as a tower, she realised, stepping into a large room that would have been circular if a partition had not been built across the inner side to cut off a curved slice. A dressing room, she supposed.

'I see Trotter is here. I will leave you.' He bent and kissed her cheek. 'May I return later?' he murmured in her ear.

'Yes,' she whispered, suddenly very shy. It was difficult to remember now that she had summoned up the courage to propose to this man.

Jessica sat up in the big bed and hugged her knees. It must have been like this for countless brides in this chamber. There was little that she could see in her surroundings that reminded her of what century she was in.

At least she was warm and bathed and could expect an equally warm clean man to enter through the archway, not some unwashed, hairy fighting man with very definite ideas on the place of women—under him in all senses— and of his rights in a marriage.

The door opened with a creak and closed with a disconcertingly final thud. Then Alex stepped out of the shadowed archway and she stopped tormenting herself with Gothic imaginings and felt those fluttering butterflies of desire again.

He was wearing a heavy robe of some dark red material and his hair was ruffled, dark and shining with damp. A very clean husband, then, even if he did look disconcertingly like his regal ancestor.

She was bathed, too, although the tub had been small. Trotter had brushed her hair dry in front of the fire, dressed her in the very plain and very thin silk nightgown that had been carefully packed in dried rose petals and Jessica had dabbed rosewater behind her ears and, daringly, between her breasts.

The old, tarnished, mirror on the dressing table showed a figure that was hazy in the candlelight. Was this how a bride was supposed to look—ethereal and pale? Trotter appeared to think not and produced a rouge pot. Jessica had waved it away. No pretence tonight. She knew herself to be passably pretty, not a great beauty. Alex had seen her waking after a night in a coach, wan, heavy-eyed and slightly dishevelled, so he was not going to be fooled now by a display of artifice. Besides, this had gone beyond batting lamp-blacked eyelashes to seduce a man.

'May I come in?' He took her nod for assent and came quietly across the stone floor to the sheepskin rug by her bed where he kicked off leather slippers. 'I have done my best to keep my feet warm for you,' he said with a smile. 'My father always used to offer guests a choice of dog to sleep on their bed to help prevent frozen toes.'

'Then in the absence of a wolfhound, perhaps you should get into bed before you freeze.' It was hardly a romantic conversation, but she found she had relaxed a little. This was her friend Alex as well as her husband. She could trust him to take care of her now.

'You are sure about this?' he asked, one hand just touching the bedcovers. 'You have had a difficult few days. I can leave you to sleep if you are tired.'

'No,' Jessica said firmly, wondering if he could feel the vibrations through his fingertips. It felt as though her whole body was shivering in anticipation of his touch.

'Candles alight? Or not?' Still he did not move.

She had seen statues, of course, and not all of them had fig leaves. Besides, the fashion was for very tight knitted evening breeches and a lady could not keep her eye line at collarbone level for an entire evening. She had seen how the male body was different from the female in other ways: the muscles, the triangle of shoulders and narrow hips, unlike the feminine hourglass. She was ready to see the reality in flesh tones and not cold white marble. But, somehow, she had never thought about his gaze on her. Darkness felt safe, but it also felt cowardly.

'Leave them,' she decided, wondering as she spoke just how much of her thoughts were showing on her face. If she was being transparent with her doubts and fears, at least Alex had the courtesy to remain unamused by her bashfulness.

He was tactful, too, in the way that he put back the bed-clothes before shrugging out of his robe and getting in to bed beside her. Even so she was startled. This was what it meant when men were said to be aroused, she realised.

Oh, my goodness.

Chapter Twenty-Two

Jessica braced herself for what was to come, but Alex appeared to be in no hurry. He came up on one elbow, leaning over her, and kissed her, gently, softly, then more firmly as she found herself reacting, opening to him and the caress of his tongue, the little nips of his teeth. She found when she responded he made sounds deep in his throat, encouraging, responsive noises. It was arousing. He liked kissing her and, she realised, she liked kissing him. It was hot and intimate and more than a little moist and she became aware that her whole body was involved.

There were interesting aches and she was certain her breasts were somehow larger and between her legs she was damp, which should be embarrassing, but which somehow wasn't.

She wriggled, which didn't help at all, but it made Alex growl, so it must have been the right thing to do. Emboldened, Jessica began to explore with her fingertips. Damp hair, springing under her touch, the shorter hairs prickling on the nape of his neck, the smooth skin over his shoulders and the muscles tensing in response to her moving hand.

Alex was exploring, too, one hand skimming down over her silk-covered flank, rucking up the long skirts of her nightgown. She lifted her hips as he pulled it upwards and that pressed her closer to him, which was exciting and made him tighten his hold, then the gown was over her head and gone and they were skin to skin.

No smooth marble here. Her breasts and thighs encountered rough hair, but she had no time to savour that sensation before Alex had begun caressing her breasts which, she realised, were thrusting shamelessly into his hands, then against his mouth as he took one nipple between his lips.

She might be an innocent, but it seemed her body knew exactly what was happening and what it wanted. He rolled the other nipple between finger and thumb and she moaned, twisting against the sensation building there and in her belly and lower, between her legs. She pressed them together, but that gave no relief and she almost sobbed when Alex slid one hand between her thighs and touched her there.

'Gently.' He lifted his mouth from her nipple and moved up the bed to kiss her again. 'Softly,' he said, pressing her thighs apart. 'Trust me.'

He shifted his weight over her and instinctively she moved until he was lodged between her thighs, pressing against the needy, aching core of her. She arched up against him and he thrust, slowly but steadily.

Jessica heard her own little cry, then he had covered her mouth with his again as he moved inexorably deeper.

It hurts, she thought, almost indignantly. *I do not like this.*

And then her body, ignoring soreness, ignoring her efforts to tense against the invasion, caught the rhythm of his thrusts and began to move, too, and either the discomfort vanished or it was swallowed up in wave after wave of pleasure. She had lost the power to tell.

She clung to the broad shoulders sheltering her, surrendered to the possession that seemed to be an equal thing—he was hers as she was his. If only this tightening, spiralling intensity would give her some relief.

And then the knot snapped and she heard herself cry out as Alex surged within her once more, and again, then he, too, went rigid. Then she was limp in his arms as he collapsed on to her and she stopped thinking and simply existed.

'Jessica?' She blinked awake out of a dream so intense, so startling, that for a moment she had no idea where she was. Then she saw Alex's face as he bent over her and remembered. And it had been no dream, it had been reality and now she was truly his wife. She smiled at him.

'Are you well?'

She considered the question. *'Well'* hardly seemed to cover it, but she did not have the vocabulary for all the things she felt, so she nodded. 'Yes, very well.' There was one question and she must ask it now while she was still half awake and had the courage. 'Is it always like that?'

'I hope so,' Alex said.

Now, what does that mean? she wondered as she pulled herself up against the pillows, aware that she was sore and rather sticky. This seemed to be a process where one simply had to leave inhibitions and embarrassment behind. He was not a virgin, she felt certain. Did it mean that it had been very good for him, too, and better than some experiences he had had? Perhaps it was because she was a virgin, though. Men appeared to set great store on virginity. Still, she would take reassurance from the compliment.

'What time is it?'

In answer the clock she had seen at the foot of the spiral stairs struck two, its echoes reverberating up the stone walls and through the heavy door.

'That clock will have to go,' Alex said as he got out of bed and shrugged on his robe. He did not bother to fasten it, although she noticed that he slid his feet into the leather slippers before venturing out on to the cold floor. He went into the dressing room and Jessica could hear him moving about and the splash of water. The partition wall, against which the bed head stood, was clearly only thin wood. Dressing rooms were apparently not a medieval luxury.

Alex came back holding a basin and set it down on the bedside table, then wrung out a cloth that was in it. 'Only just warm, I'm afraid,' he said, then threw back the covers and gently washed away the stickiness from her skin.

He had covered her before she had the chance to feel shy and, before she had the chance to say anything, he had carried the basin back and reappeared tying the belt of his robe. Lifting one candlestick from the chest against the wall, he blew out another, leaving her in the light of the one beside the bed.

'Sleep now.' He bent, kissed her forehead and was gone, leaving her wondering again if it had all been a dream.

But the disorder of the bedclothes on both sides, the dent in the mattress next to her, the lingering scent of citrus and warm man on the pillows and the unfamiliar aches in her body told her that this had been reality—the pain, the pleasure, the startling intimacy. The Duke of Malvern had finally made her his Duchess in every way.

The candle flame was flickering in the draughts that made layers of blankets necessary. Jessica blew it out, then snuggled down, pulling the covers high over her shoulders to cover her ears. She wished Alex had stayed, but fashionable husbands and wives slept apart, just as they tended to live their own separate lives, coming together to entertain or be entertained, to eat and to have sex.

It felt rather a lonely prospect, but she would adapt, she resolved as she began to drift down into sleep.

I wonder where Alex's rooms are?

Down the spiral steps of the turret, along a short passageway—cold radiating from its stone floor and walls—through a door so studded with metal that it seemed designed to hold out an army and into the room he had taken as his own when he had inherited the title.

Traditionally the Duke occupied the turret opposite the Duchess's tower, but Alex put comfort over tradition and had chosen this chamber. It was conveniently rectangular, the walls were panelled, the fireplace was of a medium size and the window was large. Once hung with tapestries and heavy curtains, the draughts had almost been vanquished. He could do something about finding Jessica a bedchamber as comfortable before she succumbed to a cold.

As he shed his robe he wondered whether it would be best if she moved in here with him while another room was prepared. Or he could offer to exchange rooms with her. Best to ask what she wanted, tempting though the thought was of a shared bed. He must remember that this was a marriage of mutual convenience, not a love match. Despite the wonderful surprise of Jessica's passionate response to his caresses, that was no reason to suppose that she would welcome the intimacy of shared rooms.

Clearly he had married a woman of natural sensuality and that was a true gift, but he must not presume on it, he reminded himself. How she would feel, and what she would think, tomorrow morning when she woke, sore and shy, remained to be seen. Even so, he was aware of an overwhelming sense of relief mingling with the lingering pleasure of their joining.

Tomorrow would bring the grief of funerals and the prospect of unremitting hard work, but now he knew he had a wife by his side who would support him with strength, intelligence and loyalty. Providing she felt she could trust him—and that morning had shown just how fragile that trust was.

As his body slipped into sleep Alex tried to clear his mind of the vague, unsettling doubts that lurked in its shadows. Tonight he would dream only good dreams.

She had fallen asleep wishing that Alex had stayed with her. Now, waking in the unfamiliar room, Jessica was glad that he had not.

Had they really done those things, felt those things? She huddled the bedcovers around her shoulders as she sat up, wondering where her nightgown had gone. Not that fine silk would be much help against the chill of a stone turret on a March morning in the Welsh Marches. Unattractive flannel seemed infinitely more attractive.

At breakfast she would have to preside over the table, pour tea and coffee, instruct the servants to replenish the toast and face her husband, all with the memory of their naked bodies intertwined, joined. And, of course, everyone in the castle would know what had happened last night.

The door opened to reveal Trotter. Someone else who knew, who might be speculating on how it had been. 'Good morning, Your Grace. I have brought hot chocolate.' She placed the tray next to the bed and fetched a folding screen that she set up between bed and door. 'The footmen are bringing the water for your bath, ma'am.'

Jessica murmured her thanks and sipped her chocolate while Trotter bustled around, just as she did every morning. She retrieved the nightgown from the floor, shook it out and laid it over her arm, quite as though finding garments scattered across the room was normal.

There was the sound of feet on the stairs, heavy breathing and considerable sloshing. It obviously took several trips to fill her bath.

Trotter produced her wrap and Jessica scurried into the dressing room. At least there the walls were panelled, the tiny window reduced the draughts and steam was rising from the bath.

The warm water was soothing, the fragrance of jasmine from the salts delicious, but Jessica felt a fleeting reluctance to wash the scent of last night from her skin.

Think about the day, not the night, or you will never be able to face him.

And today held funerals.

'Blacks this morning, Trotter. I hope we have something suitable in the luggage.'

'Yes, ma'am. The heavy luggage arrived in the early evening. Everything is pressed and I have laid out your jet parure.'

'Excellent. You will attend the services, I hope, and the other staff who came with us as well.'

'Certainly, ma'am. And I have ironed all the black neckcloths for the men and they have armbands as well.'

'Thank you, Trotter. I knew I could rely on you.'

'Yes, Your Grace. This might not be what we're used to, but we're all determined to stand by you.'

That sounded ominous, but Jessica told herself that if things seemed primitive above stairs, below they were probably medieval. That was all Trotter had meant.

Several years of managing her father's household stood her in good stead when Jessica sat down at the breakfast table.

The meal was served in a small room off the Great Hall, to her relief. It was shabby but comfortable and she was not surprised when Alex confessed that it was where he always ate unless he was entertaining.

He had risen and come to greet her with a kiss on the cheek when she had entered and pulled out her chair himself.

Jessica plunged into the familiar morning ritual and hoped that the colour on her cheeks would seem to be the result of entering a warm room, rather than shyness at confronting her husband.

'Tea or coffee?' she asked, trying not to recall what he looked like naked. What was she supposed to call him? Many of the married ladies she knew addressed their husband as Mr X or Sir Y, but surely she was not expected to call him *Your Grace* over the marmalade? *My dear*, at the other end of the spectrum of formality, seemed equally difficult.

Until Alex said, 'Coffee, if you please, my dear. Black.'

She managed that without splashing and Footman Two, the elderly one—she really must make an effort with everyone's names—carried it to the other end of the mercifully short table.

Food had been set out under covers on the sideboard. Pewter, she noticed, not silver.

'May I serve you, Your Grace?'

Brendon, that was it. 'Thank you, Peter. Some scrambled eggs and a rasher of bacon, please.'

Alex went to the sideboard himself and returned with a heaped plate of bacon, kidneys, eggs and fried potatoes. 'Your shopping expedition was clearly a success with Cook,' he remarked as he picked up his cutlery. 'James tells me that the staff are also very pleased with their provisions.'

'I am glad. At what time is the first service?' Jessica asked.

'At ten. Widow Jenkins had no family, so it will be followed immediately with that for the Bonds' baby.'

'Poor mite. Did it have a name?'

'It would have been baptised today. Michael Alexander. The second son. He had three sisters as well and fortunately all are safe and unharmed. I do not think that will make the family's grief any less, however.'

So often Jessica had heard people remark that the children of the working classes were so numerous that the parents could lose one or two without undue distress, as though poverty somehow dulled parental love. Some people spoke as though the poor had coarser feelings, felt less refined emotions than the upper classes. She was glad Alex did not share that unthinking prejudice and smiled at him warmly.

He returned the smile and she found her shyness lifting a little. 'Some more coffee, my dear?' she managed to say with what she felt was a perfectly steady voice.

Chapter Twenty-Three

It was a beautiful March morning when both coffins, one very light, the other very small, were carried together to the church with the mourners following on foot behind, the Widow Jenkins's old friends supporting the bereaved parents.

All the servants from the castle came, too, bringing up the rear, with Alex and Jessica walking in the middle of them.

'I hope you do not mind,' Alex said as they walked across the drawbridge and waited as those villagers who still had homes standing joined their disposed neighbours.

'No, of course not. This is the villagers' occasion. It would not be right to distract the Vicar from greeting them.'

Thank goodness it is not raining, she thought as they passed the sad ruins. *This is a dismal enough day as it is.*

Jessica was touched by the services, the Vicar's gentle sermon and the warmth the villagers showed to the bereaved and to each other. This had been a happy community and it would be again, she was certain, watching people. They were sad, but they were determined. When this day was over they would work to build again and they were clearly confident that they could rely on the Duke to help them do it.

* * *

Everyone had been invited back to the castle for the funeral meats and Jessica judged it time to take her courage in both hands and start introducing herself.

She joined Alex as he spoke gently to the bereaved parents and added her own quiet words to his, but did not linger. She did not want them to feel they had to be polite to the new Duchess.

It was easier mingling with the other villagers. They knew who she was by now, of course and she was taken aback by their warmth and the fact that they kept apologising for spoiling her honeymoon.

That was difficult to answer—she could hardly say she was enjoying herself—so she smiled and plunged into conversation, desperately trying to remember names and who did what. They were curious about her, too, and quite ready to ask questions, exclaiming in wonder at the news that her father was an ironmaster and that she came from Shropshire.

'Why, that's just next door,' one man said. 'I'm the smith and we use good Shropshire iron in the forge. Jeffrey Caudle.' He held out a gnarled hand, its scars and lines engraved with black despite its scrubbed cleanliness.

Jessica took it. 'It is good to shake the hand of a worker in iron, Mr Caudle. I have no doubt we will be calling on your skills once you are free to work on the castle.'

That was an important point, she remarked to Alex as they met at the long table serving food. 'My head is spinning with ideas for the castle that I would like to put to you, but we cannot take any resources away from the village.'

'I was thinking of establishing a group of parishioners so we can decide fairly on who has priority for the new housing as it is built and how they would like to see the village planned. And, even with all our skilled craftsmen employed, we will still need outside workers if we are to get this done quickly,' Alex said. 'All this means I need a secretary. Soon. The Vicar's eldest son is a possibility. He was employed by Lord Arnside, but he died recently so Goodson is out of a place. I will ask if he has accepted another position.'

'I need a secretary, too,' Jessica agreed. 'I will ask Papa if he knows of anyone. You need someone who has an understanding of society, I need one who is a down-to-earth practical man!'

Alex took her by the elbow and steered her towards a narrow arched doorway she had not noticed before. 'Give me your plate and glass and climb the stairs.'

They proved to be a short flight of spiral steps. Jessica emerged on to a wide ledge with a stone balustrade, with a view over the Great Hall below.

'The minstrels' gallery,' Alex said emerging, cautiously balancing two plates and both glasses. 'Shall we sit a while and eat our luncheon? There is something I want to say to you.'

'That sounds ominous,' she said, not entirely in jest. But she sat on a stone bench topped with a moth-eaten cushion.

'Not at all.' Alex looked out over the crowded room below and then back at her. 'I simply wanted to tell you that I cannot imagine that any woman I might have married could make a more ideal lady of the manor for this place than you, Jessica.'

'Oh.' She found herself without words. That was a serious compliment and it gave her reassurance that she was not an outsider blundering in to a small community. But, of all the things she had dreamt of hearing from Alex's lips, that was not one of them.

I desire you. I am happy being with you. I love you...

No, that was a wish too far.

As she thought it Jessica looked at her husband, at his profile as he had turned to look out over the Great Hall again and the realisation hit her.

I do love him.

It wasn't simply desire, it wasn't just liking, or admiration for his care for the people who relied on him. It was love.

How ironic. Here she was, married to a man she loved, a man whose own dream had been to marry for love. In her, he had not found that, although he had just told her she fulfilled her duties well and, last night, had surely proved that he desired her.

She felt tears welling and blinked them away, finding a smile as he turned to look at her. Alex smiled back and hoped welled up as well. Love grew. It might sometimes be instant, as he thought so romantically, but it could also unfurl slowly, like a bud. It had happened to her and it might happen to him.

'Thank you,' she said. 'That means a great deal.' There was too much else that she feared to blurt out, so she turned the conversation deliberately. 'Hasn't Cook made a wonderful spread?'

'Wait until you witness her Harvest Suppers.' Alex took a mouthful of a raised pie and chewed with obvious enjoyment, then raised his glass of cider. 'To the future.'

Jessica clinked her own glass against his. 'To the future.'

And, although it felt as though she was holding her breath for most of the time, the future did seem to be holding the prospect of happiness.

To Jessica's relief her father wrote from the iron works

to tell her that the crisis had been averted and relations with the rival firm of Bracegirdle and Sons had returned to normal. Her brothers and her father were still renegotiating their relationship, she suspected, but Joshua wrote to tell her that he was courting Prunella Wilson, the eldest daughter of a family of whom their father greatly approved and, it seemed, Ethan was taking an interest in her younger sister, Naomi.

'I suspect we may be travelling to Shropshire for a double wedding in month or so,' she said, passing the letter to Alex.

They had their desks together in what Alex was planning to be the library. Their new secretaries shared a room next door—Adam Goodson, the Vicar's son, and Charles Fielding, the young man who had been working in the ironwork's office and whom her father had picked out for her. The architect Alex had hired to design the new village had his desk there, too.

Now, a month after their wedding, she and Alex had settled into a harmonious working relationship, although that could not always be said of the architect. Mr Phelps had produced an elegant design of cottages either side of a street leading up to the drawbridge. Jessica had pointed out that half the cottages would have gardens facing north and Alex had refused point blank to have an ornate new Gothic-style gatehouse built on the village side of the drawbridge.

Eventually they had compromised on a crescent that gave everyone a good aspect for their garden. It also provided a suitably picturesque prospect for the architect, although Jessica still treasured the memory of closeting him with a delegation of village housewives who left him in no doubt about what was needed in the way of accommodation, wash houses, bake houses and privies. He had retaliated with a Gothic style of pigsty which made Alex laugh so much that he signed off the drawings without a protest.

The first families would be moving out to their new homes very soon and Jessica finally felt she could turn her attention to the castle itself. Beginning with her bedchamber. She really could not inflict those stairs on the footmen every time she wanted a bath.

'I'm glad things are settling down with your brothers,' Alex said, passing the sheet back. 'It must have been a concern for your father.'

'Yes. And now he has started fretting about the May Day parade—I keep sending him pages of notes and there is plenty of time yet.' Jessica sealed the letters she had been writing. 'I will see you later, I have some housekeeping tasks to attend to.'

He looked up and smiled at her and, as always now, something inside her warmed and softened. Alex was affectionate, passionate in bed at night, generous in sharing his thoughts and asking for her opinions. He was always pleasant and attentive during the day, although he never seemed to share her thought that a kiss, and what might follow, might be desirable, even in broad daylight. On the surface it seemed an ideal marriage, only beneath the surface did she feel its foundations tremble.

And that was her own fault, she recognised that. She was constantly waiting for Alex to realise that he had found what he had always looked for—a true love. He would not act on it, she was confident of that, she told herself. He was an honourable man. But she loved him now and that made it a deep and gnawing fear.

In all the weeks she had lived there, Jessica realised, she

had explored no further than the rooms they used daily, below stairs in the kitchens and the temporary accommodation for the displaced villagers. It was time she took possession of her new kingdom.

She closed the door behind her and set off to explore the castle thoroughly, floor by floor, staircase by staircase, beginning at the very top. At one point she thought she was lost and should have taken a thread to guide her back, like Theseus in the Minotaur's lair, but she finally discovered a door behind a mouldering tapestry and found herself on the minstrels' gallery.

It was clear that only the rooms on the first floor held any hope of being comfortable until a great deal more work was done. She had worried about the servants, but when Pitwick had arrived from London, he and Mrs Black assured her that the servants' wing, being a newer part of the castle, was quite adequate and had been properly maintained. Alex had looked after his staff's needs, even while the castle crumbled around him. New mattresses, bedding, rugs and curtains were all that were needed there and those had been ordered.

Now she began to explore the first floor, passing the stairs that led to her own turret. The first door that she opened was clearly Alex's bedchamber. She had never been into it, he had always come to her. It struck her now that somehow symbolised their marriage—apparently open and shared and yet with hidden corners, unopened doors on to private worlds of thought.

Now she stood on the threshold and took in the dark panelling, the heavy draperies at the windows and around the bed, the old Oriental carpets on the floor, which was boarded, not stone. Similar carpets had appeared in her chamber after that first night without her having to ask. In the corner was an opening which she supposed led to a dressing room.

It was gloomy and worn, but it was comfortable, she thought. Perhaps the other chambers on this floor were as good. She closed the door without entering and walked on.

Alex found her in the room next door, standing in the middle of the floor and rotating slowly. 'What on earth are you doing?'

He came in and closed the door. Jessica found herself unaccountably breathless.

'Finding myself a new bedchamber,' she said, determined not to be defensive. This was her home, too.

But there was something about Alex's smile that made her put up her chin and give him back stare for stare.

Chapter Twenty-Four

'Are you not comfortable where you are now the floor is covered? That turret has always been the Duchess's room,' Alex said, mildly enough.

'I am comfortable, and that chamber can be made more so, but the unfortunate footmen have to negotiate those stairs every time I want hot water and I expect Trotter to break her neck on them at any moment,' Jessica said. She spotted another door and went to open it, glad of something to break this odd tension. 'Oh, good, a dressing room.'

'It connects to mine next door.' Alex had followed her. She could not read his mood at all.

'I like this room,' Jessica said. 'But would you prefer that I choose another?' She meant it as a challenge and it sounded like one to her own ears. 'Does it bring me too close, liable to invade your privacy?'

'Not at all.' He sounded surprised that she might have thought so. 'It was simply that I did not want to treat you any differently from your predecessors. And this suite is even shabbier than mine.'

'Where did *your* predecessors sleep?' she asked.

'In the other turret—the one that is threatening to fall down.'

'Ah. Yes, I can see why you moved. I am afraid I put

comfort and convenience over centuries of tradition in this
case. May I have this chamber, or shall I look for another?'

'I would very much like you to sleep here.' Alex backed
out of the dressing room, drawing her with him. Now she
had no difficulty understanding his thoughts. 'It is undoubtedly convenient—for many things.' He kept going,
without looking back, until his legs met the edge of the bed
and he fell back on to it, pulling Jessica with him so that
she landed on top of him.

There was an ominous cracking sound, a cloud of dust
and feathers and they sank deeply into the musty bedding,
sneezing violently.

Jessica scrambled free and staggered off the bed. Alex
was coughing and laughing too much to lever himself out,
so she held out her hand and helped him to his feet.

'The webbing and base boards must have gone,' she
said, fanning away the dust. 'Never mind, the frame is
marvellous. Look at that carving, it must be very old. I'm
sure it can be—'

She did not finish the sentence. Alex lifted her in his arms
and backed her against the wall. 'We do not need a bed.'

Instinctively Jessica wrapped her legs around his hips
and put her hands on his shoulders. She was not at all certain that one could make love standing up, but she was definitely willing to try and clung on. With his hands free, Alex
was raising her skirts, tearing at the falls of his breeches.

It was inelegant, shocking, excitingly urgent. Jessica
felt the familiar heat and knew her body was ready for
him. More than ready and he knew it. There were none of
the careful, considerate preparations that she was used to;
this was a different man, one whose impatient desire for
her was thrilling.

As Alex sheathed himself she heard her own cry, not of pain but of triumph. This was no mild, polite marital bedding, this was raw craving for *her*, the woman, not the wife.

It was untidy, uncomfortable, noisy and ended far too quickly. Jessica felt her own peak cresting as Alex surged deeply within her and his shout of triumph mingled with her own scream of pleasure.

Alex slumped against her, his whole body pinning hers to the panelling, his forehead resting against hers as they panted in unison.

'Bed,' he managed to mutter after a minute.

'But—'

'Mine.' With her still clinging to him, Alex shouldered open the dressing room door, then the connecting one into his and finally through into his bedchamber. They collapsed on to the bed in an intertwined, overheated sprawl.

'Should I apologise for that?' Alex asked when they finally found the strength to disentangle themselves and lie together against the pillows.

'Oh, no. It was wonderful.' Jessica rolled her shoulders experimentally. 'I do not think we should do that every day, but perhaps once a week? That would be very invigorating.'

'You might be invigorated, Wife. I am a shattered man,' Alex complained, but his look of smug masculine contentment gave the lie to his complaint.

'We were so loud, though,' Jessica said worriedly as she snuggled up against his shoulder. She ought to get up. Her stays were digging in, one garter seemed to have worked its way down to her ankle, and her skirts were rucked up beneath her in a way that would create frightful creases. 'Whatever will the servants think?'

'That we are newly wedded and some exuberance is to be expected.'

'We aren't *that* newly wedded,' Jessica protested. 'It is at least five weeks. Why, we are almost an old married couple.'

'That would explain my aching legs.' Alex finally got off the bed and began to strip off his disordered clothing. Then, naked, he started on hers. 'I am old and frail and therefore need reminding how to make love to my wife in a sedate and respectable manner.'

'Oh, you ridiculous man,' she said, laughing up at him as she pulled him down to the bed. 'You may make love to me in any manner you choose, provided you release me from this infernal corset.'

Alex did both in a manner that left Jessica limp with pleasure. Even the embarrassment of climbing into her crumpled gown and having to retreat to her turret and ring for Trotter did not dampen the warm glow that lingered.

It was sensual satisfaction, of course, but it was also hope. Alex was so affectionate, so passionate. Surely love was beginning to creep up on him, just as it had ambushed her?

Chapter Twenty-Five

'This is not April Fools' Day, is it?' Jessica demanded, waving a letter at Alex across the breakfast table.

'That was a week ago. Why, is someone playing a trick on you?' He put down his coffee cup and reached to take the letter from her. 'It appears to be from Miss Beech—or, no. Mrs Locksley, I see she is styling herself.' He glanced at the top of the sheet. 'In Edinburgh, no less.'

'I never thought they would do it,' Jessica said, twitching the letter back from his hand. 'I really thought that her nervousness and his respectability would put an end to that romance, especially when I have heard virtually nothing from her for weeks. So how did they manage it?'

She read the letter through. 'Oh, they were very clever. Jane enlisted the support of her aunt, who lives in Bath. The lady wrote to Mr Beech to say she was feeling unwell and begging for Jane's company. She would, she said, send her own travelling chaise to collect her. But how clever! Jane was collected with her luggage and without raising a whisper of suspicion. Locksley was waiting around the corner with his own bags, got in and they headed north.

'They married just north of Berwick at the toll booth… Staying with Locksley's cousin who is an Edinburgh lawyer… Expecting to return to London later this month so that he can take up a position as secretary with Lord Wantage who has shown great interest in promoting his career...' Jessica read out the highlights as she went. 'And Mr Beech promptly disinherited her, went down to Bath where he had a blazing row with his sister who promptly changed her own will to leave everything to Jane and not to her unsatisfactory nephew, who is the son of their other sister and who happens to be a great favourite of Mr Beech.'

'Good for them,' Alex said, apparently losing interest in the Locksleys in favour of his sirloin steak and eggs.

'Which reminds me,' Jessica said. 'I must go up to London myself in two weeks, otherwise Papa is going to wear himself to a thread worrying about this May Day celebration.'

That did catch Alex's attention again. 'I thought everything was organised. Why do you need to go? You have put in a great deal of work on this already.'

'It *is* organised, on paper. And my friends have been helping as well, but Papa has a touching faith in my ability to ensure everything will go smoothly.'

'And so you will stay in London until May Day?'

'Yes, of course—I have not done all that work not to enjoy the results! Why, do you object?' Surely he was not going to prove to be the kind of husband who expected their wife to mind hearth and home and never venture out without him?

'Besides, everything is under control here,' she said. 'The building works are going well, almost all the villagers can expect to be rehoused by next month and there are no more decisions to be made about the rooms in the castle that we have agreed should be renovated first.'

'It is simply that I will miss you,' Alex said. 'I agree,

all is going well, but I do not think that both of us should be absent for several weeks until everyone is resettled and that wretched turret is finally stabilised. I have every expectation of it falling down the moment my back is turned.'

Jessica puzzled over his words. He would miss her—but for herself or because of her role in the work here?

'You could come up to town for a few days at the end of the month,' she suggested. 'Stay for May Day and then we can travel home together.' *Home.* That was another thing that gave her a warm glow of hope, the fact that she instinctively referred to the castle as her home now and that Alex treated her as an equal partner when decisions about it had to be made.

He nodded now as he finished his food and reached for his own post. 'Yes, that sounds ideal.'

They sat for a while in a silence punctuated only by the crack of breaking seals or the rustle of paper as they opened letters. Jessica had plenty of tradesmen's accounts to scan and pass to Charles Fielding. There was news from all her London friends, some notes from Hereford dressmakers and milliners soliciting custom and several fashionable magazines.

Alex's pile looked equally mixed, but when he had finished sorting it he passed her a handful of gilt-edged cards. 'The London Season is drawing to a close and families are returning to the Marches. We can expect more invitations soon, but these will give you a start in getting to know our neighbours.'

Jessica shuffled through the cards. 'They are all for the evening. Are the distances very great?' She was still coming to terms with living in the country—and in hilly country with poor roads, at that.

'Ten miles or so for the nearest. They will all be timed to coincide with the next full moon—you'll see that the dates are close together. If the weather turns bad, then it is expected that the host puts people up for the night. In fact, that largest card is for a full dress ball and we will be staying.'

'We will? It does not say so on the invitation.'

'The Hawksmoors are very old friends. I always stay, even though it is one of the closest estates.'

'Are they so very grand then, that they hold full dress balls the moment they return from London?' The card was certainly of very heavy stock, the gilding extensive, and it was engraved, not simply printed.

Jessica read it again with more attention.

The Viscount and Lady Hawksmoor

'He is only a viscount,' she said, pretending haughtiness.

'A wealthy one with a large family and a disposition to hospitality. Our families have always been very close.'

'But a mere lodge?' Jessica said, smiling at herself. 'See how haughty living in a castle has made me,' she added with a laugh.

'You will be surprised when you see it,' was all Alex would say. 'But it will definitely be the occasion for your very best ball gown and your sapphires.'

'A week's time to the full moon.' Jessica looked at the other cards. 'It is going to be a very busy few days.'

The Hawksmoor ball was the first of the parties and, Jessica suspected, the other hosts had deferred to them in setting their own dates.

She had expected to find them stiff and formal, arrogant

even about their status locally, especially when she saw the sprawling mansion that someone with either a wicked wit or a very humble nature had named The Lodge. But she could not have been more wrong. Alex had insisted that they arrive early so they could settle into their rooms and it was clear from their welcome that this was expected.

The Viscount wrung Alex's hand and slapped him on the back, his wife stood on tiptoe to kiss his cheek, then descended on Jessica in a flurry of lace to embrace her. 'We are so delighted that Alex has finally brought his bride home,' she said. 'Welcome to Herefordshire, my dear.'

Half a dozen people ranging from a girl still in the schoolroom to a mature man who was clearly his father's heir were introduced as, 'Some of the children, the rest will be at the ball. Do not bother with names yet, Jessica—we may call you Jessica? You will see, Alex—we have the entire family here to celebrate your return.'

It was said jovially, but Jessica thought there was some restraint in Lady Hawksmoor's smile that had not been there before. But she did not know the woman and she must have a great deal on her mind with the ball to prepare for.

Another carriage was arriving, so Alex said that he knew the way to his usual suite perfectly well and guided Jessica upstairs, followed by Trotter clutching her dressing case and James, who had been promoted to valet after admitting that he much preferred it to being a footman.

'You have your bath now, Your Grace,' Trotter said, bustling about. 'Oh, my! Look, they have *running water* in the dressing room!'

Jessica and Alex joined her to marvel over this luxury. Trotter opened another door. 'And a water closet. Why, this is a palace. Madam, could we—?'

Jessica seeing mild panic in Alex's eyes, shook her head firmly. 'One day. The castle plumbing must wait for more urgent work, Trotter. But how lovely—we will certainly take advantage of this while we have it.'

Trotter shooed Alex out, saying firmly that her lady needed to bathe and then rest, then returned, clearly determined that Jessica was going to outshine every other lady present, however magnificent this house might be.

Jessica gave in to being fussed over with good grace. After weeks of constantly feeling dusty and having nothing more glamorous to think about than upholstery colours at best, and drains at worst, she was rather looking forward to this party. Although whether she would be able to conjure up any conversation that did not involve guttering, structural underpinning or the design of piggeries remained to be seen.

Jessica and Alex joined the family and the eight other house guests for the early dinner before the other guests arrived. There were twenty-two seated at the long table, she realised, trying to get everyone straight in her head.

Lord and Lady Hawksmoor were at the head and foot of the table with Jessica as the ranking lady on her host's right and Alex by his hostess. Lord and Lady Henderson, The Right Reverend and Mrs Pomfret, Sir Aubrey and Lady Tanner and Mr and Mrs McDonald, she had managed to commit to memory. The family were more difficult. There were five unmarried siblings—three men and two young ladies and four married couples. There was also one empty seat in the middle of the side opposite her.

The family seemed determined not to draw attention to it. She saw Lady Hawksmoor's gaze flicker to the butler who gave what, in a lesser servant, would have been a shrug and her smile became more fixed.

Finally, just as their hostess nodded to the butler for service to begin, the door opened and a slight figure hurried to the vacant place. A footman pulled out the chair for her and she slid into it, keeping her head down. Ringlets the colour of mahogany fell from a central knot and effectively veiled her face from Jessica. The substantial bulk of the Rural Dean on one side, and one of the middle Hawksmoor sons on the other, served to screen her from everyone except those sitting opposite. Jessica did not think that Alex had even noticed her entrance, it had been so discreet.

It was intriguing, but none of her business. She concentrated on Lord Hawksmoor and managed not to let her conversation stray into asking his opinion on the design of pigsties.

When Lady Hawksmoor nodded to the ladies at the end of the meal and rose to lead them out to the drawing room, the latecomer slipped out behind other guests, leaving Jessica increasingly curious about why she was so shy.

Lady Hawksmoor left the ladies with the tea tray, which they all ignored, and excused herself to go to attend to the last-minute preparations for the ball.

'I will send word when enough people have gathered to make it worth coming through,' she said. 'Meanwhile, do make yourselves comfortable.'

They sat, distributing themselves around the various sofas and chairs which had been arranged into conversation groups. The mysterious young woman—she *was* young, Jessica was certain—retreated to a corner and took an embroidery frame from a basket by the chair.

Definitely a daughter of the house then. Perhaps the poor girl was simply very timid. 'Who is that?' she asked Mrs Pomfret. 'The young lady over there with the embroidery.'

The Rural Dean's wife pinched her lips disapprovingly and lowered her voice. 'Helena, now Lady Charlton. The third daughter.'

'She seems very shy,' Jessica ventured.

'I am only amazed that she is permitted to show her face at a social gathering.'

Jessica blinked. 'Indeed? Why is that?' She did not care if she was being nosy; now she had to know.

'She has left her husband,' Mrs Pomfret said, almost in a whisper. 'Can you imagine!'

'Well, I can imagine that she must have had a very powerful motive,' Jessica retorted. 'After all, she is here and not with another man, is she not?'

That caused a sharp intake of breath. 'A wife's place is with her husband. Announcing after barely a year of marriage that he does not suit you is no excuse for such a lack of duty.'

'Perhaps he was a drunk. Or violent towards her.'

'Lord Charlton is a most sober and upright gentleman. And it is a husband's right to chastise his wife.'

'Only if he is a brute,' Jessica retorted, loudly enough that several heads turned. 'Her parents have accepted her back,' she added more quietly.

'Very lax of them.' It was clear that only her title was saving Jessica from a sharp lecture on wifely behaviour.

'But charitable, do you not think?' Jessica said with a sweet smile and turned to Lady Tanner on her other side before she said something regrettable.

It was brave of Lady Charlton to attend the ball at all, she thought. It was rather too pointed to go across and intrude on her self-imposed solitude, but she would see if she could find the opportunity for a word once the ball was underway.

A footman came in and bowed. 'Ladies, her ladyship asks me to say that you may wish to join the guests in the ballroom at your convenience.' He went through to the dining room and could be heard delivering a similar message.

'I am going up to tidy my hair,' Lady Tanner said. 'Come with me?' She offered her arm, Jessica linked hers through it and they walked companionably to the stairs. Below they could hear the sound of many voices. 'The ballroom is off to one side in an annexe built in the last century,' Lady Tanner said. 'This is such a rabbit warren!'

'I am still finding my way around my own, much dustier warren,' Jessica confessed and they went off laughing to find their rooms. She was going to enjoy herself, she realised. After so much hard work she was going to dance in her husband's arms and give herself up to pleasure.

Chapter Twenty-Six

'In London this would be called a frightful squeeze,' Alex remarked half an hour later as they surveyed the crowded ballroom from a position in one corner of the room. 'I think every family of note for miles around is here.' He smiled down at her. 'Too much? These country affairs are rather more lively than town balls and we are out of practice.'

'It is less lively than a masquerade at the Pantheon,' she retorted, teasing, and laughed when he shuddered theatrically.

'Although that evening did have its moments,' he said. 'I can recall a certain dark alleyway off the Strand...'

'I seem to have forgotten that,' Jessica said demurely as a set came to its end and couples began to come off the dance floor, opening up a view across the corner to the wall. 'Perhaps you can remind me later. Alex?'

She had expected a response, but when she glanced up he was staring across to where a slender young woman with dark hair in ringlets stood quietly behind a group of gilt chairs.

It must be the late arrival at the dinner table, Lady Charlton, Jessica realised and saw in the next moment that she was very beautiful indeed, with high cheekbones, dark eyes, a sensuous mouth and those glossy ringlets.

'That is Lady Charlton,' she said sharply, and Alex started, as though she had shaken him awake.

'Charlton? Little Nella?' He still had not taken his eyes off her.

'I thought you knew them all.'

'I do, but I do not think I have seen Helena since she was about sixteen—all eyes and mouth too large for her face and hair always in tangles and as skinny as a rake,' he said without looking away. 'They sent her off to look after her grandmother when the old lady had a stroke, I think.'

'Did you not attend her wedding?'

'No. That was last year and I was not here for some reason... I forget why now.'

He looked to Jessica as though he had probably forgotten his own name as well. She was beginning to have a very bad feeling about this.

'She has left her husband,' she said tartly.

She is a married woman.

That did get his attention. 'Do you know why?'

'No.' Why did she say that? Now he was bound to go and ask the woman. *Little Nella.* A girl he had known for years and had clearly been fond of. Surely that was why he looked poleaxed now—the discovery that the plain little chit was now a beauty. That was all it was. Nothing else. *Nothing else.*

'Excuse me,' Alex said vaguely and started to make his way around the corner of the dance floor to where Lady Charlton stood.

She could, of course, go with him, ask to be introduced to an old friend of the family. Or she could stand rooted to the spot while her husband reached Lady Charlton and spoke and she turned and reached out a hand to him. Alex took it in his and she clung to it, looking up into his face and talking rapidly and urgently.

Jessica watched as Alex lifted his free hand and touched Lady Charlton gently on the cheek, saw the other woman turn her face into his palm, caught the glint of a tear as Alex moved so that he was sheltering her from the room.

She is distressed...he has known her since she was a child...his instinct is to protect...

The excuses and explanations ran through her head and all the time the voice of cold reason said, *This is what he always expected and you always dreaded. This is the* coup de foudre. *He has fallen in love.*

'Are you quite well, Your Grace?'

Jessica turned, suddenly dizzy, and realised that she must have been holding her breath. Around her guests moved and talked and laughed and a new set was forming. She had been unaware of any of it.

A gentleman stood beside her, his expression concerned. She knew him, he had been at dinner. Her mind was blank.

'Just a little light-headed,' she managed. 'The heat, you know.'

'Allow me to find you a seat.' He took her by the arm and steered her towards the nearest chair. 'May I fetch you something to drink, Duchess?'

She remembered his name as she sat. Thank goodness, her wits were returning. 'Thank you so much, Lord Henderson. I will be quite myself in a moment,' she said firmly and smiled and he gave a little bow and, mercifully, went away.

Her fan, with its ebony sticks and its hand-painted leaf, gave her some privacy as she fluttered it, keeping it close to her face. She looked across and saw, through the weaving pattern of dancers, glimpses of Alex's back turned squarely to the room.

They would have a great deal to catch up on, she thought, striving to keep calm. And he would want to give Lady Charlton time to compose herself. She would sit here where he had left her while this set came to its conclusion. Alex had asked for the next one, teasing her as he had pencilled it in on her card—the first opportunity to waltz with his wife—so he would come back then.

The final dance ended and, as the dancers left the floor, going this way and that, stopping to chat, she lost sight of Alex. When she could see clearly, he had gone and so had Lady Charlton whose seat was occupied by a flushed young woman fanning herself vigorously and laughing rather too loudly with her companion.

There, she told herself. *He is coming to claim you for the next dance.*

Only, he did not. Everyone was on the floor, she could see the string players in the orchestra lifting their bows, and there was still no sign of Alex.

'May I have the pleasure, Duchess?' It was one of the older Hawksmoor sons.

'Of course. I would be delighted.'

Jessica wished she could recall his name, but he danced well, sweeping her elegantly around the room and maintaining just the right level of conversation. Years of training in deportment helped her outward composure and having to think about answering him, as well as minding her steps, was calming.

Then she saw them. Alex was waltzing with Lady Charlton, holding her close, his head bent to listen as she talked.

'Oh, I am so sorry. Did I step on your toe?' She had stumbled, but her partner held her firmly and kept the rhythm.

'Quite all right.'

'Is that your sister dancing with my...dancing with the Duke? Lady Charlton, is it not?'

He glanced across and frowned. 'Yes. She is not quite herself at the moment. I am glad Demeral has persuaded her to dance.'

'She is very beautiful.' A sweeping turn took them out of sight.

'Yes.' Mr Hawksmoor chuckled. 'Helena was rather a late developer.'

'And is she married?' Jessica persisted, striving to sound as though she was making polite conversation. 'I imagine she must have been a great success at her come-out.'

'To Viscount Charlton, the heir of the Earl of Strickland.' His smile was definitely forced as he spoke. No amusement now.

'I have never met him. Is he here tonight?'

'No.' That was curt.

'What a very fine ballroom this is,' Jessica said brightly. Clearly time for a change of subject and her spinning brain was incapable of coming up with anything more original.

'Indeed. We are most fortunate.' Mr Hawksmoor had relaxed again.

Somehow Jessica got though that set and the ones that followed. Alex reappeared—alone—to take her in to supper and she managed to smile brightly and not to make any mention of missed dances, or of Lady Charlton.

If she had not seen him with the other she would not have known anything was wrong, but now she was alert to the slightest change in him.

Eventually she could not bear it any longer. 'Lady Charlton appeared upset,' she remarked lightly, pretending indecision over the choice of savouries on her plate. 'But I saw you waltzing, so you obviously lifted her mood.'

'It is hardly a question of mood,' Alex said, lowering his voice. He looked sombre. 'She tells me that her husband is a brute, frequently in his cups and unfaithful into the bargain.'

'That is dreadful,' Jessica said and meant it. A married woman was, effectively, the property of her husband and had few rights. Lady Charlton's flight to her family might be frowned on by society, but was completely understandable. At least they had taken her in: Jessica had heard of families where the door could have been slammed in the face of a daughter trying to leave her husband.

But Helena had her large, wealthy and influential family. She did not need Jessica's husband, except as a friend.

'What will happen to her now?' Divorce was prohibitively expensive, involved an Act of Parliament and, as far as Jessica was aware, no woman had ever managed to divorce her husband. 'Are there children?' They would legally have to remain with their father, another crushing blow to the distressed wife.

'No, thank goodness. I assume she will stay here while her father negotiates a separation with Charlton who may, eventually, divorce her. But neither of them can remarry if that happens—this will deprive Charlton of an heir.'

'Serves him right,' Jessica muttered.

Alex gave a grunt of agreement. 'But it will not make him any easier to deal with. He will want her back.'

'A horrible situation. Still, I am sure the good wishes of old friends such as yourself will help raise her spirits,' she said with determined cheerfulness and swallowed her champagne.

Something in her tone must have struck him as false because Alex glanced at her, a slight frown on his face. 'I hope so.' His expression lightened. 'She is not the girl I recall from our childhood. Seeing Helena was quite a…a revelation.'

I could see that.

Jessica told herself that jealousy was unattractive, that it was feeble to feel so insecure and that it was simply Alex's gallant nature and warm heart that had drawn him to Lady Charlton.

'That was a deep sigh,' he remarked.

'I was simply making a resolution. Please pass me one of those cheesecakes.'

They retired well into the small hours, but Jessica lay awake, unable to sleep. It seemed Alex was not going to come to her bed. Was that because he was tired and was already sleeping or because he was lying awake thinking about the lovely Lady Charlton? Was he facing the fact that he had fallen in love, as he had always expected he would?

If he had, she was sure he would pretend it had not happened, would not let her see what had occurred. And he would not act on his feelings. At least, she was almost certain of that. Alex was a gentleman, a man of honour. And he was kind. He would not want to hurt her. He had been angry when he had realised she thought he had deceived her over the fire and the reason for his proposal. He had expected her trust and she had failed to give it. Now she must remember that. If only that small nagging ache of doubt would leave her.

* * *

There was no sign of Alex the next morning when she came down for breakfast to find the other house guests and the family as heavy-eyed as she was. But then, there were only half the places at the table occupied.

He might still be sleeping, or have ordered a tray in his room or gone out for a walk to clear his head. But that meant nothing. They were expected to remain for a light luncheon before travelling home, so there was really no need for Alex to be up and about yet.

There was no sign of Lady Charlton either.

After she had managed to finish a slice of toast and two cups of tea Jessica went upstairs. She would go for a walk, she decided, asking Trotter for a bonnet and warm cloak. But on her way out she would just look in on Alex.

His bedchamber was empty. She walked in to the dressing room and made James jump. 'I'm sorry, I was wondering whether His Grace was coming down for breakfast.'

'He was up at daybreak, Your Grace,' the valet said, his arms full of the previous night's clothing. 'I haven't seen him since.'

'I expect he has gone for a walk, which is what I am about to do.' She smiled and made her way downstairs. Alex was up early every morning at the castle and it had probably become such a habit that lying in bed once awake was not restful.

A footman directed her to the nearest door to reach the gardens and she stepped out into sunshine. It was cool and the air was damp, but there was a scent in the air that held the promise of spring and of growing things, of a brown world turning green again.

A lawn stretched out in front of her, ending in a ha-ha

which allowed the view to be open to the parkland beyond. Paths led off from the terrace left and right and on a whim she took the left-hand one. It led to a shrubbery, not so overgrown as to be dismal, and wound its way between artfully placed shrubs and small trees. In gaps between the branches she could see the roof of what must be a summerhouse of some kind and made her way towards it, walking quietly in the hope of seeing wildlife. Rabbits, perhaps, or a squirrel or even deer.

She was almost on the little building now. As she approached it from the side it appeared to be an open-fronted shelter. It was positioned so that it looked out over an open glade with a pond in the centre and would, once the weather was warm, be a charming place for a picnic.

The path led up to it and then turned to follow its wall around to the front. Jessica stopped and looked at how it had been built, thinking it would be simple enough to have one made for the castle grounds. There was a perfect spot—

'But he will find me if I go with you,' a woman said.

Jessica froze, her hand resting on the lapped boards of the hut.

'No one need know. I can get you away in secret, find you a house in some small town. You can become a widow.' That was Alex's voice. Jessica's fingers cramped on the rough wood. 'There are plenty of market towns near London where you could be quite unknown.'

'I would know nobody. I would be alone.' The woman's voice cracked. She was crying.

'You would have me,' Alex said, his voice warm. 'You would always have me, Helena.'

Chapter Twenty-Seven

'Swear you would tell nobody? Your wife will guess, surely?' the woman said.

'No,' Alex said. 'No, Jessica trusts me.' There was regret in his voice, she could hear it even through the buzzing in her head that warned her that any moment she might faint.

Jessica sat down abruptly on the damp ground, but Alex's voice went on relentlessly. 'Ours was not a love match for her, you see. And she believes that I had given up on my foolish dream of falling for someone, heart and soul, so she will not be suspicious.'

'But she was wrong.'

'She was wrong,' Alex said. 'But how can I tell her that?'

Silence, the sound of soft weeping. Then he said, 'Don't cry, Helena.'

'Then kiss me.'

'Oh, Helena.' There was a world of feeling in Alex's voice.

It brought Jessica to her feet. She took a step towards the front of the shelter. She would confront them…

But she had married Alex knowing this might happen one day. Many men kept their mistresses in a discreet house somewhere convenient and their wives never knew, or perhaps did and chose not to confront the situation.

She should never have agreed to marry him without deciding what she would do if this happened, and now it had and the man she loved...loved another.

How did one remain a complacent wife in the face of this? How did you welcome your husband into your bed knowing he might have lain with another woman, the one he loved, only hours before?

Walk away. Walk away now, before this can become any worse than it already is.

Jessica began to walk back the way she had come, dry-eyed, sick at heart, her mind in turmoil.

Alex shook his head ruefully. Kissing away tears as he had done when they were both children was not going to help now, however effective his old nanny's advice for soothing childish upsets had been.

But he dropped a kiss on to each of Helena's tear-soaked eyelids even so and tightened his arm around her shoulders in a fierce hug.

'You must stay here and decide what you will need to take with you,' he said when Helena's tears had finally dried and she was sitting upright, a look of determination replacing the hopelessness on her face. 'How likely is your husband to come and try to remove you, do you think?'

'He will not come. Papa wrote and told him that I am with the family and that I will stay under this roof for as long as I want. He is very upset, very disapproving but, when I told him that Charlton had struck me, he said nothing more about me returning to him. He will not hear of me living anywhere else, though. He thinks that by hiding me away here it will somehow hide the scandal, too.'

'In that case you are safe for a few weeks. It will take

me a while to find the right house for you.' And a while to raise the money for it. This was not something he could use Jessica's money for, even though she would never know.

'You must not pay for it,' Helena said, as though reading his thoughts. 'I have my diamonds, left to me by my great-aunt. They are worth a lot of money, enough for a house, I know, because Mama told me that when I inherited them. But they are quite hideous, I never wear them and they are here, in the safe in my dressing room.'

She broke off and sat, clearly thinking. 'I will not give them to you to sell, because they might be traced back to you and that could put you in a most difficult position. But Mr Evers, our Vicar, is travelling up to London next week. I will give them to him, parcelled up, and let him think it is some simple piece that I want Rundell, Bridge & Rundell to clean and reset.

'I will enclose a note saying that I want to sell them. They know they are mine because they cleaned them when I inherited the set.'

Planning had improved her spirits, Alex could see. She was determined now that she could see a way to escape and the means to do it.

'Then I will write when I have found a suitable house. I have to go up to London soon, so I can look at possibilities then. We can agree a date and I will send a hired carriage to collect you. But, Helena, I must tell Jessica about this, I cannot keep secrets from her. And I may have to tell Robert and Anna as the plan to get you away develops but you know you can trust them.' It would need more subterfuge than that, of course—several changes of vehicle, for a start. But that could be dealt with nearer the time.

'Oh, thank you. I understand about Jessica and of course

I know the Chandlers would help.' Helena's eyes were pink with weeping and so was her nose, but she was still the most beautiful woman he had ever seen.

And, he recognised very clearly, she meant nothing to him beyond an old friend who desperately needed help. She would never be more lovely to him than Jessica. Jessica, whom he loved and who gave him no hint that her feelings for him might be turning into love.

But she was his and they were together. There was always hope.

'You go back first,' he said to Helena. 'They will be wondering where you are. I will go for a walk and come back from a quite different direction.'

He sat for a while, wishing he could tell Jessica about this, ask for her help. But Helena had become almost hysterical when he had suggested it and he had sworn to tell no one else in order to calm her.

There were things he could do immediately, he decided. He would write to his London lawyers, tell them he had to find a home for a distant relative, respectable but in straitened circumstances. Then, when he joined Jessica in London for May Day, he would have time to inspect what they had found.

After a while he stood up and stretched and strolled out across the glade, following a winding path that, if he remembered rightly, led down to the river bank. From there he could cut across a meadow, circle around to the other side of the house and no one would know he had been with Helena.

Over an hour later Alex entered the hall through a side door and encountered his host.

'Ah, there you are, Demeral.' Lord Hawksmoor looked concerned.

'I went for a walk. Is there a problem?'

'Your wife has left—she said she must get back to the castle urgently.'

'Had a message come?'

'No, although that only struck us after she had left. Perhaps she had recalled something.'

'How strange.' Alex thought back to the previous evening. Now he came to think about it, Jessica had seemed somewhat subdued, brittle almost. He had put it down to tiredness and the impact of the Hawksmoors, who tended to be somewhat overwhelming until one got to know them. 'She will have taken the carriage, I suppose.'

'Yes. I must say she seemed rather distracted—I expect she intends to send it back for you. Or you can borrow a horse and gig from the stables if you don't want to wait.'

Odder and odder. 'Thank you, I'll do that. One of the grooms can return it tomorrow. Excuse me, I'll get my man to pack.'

There would be a good reason, of course. Jessica would not leave her hosts so abruptly, let alone him, without a word. Was she feeling unwell? An unpleasant sense of foreboding gripped him and he tried to shake it off as he walked into his bedchamber.

'We need to leave right away, James.' Then he saw the valet was just closing his valises.

'Yes, Your Grace. I intimated as much from the departure of Her Grace and Miss Trotter. Her Grace left a note.'

Good. That would explain everything. It was sealed with a wafer which Alex tore open. He read what it said, then sat down on the bed to read it again because his legs no longer seemed able to support him.

The second time the words sank in and made horrible sense.

> *I think I realised as soon as I saw you set eyes upon her that you recognised Lady Charlton as the one you had been waiting for, hoping for. I thought I was prepared for this, for you finding your true love, but it seems I need time to accustom myself.*
>
> *Please do not come after me. I do not want this to become some hideous confrontation when we both will say things we will regret one day.*
>
> *I married you knowing this might happen and knowing that, when it did, I must do my duty as Duchess of Malvern. I will return. Of course I will. I do not break my promises and I know, of course, that you can never marry her and nor can she give you an heir. But for now, do not ask it of me. I do not think I could bear it.*
> *Jessica*

The anger that flared through him shook Alex almost as much as the letter that he held crumpled in his hand.

On the evidence of his concern for Helena last night Jessica had decided that he had fallen in love with the woman? She had reacted to his distraction and his neglect of her by leaping to the conclusion that he would be unfaithful to her?

How could she have so little faith in him? But she had shown that she did not trust him when she had assumed that he had hidden the destruction at the castle from her in order to win her wealth.

It hurt this badly because he loved her; he retained enough control to recognise that. And she did not love him. She thought she was the injured party here when, in fact, he was the one who, because of his concern for an old friend, was the one who had been abandoned. Blamed.

Alex strode out of the room and into the bedchamber she had occupied, managing not to slam the door behind him. He could not let James see his emotions or sense that anything was amiss with the marriage.

He flung open the window and stood, hands on the sill, breathing in the cool air until his heart rate returned to something like normal and he could think straight.

I love her.

He loved his wife. This was not friendship, or desire or any other form of attraction that he could think of. He was in love and he loved. How had that happened? How could he have been so wrong about himself and his emotions? But this had to be love because, surely, nothing else could hurt so savagely?

He had been wrong all along—love *could* grow, slowly, subtly. It had developed as he learned to know Jessica, as she had become as essential to him as breathing. And, obsessed with the idea of recognising his one true love, he had not realised what the affection and desire and feelings of warmth and closeness meant as they wove their way into his heart and mind.

After a minute or so he found he could begin to think through what he must do. He would go back to the castle and he would wait. Wait until Jessica came back. She would do; he trusted her word, as, it seemed, she did not trust his. But he would not write—this was not something that could be mended with words on paper.

Then, somehow, they must make this marriage work, even if its public face was a mask fit for the Pantheon masquerade, because if she had so little trust in him, he would never believe protestations of love—not after this.

It was a plan, but one that held none of the hope he had experienced only a few hours before.

Jessica arrived back in London three days later. She had deliberately not forced the pace, not wanting Trotter, or the driver and grooms, to realise that she was leaving in such circumstances. They believed what she had told them, that her father needed her and she was concerned about him, so had decided to return a little earlier than planned. Also, she informed Trotter, as the work was proceeding so well on the castle, she thought that it was time to improve things at the town house.

Inside she felt as though she was bleeding. It was her own fault, of course. Once she realised that she loved Alex the last thing she should have done was to marry him, risking this heartbreak.

And somewhere beside the pain there was anger. He had been furious that she had not trusted him when they arrived at the castle to find the smoking ruins of the village and she had chastised herself for that lack of trust. She had believed that, even if he did fall in love with another woman he would be too much a gentleman to act on it.

Now she knew he would act. He would kiss his true love, he would plan to set her up in a convenient house where he could visit her. He would make her his mistress. Perhaps she already was. Perhaps on the night of the ball he had not come to his wife's bed because he was weary, but because he was in Lady Charlton's.

Why had she not read her own future in that moment when Miss Fawcett had thrown herself into the arms of Lord Branscombe and they had realised that a childhood friendship had blossomed into something else entirely?

Her father greeted her with delight, but expressed concern about the dark circles under her eyes. 'You have lost weight,' he accused, ringing for hot chocolate and cake.

'It is tiring, the work on the castle and village,' Jessica explained. 'I thought London would make a pleasant change. Alex, however, will probably be unable to spare the time. He takes his responsibilities very seriously.'

Except those to his wife.

Chapter Twenty-Eight

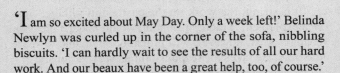

'I am so excited about May Day. Only a week left!' Belinda Newlyn was curled up in the corner of the sofa, nibbling biscuits. 'I can hardly wait to see the results of all our hard work. And our beaux have been a great help, too, of course.'

'And now we have decided on the final order of the floats, which is really the last major decision, I think,' Anthea said.

Jessica made herself sit up and pay attention. Nine days since she had overheard Alex and Helena in the shrubbery. A week in London presenting a cheerful face to her father and her friends. Thank heavens for the May Day planning: at least it gave her mind something to occupy it instead of spinning like a dog in a turnspit wheel.

'Oh, and we do need chimney sweeps after all, because the ironmongers decided to have a float with their various domestic equipment like dust pans and fire irons and coal scuttles, so there will be a float with a hearth and a sweep and some of the girls dressed as maids. But it is all right because our housekeeper asked our sweep and he is organising that.'

'The other floats will be as we agreed,' Lucinda chimed in, making check marks on a list. 'There's the tower of greenery with the maiden at the top and the knight in armour—signifying ironmongery generally—riding along-side and the one with flowers and our pretend milkmaids who will all have various metal items of equipment—cream skimmers and pails and bowls and so forth.'

'What about the apprentices?' Anthea asked. The management of a mob of over-excited youths had been worrying all of them. They were to be dressed as spirits of the forest and would caper alongside the floats with pipes and drums.

'Papa says that they will be supervised by the journeymen who, one can only hope, are old enough to keep some kind of order. The Ironmongers themselves, those who feel able to, will process behind.'

'Apparently the sweeps' boys run riot at May Day,' Belinda added. 'They dress up as girls, toss brick dust about and bang their brushes and shovels. We do not have to do anything about those—they will plague everyone equally, I believe!'

'I have a letter here to Papa from the Master of the Guild giving the time for everything to assemble in the yard at Ironmongers' Hall,' Jessica reported. 'Have you all decided whether you want to take part?'

'Goodness, yes,' Belinda said. 'We are all joining in as milkmaids and Major Rowlands has agreed to be the knight in armour because his horse is accustomed to battle so will not be alarmed at the noise. Will you be with us on the float, Jessica? Or is it too much of a romp now you are a duchess?'

Jessica's stomach gave the unpleasant lurch that it produced whenever she was reminded of her marriage. 'Um, I had not thought. No, I had better be with Papa—he wants to be in the yard to make certain everything sets off properly and then we were going to take the carriage by back streets to where he is joining a party with a large balcony overlooking the route.'

'But you will join us in Green Park at dawn?' Lucinda asked. 'We are going to bathe our faces in the dew which, I am reliably informed by our housekeeper, will render us ravishingly beautiful.'

'You *are* ravishingly beautiful, dear,' Belinda teased. 'Or so a certain viscount believes.'

Lady Lucinda threw a cushion at her friend. 'And a certain baronet thinks the same about you.'

'Spring is in the air, two of us are married and we are all in love. Isn't it wonderful?' Belinda caught the cushion.

'Wonderful,' Jessica echoed, her smile fixed firmly in place. Where was Alex? There had been no reply to her note and there was no sign of him in London, certainly not at his town house. She had made quite certain that the staff there knew where she was and that they must send all post around to Adam Street the moment it arrived.

Was he with Lady Charlton, or had he simply stayed at the castle, too angry with her for leaving to communicate in any way? Or was he too ashamed of himself to face her? No, it could not be that. Whatever Alex's faults, cowardice was not one of them.

Had she done the right thing, leaving? It felt more and more difficult to contemplate returning with each day that passed. But she must, it was her duty. She was the Duchess, people depended on her and she had made vows which she took very seriously, even if her husband did not.

Alex paced along as much of the battlements as he could before the way was blocked with scaffolding poles, buckets of lime mortar and piles of stone. The masons had taken one look at his expression and had moved to the far end where they were working with none of their usual jests and whistling. Even the sharp orders thrown at the apprentices were muted.

One week until May Day. He should be travelling up to London today, as they had agreed. He had resolved not to go, but now he wondered. What would he find if he did? A wife consumed by jealousy? He wondered again how he could explain what had happened and be believed.

Yes, he had been taken aback at the sight of Helena, his childhood friend, grown up and beautiful, and he would have come back to Jessica immediately and apologised, laughing at himself for his instinctive male reaction.

But he had seen the misery in Helena's eyes and he could no more have walked away from that than he could from an animal lying injured in the road. Yes, he had been so absorbed in Helena's story and in trying to cheer her that he had forgotten a dance with Jessica—and had not remembered that until after he had read her letter—but surely husbands committed worse crimes than that, with only a china ornament thrown at their heads in retribution?

So was it jealousy? Or did Jessica, after all, care more for him than he thought? Had he been blind, or was this flickering flame of hope false?

He passed back, kicking shards of stone out of his path as he went. The masons' hammers were like an echo of his churning thoughts.

I love her. She has left me. She does not trust me. I love her. Could she possibly, after all, care for me?

There was no one he could talk to about this, because it would feel like a betrayal of Jessica. Even if he could, his closest friends were at the Lodge and the very nature of the split meant that any mention of it was impossible in the Hawksmoor household.

Robert and Anna were the only people he felt he could trust with this and they were in London. And so was Jessica.

The anger had left him now, replaced with confusion and a dull ache under his breastbone which, if he was a fanciful romantic, he might call a broken heart. But he was no longer a romantic, daydreaming of love. He was a man in love with his wife and, he realised suddenly, he would do anything to get her back.

To hell with his hurt feelings, with the feeling of betrayal that Jessica did not trust him, although that still stung. He was her husband and he loved her.

And I never told her.

Alex stopped dead, one hand on the ring handle of the tower door. He had never risked telling her he loved her. 'Coward,' he said now, out loud. What had stopped him? The fear that she would pity him and be kind about it? The risk of looking a fool for his romantic theories of love at first sight when it had happened to him so slowly, so gently, that he had hardly realised what was happening?

She did not know and all she had seen was what he had said he wanted to happen—a glimpse of someone across a room and, apparently, her husband falling for a lovely woman.

The handle turned in his hand and he was halfway down the spiral stairs before he realised what he was doing. 'James!' he yelled as he reached the first floor.

'Your Grace?' The valet shot out of the bedchamber, his hands full of neckcloths.

'Pack. I am going to London.'

'Now, Your Grace? Only it is three in the afternoon and—'

'Now.' Alex took the main stairs two at a time. 'Goodson!' The secretary appeared. 'Sir?'

'We leave as soon as bags can be packed. Ah, Pitwick, have the carriage brought round. Two drivers, two grooms. I am leaving for London immediately.'

The staff scattered, leaving Alex standing in the middle of the Great Hall feeling, he realised, more like himself than he had since the morning after the ball. Was this what it was like going in to battle once the decision had been made to charge? Everything became quite clear-cut—live or die. Or, in this case, win or lose.

He was still standing there when Goodson came and deposited a portable writing slope and a portfolio of papers on the table, then ran for the stairs.

An hour later they were on the road, a large hamper of food on the seat beside James, Goodson sorting papers beside Alex and a spare driver and groom outside trying to snatch some rest before they took over for the next stage.

'I have brought the correspondence relating to that house you wished to acquire, sir. Do you wish to review it now?'

Alex stared at him, then realised what he was talking about. 'No, that doesn't matter now.' He would think about that later. Helena was safe where she was—all he had room to worry about was Jessica.

As Alex had expected, Jessica was not at the London house when they arrived fifteen hours after they had left. That did not prevent the sharp stab of disappointment.

'Her Grace is at her father's house, Your Grace,' Cook reported. She was more than a little flustered by the arrival on the doorstep of her employer, unannounced and unshaven. 'She is helping him with this May Day affair, sir, but she said to send all the post around to her.' She turned to shout down the back stairs. 'Milly! Hot water for His Grace and the gentleman.'

'Mr Goodson, my secretary,' Alex said, stripping off his greatcoat. 'James, you go and get some food and sleep. You, too, Goodson.' It was tempting to simply take the coach and driver to Adam Street, but he knew that would be a mistake.

A weary, dirty, unshaven husband arriving without warning and announcing that he loved her was no way to court a wife. He needed his wits about him, every single one that he could muster.

'I will bathe, shave and I would welcome some food, Mrs Dobson. Anything you can prepare easily. Then I shall rest. I shall be out this evening.' Not to Adam Street, but to the Chandlers' house and, he fervently hoped, the chance to work out just what had gone so very wrong with his marriage.

'Alex! What a lovely surprise. Come in.' Anna appeared in the hallway behind their footman and waved him through to the drawing room.

'Are you free this evening?' He kissed her cheek, then shook hands with Robert who had put down a book and got to his feet. It had only just occurred to him that they might be out, or entertaining.

'We are, unless a patient staggers thought the door,' Robert said. 'Sit down. You look as though you need a stiff drink.'

'Food, rather, I would say.' Anna tugged the bell pull and when the footman appeared, told him to tell Cook they had one more for dinner. 'Roast chicken,' she said when the man had left. 'That can stretch to any number of guests. What is wrong?' she added when they were all sitting down.

'I am tired. I did the journey from Herefordshire without stopping except to change horses.'

'I can see that.' Anna did not exactly roll her eyes, but it was close. 'Jessica is in town and has been for over a week. She has not called and when I saw her by chance in the street I thought she looked like a woman who was doing a great deal of weeping into her pillow, despite the very brave face she was showing to the friends who were with her. Now here you are. And you are with us, not at home, not at her father's house. You are looking, I have to say, like death warmed over.'

'Thank you for that description,' Alex said. 'It makes me feel so much better.'

'Then eat, drink a little and then talk,' Robert said as the door opened and dinner was announced.

Onion soup, roast chicken washed down with two glasses of good claret and lemon tart to follow certainly stopped him feeling quite so light-headed. Robert and Anna's questions when they were back in the drawing room were sufficiently sharp to complete his revival.

'What happened?' Anna asked.

'I encountered an old friend at a ball. She had…she was in considerable trouble. I was so absorbed in talking to her that I forgot a dance I had promised Jessica. She was very cool about it. I do not think it helped that Hel—that the old friend is very beautiful.'

'Lady Charlton,' Anna said. 'Of course I remember her,

we were always friendly, and we know about what has happened to her—her sister Marjorie and I correspond.'

'Go on,' said Robert.

'The next day Jessica had gone. To London. She left a letter that said she realised that I was in love with Helena, that it had struck me just as I had always thought it would, fool that I am. That she had to come to terms with it, but would come back when she had, because she recognises her duty.'

Robert said something short under his breath, then, 'Her duty.'

'What else happened?' Anna asked. 'Jessica is a sensible woman with feelings for you that go beyond duty. She might have lost her temper with you if you have been flirting with a beautiful young lady, but she is not going to react in such a dramatic manner as that.'

He shrugged. 'I met Helena the next morning and I promised her that I would find her a house near London and help her escape to it without anyone else knowing. By the time I got back to the house Jessica had left.'

'And since then the pair of you have been nursing your wounded feelings and misunderstandings at a distance of over a hundred miles and are both too proud to try to work out what has gone wrong?'

'Yes,' Alex admitted. 'I was angry. And hurt.'

'And had you told her that you love her?' Anna demanded. When he did not answer, she did roll her eyes. '*Men*. Sort out Helena's problem so that when you do work out what to tell your wife you can give her the facts. Find Helena a lawyer so you will not be involved so closely with her until you are sure Jessica accepts her as your friend.'

'I promised I would get her away from home.' He had

given his word, but he could see now that he must keep a distance, at least until Jessica's faith in him was restored. If it ever was.

'We will do that,' Robert said. 'Go home and sleep.'

He saw Alex to the door. 'Good luck.'

'Thank you, both. I think I will need it.'

The next day Alex approved the house Goodson had picked out. He found a lawyer to deal with matters and he wrote to Helena, telling her that the Chandlers would help her and that the lawyer would manage her affairs for her. And he told her frankly that their friendship had caused a misunderstanding with Jessica that he must put right.

The day after that he called at the house in Adam Street at two in the afternoon. The door was answered by Alfred. He did not step back to allow Alex to enter.

'Is Her Grace at home?'

Alfred went red, but said firmly, 'No, Your Grace.'

'Not at home or not receiving?'

'Not receiving, Your Grace.' Now even the tips of his ears were scarlet. 'I am sorry, Your Grace.'

Alex nodded and walked steadily the short distance to the junction with the Strand. A carriage passed him and he looked back. It drew up outside Mr Danby's house and Lady Anthea and Miss Newlyn got out. They were admitted immediately.

Chapter Twenty-Nine

May 1st, just before dawn

Alex set his booted toe into a crack in the brickwork, reached up, put his hat on top of the wall between the alleyway and the back yard of the Danbys' house and hauled himself up.

There were lights on in the kitchen and on the upper floor. So, the servants were about. He jumped down into the yard, retrieved his hat, then walked to the back door, not troubling to be quiet about it. His feet crunched on spilt coal and as he reached it the door opened to reveal a scullery maid clutching a coal scuttle and shovel on her way out to refill it.

She gave a shrill scream and dropped them both with a crash.

Alex lifted his hat. 'Good morning. I do apologise for alarming you.' He walked past into the kitchen to confront a woman in a vast apron, a kettle in one hand. 'Good morning,' he repeated. 'This way for the back stairs?' and was gone before she could speak.

He encountered Alfred just reaching the foot of the stairs. The footman opened his mouth, closed it again and said, 'Miss Jessica's gone out, Your Grace.'

'At quarter to five in the morning? You'll have to do better than that, Alfred.' Half expecting the man to try to stop him he stepped to one side, but Alfred just shook his head and let him pass. 'Miss Trotter'll tell you. Dabbling in the dew. My ma always used to do it and my sisters. Used to swear by it for their skin or some such.'

And so did the village girls on May Day, although more, Alex had always suspected, to meet their swains than for a beauty treatment. And where, exactly, would someone living off the Strand go for wholesome dew?

'Which door?'

'Second on the right.' Alfred caught the sovereign that Alex tossed him neatly in one hand. 'Thank you, Your Grace.'

Alex took the stairs with more care. He had no wish to come face to face with his father-in-law at this hour of the morning.

The second door on the right was ajar and he went in, closing it behind him.

Trotter, clad in a sensible flannel robe and with her hair in curl papers, gaped at him. 'Your Grace?'

'Indeed.'

Trotter sat down on the bed, threw up her hands and said, 'Thank goodness!' She bounced up again and Alex could see her blush in the candlelight. 'I beg Your Grace's pardon, I'm sure. She's gone to Green Park, Your Grace. Driving herself in the phaeton with a groom and off to meet her friends. It is going to be all right, isn't it, Your Grace? Only I've been that worried.'

'If I can make it so, Trotter. I might make a mull of it yet because I feel I'm groping in one of London's famous fogs.'

Trotter's only answer was to produce a large handkerchief and burst into tears. Alex beat a hasty retreat, down the stairs, through the kitchen, out of the back gate that Alfred was obligingly holding open and up to where Will was waiting with the curricle.

'Green Park, Will. Go to Cleveland Row.' That was the most direct route, less than a mile and passing St James's Palace. He would leave the curricle there and cut through by foot.

Despite the hour there was enough traffic—and most of it heavy vehicles and delivery carts—to slow them. The clock over the great Tudor gatehouse of the Palace was chiming five as they passed it and the first glimmerings of dawn were breaking through the clouds.

It would be a fine day. Alex only hoped it would be a good omen as he strode out into the Park.

There was the holly bush they had hidden behind when they saw Anthea kissing Major Rowlands. How idiotic to feel sentimental about a small prickly shrub. Better that than a large, prickly husband, she supposed.

'David, stop here,' she told the groom. 'You go home and I will drive back with my friends. They are only over there—see?'

He looked across and, indeed, there were Belinda, Anthea and Lucinda, close enough that their laughter and shrieks as they patted their faces with cold dew was perfectly audible. 'If you're sure, Your Grace. There doesn't seem to be anyone else about…'

'Exactly, and they have their grooms with them. Off you go back to Adam Street.'

As he drove away Jessica walked over to the holly bush and sat down on a tree stump next to it. What on earth was she doing here? No amount of May Morning dew was going to make her beautiful. She would probably catch a cold on the chest and perish, which would leave Alex a wealthy widower. Then he could live in sin with Lady Charlton and they could have beautiful children together.

Oh, don't be such a feeble creature, she told herself savagely, brushing her hand across her cheeks, which were quite damp enough without any dew. *You agreed to be a duchess, now behave like one. You* will *make this marriage work, somehow. You will learn to pretend that there is nothing wrong. You will do your duty and keep your vows.*

'Jessica?'

She was so started that she reeled back and almost fell off the stump.

Alex—or this figment of her miserable imagination—went down on one knee on the wet grass and took her hand. 'Jessica. What are you doing here?'

'Dabbling in the dew,' she said defiantly. He was real, his bare hands warm on her chilly ones.

'That is not dew.' He raised one hand and brushed the pad of his thumb along under her eyes. 'I don't think that works. I mean, why are you in London? Not because I forgot one dance, surely?'

Of course, she realised, he did not know what she had overheard, she had been too distressed to put that in the note. She pushed his hand away. 'I was in the shrubbery the morning after the ball. I heard everything. About the house, about seeing her. I know you kissed her.'

That set him back on his heels. She took the chance and jumped to her feet, took two strides away until the holly bush was between them.

'You were in the shrubbery?' Alex got to his feet slowly.

Giving himself time to decide what to say, she thought miserably.

'I went for a walk after breakfast. I saw that little shelter in the glade and thought it might be nice to build one in the castle grounds. For…for picnics. I had no idea anyone was inside, but I was standing there and then I heard everything, very clearly indeed.'

He was watching her, his face very grave. 'So that explains it. I knew you were not a woman who would do something so drastic over a missed dance and the possibility that I was flirting with a pretty girl.'

'And you were quite correct,' she threw back at him. 'But I am a woman who finds it hard to come to terms with seeing my husband fall head over heels, to hear him making arrangements to set up his mistress close to London, to hear him kissing her.'

There was a long silence, then Alex said, 'When I was a small boy my old nurse's sovereign remedy for tears was to kiss the eyelids. I did it to Helena once when she fell over and grazed her knee. I think she was eight at the time. That was what she asked me to do, because she was weeping.' He watched her face in the growing light, his own tipped a little to one side. 'Did you leave at that point?'

'Of course.' Jessica sounded defiant, but there was doubt on her face now.

'If you had stayed, you would have heard me making practical arrangements about Helena's house. You would have heard that she is going to pay for it by selling jewellery, not from any money I might give her. I have found the house now and a lawyer to administer her affairs for her and Robert and Anna Chandler, who are old friends of her, will help her escape from home and settle there.

'I understand why you believed what you did, having overheard our conversation as far as that very innocent kiss, but I give you my word, Jessica, I have no desire to make Helena my mistress, although I hope she will always be my friend. I have no desire for any mistress.'

'You are not in love with her?'

'No. How could I be, when I am in love with another lady altogether?'

He couldn't mean... No, it could not be true. 'Who?' she managed to ask.

'You. My wife,' Alex said simply. 'I was quite wrong— I didn't fall in love at first sight, or even fifth or sixth or seventh sight. I fell in love slowly, so gradually that I did not realise what had happened to me.'

'But you didn't tell me. You said nothing.'

'Because you did not love me. I did not ask you to, I married you knowing why you agreed to wed me, just as you understood my motives. Only they changed. I changed. But I couldn't put that burden on your shoulders of having to be kind to your husband who loved you.'

'Oh.' It seemed her feet were rooted to the ground and then suddenly she could move, could rush into his arms and wrap her own around him. 'Oh, we have been so blind! I love you, Alex. I have loved you for so long and I couldn't tell you. Alex! What are you doing?'

He scooped her up in his arms and strode off towards the Palace. 'Taking you home.'

His groom looked bewildered, but touched his cap politely. 'Good morning, Your Grace.'

'Home, Will, and then go around to Mr Danby's house and tell him his daughter is with her husband and will doubtless see him later this morning.'

* * *

Alex carried her up the steps, over the threshold and up the stairs to the bedchamber she had never seen, passing poker-faced staff as he went. He turned the key in the lock and looked at her as she lay getting grass and mud from her shoes on the handsome blue coverlet.

'What time must you be at the Ironmongers' Hall?'

'Eight,' she said.

'Then we do not have much time.' He began to strip off his clothing, letting it fly anywhere. 'But first I fully intend to make love to my wife—whom I love—very thoroughly indeed.'

'Oh, yes, please.' Jessica began to struggle with pins and laces until he helped her. They tumbled together on the silk, laughing and kissing.

'If only your letter had told me that you had overheard us—'

'If only you had swallowed your pride and come to London to confront me—' She smiled up at him as he came over her, his weight on his elbows. 'If only we were perfect instead of two poor mortals in love and very insecure with it.'

'Just at this moment I do not feel in the slightest insecure,' Alex said as he took her slowly, inexorably sinking into her welcoming heat, and she closed around him, caressing him with the muscles she had discovered over weeks of intimacy, finding new pleasures in the emotion she could see in his eyes.

He had said there was not much time, but Jessica was unaware of it passing, only of the slow slide of skin against skin, the pressure of lip against lip, the strength of the body joined to hers and the spiralling pleasure his caresses brought.

She could say it now. 'I love you. I love you, Alex. Now and always.'

And the words she heard as everything broke and splintered into the intensity of pleasure, were his, gasped out as he came with her. 'I love you, Jessica. *Jessica.*'

Mr Danby's well-trained staff did not turn a hair at the return of the daughter of the house, dishevelled, creased, smiling and in a desperate hurry.

'Trotter, where is my gown and my garland? Trotter—I am going to be late. Oh, Papa, Alex is in London. Do you mind dreadfully if I see the parade with him?'

Her father in his Sunday best with a huge nosegay for a buttonhole, kissed her cheek and made for the front door. 'Of course not, my dear. Off you go and get changed.'

Trotter, who for some reason seemed rather red about the eyes, was ready with the leaf-green gown, the darker green slippers and the circlet of spring flowers. She thrust Jessica into the dressing room with a cry of, 'No time for a bath! The water's warm.' When she emerged after a hasty wash, Trotter got her into petticoats, stockings and gown before attacking her hair.

'Pearl and aquamarines, I think,' Jessica managed to say between yelps as the circlet was ruthlessly pinned into place. 'Papa has found all the staff a good place to view the celebrations from, hasn't he?'

'Oh, yes, ma'am. A lovely balcony and a hamper of food from Gunther's so Cook can come, too.' She pushed in the last pin. 'Oh, you look a picture. His Grace is going to be so proud of you.'

'You know he is in London?' Of course, Alex must have

come here first, no wonder he had known where to find her. 'Have a lovely day, Trotter.'

The yard of Ironmongers' Hall off Fenchurch Street was a scene of apparent chaos. Horses neighed, people, all draped in flowers and greenery, ran back and forth, everyone was shouting and the horses were neighing. Jessica almost panicked, then she saw that Major Percy, in armour on horseback, was directing the floats to line up in order and that Alex and his other friends were lifting the faux milkmaids on to the carts and marshalling the apprentices and journeymen.

The clock stuck the quarter-hour: it was almost time to leave. Then she saw that the float that had had the scene of housemaids and a chimney with a sweep by it had a large throne-like chair placed where it looked out from the back. It was covered in greenery and bunches of flowers.

'Here she is!' Alex fought his way towards her through the throng. 'Come along. You are to be the Queen of the May.'

Before she could protest he started unpinning her wreath, draped a vast fragile white silk veil over her head and replaced the coronet. Then he picked her up and lifted her on to the float, got up beside her and handed her on to her throne. 'Your sceptre, ma'am.' She took the wand decorated with flowers and trailing ivy.

'Here's your costume, Demeral.' Viscount Oakham, almost unrecognisable beneath green paint and a long green wig handed Alex a strange structure like a domed basket with a hole at the front. It was absolutely covered in foliage, but no flowers. 'And here's the mask,' he said as Alex upended the structure over his head.

'I am the Green Man,' said this rather scary apparition. 'Lord to the Queen of the May.'

There was a very military shout from Major Percy and suddenly they were in motion. The gates opened and the roar of the crowd greeted them. All around was music, singing, cheers, catcalls. Small boys—the sweeping lads—ran back and forth, hurling their brick dust, onlookers, many of them dressed in green, joined in, dancing alongside for a while before they fell back to greet the next float.

Following her, Jessica could see the maiden in her tower and catch a glimpse of cocked hats and gold chains as the Ironmongers fell in at the rear.

It was chaos, it was almost anarchy, but it was joyful. Spring had come, green shoots were bursting out between cracks in old paving, soot-laden plane trees were decked once more in fresh leaves. Everyone was having the most marvellous time. Small boys were everywhere, hands held out for money, calling, 'Sir, remember the Bough!'

She saw the crowded balconies, saw her father who was brandishing his hat and tossing coins to the lads and milkmaid.

Jessica waved and kissed her hand and was pelted with flowers, some money—which small dirty hands rapidly scooped up—and some brick dust.

Behind her Alex rested one hand on her shoulder, his fingers tracing caresses on her bare skin. He was laughing, throwing back flowers as they hit him, but she could hear his voice, pitched to reach only her ears.

'Queen of the May, queen of my castle, queen of my heart. True love of my life.'

* * * * *

Author Note

Modern Ironmongers' Hall, rebuilt in 1922 after a bomb destroyed the building in 1917, is in Aldersgate. The Hall that Jessica knew was in Fenchurch Street and was built in 1745, replacing the medieval halls on that site.

Maypoles had disappeared from London by the Regency, although they persisted—and can still be seen—on village greens throughout the country.

Mr Brand, in his *Observations on Popular Antiquities... Vulgar Customs, Ceremonies and Superstitions* recorded:

> *In the* Morning Post, *Monday May 2nd, 1791, it was mentioned that yesterday, being the first of May, according to annual and superstitious custom, a number of persons went into the fields and bathed their faces with the dew on the grass, under the idea that it would render them beautiful... The Mayings are in some sort yet kept up by the milkmaids at London, who go about the streets with their garlands and musick, dancing...*

And as for the chimney sweeps' boys—those he describes as *'the most striking objects in the celebration of May Day in the streets of London'.*

Don't miss the stories in this mini series!

A SEASON OF CELEBRATION

MILLS & BOON

The Marquess's Year To Wed

Paulia Belgado

MILLS & BOON

Born and raised in the Philippines, **Paulia Belgado** has worn many hats over the years, from office assistant, flyer distributor, singer, nanny to farm worker. Now she's proud to add romance author to that list. After decades of dreaming of seeing her name on the shelves next to her favorite romance authors, she finally found the courage (and time—thanks, 2020!) to write her first book. Paulia lives in Malaysia with her husband, Jason, Jessie the poodle and an embarrassing amount of pens and stationery art supplies. Follow her on Twitter @pauliabelgado or on Facebook.com/pauliabelgado.

Visit the Author Profile page
at millsandboon.com.au.

Author Note

Numerous women have made great contributions to mathematics—too many to mention, in fact, but I'll try to name notable ones who have inspired this book or me personally throughout my research.

M. Lenoire was not a real historical figure, but she was inspired by Sophie Germain. In 1816, after three attempts, she became the first woman to win a prize from the Paris Academy of Sciences for her paper "Recherches sur la théorie des surfaces élastiques" published under the pseudonym M. Le Blanc. Her later work was also crucial in proving the first case of Fermat's Last Theorem.

Ada Byron, Lady Lovelace, is perhaps one of the most famous mathematicians in history and considered the first computer programmer in the world. While translating an article about Charles Babbage's work on his "analytical engine," Lovelace provided additional notes that theorized machines could do more than crunch numbers, like follow instructions. These notes were eventually published in a science journal in 1843, and her revolutionary ideas paved the way for the use of computers outside mathematics.

In 1943, Euphemia Lofton Haynes became the first African American woman to earn a PhD in mathematics. She taught at public schools in Washington, DC, and was the first woman to become chair of the DC Board of Education in 1966. While there, she argued against the "track system," which discriminated against African American students. Thanks to her efforts and contributions, the system was eventually abolished in 1967.

Thank you, ladies, for your persistence, vision and inspiration.

DEDICATION

This book is dedicated to my nieces and nephews,
Dana, Mikk, Martine, Raj, Yssa and Sophie.

You make my world better and brighter.
Love always,
Tita P

PS: You're still kids to me no matter how old you are,
so chapters seven, eight, nine and eleven
don't exist to you, okay?

Chapter One

Archimedes once said, *'There are things which seem incredible to most men who have not studied Mathematics.'*

While she greatly admired the ancient Greek mathematician's work, Miss Violet Avery doubted this particular piece of wisdom. While she had studied the discipline of numbers and formulas since the tender age of nine, there were many things that Violet still found incredible.

Or at the very least inexplicable.

Indeed, there were many, many things she could not explain.

Number one: Why was it necessary for ladies like her to wear numerous layers of itchy and uncomfortable clothing—a dress over a petticoat, over a camisole, over a corset, over a chemise, over drawers, not to mention stockings and shoes? Not that she would have liked to be naked, but surely one or even two layers of clothing were enough to retain one's modesty?

Number two: why were dinner parties such long, tedious affairs? Course after course of various foodstuffs, brought into the dining room by liveried footman who uncovered each dish with a flourish. Food was nourishment—nutrients to keep the body and mind alive—not entertainment. A simple meal could be finished in minutes. And then there was the social aspect of it. So much chatter and conversation and discourse that extended what should have been a perfectly normal biological function.

And number three—

'Violet, I cannot express how important this event is.'

Ah, yes, number three.

Lady Avery.

Violet's incredible, inexplicable mother.

Since Archimedes had never met Lady Avery, perhaps Violet had to forgive his error.

Her mother marched towards the dressing table where Violet currently sat as she waited for her maid, Gertrude, who was bent over the fireplace, heating up a pair of curling tongs. 'This is our first dinner party at Highfield Park. You must make a good impression on our hosts.'

Why they had even travelled all the way to Surrey from their home in Hampshire to attend a dinner party, Violet did not know. Well, it wasn't just to attend a dinner party, of course. They'd been here for over a week, as guests of the Dowager Duchess of Mabury, an old acquaintance of her father's. Violet and her mother were staying at the dower house, located on the estate of their hostess's son and daughter-in-law, the current Duke and Duchess of Mabury, but tonight was the first formal event up at the main house.

'Did you hear what I said, child?'

Violet turned her head up, focusing on Lady Avery's forehead before forcing her gaze to meet her mother's.

'First of all, Mother, I am not deaf, therefore I did hear you. Second, the word "important" usually signifies something consequential, substantial and life-changing. Yet you have called every dinner, ball and occasion we have attended in the last six months "important". Therefore, if every event we go to is important, then doesn't that dilute the significance of all those occasions?'

'I have not called all of them important,' Lady Avery protested with a huff.

'You have. All twenty-three of them, if you count tea with the vicar and his family.'

Her eyes slid to the heavens. 'Oh, Sir Gregory, whatever am I to do?'

'Papa is dead,' Violet said flatly. 'He's been dead for over two years. I doubt very much he'll hear you.'

Her mother's face crumpled like a balled-up piece of parchment. 'Violet!'

'What?' She shrugged.

'He was your father!' Lady Avery cried.

'He was. One day he was alive, then he went to sleep and didn't wake up.'

'Violet!'

'It's the truth.'

And why people didn't like hearing the truth was, perhaps, the *most* inexplicable thing to Violet. The truth was pure, inescapable and inevitable.

But for some reason many people did not like hearing the truth. In fact, when Violet pointed out the truth, they often acted horrified.

Or offended.

Or both.

Perhaps that was why Mother preferred to forget that tea with the vicar.

Lady Avery shook her head and sank down on the stool next to Violet. Turning her head, she dismissed Gertrude, who scuttled out of the room, hot tongs in hand. 'You want the truth, child? Allow me to lay it out for you. If you don't find a husband, you will learn the *true* meaning of consequential, substantial and life-changing.'

'Husband?' Mama could not be *serious*. 'What are you—'

'I have not finished.' Straightening her spine, Lady Avery continued. 'In the past two years I've been indulging you, as you father did, but I can no longer hide the truth from you. Violet, we are in dire straits.'

Violet knitted her brows together. 'What do you mean?'

Lady Avery's lower lip quivered. 'Wh-when your father died, he didn't leave us with much. Not much. Very little, in fact.'

'Very little? How little?'

'Probably not enough to keep our home.'

'We've lost Oakwood Cottage?' A feeling crept into her chest—a tightness that made it difficult to breathe.

'Not yet, but we will.'

'B-but Papa…he was a scholar! One of the most celebrated of his generation.' Her hands tightened into fists. 'He wrote so many papers…published four books. He had invitations to speak at all the top universities in England and on the Continent.'

'Just because he was intelligent, it does not mean he was wise.' Lady Avery's shoulders sank. 'I only found out we were deep in debt after his death.'

'I don't understand. What happened? And Oakwood Cottage!' Violet shot to her feet. 'Did you know we weren't going back when came here? Is that why we have brought so many clothes? Is someone else living in our house? What about our things?' The very thought of strangers pawing through their things—especially her father's study and his books—made Violet's stomach lurch. 'What if they touch his books and don't return them—'

'Calm yourself and have a seat—'

'No, I will not,' she shouted, then grabbed the first thing she could—a hairbrush.

Lady Avery grabbed her arm and tugged her back down. 'Violet Melissa Avery, you are no longer a child. You will control yourself this instant.'

Violet put the brush down. When she was younger, she'd been prone to fits, especially when frustrated. Often those episodes had turned violent, with her throwing things at the walls or even herself to the ground. Numerous nannies and governesses had given up on her—everyone had.

Everyone except her father.

One day, after a particularly ferocious tantrum when she was eight—which had caused another governess to resign—her father had walked through the door of the nursery. At first, she hadn't been sure who he was; she hadn't really seen much of him in her younger years, and could barely recognise him except for his bushy white beard and eyebrows.

But on that day... She could picture him clearly—his hair dishevelled, cravat loosened, shirtsleeves rolled back to his elbows as he knelt down next to her to place a calming hand on her back. Pure shock at seeing him had quieted her outburst and she could remember the sensation of weightlessness as he picked her up and took her to his study. Violet had never been there before, but there had been something about it—the smell of paper and leather and tobacco, the dark wood furniture, the massive desk piled with books and ledgers and scattered pens—that had comforted her. To this day, she had never felt more at home in any other place than Papa's study.

'*Violet,*' he'd begun as he'd sat her down on a massive overstuffed armchair by the fireplace. '*Look at me.*'

She hadn't been able to. She'd always had a hard time looking people in the eye.

'It's all right, my Vi.'

The pet name had sent a strange sensation through her, and so she'd forced herself to lift her head, even though the very idea of meeting his gaze had sent her skin crawling.

'Like me, you are different, my Vi.'

His voice had been like the softest silk brushing against her.

'The world is unkind to different people like us, but even more so to the female sex. So you must control your emotions. Learn to act like them. And mimic their ways.'

'Who's "them"?'

The corners of Papa's mouth had stretched back. *'Them, my dear child. Everyone but* us. *Do not worry. I will help you.'*

And so Papa had. Every day, he would take her to his study to teach her how to quiet the outbursts that seemed to come out of nowhere. He'd never given up on her. He had taught her tricks to mask how different she was. How to copy the way other girls walked, talked and acted. How she could be like everyone else.

How to be...normal.

As he'd taught her these tricks, however, he had also discovered her interest in mathematics and philosophy, and soon she had begun to spend hours with Papa, solving equations or reading through the works of Aristotle and Socrates, Descartes and Hume.

Papa's study had been an oasis from an outside world that she could not understand and which could not understand her.

And now—

'Are you finished?'

Mama's hands, clawing over hers, startled Violet. She hated unexpected touches, but fought the urge to pull away as she needed to know more.

She nodded.

'Now, there is a way to save Oakwood Cottage. You must—'

'Find a rich husband.'

'So you do understand?'

Papa had had some geographical dissected puzzles in his study that he'd let Violet play with. She'd enjoyed putting the pieces together to make one whole map, loved the way the wood clicked when they snapped into place.

And once she'd seen all the pieces, Violet's mind had always quickly put them together.

Dead father.

Click.

No money.

Click.

Attend parties and balls.

Click.

Push Violet towards any available gentlemen.

It all made sense now.

Violet should have had her coming out four years ago, when she'd turned seventeen, but her mother had delayed it.

'Perhaps she needs more time to…er…mature,' Mama had said.

Violet hadn't cared one way or another—only that she didn't have to disrupt her routine or take time away from her readings. Another year had gone by with no mention of her coming out and then Papa had died…

'Why have you never said anything before?' Violet asked. 'All this time you've been forcing me to go to balls and meeting all these strangers…you should have told me when Papa passed away.'

'We were in mourning,' Mama reminded her. 'And it was only after everything was settled that the solicitors told me about our…situation. The only thing we had left was your small dowry, and—'

'Me,' Violet finished. 'Yet you didn't say anything about the need for me to find a husband.'

'You would have fought me. I could barely get you out of the house to attend all those events. I thought perhaps some gentleman would offer for you once you'd had enough time to…settle yourself.'

It took all Violet's strength and all the training from her father not to scoff at Mama.

'You see, Violet,' Papa had said, *'it's often the ones who love us most who can be hurt by our frank words and reactions.'*

Mama squeezed her fingers tighter, making Violet's chest tighten, as if her mother's hands were wrapped around her lungs instead.

'I've done my best in the past year to find you a gentleman to wed, but alas we've had no luck on our own.'

Of course what Mama truly meant was that Violet had somehow managed to offend—or, in the case of the vicar's son, horrify—any eligible man who came within hearing distance of her.

Lady Avery continued. 'We are so fortunate that the Dowager has agreed to sponsor you for the Season. With her influence, I'm certain many men will overlook your… flaws.' Her lips pursed. 'Do your best, Violet. You are such a beauty you can capture any gentleman's attention even without a sizable dowry.'

Violet had been told on numerous occasions that she

was, indeed, beautiful. She often stared at herself in the mirror, sometimes for hours a day, but not because she was admiring her supposed looks—no, it was another of her father's lessons. He would practise different expressions with her, teaching her how to smile 'sincerely', or look surprised or shocked when called for. Unfortunately, it was one of the more difficult of his teachings, as the range of human emotions was wider and more complex than all thirteen books of Euclid's *Elements*.

'You just need to control what you say…think before you say anything.'

Violet had heard it a hundred times before from her mother, as well as from her governesses and tutors. The only problem was, she *did* think before she opened her mouth, and yet there were still times when she simply could not stop herself from saying what was on her mind.

But Oakwood Cottage… Papa's study…the furniture… the books and ledgers and scattered pens.

We haven't lost it, she reminded herself. *Not yet.*

'I…I will do my best, Mama.'

Lady Avery's smile widened into what Violet could tell was a genuine, happy smile—one that caused the lines at the corners of her eyes to crinkle.

'Wonderful, my dear. Let me call Gertrude so she can continue with your hair.'

Once her mother had left the room, Violet stared at the mirror, forcing herself to look into her own light blue eyes. 'This is for the best,' she said aloud, her voice sounding even more flat and loud than usual.

Papa had always said she had to learn to control the volume of her voice and her tone and…

Papa.

Long dead and gone.

It seemed illogical to miss him or even grieve for him. The time of mourning was over. One year, they said, and then she was supposed to be finished with mourning. So, after an entire year had passed since his death, Violet had locked up those feelings of sadness and grief. Yet they still escaped somehow, lingering in the corners of her mind.

The door opened and Gertrude crept in, those torturous tongs in hand.

This is for Oakwood Cottage, she told herself silently as she prepared for the upcoming torment.

Find a rich husband.

Save Oakwood Cottage.

Save Papa's books and study.

After what seemed like hours, Gertrude proclaimed that she was ready. A quick glance at her reflection showed Violet the familiar young woman everyone proclaimed was beautiful—dark sable curls piled elegantly on top of her head, heart-shaped face, light blue eyes, and a small mole just above the corner of the left side of her lip.

The light violet silk gown was her best, or so Mama said. She'd last worn it at a ball five months ago, given by Mr William Hollister, a wealthy widower who lived twenty miles down the road. Violet recalled how uncomfortable she had been—more than usual—as Mr Hollister's gaze had slid over her, and how he had said he was surprised at how she'd grown into a lovely young woman. Violet had retorted by reminding Mr Hollister that time worked in a forward motion, and then asked him how old he was—though she'd guessed he was probably older than her father had been. Her mother had turned the most unusual shade of purple and hurriedly ushered her away, much to Violet's relief.

She pressed her lips together, thinking of that encounter and all the others she'd had before that, as it dawned on her that they had all been attempts to find her a husband.

Mama should have told me.

But then again, she was correct in her thinking that Violet might have resisted.

She did not want a husband.

A husband meant leaving Oakwood Cottage for ever.

A husband would expect many things of her, like attending balls and parties and perhaps listening to whatever boring things he had to say.

A husband also meant having children…and the begetting of children.

Unexpected touches. Contact with bare skin. Possibly kissing.

Some time ago, when she had started her monthly flow, Papa had given her a book that explained the process. It had all sounded dreadful to her, and she had put that book back on his shelf and never touched it again.

But to save Oakwood Cottage and Papa's library she would endure anything. When the time came, she would just lie back, close her eyes, endure her husband's unwanted touches and think of something to distract her—like the Pythagorean Theorem or the Euler-Lagrange Equation.

'How lovely you look,' Mama said as she re-entered Violet's room, then escorted her out. 'Now, come. The Dowager has gone ahead to the main house, but she has sent her carriage back to fetch us.'

Due to her busy schedule, Violet had only met their host a handful times in the past week. She'd rather liked Miranda, the Dowager Duchess of Mabury, from the moment they were introduced. When Mama had first announced that they would be visiting the Dowager, Violet had pictured a stern matron with steely white hair. She'd imag-

ined such a high-ranking member of the Ton would look
down her nose at Violet and her mother, and perhaps dis-
miss them with a cold word or two. To her surprise, the
Dowager had turned out to be warm and welcoming, and
Violet found looking directly in her kind, dark eyes only
mildly disconcerting.

'I'm so delighted to finally meet you, Violet,' she had
said. *'Your father told me so much about you through our
letters. I hope you enjoy your stay here.'*

During the few meals they'd shared together, she'd never
treated Violet as if she was different. She'd asked Violet
questions, and if she had found any of her answers offensive, she'd never shown it.

Now that Violet knew the real reason she and Mama
were at Highfield Park, she wondered what the Dowager
truly thought of her. And how she could possibly have
agreed to sponsor her after meeting her. Except for Papa,
most people dismissed her for her oddness.

'We're here,' Mama announced as the carriage stopped.

Violet blinked. Time had seemingly moved without her
noticing, and now they were outside the main house. As
they alighted from the carriage Violet stared up at the imposing structure before them. Though they had driven by
the manor on their way to the dower house, seeing it up
close was quite different. It was nothing like Oakwood
Cottage—no, this manor projected opulence and wealth,
with its four-columned entrance, high archways, imposing
stone walls and perfectly manicured lawn. Having such a
large home seemed impractical to Violet—how long did
it take to navigate such a place, for one thing?—but then
again the Duke was likely a very important and wealthy
man, and society dictated that important and wealthy men
had significant and large homes.

'Fiddlesticks!' Mama exclaimed when they were half-way towards the door. 'I've left my reticule in the carriage.' She hesitated and looked back. 'I should—'

'Don't be silly, Mama.' Violet picked up her skirts. 'I shall go and fetch it.' Night had fallen and the air around them had cooled considerably. 'You should go inside before you catch a chill.'

Before Mama could protest, she hurried back towards the end of the torchlit walkway where the carriage awaited. She could at least delay the inevitable, even for a few minutes. The thought of being inside an enclosed, stuffy room surrounded by strangers making all kinds of chewing and slurping noises made her want to crawl out of her skin. How was she supposed to find a husband with all those distractions?

Slowing her steps, Violet loosened the shawl around her shoulders, took a deep breath and recalled her father's words.

'One step at a time, Violet. Be methodical. Logical.'

Retrieve Mama's reticule.

Return to the manor.

Sit through a torturous dinner.

Find a husband.

Step one first.

As she reached the end of the pathway, however, she saw the Dowager's carriage was gone, and another stood in its place—a sleek, shiny black carriage, trimmed in crimson, with a team of all-black stallions in the lead. Two liveried footmen dressed in red and black stepped off the rear and made their way to the side.

Violet froze, unsure what to do as she blocked the path. At any moment a stranger would come out of the carriage and she would have to subject herself to said stranger's scrutiny. Her only other option was to turn around and run back into the manor. Before she could make a decision, however, the doors opened and a shiny black boot landed on the carriage step, then a second boot met its twin on the gravel.

For some reason Violet could not keep her eyes off the glossy leather tips of the shoes, not even as they came closer.

'Oh, hello.'

The sound of the stranger's voice was not unpleasant, Violet supposed. In fact, there was a rich, deep quality to it that sent a warm feeling across her chest and warded off the chill of the evening air.

'My lady?'

'I'm not a lady.'

'Miss, then?'

Violet managed a nod, even as her gaze remained fixed on the stranger's boots.

'Tell me, miss, is there a spot of mud on my boots? Or is there something else fascinating down there that has kept your attention?'

Swallowing, she slowly raised her head, tracing her gaze up his dark trousers to the well-fitting waistcoat under his coat, up the snowy white shirt and cravat, until it reached a chiselled jaw. The next part was the most difficult—staring people in the eye. But Papa had said it was one of the most important skills she had to learn. And so, no matter how uncomfortable it was, she always looked people in the eyes.

Preparing herself, Violet lifted her gaze—and found herself staring up at the most striking pair of eyes the colour of glittering sapphires. The crinkling at the corners told her the smile he flashed her was genuine but, unable to hold his gaze, she focused her attention on the rest of him, starting with the sharp cheekbones, then his straight, aristocratic nose, then his full, firm lips.

He was unlike any person she'd ever seen before, which prompted her to blurt out the first words that came to her mind.

'You're beautiful.'

His mouth opened and he threw his head back and barked out a laugh.

No one ever laughed when she spoke the truth.

'Why is that funny?'

'I've been called many things, but this is the first time I've been described with that word.'

'Surely that can't be true.' With a quick intake of breath, she briefly locked eyes with him, before focusing on the point between his eyebrows. 'You're probably the most beautiful man I've ever seen.'

'No one calls me beautiful. Handsome and attractive, yes. But never beautiful.'

'Not to your face, perhaps.'

Your beautiful face.

It reminded her of angels painted by the Italian Masters.

'But people say all kinds of things when they think no one is listening.'

'Really?' He leaned forward. 'What kinds of things?'

'Well…mostly what they truly think about a person. It's baffling to me that people only say the truth when they think no one is listening.'

'I should like to know more of these truths. But we should probably go inside. I assume you are a guest of His Grace, the Duke of Mabury?'

'I am.'

'Excellent—as am I. He's one of my best friends, you know.'

'One of them? You have more than one?' Her mouth twisted. 'But the word best implies a superlative—the leading, the top-ranking. How can you possibly categorise His Grace as your "best" friend if there are others sharing the position with him?'

'Yes,' he replied, as if that single word offered any explanation to the paradox she'd laid before him.

When the corner of his mouth quirked up, Violet quickly rifled through her mental catalogue of facial expressions, trying to find its meaning—and coming up short.

'I must say, you are quite refreshing,' he said. 'And since we are both guests at Highfield Park, would you do me the honour of allowing me to escort you inside?'

She stared at the arm he offered. Courtesy would dictate that she take it, and, so she did. Contact with someone else was not always uncomfortable, as long as she did the touching. 'All right.'

His arm was surprisingly firm underneath the fabric of his coat.

'Tell me,' he began as they made their way towards the manor, 'what other truths would you like to share with me?'

'You really want to know?'

He chuckled. 'From the expression on your face, I can guess no one else asks you to share such things.'

She shook her head. 'No. And when I do… Well, it often ends in disaster.'

'Disaster? How so?'

'I danced the quadrille with Mr Jonathan Eldridge a few months ago at a ball. When we had finished, and he asked me if I enjoyed myself, I told him that while the dancing had been tolerable, the stench from his person had not.'

He burst out laughing. 'I hope my scent isn't as unpleasant as Mr Eldridge's?'

Violet lifted her nose and sniffed. 'Not at all, my lord.'

Most manufactured scents offended her senses, but as long as they did not emit a foul smell like Mr Eldridge she had learned to tolerate them.

'I'm glad.' He stopped when they reached the door, which promptly opened. 'Ah, Eames,' he greeted the butler on the other side of the threshold. 'No need to announce me. I'll make my way in. Refreshments in the drawing room?'

The butler's eyes landed briefly on Violet before he spoke, 'Perhaps I should inform——'

He waved him away. 'Thank you, Eames.'

'You've been here before,' Violet observed.

'Sebastian *is* one of my best friends after all,' he said. 'I was best man at his wedding.'

'And I assume there was more than one best man at this wedding?'

He barked out a laugh.

A tight, hot ball formed in Violet's chest. She supposed she should be used to people laughing at her—and in some ways, she was. But coming from him it made her want to run away and hide.

'Lord, I can't remember the last time a woman made me laugh so much.'

Her steps faltered.

He wasn't laughing *at* her.

He was laughing at something she'd said.

She made him laugh.

The most curious warmth spread across her belly, and for a brief moment she didn't quite find looking into his sapphire eyes so excruciating.

'Ah, here we are,' he declared as he steered them towards an open entryway just to the left of the front door.

Violet's chest tightened and sweat built on her palms inside her gloves. The din coming from the room, the mix of smells, and the thought of being among so many strangers made her want to jump out of the window. No matter how many times she'd been in such situations, the initial assault to her senses always threw her off.

Remember what Papa taught you, she told herself.

Briefly, she closed her eyes, then took a deep breath, and then, using her free hand, she began to touch her thumb to each finger as she counted.

'Are you all right?'

She blew out a breath. 'I…yes.'

'You seem a tad pale.' He frowned. 'I did not even think… Surely you didn't come alone? Do you have a companion… a husband?'

She shook her head, tried to speak, but her throat was too dry.

'Would you like a drink? Perhaps some water?'

She answered with a nod. 'P-please.'

'Wait here.'

Her protest remained stuck in her throat as he walked away. Violet wanted to go after him, but he strode into the crowded room. Seconds and then minutes passed by, but she could not bring herself to proceed. It was as if she was stuck in time while the rest of the world continued to move.

'There you are.'

Spinning around, she found her mother behind her, along with the Dowager. 'Your Grace,' she greeted her, curtseying to their hostess.

'Good evening, Miss Avery, how lovely you look,' the Dowager remarked.

'Did I see you speaking with a man?' Mama asked, her gaze narrowing. 'Who was that?'

'I…I don't know.' How on earth had she had an entire

conversation with a man whose name she didn't even know? 'I was chasing after the carriage when he appeared. Then he escorted me inside. He said the Duke is one of his best friends.'

The Dowager's face lit up. 'Ah, that must be Ash.'

'Ash?' Mama asked.

'Devon St James, the Marquess of Ashbrooke,' the Dowager explained.

Mama's eyes turned as large as saucers. 'Your Grace, does the Marquess have a wife?'

'Er...no.'

'An unmarried marquess.' Mama's fingers steepled together. 'And do you think he's suitable for my Violet?'

The Dowager hesitated. 'I suppose... But I'm not sure if he's in search of a wife. Not at this time.'

'Why not? He's a marquess, isn't he? Surely he must need to produce an heir. And my Violet would be suited to such a task.'

'Me?'

Married to that beautiful man?

The very idea had Violet's heart lurching, though not out of terror. No, this was a different feeling altogether, and just the thought of his handsome face was enough to soothe the anxiousness in her.

Mama laughed aloud. 'Yes, and why not? Violet, what great luck—catching the eye of a marquess before the night has even begun.'

'Mama—'

'Soon people will be calling you "my lady". My daughter...the Marchioness of Ashbrooke! You can have all the fine things in life.'

Before she could protest that the only thing she wanted was to save Oakwood Cottage and her father's library, someone clearing his throat caught their attention. Slowly, she turned her head, her gaze briefly meeting twin sapphire jewels.

'Your Grace,' he murmured, bowing his head towards the Dowager. In his hand was a glass of water, but he didn't offer it to Violet. Instead, his gloved fingers tightened around it.

'Ash, how lovely to see you here tonight. I don't believe you've been introduced to our guests,' the Dowager said. 'This is Lady Avery and her daughter Miss Violet Avery. Lady Avery, Miss Avery, this is Devon St James, Marquess of Ashbrooke.'

Violet wasn't sure what had happened, but it was as if all the air in the room had been siphoned away. Ashbrooke's entire body stiffened as he briefly glanced at her. His expression, however, was one Violet could easily read, because she'd seen it many times before—disdain.

'My lord,' Lady Avery fawned. 'My daughter tells me you found her outside all by herself. I had sent her to retrieve my reticule, and when she didn't return I thought I'd lost her. Thank you for finding her. We owe you a debt of gratitude.'

'I'm sure Miss Avery would have found another saviour,' he muttered.

'My lord—'

'If you excuse me, I see someone I must speak with,' he said, cutting her off by turning on his heel and then walking away.

He was barely out of earshot when Lady Avery exclaimed, 'Oh, he's so handsome—and young too. He will make a fine husband.'

'Um…shall we move inside for refreshments?' the Dowager suggested.

'Do you think Violet could be seated next to the Marquess?' Mama asked. 'Surely now that he's acquainted with her, he'll want to be near her?'

'I believe Eames has already settled the seating arrangements,' the Dowager explained. 'And he does work so hard on these things.'

'Perhaps we could switch with someone...'

Violet watched as Ashbrooke continued to walk way. He hadn't even given her the glass of water in his hand. What could have changed in the time since he'd walked away from her and then come back?

As she followed her mother and the Dowager into the drawing room, she couldn't help but search for him amongst the throng of guests. When she did find him, she almost regretted it. The Marquess was standing by the fireplace mantel, drink in hand, as he spoke to a pretty blonde woman in a blue satin dress. As she continued to stare at them he turned his head towards her, then frowned, his lips twisting into a cruel line, before resuming his conversation.

Anxiety rose in Violet, growing three, four, five-fold as the evening dragged on. But it wasn't the people, the noise, or even the smells that caused her nerves to fray.

No, it was the presence of a single man, seated all the way at the other end of the table with their host and hostess, that caused the discomfort in her.

'How are you supposed to continue your acquaintance with the Marquess from all the way down here?' Mama said with a pout. 'Really... I was the wife of a gentleman. We should be seated further up. Violet, you must do something.'

Violet looked down at her roasted pheasant. She didn't dare look towards the Marquess. She could not bear to see the scorn on his face again.

I suppose I should be used to it by now.

But it was difficult to ignore this time, and even harder to brush off—like burrs stuck on the hem of her dress.

When dinner was finally over, the Duke announced that the men would head to the library for cigars and port and the women would go to the parlour for tea and sherry. As the guests began to file out, Violet breathed out a sigh of relief, thinking she was finally being granted a reprieve. Mama, however, had other thoughts, and she dragged Violet away, blocking the remaining gentlemen—and effectively Ashbrooke—from leaving.

'My lord!' Lady Avery exclaimed. 'You did not get a chance to converse with Violet during dinner.'

The Marquess, who was flanked by a group of equally well-dressed gentlemen, lifted a blond eyebrow. 'You must be lost, Lady Avery.' Someone behind him guffawed. 'The parlour is that way.' He gestured behind Violet.

Lady Avery's cheeks turned pink. 'Ah, yes, indeed. I must have been mistaken.'

She sidestepped, tugging at Violet's arm. And as the gentlemen passed, she couldn't help but feel their gazes upon her. One of them even poked his elbow into Ashbrooke's side, whispering loudly enough for Violet to hear. 'They do grow more desperate each year, don't they, Ash?'

'All the more reason not to let their hooks get into you,' another replied—which caused the others to agree, with mocking laughs.

A sinking pit opened up in Violet's chest and she desperately wished for her entire body to shrink until it turned into a minuscule speck of dust, imperceptible to the naked eye.

Mama's fingers grasped at her hand, but she was too numb to pull away.

'I think you've made an impression.'

'That is one way to put it.'

But Violet had a feeling that the Marquess would never look her way again. He would never give her another genuine smile, nor laugh at something she said.

'Come, we should make our way to the parlour with the other ladies.'

Violet allowed her mother to lead her towards the parlour, though she desperately wanted to run back to the dower house and hide in her room.

'There you are,' the Dowager greeted them as they entered the parlour. Thankfully, it was only half as raucous as it had been in the dining room, which was a relief for Violet. 'I want you to meet my daughter-in-law. Kate, this is Lady Avery and Miss Violet Avery. Lady Avery, Miss Avery, this is Kate, Duchess of Mabury.'

'What an honour to meet you, Your Grace,' Mama greeted her as they curtseyed.

Violet sneaked a quick glance at the pretty Duchess, who was much younger than she had imagined—perhaps only a year or two older than herself—with dark brown hair and blue eyes. Her hand lay on top of the noticeable bump of her belly.

'It's my pleasure,' the Duchess said. 'Are you enjoying your time here at Highfield Park? I do hope you're comfortable at the dower house. If there is anything at all you need, you have only to ask.'

The Duchess's canorous tone and rounded, prolonged vowels pricked at Violet's ears. 'You are not English.'

'I am not,' she said with a warm laugh. 'I'm American.'

'Violet…' Mama warned. 'Forgive her forwardness, Your Grace. She is…tired.'

'There is nothing to forgive, Lady Avery.' The corner of the Duchess's mouth tugged up. 'We Americans happen to find candour admirable and efficient.'

'That's what I have always thought,' Violet added. 'Why waste time using twenty words when you can convey the same meaning in ten?'

The Duchess looked at the Dowager, who smiled back at her. 'I regret that it has taken me so long to meet with you. I have been occupied for the last few months.'

'Of course, Your Grace. Quite understandable.' Lady Avery's eyes quickly darted to the Duchess's middle. 'I'm sure His Grace insists you take as much rest as possible.'

The Duchess let out a burst of laughter. 'Sebastian *wishes* he could tell me what to do,' she said wryly. 'But I can't possibly stay in bed—not when I'm so close to finishing my prototype.'

'Prototype?' Violet asked.

'My daughter-in-law is a locomotive engineer,' the Dowager began, and then proceeded to tell them about how the Duchess's family owned the most successful railway company in America, and that she and the Duke had their own locomotives factory just outside London.

'I've been around steam engines all my life,' the Duchess declared. 'I helped my grandfather, Henry Mason, design his greatest creation—'

'You helped design the Andersen?' Violet interrupted.

The Duchess's jaw dropped. 'You've heard of it?'

'I read about the Andersen in a journal from a few years ago. It's supposed to be one of the most advanced steam locomotives today. And you had a hand in making it?'

'It was mostly Pap's work—that's my grandfather—but he taught me everything I know. He worked as an engineer in the coal mines in West Virginia, you see. Once my father had made his fortune in real estate, he brought us to New York and financed the factory. And, well… Pap had this idea for a steam engine, and after a few years of working on it together we were able to build a prototype, and then eventually it went into production. And now I'm building my own—bigger and better than the Andersen.'

'Oh, I wish I could see it,' Violet said. 'How are you planning to maximise efficiency in the engine?'

The Duchess flashed her a genuine smile, then looped her arm through Violet's. 'Miss Avery, I think we are going to get along quite well. It will be nice to have a new friend around.'

Friend. The word was not something Violet heard often—especially not being applied to herself.

'How wonderful.' Mama clapped her hands together. 'And perhaps we could accompany Her Grace to various functions around London sometimes? For example, a ball?'

Violet's elation quickly deflated at Mama's words, reminding her that she had to find a rich husband in order to save Oakwood Cottage. That sinking pit in her chest returned too, as she remembered the Marquess's sudden cold demeanour towards her.

'There will be plenty of time for that,' the Duchess said diplomatically. 'But, come. Let's sit down for some sherry and we can talk more about my prototype.'

There's nothing you can do for now…not about the Marquess or Oakwood Cottage.

So Violet decided then and there that she would put thoughts of saving Papa's library aside for now, and of the Marquess—permanently.

Violet had thought that the whole business with the Marquess was well and truly over and she would never see him again.

Hours and hours of discourse and debate with her father had honed Violet's logical mind. While there were many mysteries in the world she did not comprehend, she did lean towards the belief that man created his own fate instead of the idea that fate controlled man.

But perhaps, just this once, fate—or some higher power—did indeed control Violet's life. Because she encountered the Marquess of Ashbrooke once again, not even a fortnight later, this time in Hyde Park.

Violet had got along splendidly with the Duchess—Kate, as she had insisted on being called—in the days since they'd met. And when Kate and the Duke had returned to London, the Dowager had suggested they come along and stay at Mabury House, much to Mama's delight. Violet had been to Town once in her life and vowed never to return. The smells, sounds and general chaos there made her want to pull out her hair. This time, however, she had looked forward to it, as Kate had promised to take her to see the locomotives factory.

Alas, as soon as they'd arrived Kate and the Dowager had been called away, as a dear friend of theirs had been injured in some kind of house fire. That had been days ago, and due to Kate's busy schedule and her visits to her injured friend, Persephone, there had been no time for Violet to visit the factory. So today, tired of being inside, Mama had decided they should go Hyde Park.

'Finally, some fresh air,' Mama declared as they walked along one of the tree-lined paths inside the lush parkland. 'We've been indoors for so long... This will do wonders for your health.'

'The air here is hardly fresh compared to Surrey or Hampshire.' Violet's nose wrinkled. Still, Hyde Park was one of the more peaceful places in raucous London. 'And isn't the sun bad for my complexion?'

'That's why you should carry— Oh! What luck.'

'Luck?'

Mama's eyes gleamed, then she nodded ahead. 'Look who it is.'

Violet followed Lady Avery's gaze—and nearly stumbled as she spotted the familiar tall and lean form of the Marquess of Ashbrooke.

'Oh, no.'

He was not alone, either. No, he was surrounded once again by a group of well-heeled people, with servants and chaperons trailing behind them. Most of them were men, but a beautiful young blonde woman dressed in an emerald-green gown embroidered with peacock feathers clung to Ashbrooke's arm. She leaned close as she whispered something to the Marquess, causing him to throw his head back and laugh.

Violet was too far away to confirm if his laugh was genuine or not, but still an unknown emotion stabbed her in the chest, reminding her that when they'd first met she herself had been in the same position as the young woman—before the Marquess's countenance had changed.

'He's coming this way,' Mama announced. 'We must meet him head-on.'

Violet's inner voice screamed in protest, but it was too late as Mama dragged her forward. Violet nearly toppled over as her mother practically threw her at the unsuspecting Marquess. His sapphire eyes grew wide as she collided with him. His arms darted out to catch her. Firm hands wrapped around her bare upper arms, keeping her upright. The unexpected contact sent a jolt through her.

A murmur grew among his friends, and some of them were whispering amongst themselves as they stared at Violet.

Ashbrooke quickly released her. Though his hands had been gloved, they left a brand on her she could not explain.

'Are you mad?' he muttered.

She could understand why he would think that. Most people thought she was. Papa had said it wasn't her fault, but sometimes she thought…maybe it was. Perhaps there was something fundamentally broken within her and she just couldn't understand the world around her.

'My lord, once again you have saved my daughter!' Mama tittered. 'She might have fallen and hurt herself.'

'She does seem to be in the habit of getting in people's way,' someone quipped.

Violet recognised the speaker as one of the guests from the dinner party at Highfield Park.

The young woman who had been on Ashbrooke's arm covered her mouth and giggled. 'Oh, is this *her*?' She eyed Lady Avery. 'And this is the mother?'

Violet's gaze snapped to her and she blurted out, 'Did you know in some cultures peacock feathers are considered a bad omen?'

Mama's face turned a deep shade of red. 'Violet!'

She bit her lip. She couldn't help it, after all. When faced with a situation that she could not easily comprehend, she tended to spout random facts she'd recalled from Papa's books.

The Marquess's expression had turned inscrutable. 'Perhaps we should be on our way, or else the best areas for our picnic shall be occupied.'

Without even a nod, he sidestepped Violet and Lady Avery, then continued down the path, his entourage trailing behind.

Violet stared after them, wondering if she'd done something wrong. But it wasn't her fault; Mama had been the one to fling her at him.

'Well, I never,' Mama said with a click of her tongue. 'And I thought he was a lovely young man… Don't worry, Violet, we are in London now, and there will be plenty of eligible gentlemen vying to court you.'

Unfortunately, Mama's prediction did not come true— not even a little bit.

Violet attended a few more events over the next few days—tea at Lady Highbridge's, the opera, a play at the Adelphi, and even a ball—but she had no gentlemen callers. That would usually have been a relief for Violet, except Mama's constant reminders of their dire situation were difficult to ignore.

'I don't understand,' Mama cried, wringing her hands together. 'We've been here two hours and you've only danced once.'

This evening they were attending a ball at the fashionable home of Viscount and Viscountess Walden, with not only the Dowager, but also the Duke of Mabury and Kate. Many members of the Ton had approached their group, but mostly to speak with Mabury. A few had glanced over at Violet and her mother, murmuring greetings when they were introduced, but all of them had quickly found excuses to leave.

Despite her aversion to touch, dancing did not pose a problem for Violet. In fact, she found it rather soothing: she knew what to expect and could anticipate where her partner's hands would rest upon her. But, more importantly, dancing had rules in place, steps to follow, and everything was based on counting. Papa had once declared it as just another way numbers and maths kept things in order.

Even so, while dancing at balls did not unnerve her, she had only danced twice since coming to London. The one gentleman she had danced with was an old acquaintance of the Dowager. And Lord Hornsby was indeed old—Violet guessed he was at least seventy—and had seemed offended when she'd asked if he would be able to finish the reel, seeing as he seemed to be suffering from stiff limbs. As soon as the dance had ended he had brought her back to her mother and limped off in a huff.

'Violet has only been London for a little over a fortnight,' the Dowager reasoned. 'Perhaps the gentlemen require some time to…to warm to her presence.'

Violet had counted seven men who'd asked for an introduction at Lady Highbridge's tea, five at the opera, three at the Adelphi, and two dances at her last ball. With each outing in London, it seemed, the amount of gentlemen who approached dwindled. Seeing such a downward trend, Violet suspected she could radiate the same heat as the sun and the Ton's shoulders would remain frozen as snow.

'If you will excuse me? I require the retiring room,' she announced.

'As do I.' Kate looped her arm through Violet's. 'Come, let us go together.'

The two women made their way together across the room, and when they reached the parlour which had been assigned as the ladies' retiring room a footman opened the door for them.

Please be empty. Please be empty.

When she stepped in and found the room unoccupied, Violet let out a sigh of relief, then plopped down on the nearest settee. 'It's hopeless,' she declared. 'I will never find a husband.'

Kate blew out a breath. 'Oh, Violet, don't say that. Like Mama said, perhaps you just need some time.'

'I'm not upset. At least, not about the lack of suitors.'

The Duchess sat down next to her. 'You're not? But you have just said you'll never find a husband.'

'I don't *want* a husband,' she declared flatly.

'You don't?'

'No. But I need one. Preferably with means.'

Very substantial means.

Frowning, the Duchess said, 'Explain.'

And so Violet did, starting with the death of her father and finishing with the dire straits she and Mama were now in.

'She will not tell me how much time we have, exactly, but I suspect it is not a lot. That's why I require a husband, a rich one, so that I may save Oakwood Cottage.'

If she did not find a wealthy husband she would completely lose the last links to her father.

'I didn't realise…' Kate straightened her shoulders. 'Then we must do what we can to find you a husband. Mama was able to help me find one, and she'll do the same for you.'

'The Dowager wouldn't happen to have another son hidden away somewhere, would she?'

'I'm afraid not.'

'I didn't think so.' Crossing her arms over her chest, she blew out a breath. 'It is hopeless.'

'Don't give up yet; you've only just started your London Season. There's plenty of time. I do hate to see you like this, Violet… How about we go to the factory tomorrow?' Kate suggested. 'Would that lift your spirits?'

Violet took a deep breath. 'Truly?'

Her friend's head bobbed up and down vigorously. 'Yes.

Persephone's on the mend, and I've finally caught up with my work. We could spend the afternoon there, if you like.'

For the first time in days, Violet's spirits lifted. 'That would be wonderful.'

Perhaps, just for tomorrow, she could put aside all thoughts of searching for a husband and distract herself at the factory.

Chapter Two

~~~~~~~~~~~~~~~

London,
New Year's Eve, 1843

Devon St James, Marquess of Ashbrooke—Ash to those who considered him a friend and an assortment of names that could never be uttered in polite society to those who did not—stepped into the grand hall of the large house on Upper Brook Street as soon as the door opened. To his surprise, his host was waiting on the other side, tapping his foot impatiently.

'What a magnificent house, Your Grace,' Ash teased. 'You truly have moved up in the world. Or should I say up from The Underworld?'

'Hello to you too, Ash,' replied Ransom, Duke of Winford, with a sardonic lift of a dark eyebrow. 'And Happy New Year.'

'I know you and Persephone value your privacy at home—even this temporary one.' Ash removed his coat and handed it to the footman standing by the door. 'So imagine my surprise when I received your invitation to this party. I didn't think you'd invite *me*, of all people.'

'Well...' Ransom crossed his arms over his chest. 'You are my best friend after all.'

Ash stumbled on the marble floor, nearly toppling forward, but managed to find his footing. He'd expected Ransom would bite out some cynical reply, or imply Ash hadn't been invited, but his actual words had caught him off guard. However, when he saw the corner of the other man's mouth lift, he barked out a laugh.

'You did that on purpose.'

Ransom, out of the three men he considered his best friends, would be the last one ever to admit the existence of their friendship.

Ransom merely smirked. 'Come. You're fashionably late, as usual, and everyone is waiting.'

As he followed Ransom down the corridor, Ash let out a whistle as he glanced around the sumptuous surroundings. 'This truly is a magnificent home. How did you manage to snag it? Did some degenerate who owed you thousands of pounds hand it over?'

Aside from holding a prestigious title, Ransom also owned a popular gentleman's club in London, making him perhaps one of the richest and most powerful men in England. Not that Ash resented him for that—after all, he himself had a respected title and, while not as rich as Croesus, like Ransom, was wealthy enough to indulge in all the activities a peer like himself needed and wanted to pursue.

'Something like that,' Ransom answered immediately. 'We couldn't keep staying at a hotel after the fire.'

A few weeks back Ransom's home and his club, The Underworld, had burned down, when the kitchen boiler had exploded. Thankfully, no one had perished during the incident. Despite not being in Town when it had happened, Ash still felt a knot tighten in his chest at the knowledge that both Ransom and Persephone had been inside during the disaster.

'Ransom, I truly am glad you and Persephone are safe,' he said, his tone sombre.

The Duke's back stiffened, then relaxed. 'Thank you, Ash.'

Clearing his throat, he clapped Ransom on the shoulder. 'And how *is* your lovely wife?'

Ransom's face lit up at the mention of his duchess. 'She's well and fully recovered. And for some reason she's looking forward to seeing you, so we should hurry along.'

That only made him chuckle. 'I've been told I have that effect on women.'

Ash wasn't blind, of course, nor dull-witted. He knew he was handsome and charming, and it was a fact he fully exploited, allowing him to seduce any woman into his bed. Indeed, no female below the age of eighty could resist his charms, and he wasn't ashamed of his 'accomplishments'. In fact, he fully intended to take advantage of his bachelorhood until his hair and his teeth fell out. And, while all three of his best friends seemed happy enough with their wives, Ash knew he would never find himself shackled in the bonds of matrimony.

A memory from long ago threatened to rise up.

A vivid image of a beautiful summer day.

The swish of cotton and silk.

The slamming of a door.

Ash quickly quashed the image. 'Where is everybody?' he asked as they entered the empty parlour.

'Already seated for dinner.' Ransom gestured to the doorway across the room. 'Kate, Sebastian, and the Dowager arrived over an hour ago.'

'Such a formal affair for six people?'

Ash had guessed that it would just be their hosts, Kate, Mabury and the Dowager tonight. The last grand affair

Ransom had hosted had been his own wedding, and he had hardly been able to stand being around the members of the Ton then. No, judging from the handwritten note he had received a few days ago, this had to be an intimate affair.

'Eight, actually,' Ransom corrected him. 'The Dowager has invited her protégée and her mother.'

'Protégée? I didn't realise the Dowager had taken another debutante under her wing.'

In past year or so the Dowager Duchess of Mabury had sponsored a few young misses for the London Season. Kate and Persephone had been two such debutantes.

'And who—'

Once again Ash found himself nearly stumbling as he missed the small step leading into the dining room because his gaze had landed on the familiar woman sitting at the dining table, staring up at him with those mesmerising eyes before quickly turning away.

Miss Violet Avery.

A roaring sound filled his ears and his heart slammed into his chest at the sight of her, just as it had the first time he'd seen her that night on the torchlit pathway at Highfield Park.

Even now, the damned organ trapped behind his ribcage was beating out a rhythm not unlike the drums of the young men out wassailing tonight, hoping to ward off evil spirits before the New Year arrived.

He had never encountered anyone so breathtakingly lovely. Despite his years of experience and countless lovers over the last decade, he could not remember a single woman who could compare to Miss Violet Avery's beauty—thick sable hair, light blue eyes ringed with dark navy, a sensuous pink mouth and that tempting beauty mark over her lip. She was so achingly beautiful he'd thought he must be hallucinating.

But more than her physical attributes, there was something else about her that he just couldn't put his finger on. She had made quite an impression on him in the short time during that walk between his carriage and the door. Her wit and unique charm had made him laugh—truly laugh aloud, not pretend to for the sake of trying to lure in a beautiful woman. For the first time in his life he'd found he was actually listening to what she was saying and wanting to hear her talk.

But as it turned out she was just like any other debutante on London's notorious marriage mart and had her sights set on him. Why, her audacious mother had practically declared him in the bag, calling her 'the Marchioness of Ashbrooke' to everyone within earshot.

Had she known he was coming tonight? Perhaps she'd waited for his carriage to arrive so she could position herself at the right place to bump into him that night they met. It wouldn't be the first time some brazen husband-hunter had schemed to entrap him.

'You're beautiful.'

Those had been the first words she had said to him.

It had caught him off guard, to say the least. Was that part of her plan? It irritated the hell out of Ash that she'd fooled him—*him*, of all people—into thinking she was different from all the other women of the Ton.

But what the devil was she doing here?

'Ash,' Persephone, Duchess of Winford, greeted him. 'I see you've finally arrived,' she said playfully, in her lilting Scottish burr.

He tore his eyes away from Miss Avery and turned to

the Duchess. 'Persephone, you look ravishing tonight. Forgive me for my tardiness. Thank you for the invitation.'

Of course, had he known who else was on the guest list, he would have instantly declined.

Ransom cleared his throat. 'Perhaps we could get back to eating? My dinner is getting cold.'

'Of course. But first, do introduce our guests to Ash.'

Ah, so Miss Avery was the Dowager's new protégée. *What a pity.*

'We've met, actually,' he said curtly. 'At Highfield Park. Lady Avery… Miss Avery.'

'My lord,' Lady Avery chittered, her cheeks puffing excitedly. 'How wonderful to see you again after all this time.'

Miss Avery, on the other hand, seemed to find something on her lap riveting as her head lowered to avoid his gaze.

Ah, so she does feel some shame.

'I'm sure it is,' he replied coolly. 'Now, where shall I sit?'

'Beside Mabury,' Persephone instructed. 'We're not seated formally for tonight. I missed having cosy family New Year's Eve dinners like we did back in Scotland with my brothers and I, so I told Ransom I wanted a small affair with just all of us.'

'And I, for one, am glad we don't have to sit through a boring, stuffy dinner with people we don't even like.' Kate raised a glass. 'Come, Ash, have a seat.'

'Kate… Sebastian,' he greeted them. 'Congratulations on the birth of Henry. How is the little one? I apologise for not coming to visit yet.'

Sebastian glowered at his wife. 'He's at home, sleeping. Unlike *some* people.'

'Don't look at me like that, Sebastian,' Kate retorted. 'I don't even know why I'm supposed to stay at home for a whole six weeks when I'm perfectly fine. I simply gave birth, for God's sake. Women have been doing it since the dawn of time. Besides, he's just a few doors away. The nanny will send for us if there's anything wrong.'

'Ah…perhaps I can stop by later to see my godson?' Ash enquired.

'I don't recall asking you to be my son's godfather,' Sebastian said.

'Tut-tut…minor details.'

He took his place at the empty chair between Sebastian and the Dowager. Unfortunately, that meant he was seated across from Miss Avery, but thankfully, throughout the meal, Ash only had to converse with his friends. Lady Avery tried to catch his attention a few times, but Ash pretended not to hear her when she called his name.

Still, when he thought no one was looking, Ash allowed his gaze to stray towards Miss Avery. She looked calm as a millpond, eating her food methodically, almost mechanically, cutting it into even-sized pieces before lifting each morsel to that plump mouth. He scrutinised the way her long lashes cast shadows over her high cheekbones. Even let his gaze stray lower, down to the tempting low neckline—

'Ash, did you hear what I said?'

Ash's head snapped back towards his host. 'Yes?'

'Never mind.'

But Ransom sent him a silent, warning look.

Ash sank back into his seat. It wasn't his fault Miss Avery was so damned tempting—even if she *was* a deceitful little schemer. Why, the chit and her mother had even had the gall to stalk him at Hyde Park.

Ash had planned a picnic outing there, with his old university friends. At least it should have just been him and his friends, but one of them—Lord George Jacobs—had brought his sister Lady Helen along at the last minute. Ash hadn't been able to tell her to leave, even though he'd suspected she had had her eye on him since her coming out earlier that year, and she had clung to his arm as they'd made their way into the park.

As she'd chattered on about nothing, Ash had found his mind and attention drifting away—which was why he hadn't noticed Miss Avery careering towards him until it had been too late. While he should have let her crash to the ground for attempting such a brazen stunt, he'd nonetheless found himself catching her anyway. Besides, it had been a good excuse to prise Lady Helen's claws from his arm.

He had not been prepared, however, to have Miss Avery so close that she'd practically been in his embrace. The smell of her lavender and powder-scented perfume had been enough to send his heart racing like mad once again. When his friends had begun to mock her, he had done his best to steer them away, but of course Miss Avery, her strange behaviour and her outrageous mother, had been a topic of conversation for the rest of the day.

'She must truly be fixated on bagging you, Ash,' Lord George had remarked. *'Twice now she has schemed to catch your attention.'*

Damn George. He'd forgotten that he had been at Highfield Park and witnessed that incident after dinner when Lady Avery had tried to block his way.

'And what a strange girl,' Lady Helen had said with a huff, plucking an imaginary piece of lint from the blue-green embroidery on her gown. *'Going on about peacock feathers and bad omens.'*

That had actually made Ash want to laugh so badly that he'd had to bite the inside of his cheek until it had nearly bled to stop himself.

'Bizarre,' Lord George had harrumphed.

'But you must admit she is a beauty,' someone else had remarked.

'A bizarre beauty.'

Ash had blurted it out thoughtlessly, but it had nonetheless made his companions break into fits of laughter.

That incident had been weeks ago, and frankly Ash had mostly forgotten about it. But he had not forgotten Miss Avery. Though he hadn't run into her again, she was like a gnat, buzzing around him, and the memory of her eyes or her laugh landed in his mind at random times of the day.

He'd thought that after some time he would forget about her. But now it seemed, because of her connection to the Dowager, if he wanted to spend time with his friends, he must also endure her company and that of her mama.

'That was a splendid dinner.' Kate wiped her mouth with her napkin and placed it on her plate. 'Thank you, Ransom, Persephone, for this invitation.'

'The night isn't over yet.' As Persephone stood, all the men were prompted to follow suit. 'We must now wait for midnight which is...' she glanced at the clock '...only two hours from now. I've arranged treats and amusements for us in the library.'

As Persephone had promised, there were indeed treats in the library. Aside from the usual refreshments—port, sherry, tea and coffee—there was a table laden with sweetmeats, gingerbread, four kinds of pudding, mincemeat pies, sugar plums and wassail punch. The household staff had also prepared board games, parlour games, and a card table was set up in the middle of the room.

Kate, Sebastian, Persephone and Miss Avery decided to sit down to a game of whist, while the Dowager and Lady Avery enjoyed some sherry as they watched on.

Ash joined Ransom by the fireplace for port and cigars,

making sure to keep his back towards the room. From the look his friend had given him earlier, he wouldn't be surprised if Ransom suspected he was gawking at Miss Avery, and he didn't want to give his friend the wrong impression.

Well, he *was* gawking—but it was Miss Avery's fault.

Once they had glasses in hand and cigars lit, Ash launched into conversation, hoping Ransom wouldn't ask him about his non-gawking.

'How are the renovations at The Underworld progressing?'

'Very well.' Ransom took a sip from his glass. 'I'm just glad the clean-up is done now and we can finally start building. Seeing it straight after the explosion was heartbreaking.' His eyes drifted somewhere over Ash's left shoulder—most likely towards his wife. 'Persephone was inconsolable for days. But moving here and planning our honeymoon has been a good distraction for her.

'When do you start building?'

'As soon as we can. I need to get The Underworld back in business as soon as possible. But finding the right company is exhausting and no one can get—' He frowned.

'No one can get what?'

Ransom didn't answer. Instead, his hawk-like gaze focused on something behind Ash.

'Ransom?'

'Hmmm…' The Duke's lips pressed together. 'Card-counting.'

Ash glanced over his shoulder towards the card players. 'Oh, yes. Mabury's good at that.'

'Not him.'

Ransom brushed past him and strode off towards the players.

Not him?

Intrigued, Ash followed suit, walking to where Ransom hovered by the card table. Kate and Miss Avery were paired up, while Sebastian and Persephone played together. Normally in such settings, whist was a fun, social activity. However, a thick tension hung in the air as the players rapidly played trick after trick. Or rather it was Sebastian and Miss Avery who were quickly dominating the game, their eyes darting back and forth from their hands to the cards on the table, each one winning every other trick or so.

Damn. Ash didn't play much whist, but it was dizzying watching them play. He'd only seen this magnitude of intensity in gaming halls, where whole fortunes were at stake.

Once the last trick was played and all the cards were gone, Sebastian turned to his opponent. 'Good game, Miss Avery.'

Kate looked at the young miss, then at Sebastian, with disbelief. 'But we haven't tallied the points yet.'

'I assure you, your team has won, my love.' Sebastian flashed her a smile. 'Isn't that right, Miss Avery?'

She nodded.

Kate's jaw dropped, then a grin spread across her face. 'I can't believe it. Someone has finally beaten you at cards. Splendid job, Violet. I knew you could do it.'

Ash scrutinised Sebastian, searching his face for anything that might indicate that he had let the girl win, but found no such clue. In fact, the Duke looked amused that he'd been defeated by a woman.

Lady Avery scrambled towards her daughter. 'Your Grace, you must forgive her…'

'There is nothing to forgive, Lady Avery. Your daughter won the game.'

Horror crossed her face. 'Violet, you should not have done that.'

'Done what, Mama?'

The low, husky voice jolted Ash into attention, and he realised this was the first time he'd heard her speak all evening.

'Defeated His Grace at cards. It's…unladylike.'

She blinked up at her mother. 'How so?'

'Oh, child, this is exactly why you…' She drifted off, then shook her head. 'A wife must humble herself to her husband. If you hurt his pride, no man will want you.'

A protest rose in Ash, but before he could say anything Miss Avery spoke up. 'First of all, Mama, His Grace is already married, so there is no need for me to "humble" myself to him.'

Ash found himself mesmerised by the throaty, smooth quality of her voice…like dark velvet brushing on his skin.

'And secondly,' she continued, 'why should I hide my skill and knowledge just to save a man's pride?'

'What good is skill and knowledge if you end up as a spinster?'

Without a beat, she retorted, '"There is only one good, knowledge, and one evil, ignorance."'

'Socrates,' Kate and Persephone said at the same time.

Lady Avery pressed the back of her hand to her forehead. 'Violet, you will be the—'

The doors opening to admit two footmen carrying trays of champagne flutes interrupted them.

Persephone glanced at the clock. 'It's almost midnight.' Walking over to the pianoforte, she waved at the Dowager. 'Your Grace, would you do us the honour?'

As everyone gathered around when the Dowager played the first few notes to 'Auld Lang Syne', Ash couldn't help but study Miss Avery once again, his mind drifting back to that torchlit path that very first evening they'd met. For a moment it was as if everything that had happened between that short conversation and now had never occurred, and he was once again staring at the breathtaking beauty who had made him laugh and captivated him with her refreshing wit.

Ash shook his head mentally and took a swig of champagne.

No, that couldn't be right.

He could not allow himself to think that way. She might be a beauty, and perhaps possessed an ounce more intelligence than most, but Miss Avery was no different from all the opportunistic husband-hunters in London. He would be damned before he allowed himself to be caught in her trap. His reaction to her was merely a case of lust from not having had a woman in his bed these last few weeks.

Yes, that was it, Ash thought to himself as he took another sip of champagne. This was simply a case of pent-up frustration.

'Happy New Year!' everyone shouted as the clock struck twelve and began to chime.

As all the guests cheered and clicked their wine glasses, Ash decided that now it was the New Year, it was time to seek out some new, friendly company.

'There must be something amiss. Or perhaps something we haven't done yet to attract a suitable husband for Violet,' Lady Avery said. 'It just doesn't seem right that my daughter hasn't had a single suitor in all this time.'

The Dowager placed a comforting hand on Lady Avery's arm. 'Not every girl is a success in the first few weeks of her Season.'

'But we've been in London for nearly four months now, and we've attended dozens of events. And aside from a few conversations here and there, no one has paid her a call or even shown interest in courting her. There *must* be something wrong.'

While Lady Avery did not always act within the bounds of reason and logic, Violet found herself agreeing with her mother because the evidence did seem to support her theory. By her count, in almost four months in London, she had attended fifty-two events, including ten balls.

She had been introduced to thirty-seven gentlemen, although only twenty-three of them were unmarried, and danced thirteen and a half times—the half was due to the fact that her partner during ball number eight, the Honourable Gregory Talbot, had seemingly lost his way after changing partners during a quadrille and had not returned to her. She could only assume he was still out there, wandering about London.

And she had exactly zero prospects.

To Violet, the numbers simply did not add up. Surely by this time she should have had at least one call from a gentleman.

Perhaps Mama was correct: something was definitely wrong.

Kate sent her a sympathetic look. 'Do not fret, Violet. I'm certain you will find a suitor. Maybe even tonight. There are so many more gentlemen here, and now we've expanded our search to include a few international prospects.'

Tonight, she, Mama, the Dowager and the Duke and Duchess were in attendance at a gathering at the Spanish Ambassador's house. Violet had dreaded the prospect of attempting to mingle with the diplomatic set. After her months in London she was now able to observe the rhythms of London society, making it less daunting to navigate. The people tonight, however, with their own ways and pace and patterns, were an entirely new variable to her. However, she'd had no choice in the matter.

'Violet, please be careful with what you say,' Mama warned her. 'You cannot risk offending more people.'

'Only half the guests here can even understand me, so I'm quite certain that there is a lower chance of me offending anyone.'

Mama let out an impatient breath. 'Still, you must try to keep your thoughts to yourself.'

Violet tried. She really, truly tried. Each time a thought popped into her head she kept it to herself. And it worked—most of the time. There were instances where she just could not help herself, however—like when she'd asked Lady Katherine Pearson to please stop playing the pianoforte because it sounded like a dying warbler being trampled by a cart. The noise had been unbearable, and had driven her to breaking point.

Mama continued. 'And Violet, don't forget to—'

Kate cleared her throat and stood up. 'I must visit the necessary. Violet, would you be so kind as to accompany me?'

'Yes.' Violet practically leapt up from her seat. 'I would very much like that.'

Once they were out of earshot of Violet's mother, Kate said, 'I don't really require the necessary. But I thought maybe you'd like a few minutes away from your mother.'

'Thank you.' She breathed a sigh of relief. 'I really am trying, Kate.'

'I know.' She bit her lip. 'I mean…if I may be frank?'

'Always.'

'Violet, you're a stunning beauty. You may not be perfect, but I still cannot fathom why you have no prospects after all this time. Even if they aren't rich or titled, surely at least one man should have shown interest in you.' Her dark eyebrows furrowed. 'While I know I was not raised here in England, some things work the same way in New York. If a marriageable woman out in society has not had a single caller, then perhaps there is something else at work.'

'You think there are other reasons why I cannot find a suitor?'

'It's possible.' Kate tapped a finger to her chin. 'For example, in my case, I was simply shut out by the elite of New York society because my father had made his own fortune instead of inheriting it.'

'That seems illogical. Money is money.'

The corner of Kate's mouth lifted up. 'The rules of society are hardly ever logical. But in any case… Perhaps we can investigate and find out what is going on.' She paused. 'I shall write to my former companion and chaperon. She guided me in navigating the waters of London society. She'll be able to help us.'

'Another perspective on the matter? That sounds like a fairly reasonable plan.'

'I shall write to her in the morning. In the meanwhile…' Halting, Kate pulled her aside and lowered her voice. 'I have some excellent news for you. We will be ready to test the locomotive in a few weeks' time.'

The very prospect of seeing Kate's locomotive in action sent a thrill through her. 'That soon?'

'Yes—and it's all thanks to you and your assistance.'

Violet shrugged. 'You did all the hard work in the beginning. All I did was assist with your calculations.'

When she hadn't been attending the aforementioned fifty-two events, Violet had spent most of her time at Kate's locomotives factory—Mason & Wakefield Railway Works. During their initial visit the Duchess had shown her the initial designs, as well as the prototype, and while Violet did not know much about steam engines, she had noticed that a few of Kate's figures in one of the plans were inaccurate. Initially, she had feared her friend would be insulted when she pointed out the error, but Kate had been ecstatic.

'I've been going mad trying to figure it out. Thank you, Violet.'

That had led Kate to ask her to look over other plans and calculations—and that had meant she was at the factory nearly every day. It was her place of solace—not even the loud noises and all the people milling about bothered her. No, when she was sitting down and working on torque diagrams and calculating tractive force formulas, the world outside simply disappeared.

'There's one more thing I want to speak to you about, Violet.'

'What is it?'

Kate hesitated. 'I have had a thought… What if…? I mean, just on the small chance you can't find a husband… What if you stay in London and work for me? At the factory?'

Violet inhaled a breath. 'W-work for you?'

'Yes. I would pay you a salary, of course. I'm afraid it won't be enough to save your Oakwood Cottage, but you and your mother could have a comfortable life. And this first locomotive is just the beginning. We could work together, and you would co-own any patents we create. What do you think?'

Stunned at the offer, Violet couldn't form the words to speak. 'I…'

A movement—no, a presence—caught her attention from just over Kate's left shoulder. It was the Marquess of Ashbrooke.

After their encounter in the park, she'd been certain she would never see him again. When he'd arrived at the Duke and Duchess of Winford's New Year's Eve dinner less than a fortnight ago, Violet had thought she was hallucinating.

Truth be told, the Marquess had always been there…just at the edges of her mind. How could she forget the beautiful man who'd said she was refreshing and had wanted to hear the truth from her? Who hadn't laughed at her, but at something she'd said?

Violet had tried to completely banish him from her mind, because it was evident from his dismissive behaviour that he didn't think much of her. And it had worked for a time—especially when she'd tried hard not to think about him.

Now here he was again…reminding her of his existence.

And he was not alone.

The Marquess stood in an inconspicuous corner of the room, next to a stunning brunette.

Violet wanted to turn away, but she couldn't. So she watched as Ashbrooke leaned over and whispered in the woman's ear, his hand disappearing behind her. Narrowing her gaze, she scrutinised the woman. There was something familiar about her…as if she'd seen her before. But from this distance Violet couldn't see her features.

The woman's lips curled up into a smile and she nodded at the Marquess, then he caught her hand and dragged her towards one of the glass doors leading out to a balcony.

A strange, stabbing sensation pierced Violet's chest, making it hard to breathe—just like that day in Hyde Park, when the blonde woman in the peacock dress had clung to his arm.

'Violet?'

'I…I need the necessary.'

Her stomach turned, and suddenly everything around

her was too loud, the lights overhead too bright. She rushed away from Kate and quickly crossed the room to her intended destination. Pushing at the door, Violet took one step in—but stopped when voices from inside filtered out.

Drat.

'I'm quite sure that's her…the strange one,' a voice said. 'She was wearing the same pink gown at the Adelphi.'

Violet's eyes darted down to her own pink evening gown.

Surely they couldn't mean…?

'And that's the mother?'

'Who else could she be, Lydia? Do you see her eyes light up like some poor street urchin peering into a sweet shop each time a man approaches her daughter? She's probably imagining their wedding day. How utterly desperate!'

A hand squeezed her shoulder. 'Violet…' Kate whispered. 'I'm sure they don't mean—'

'Me?' Violet pursed her lips together, resisting the urge to shrug off what Kate probably thought was a reassuring gesture.

The chatter continued. 'Apparently during the intermission at the opera she went on and on about whale oil.'

Now she was certain those women were talking about her. She recalled that conversation. She'd been talking with Lord Banks when he'd complained about his opera glasses being broken and she'd suggested he clean them with whale oil. Then she'd proceeded to tell him about how the oil was harvested, from the spermaceti organ, and the way sailors persevered it during the long months at sea.

'She spouted something about peacock feathers when we crossed paths at Hyde Park,' a new speaker said.

'Peacocks? Why would she say anything about that, Lady Helen?'

'Who knows? No wonder Ash thinks she's bizarre. The Bizarre Beauty,' she added with a sneer.

Ash.

The Marquess of Ashbrooke thought she was bizarre.

Despite his cold indifference to her, she could not help but still find him beautiful. Out of all the gentlemen she'd been introduced to, none could compare to him. She had decided that perhaps it was better just to admire him for his looks. He didn't care for her, so why should she care for him?

But hearing these words made something fierce pierce her chest.

Mad, he'd called her.

Strange.

And now bizarre too.

'Word about her has spread, and no man will even go near her,' Lady Helen guffawed.

'You mean, *you* helped spread the word?'

Lady Helen harrumphed. 'It's all true—and her continuing to act in such peculiar ways does not help her at all.'

'Such a waste, really. She is stunning. What I wouldn't give to have her complexion.'

'Or her eyes. Mine are just plain brown.'

'Mama says blondes are no longer in fashion. Do you think that's true, Lady Helen?'

'Blondes will always be in fashion,' she replied snidely. 'But odd girls who cannot fit into society will never be.'

Without a word, Violet took a step back, spun on her heel, then marched away from the door.

'What those women said…it simply isn't true,' Kate assured Violet as she walked beside her. 'I had a difficult time too, when I first came to London. I was too different. Too American.' She wrinkled her nose.

'But that's not the same, is it?' Violet stopped short and faced Kate. 'I'm not just different. I am *bizarre*.'

She could practically hear the Marquess's deep, rich voice uttering the word.

'No, you're not—'

'Yes, I am, Kate. Please, I thought we admired each other's candour. Except I am not just candid. I lack restraint and I simply cannot act normally.'

'Do not talk like that.' Kate placed her hands on her hips. 'Violet, you are brilliant and lovely, and if "normal" means you'd be just like all those snooty Englishwomen who acted like I was dirt under their heels when I first arrived here, then I'd rather have you abnormal.'

Abnormal.

Yes, that was what she was.

Bizarre.

Mad.

Not normal.

Never normal.

Kate's eyes widened. 'No, wait…that's not what I meant.' She clicked her tongue. 'And Ash… I can't believe he would say something like that. And in front of other people too. Perhaps they misheard him?'

Violet blinked as once again the puzzle pieces began to click into place.

Bizarre Beauty.

Click.

The Marquess had called her that and now everyone called her that.

Click.

Fifty-two events, twenty-three unmarried gentlemen, thirteen and a half dances.

Click.

Exactly zero prospects.

Click.

It was *him.*

Ashbrooke was the reason she had no suitors. Because of him she would be unable to save Oakwood Cottage and Papa's library.

A cold, silent rage rose up in Violet. Try as she might, she couldn't stop it. It was a like a wave, washing over her. Even her father's words rang hollow in her mind, unable to penetrate the fury wrapping around her.

'Violet? What are you— Where are you going?'

Her hands forming into fists, she spun on her heel and marched off, devouring the space between her and the balcony door across the room. Grabbing the handle, she flung it open.

'You!'

Ashbrooke and his companion—whose hair looked mysteriously dishevelled—jumped away from each other.

'What— Miss Avery…?'

The brunette shrieked. 'How *dare* you come out here?'

Ignoring the woman, Violet marched towards until she stood toe to toe with the Marquess. Craning her head back, she somehow found the resolve to look him straight in the eye.

'This is all your fault.'

'My fault?' He raised his palms. 'Whatever do you mean?'

'It's because of you that I don't have any suitors!' She poked him in the chest.

'I have no idea—'

'Violet? Where have you— Ash…?'

Violet spun her head and saw Kate in the doorway.

The Duchess gasped. 'What's going on here?' Her gaze darted from Ash, to Violet, then to the brunette. 'Ash, what in God's name are you doing out here?' Slamming the door behind her, she strode over to him. 'I can't believe you'd plan a tryst here, of all places.'

'The Spanish Ambassador's house is one of the best places to plan trysts,' he said casually. 'So many balconies.'

Kate narrowed her eyes at the brunette. 'Mrs Bancroft?'

It dawned on Violet why the woman seemed familiar. They'd been introduced the previous week at a charity function.

'Ah, I see you're already acquainted with Emma,' the Marquess said cheerfully. 'That should save me the awkward introductions.'

'Yes, we are acquainted indeed.' The Duchess's nostrils flared. 'We both attended that fundraising event for war widows. She was there—along with her husband. How *is* Mr Bancroft, by the way?'

The woman's face turned pale.

'Husband?' His expression shifted completely. It was like storm clouds swooping across a sunny sky. 'You're married?' His voice was measured and controlled, with a knife-like edge.

'M-my lord.' Mrs Bancroft let out a nervous laugh. 'This is merely a misunderstanding—'

'You lied to me.' His teeth ground together audibly. 'You said you were widowed.'

'Well, she was at a war widows' charity event,' Violet stated. 'Perhaps she was trying to imagine herself in their place.'

Ashbrooke's head snapped towards her, his sapphire eyes blazing.

Was he angry with her? When she was the injured party here?

Mrs Bancroft's face flushed. 'Miss Violet Avery,' she sneered. 'You truly are as ravishing as they say. I thought as much when we were introduced. And then you insulted our hostess by asking her to stop playing the pianoforte—in her own home.'

'She was a terrible piano player,' Violet stated. 'No sense of rhythm, and her fingers landed on the wrong key with every fifth note.'

'Everyone was talking about you afterwards—you and your desperate mother. I hear she's been flaunting you all about Town, trying to get you married off.' She clicked her tongue. 'It's such a tragedy that no man will come near you because you're truly…what do they call you? Ah, yes. The Bizarre Beauty.'

'Emma!' the Marquess barked.

The cold fury that had earlier fuelled Violet drained away as the other woman's words confirmed everything she had learned tonight. The entire Ton did, indeed, consider her a laughing stock. A mad, bizarre woman whom no man would ever want to marry.

Slowly, she turned to face Ashbrooke.

'I hate you.' Violet once again managed to look him straight in the eye. 'I hate you and I never want to see you again.'

An arm slipped around her shoulders. The unwelcome touch made her flinch, but the arm didn't move.

'Violet,' came Kate's soft voice. 'We should leave.'

'Kate—'

'Ash, for once in your life, keep your mouth shut,' the Duchess hissed.

'But—'

'Shush!'

Everything from that moment on passed in a blur for Violet. She had a vague memory of being led off the balcony, of people staring and whispering, and being whisked away to a carriage.

The one thing she knew she would never forget from that night was her feeling of loathing towards the Marquess of Ashbrooke. She had truly meant the words she'd thrown at him, and if she ever did see him again it would be far too soon.

Chapter Three

Ash had had some terrible evenings in his life, but tonight was undoubtedly the worst.

After he'd escaped the Spanish Ambassador's party, he quickly found his carriage. Upon reaching his home, he stormed in without even waiting for his butler, Hargrove, to open the door and then proceeded to his study to retrieve the bottle of aged Glenbaire Whisky he'd hidden under his desk. His best friend Cam, who owned the Glenbaire Whisky Distillery, had told him it was one of the finest bottles they had produced and to save it for a special occasion or—this added jokingly—for an emergency.

Well, if this wasn't an emergency Ash didn't know what was, so he uncapped the bottle, took a healthy swig, then collapsed on the leather chair behind the desk.

Christ Almighty.

The evening had begun smashingly enough. After days of heavy flirting and getting to know each other, he had set up a meeting with his potential new paramour at the Spanish Ambassador's party. Everything had been going splendidly, and he'd managed to find an empty balcony where they could continue their 'acquaintance'.

Then Miss Violet Avery had come along and it had turned into a disaster.

Ash took another gulp of the whisky, the smooth liquor sending a warm path to his gut. When they'd met at Covent Garden the week before, Emma Bancroft had told him she was a widow and that her husband had been gone five years now. There couldn't have been a misunderstanding, and nor did he misremember because, despite his appetites, there was one kind of woman he didn't touch—one line he did not cross.

Ash did not sleep with married women.

At least that was one consolation from tonight's debacle. Miss Violet Avery had saved him from breaking his own cardinal rule. He should thank her—except he would never get the chance.

'I hate you and I never want to see you again.'

Tossing his head back, he tipped the bottle up and allowed the liquid fire to burn his throat until his eyes watered.

'Blasted...hell,' he spat, slamming the bottle on top of his desk.

Slumping back in his seat, he blew out a breath.

What did I do to deserve this?

He'd never done anything to her—had barely interacted with her since that first night. After the champagne had been drunk at Ransom's New Year's Eve party he'd left right away.

But tonight, when she'd charged out onto the balcony, she had said something about her lack of suitors being his fault.

'How in blazes am I to blame for that?' he muttered.

But another more pressing thought niggled at him—how could she not have any suitors? Between her scheming and her good looks, surely by now she should have roped some poor, besotted fool into proposing? Were the men of London blind? The young, healthy bucks of the Ton should all be falling over themselves and elbowing each other to fawn over her—Miss Avery was gorgeous, after all. Even if her dowry was small, some rich old lord looking for a young, healthy third or fourth wife to parade on his arm should have snapped her up. Miss Avery's standards couldn't be that high, considering she was not wealthy nor the daughter of a peer.

A knot formed in his chest as he imagined her married to some man who probably wouldn't be able to appreciate her wit.

Shrugging, he put it out of his mind. In any case, it was not any of his concern—though the very thought of her in someone else's bed had him reaching for the bottle and chugging down another healthy measure of whisky.

Dong! Dong! Dong!

Ash glanced up at the grandfather clock as it chimed away the hour—midnight.

It was a new day.

His thirtieth birthday, to be precise.

He had hoped to ring in *his* new year between the sheets with the luscious Emma Bancroft.

Happy birthday to me.

Taking one last pull from the bottle, he leaned back, closed his eyes, intending to rest for a few minutes before he called his valet to help him prepare for bed...

'My lord!'

Ash shot up to his feet. 'What the blazes—' His head felt as if it had been split open with a dull axe, and he fell back onto his chair.

Chair?

Glancing around, he saw that he had, indeed, fallen asleep in his study. He dropped down again, closed his eyes, and reached back to massage his nape with his fingers.

That crick will be there all day.

'My lord?'

Bleary-eyed, he cracked an eye open. 'Yes, Hargrove?'

The white-haired butler was standing in the doorway, posture stiff as a board. 'My lord, you have guests.'

'Guests? Who?'

'I don't know all of them, my lord, but Mr Madison accompanied them here.'

'My solicitor?' What the devil was *he* doing here? 'Did he say what this is about?'

Hargrove shook his head. 'No, my lord. Only that it is of the utmost importance and that you must see them right away. Mr Madison said that I should haul you out of bed as if your life depended on it.'

Arthur Madison was a stodgy old chap who never minced words. Ash only saw him at most twice a year, so if he was knocking on his door this early it must truly be important.

With a frustrated groan, he hauled himself upright. 'Invite them into the parlour, then send Holmes to me with a strong pot of coffee.'

Thanks to the miraculous work of his valet, Holmes, Ash appeared presentable within fifteen minutes and found himself walking into the parlour just a short time after that.

'Good morning,' he greeted his guests.

Madison spoke first. 'My lord.' The solicitor's face was drawn into a grave expression as he stood up. 'Forgive me for imposing upon you at home at such an inconvenient hour. The Canfields and Mr Gallaway came to my office this morning with a concerning matter and I thought it best to come straight to you.'

'I see.' He glanced over at the other three occupants. 'Good morning.'

An older woman, perhaps in her late fifties or early sixties, sat in the middle of the settee. She was dressed in pink velvet and fur, with a garish feather hat on top of her head and several strands of pearls wound around her neck. To her right was a tall, skinny young man who was probably just out of university, wringing his hands in his lap, and across from them was a balding man in a flashy wine-red coat.

'My lord, allow me to introduce Mrs Alberta Canfield, her son Mr Richard Canfield, and their solicitor, Mr James Gallaway. Madam, sirs, this is Devon St James, Marquess of Ashbrooke.'

'Now, now, no need to be so formal.' Mrs Canfield rose up and walked over to him, then—to his utter surprise— enveloped him in a hug. 'After all, we're family.'

'Family?' Ash gently wriggled away from her embrace. 'I have no family. Only a distant relative who lives in Shropshire. My father's second cousin, twice removed.'

And the only reason he even knew about said cousin was because he would eventually inherit the marquessate, since Ash did not plan to marry.

'We're from a different branch of the family, my dear.' Mrs Canfield smirked. She turned to her solicitor. 'Mr Gallaway, if you please?'

The solicitor cleared his throat as he retrieved a sheaf of papers from his briefcase. 'My lord, are you aware of the marriage contract between your great-grandfather, the Third Marquess of Ashbrooke, and your great-grandmother, Mrs Hannah Canfield?'

'A contract three generations old? Why would I know of such a thing?' He looked to Madison. 'What is going on?'

His solicitor's bushy white brows drew together. 'Please keep listening, my lord.'

Gallaway continued. 'Allow me to give you a summary, my lord. Your great-grandfather signed a betrothal contract for his eldest son, your grandfather, to marry Hannah Canfield's daughter. Aside from a substantial sum of money, her dowry included all the lands around the marquessate seat, Chatsworth Manor. Upon their marriage, the original estate and the Canfield properties were joined together, and all of it now belongs to the marquessate, to be passed on to the eldest St James son.'

'Yes, that's generally how primogeniture works.' Ash could not help the sarcasm in his tone. The effects of the coffee he'd gulped down were beginning to wear off and the pounding in his temple had resumed. 'But I presume you're not here for a family history lesson?'

Mrs Canfield barked out a laugh. 'No, we are not. Go on then, Mr Gallaway.'

'Er...yes, of course, madam.' He waved the papers he had taken out from his briefcase. 'This is the Canfields' copy of the betrothal contract and the marriage certificate. You should also have one somewhere in your estate, or filed with whomever your great-grandfather's solicitors were at the time. In any case, there is an extra clause here, regarding the lands.'

'And what clause is that?'

'The lands that form the original estate may only be passed on to the first-born male heir, and each future marquess must produce a male heir by his thirty-first birthday. Otherwise, these lands will revert back to the Canfields.'

'I beg your pardon? Is this true?' Ash looked to Madison, who only nodded. 'It can't be. Who— Why would anyone add that clause and why would my great-grandfather agree to it?'

'Hannah Canfield was an eccentric old woman.' It was Mrs Alberta Canfield who answered. 'She grew up poor, scraping by for her entire life. However, after years of saving and scrimping, she and her husband were able to start their own cotton factory, where they made their fortune. Despite all their money, the Canfields were shut out by the hoity-toity people of the Ton, but Hannah was determined that her only daughter should have the respect and status she'd never had herself, so she married her off to the reputable but insolvent Marquess. However, Hannah didn't agree with the way inheritance favours only the male heir. So, to ensure the wealth and lands stayed in the Canfield family, she had that clause added. She didn't want some distant relation of the St James's to benefit from her hard work and sacrifice.'

'That's utter madness.' Ash rubbed a hand down his face. 'Why would she force members of my family to produce heirs?'

'No one's forcing anyone, are they?' Mrs Canfield pointed out. 'You're free to go about as you please—just not with Canfield money. Hannah wanted only those of her blood—' she looked meaningfully at her son '—to enjoy the fruits of her labour. Not some distant relations who have no connection to her.'

Ash turned to Madison. 'And how much of the estate would go to the Canfields?'

'Most of it.'

'Most? Meaning…?'

'All the income-generating portions, my lord. You would, of course, be left with the manor house and the gardens, as well as this townhouse.'

Dread pooled in his chest. Without the lands he would not have enough income for the upkeep of either home. Or himself. Whatever money he had would only last him a few years, and that was if he tightened his belt.

'Madison, is this legal?'

'I assure you, it is,' Gallaway interjected, then shoved the papers back in his briefcase. 'And might I remind you, my lord—with all due respect—that neither the Canfields nor I were legally required to inform you of this. Your great-grandfather should have taken the steps necessary to inform all future marquesses of this clause. Your own father should have told you.'

'Well, my father was busy dying when I was ten years old, so I'm afraid he didn't have the time.'

'My condolences.' He stood up, as did Mrs Canfield and her son. 'Thank you for your time, my lord. We shall see ourselves out.'

'And, happy birthday, my dear.' Mrs Canfield had the look of the proverbial cat that had got the cream. 'We will see you in a year. Come, Richard.' The man—boy, really—who had said nothing the entire time, sprang up like a trained puppy and followed his mother.

'Not legally required to inform me—like hell!' Ash exclaimed once he and his solicitor were alone. He kicked the closest thing he could reach—which was thankfully the padded armchair Gallaway had been sitting on. 'That woman has deliberately waited until the very last year to tell me of that clause! Madison, surely it isn't binding.'

'I'm afraid it is, my lord. I made sure to read every single line before coming here.' Madison clasped his hands together. 'If you want to keep the lands around Chatsworth, you must produce an heir within the next year.'

An heir.

Which meant he needed to get married.

For a moment Ash considered just letting that horrid woman and her milksop son take the lot. It would be worth it so that he didn't have to be shackled to some woman for the rest of his life.

'Damn.'

He kicked the armchair once more before sinking down on it. There had to be a way to get around the clause. But if Madison was correct, there might not be any legal way to do it.

Drumming his fingers on his knees, Ash considered his options.

'For heaven's sake, Ash, I'm leaving for my honeymoon in sixteen hours,' Ransom roared as he charged into Ash's study later that day. He hadn't even bothered to remove his hat and coat. 'What's this life and death situation? And if I miss my honeymoon, someone *will* be dead.' He eyed Ash, who sat behind his desk, menacingly.

Sebastian, who had already made himself comfortable on the chair in front of Ash's desk, gestured to the seat beside him, then poured some whisky into two glasses from a nearly empty bottle. 'Come and sit, Ransom. There's at least enough in here for both of us.'

Ransom plopped down. 'What's this all about?'

'A tragedy, my dear best friends.' Ash sighed exaggeratedly. 'I have the most distressing news.'

He then proceeded to tell them what had transpired that morning with the Canfields.

'And it's all binding?' Sebastian asked. 'There's no way around it?'

'Not according to Madison—though he said he would speak with his colleagues, along with a judge, to see if there's any loophole or legal manoeuvre to invalidate the clause.'

Ransom finished his half-measure of whisky. 'Then what do you need from us?'

'Moral support? Ideas? Someone to kick the stool from under my feet while I hang myself?' Leaning back on his chair, Ash massaged his temples with his fingers.

'Could you not purchase the lands?' Sebastian asked.

'I've already withdrawn all my income from last year, and most of it has been accounted for, with upkeep and salaries and whatnot.'

He'd had his man of business, Mr Bevis, come over that afternoon to explain his current financial standing. The situation was just as he'd thought—if he were to lose the lands he would be left without any means of income to support himself.

'You could get a job,' Ransom pointed out.

'A *what*?' Ash scoffed. 'Marquesses do not work.'

Both men rolled their eyes.

'I should have invested with you, Sebastian.'

The Duke had been in similar straits when his father had passed away, but through smart investments Sebastian had not only paid back his father's debtors but increased his wealth tenfold.

'All this wasted time...'

Ash was not the type to worry about the future. Indeed, as long as his tenants were comfortable and he had a healthy estate, that was all that mattered. He was used to being wealthy, to having his solicitor and his employees attend to the boring parts of life while he enjoyed the fruits of his lands. He hadn't expected a disaster such as this to strike.

'I don't see what the problem is,' Ransom said matter-of-factly. 'You have exactly one year to produce an heir. So...produce. You're very good at that, or so I've heard.'

Ash let out a breath. 'In case either of you did not re-alise it, to produce a legitimate heir there is another crucial step. Marriage.' The word left a bitter taste in his mouth.

'So?' Sebastian tutted. 'Every woman of marriageable age in London is after you. Choose any one of them. I'm sure many would be happy to marry you tomorrow if it meant becoming the Marchioness of Ashbrooke and bagging the most elusive bachelor in all of England.'

They made it sound so simple.

And yet it wasn't.

Not to Ash.

He closed his eyes as memory threatened to rise again.

But this time he allowed the scene in his mind to surface…

A vivid image of a beautiful summer day.

The swish of cotton and silk.

The slamming of the door.

'The witch is finally gone.'

The little boy—not little, not really, after all he was nine years old this year—turned around. *'Father?'*

His father stood at the top of the steps. His shirt was open at the throat, hair dishevelled, eyes red and wet. *'Your mama, Devon, has packed up and left us.'*

The boy turned back to the door. *'Mama…?'*

'Has left me—us—for her lover. Joining him on the Continent. She's going to his villa in Italy.'

'No! Mama!'

Mama wouldn't leave me.

He began to run towards the door.

Father moved down the steps, catching him just before he reached his destination.

'Stop this snivelling.' His hands gripped the boy's shoulders tightly. *'You are the future Marquess of Ashbrooke, and marquesses do not cry.'*

'But Mama…'

'She does not deserve any tears. From now on you must learn to live without your mama. You don't need her anyway,' Father sneered, looking towards the door. *'You don't need anyone, Devon.'*

'Ash? *Ash?*'

Ash jolted back into the present. 'Yes?'

'What are you going to do?' Sebastian clasped his hands together and rested his chin on his fingers.

'What the hell else?' He threw his hands up. 'Get married, I suppose. Produce an heir.'

'You know, just because you're married—'

'Doesn't mean I'll be able to produce a male heir?' Ash rose and walked over to the window, then stared out into the busy street. 'And I could be saddled with an unwanted wife for the rest of my life? I know that, of course, but what choice do I have?'

'You don't need anyone, Devon.'

The words had stuck in his mind. They had allowed him to become self-sufficient, even after Father's death a year later.

Ash didn't need anyone and certainly not a wife.

'Not all marriages have to be terrible,' Sebastian said in a quiet voice. 'Having a wife to love and to love you back might not be a bad thing.'

A shudder ran down Ash's spine. If Sebastian thought the idea of love would encourage Ash to marry he was dead wrong. It only accomplished the opposite. Love was even more dangerous than needing someone. His mother had loved his father, yet it hadn't been enough to stop his fits of jealousy that had eventually consumed their relationship and pushed her to have affairs. And his father had loved his mother so much that when she'd left it had destroyed him.

Ash had vowed never to make the same mistake.

'I'd rather have a wife who won't fall in love with me and with whom I will never fall in love.'

Never fall in love.

Never…

'That's it!' Ash spun around so fast he knocked over the bust of Shakespeare behind him, but caught it in time. 'Oops, my apologies, Will.' He replaced the Bard on his pedestal.

'What's "it"?' Ransom asked.

'If I must wed, then it must be to someone with whom I will never fall in love. Someone I don't particularly like, maybe am even repulsed by.' He stuck out his tongue. 'No, no, she needs to be pleasant enough if I must beget an heir. Young and healthy. Someone like…'

Well, truly there was only one person in his mind.

Perhaps she'd been lurking there all this time, ever since he'd found out about the clause.

Sebastian slapped his hand on the table to catch his attention. 'Someone like who?'

'Gentlemen, I know exactly whom I shall wed. Miss Violet Avery.'

'The Dowager's protégée?' said Ransom.

'Miss Avery?' Sebastian exclaimed at the same time, in a louder voice. 'You can't be serious, Ash.'

'I am. It's perfect. She's perfect.'

Miss Avery was looking for a husband and Ash was certain he would never fall in love with her.

'She's the one.'

'Aren't you forgetting something, Ash?' Sebastian narrowed his gaze at him. 'Last night? The Spanish Ambassador's party?'

'The what?' Ransom scrubbed a hand down his face. 'Ash, what have you done this time?'

Sebastian rolled his eyes and explained the events of the previous night to Ransom.

'Ash, you monster!' Ransom roared. 'Did you drag the

poor girl into scandal because you couldn't keep it in your trousers for one night?'

'Excuse me, I did not drag her into a scandal. And I certainly stayed within the confines of my trousers.' Ash pursed his lips together. 'Though apparently it's my fault the chit doesn't have any suitors. I don't even know why she would accuse me of such a thing.'

'I do,' Sebastian offered. 'Kate told me. She said you had started rumours about her and given her the nickname of the Bizarre Beauty. Now no man will go near her.'

'I did no such thing,' Ash retorted indignantly. Certainly he had not particularly enjoyed being deceived by her and her mother, but he couldn't care a whit who courted her. 'And nickname? Where would I come up with such…? *Oh.*'

Hyde Park.

Lady Helen.

Bizarre Beauty.

Unease crept across his chest. 'Oh, dear.'

'So it's true?' Sebastian's tone did not denote a question. He had obviously deduced the answer from the expression on Ash's face.

'Not on purpose.' *Hell.* No wonder she was furious. 'Of course, there is an upside to all this.'

'And that is?'

'I don't have any competition for the girl.'

'Thanks to your thoughtlessness.'

'I'll take that as a compliment.'

'It was not meant to be one,' Sebastian replied, exasperated.

Ash straightened his shoulders. 'In any case, it's the best solution.'

'She hates you, Ash,' Sebastian pointed out.

'You don't know that.'

'I was standing on that balcony. She said, and I quote, "I hate you and I never want to see you again."'

Ash waved a hand dismissively. 'Pish-posh…minor details.'

He was confident he could overcome this small matter—after all, he was Devon St James, Marquess of Ashbrooke. No woman could resist him. Besides, all they needed to do was marry and conceive, which he could accomplish quickly.

'Sebastian, are you headed back to Highfield Park?'

'Tomorrow, yes. Kate and the rest of the ladies left this morning, thanks to you and your antics. We'll be staying for at least a fortnight, or until the gossip dies down.'

'Excellent. Invite me to stay with you.'

'What? Why?'

'So I may woo Miss Avery, of course.'

'Kate will not allow it.' Sebastian folded his arms over his chest. 'She was there last night too, remember?'

'You're the Duke of Mabury—why would you allow your wife to dictate who can and cannot stay at your estate?'

'Ash…'

'Think of it as your birthday gift to me,' he pleaded. 'You've never given me one, ever, by the way.' Planting his hands on the table, he leaned forward. 'Besides, if I become destitute and lose my homes, you know you'll have to deal with me? I'll become your permanent house guest and sponge off you.' He grinned at Sebastian. 'For ever.'

Ransom smirked. 'Why don't you let him try, Sebastian? You're not forcing the girl to marry him. I almost wish I wasn't leaving for my honeymoon. I'd pay good money to watch you pursue a woman.'

'I suppose it would be an amusing sight.' Sebastian smiled wryly. 'I will not invite you to stay, as I already know Kate will never forgive me. However, I know better than to try and dissuade you, Ash. So, if you somehow find a way to invite yourself, I won't stop you.'

'Now I really am tempted to cancel my honeymoon.'

'What? Have you no faith in me?' Ash blew out a breath. 'Some best friends you are… Besides, the two of you have already done it. How hard could it possibly be to convince one woman to marry me?'

The two men looked at each other and laughed.

Chapter Four

❧

Violet was deep into her calculations on the required boiler pressure for varying locomotive engines sizes when Mama burst into Kate's office.

'There you are.' Mama hurried to her side. 'It's nearly dinner time—hurry up…we must get you dressed.'

'Dinner?'

'Yes, dinner.' She tutted. 'What in the world are you doing here in the Duchess's private sitting room?'

Glancing down at the desk, Violet considered hiding the papers strewn about. Mama shouldn't find out what she was doing. But, then again, she didn't seem concerned about the scribblings. 'The Duchess is teaching me how to…' she scrambled to find something that would placate her mother '…to balance chicken accounts.'

'Chicken accounts?'

'*Kitchen*. I mean, kitchen accounts.'

Chickens were found in kitchens, weren't they? That sounded logical, at least to her ears.

'Oh, I see. How thoughtful of Her Grace to train you in such matters.' Mama clapped her hands together. 'Yes, soon you will be running your own household—perhaps even one as grand as this one. You must be prepared, so as not to disappoint your husband.'

'Of course, Mama.'

By some miracle, Lady Avery did not have any inkling about what had happened during the Spanish Ambassador's party. As Kate and the Duke had whisked Violet off, the quick-thinking Dowager had hidden Lady Avery away in her own carriage before whispers spread among the guests. They had further delayed any gossip from reaching her ears by fleeing to Highfield early the next day, citing the foul air in London as their primary reason for leaving.

As soon as they'd arrived, Violet had joined Kate in her office and immersed herself in her work.

It was the only way she could stop from thinking about *him*.

She couldn't even bear to say his name.

'Still, we must be off, child. Dinner is in one hour, and I cannot allow you to miss another one. I know you were feeling poorly after the long journey yesterday, but you must pull yourself together and make an appearance at dinner, lest we offend our hosts.'

Violet knew she could barricade herself in the office for ever and Kate and the Duke would never be offended, but she couldn't let Mama become suspicious. After all, she'd already made her decision. In between all the calculating and measuring, she had concluded that there was only one logical solution to her predicament: accept Kate's offer of a job to save herself and her mother from a life of genteel poverty.

But Mama couldn't know about her plan because Violet knew she would try to force her to marry. She might even attempt to take Violet away from Highfield Park, and then they truly would have no other option.

No, the only thing she could do was wait. Wait for their creditors to take hold of Oakwood Cottage, along with

Papa's books and other things. There was no denying it: her father's library was lost to her. The pain of it was indescribable, as if she was losing him once again.

'Violet,' Mama began again as she dragged her out of the office and towards their rooms. 'That new gown you were fitted for last week has just arrived. I cannot wait for you to wear it at your next ball. You do look so stunning in blue.'

Violet swallowed the lump in her throat as moisture formed on her palms. How she hated lying—and yet it was only now she understood that perhaps telling a few fibs was not a bad thing, especially if it meant protecting someone you loved.

So all she said was, 'Yes, Mama.'

After her bath, and half an hour of torture with dressing, and pulling hair and corset strings, Violet was finally ready, so she made her way down the main floor. Thankfully this was just the usual dinner with Kate and the Duke, and the staff at Highfield Park already knew how she liked her food prepared and her routines when dining. It would be a nice, quiet dinner with no surprises.

'My lord, you are here! I didn't know you were invited—what a wonderful surprise!'

Violet halted as she neared the bottom of the stairs. Who was Mama speaking to?

'Good evening, Lady Avery. Is that a new gown? It does suit your complexion. But then you are always the epitome of style and grace in any room.'

No.

'Oh…you flatter me, my lord.'

Violet shook her head.

No, no.

'Only because you deserve it.'

No, no, no.

Air rushed out of Violet's lungs.

Not him.

The need to flee was overwhelmed by shock, forcing her feet to stay in place. It was far too late, in any case, as the Marquess of Ashbrooke had stepped out of the doorway and into the main hall. His head immediately snapped up, and he flashed her a bright smile.

'Violet, look!' Mama yelped. 'The Marquess of Ashbrooke is here.'

'Miss Avery.' He bowed his head. 'Good evening to you.'

She stared at him, unable to speak or to move. What was he doing here? Had Kate and the Duke invited him? After what had happened?

'Child, don't just stand there.' Mama laughed nervously. 'Come down and greet His Lordship.'

Fearing her mother would drag her down by force otherwise, Violet pushed herself to walk down, taking each step slowly and deliberately, as if delaying the inevitable.

'My lord,' she managed to murmur, lowering her gaze.

'Miss Avery, you're as lovely as the day.' His smile did not waver. 'I'm happy to see you.'

Violet jerked her head up. The crinkles at the corners of his eyes told her the smile was genuine. But why was he here?

'Will you be joining us for dinner?' Mama enquired.

'Oh, is it dinnertime?' Ashbrooke turned to the butler, Eames.

'Yes, my lord. His Grace and the Duchess are already in the dining room.'

'What are you doing here?' Violet asked, finally finding her voice.

'Don't be rude, Violet,' Mama said.

'It's quite all right, Lady Avery.' He grinned at her. 'I'm

afraid a tragedy has befallen me. My carriage has broken down, you see. My coachman has said we will not be able to find a replacement, and it was getting dark, so I took one of the horses to find an inn for the evening. But then I remembered that my best friend the Duke of Mabury's home was only five miles down the road, so I thought I would come here instead.'

'How fortunate.' Mama sighed. 'And it's a good thing too, as you could have been set upon by bandits at this hour.'

He would have deserved it, Violet sulked silently.

'So, Eames, do you think I could impose upon you for dinner? I hate to disrupt your carefully planned meals...'

'Not all, my lord. Please follow me and I'll announce—'

'No, need.' The Marquess waved a hand. 'I shall announce myself.'

'Very well, my lord. I'll instruct Chef Pierre to prepare for an additional diner.'

'Lady Avery... Miss Avery...' Ashbrooke offered them one arm each. 'Shall we?'

'Yes, my lord!' Mama tittered. 'Violet?'

Violet would have rather cut off her own hand than touch him.

'Violet.'

Defeated, she gingerly placed a hand over his arm and allowed him to lead them to the dining room. She continued to fume as they entered.

'Lady Avery, we were just— Ash?' Kate's lips pressed together tightly as her gaze landed on the Marquess, then she turned to her husband. 'Sebastian, what is he doing here?'

The Duke leaned back in his chair. 'I'd love to hear an explanation too.'

'Ah, Kate, Sebastian...good evening to you too,' Ashbrooke said. 'Well, you see there has been an unfortunate incident.' He went on and explained the situation with his carriage. 'And now I must impose upon you for the evening. I hope you don't mind? Seeing as we're friends and such. You wouldn't want me to ride back to London on my own. I could be set upon by bandits.'

'Oh, you really could,' Lady Avery added.

The Duchess's nostrils flared, but she remained silent.

'I suppose it's just for one night.' The Duke motioned for one of the footmen to add a setting for Ashbrooke, which unfortunately meant he was placed beside Violet.

'Thank you.'

Everyone sat down to dinner, and the footmen brought in their first course.

'I always look forward to meals at Highfield Park.' Ashbrooke took a spoonful of the soup. 'Ah…my compliments to Chef Pierre. Miss Avery, are you not hungry?'

Violet had kept her hands under the table as she continued to touch her fingers to her thumbs one by one. 'What part of your carriage had broken?'

'I beg your pardon.'

She turned her head to face him. 'What. Part.' She could feel Mama's stare burning into her, but she ignored it.

Ashbrooke's eyes widened. 'You know…the thing…'

'What thing?'

'The *thing*.'

She straightened up and placed her hands on the table. 'The axle?'

'Yes, exactly that.'

'Which one?'

'Which what?'

'Which axle?' She narrowed her gaze at him. 'The topside or downside?'

'The downside.'

He said it with so much confidence that Violet might have believed him—if she hadn't known there was no such thing as a downside or an upside axle.

'Tell me, Ash,' the Duchess began, eyeing him. 'What business brings you to Surrey in the first place?'

'The smog in London was getting far too thick. I needed some fresh country air,' he replied cheerfully.

'Thirty miles from London? Surely there are places much closer...like Stratford?'

'It's a very thick smog, Kate.'

'That's why we left,' Lady Avery informed him. 'All that smoke was making Her Grace ill.'

'Ah, I see we are of the same mind, Kate.' Ashbrooke winked at her.

Violet gripped the edge of the table so hard her knuckles turned white. She would rather die than have to exist in the same space as him. Her fury from the other night began to build in her, and she opened her mouth to tell him to leave, but Mama interrupted.

'How wonderful it would be if you could stay,' Lady Avery fawned. 'Isn't that true, Your Grace? I'm sure you will very much enjoy the Marquess's company, seeing as you are best friends.'

Ashbrooke raised his wine glass to the Duke. 'The very best.'

Drat.

Violet couldn't very well tell Ashbrooke off—even if the oaf deserved it. It would be rude to shout at a guest in the Duke's own home. Besides, if Mama found out the reason she abhorred the Marquess, she would also eventually discover Violet's plan to work at the factory with Kate.

So she would have to stay silent, at least for now.

Besides, he couldn't stay here for ever, could he?

Chapter Five

'I think it went well,' Ash said to Sebastian as they enjoyed their after-dinner cigars and port in the library.

'The girl hardly spoke to you, and when she did she interrogated you and caught you in a lie.' Sebastian sat down on the wingback chair by the fireplace. 'Only you would think this evening has gone "well".'

'I can always chalk it up to the fact that I don't know a damn thing about axles.' She was smart—he had to give her that. 'And now I have an excuse to stay here for a few days.'

'A few days? Ash, you do know we have at least three carriages that could take you back to London.'

'And? Just say all your coachmen are indisposed.'

'So now I'll have to lie to my wife about why I can't send you packing in the morning?'

'It's not a lie… You're just withholding the truth from her for a little bit.'

'That's the same, Ash.' Sebastian shook his head.

'If it makes you feel any better, you may tell her the truth of why I'm here.'

'Because you wish to force her friend into marriage after you destroyed her reputation?'

'When you put it that way…' Ash took a seat opposite him. 'But I'm running out of time, Sebastian. With each day that passes, the possibility of that horrid woman and her son taking my lands and impoverishing me increases. Besides, it's not like I'm some fortune-hunter, trying to get my hands on Miss Avery's dowry. In fact, with this marriage, I'll be elevating her status and making her into a wealthy woman.'

'If you produce an heir.'

'Which I will. But you must help me now.'

'If Kate demands an explanation of why I'm letting you stay, I won't lie to her.'

'In the first place, the decision will be Miss Avery's,' Ash pointed out. 'I plan to ask her to marry me, and if she rejects my proposal then I'll leave and find someone else.'

His gut twisted at the thought.

'Promise me you'll court her properly and you won't force or trick her. And if she says no, you will leave her be.'

Ash sniffed, indignant. 'I do not force or trick women. I promise you, if she accepts, it will be of her own free will.'

Sebastian finished off his port. 'Then I suggest you work as fast as you can.'

Ash took Sebastian's words to heart. The following day he avoided the breakfast table and skulked around the manor—lest he run into Kate and receive an ear-bashing—then went in search of Miss Avery.

That, however, proved to be a monumental task in itself, as no one could seem to find her. According to Eames, Lady Avery was feeling tired and had retired to her room, but as far as he knew Miss Avery had not followed suit. He checked the sitting room, the library, the morning room, the drawing room, the gardens and even the orangery—still no Miss Avery. He supposed he could find out where her bedroom was and seek her out, but he had promised Sebastian he'd be on his best behaviour.

'You,' he called to passing footman as he found himself circling back to the hall for the third time. 'Have you seen Miss Avery?'

'Miss Avery?'

'Yes—you know. His Grace's guest. There can't be many young unmarried women scurrying about here, can there?'

'I…er…' The young man gulped. 'I think I've seen her.'

'Where?'

'Her Grace's office?'

'Are you asking me or telling me?'

'T-telling you, milord. I mean, yes… I believe that's where she is. I heard the maids say they were bringing her tea.'

'Excellent. Show me.'

Ash followed the footman as he led him to a room on the east side of the manor. It could only be accessed through the drawing room, which was why he'd missed it.

'Thank you,' he said, dismissing the footman.

Once he was alone, he raised his hand to knock at the door, but stopped.

What should he say to her?

It hadn't occurred to him to prepare a speech, but there was no time to sit down and outline a plan now. Should he declare his intentions?

No, that would scare her off.

Besides, if last night was any indication, she was still miffed about the whole Bizarre Beauty thing.

He had never proposed to a woman—propositioned them, yes, but never actually offered marriage. For a moment he thought to forget the whole thing altogether, but then he reminded himself that he was not built for poverty.

Screwing up his courage, he knocked on the door. No one answered, so he rapped his knuckles on the wood once again, this time much harder.

There was a pause before a familiar husky voice said, 'Who is it?'

'It's me. I mean, Devon. Er… Ashbrooke.'

Lord, he sounded like a fool. But for some reason his heart raced like a thoroughbred at Royal Ascot.

'Go away!' came the muffled reply.

'Can I come—'

'I said, go away.' Loud footsteps told him that she was coming towards the door. 'And don't come back.'

'Miss Avery, I only want to speak—'

'No, I am not speaking with you. Besides, I'm alone in here and we have no chaperon. It's not proper.'

Ash thought that sounded like a great idea—if they were discovered then they'd be forced to marry—but then he recalled his promise to Sebastian.

Damn.

'I only want to—'

'No!'

It was obvious that unless he barged in he would not be able to coax her out of the room. So he decided to change his tactics.

'Perhaps I will fetch Lady Avery? Then she could chaperon us.'

'You wouldn't dare.'

Ah, so she didn't want her mother around. He had to admit charming the older woman had been much easier, and he knew she would be on his side once he'd pleaded his case to Violet.

'She did seem genuinely happy to see me here. Let me fetch—'

'No!' The door was flung open. 'Do not fetch my mother.'

Once again, blood roared in his ears and his heart careered into his ribcage at the sight of her. She looked especially ravishing this morning, in a light blue gown that matched her eyes. Her cheeks were flushed pink, and a long sable lock had loosened from the knot in her hair and now curled over the low neckline that revealed the tops of her bosom, as her shawl had loosened and fallen away.

'What do you want?'

The low, husky tone of her voice sent a sharp rush of desire though his body. 'Huh...?'

'I said, what do you want?'

He could only think of one thing he wanted right at this moment. 'Um... A walk in the orangery. With you.'

'And then you will leave me alone?'

'Yes.'

At least he would until luncheon, at least.

The door slammed in his face, but moments later it opened again and—much to his disappointment—he saw she'd secured the shawl around her shoulders and swept up a stray curl back into the knot and under a warm hat.

'Let's go.'

'Where is your cape?'

'No need.'

She marched through the parlour and down the corridor to the glass doors that led out into the garden. Once they were on the path, he caught up with her.

'What a lovely winter day—'

Miss Avery continued on, blazing through the hedgerows like a soldier on the warpath, moving towards the brick and glass building at the top of the garden. Warm, humid air greeted them as they stepped inside, and exotic plants surrounded them, bringing them into a lush, tropical garden. However, they barely had time to enjoy the greenery as she stamped down the tiled path, crossed over to where a beautiful fountain stood in the middle, circled around, then brushed past him.

Blowing out an exasperated breath, he followed her as she left the orangery. The blast of cold air slapped his face. She was already halfway back through the garden.

How the devil did she move so fast?

He ran across the garden, catching up with her again as she re-entered the manor. 'Miss Avery!'

She continued on, stopping only once she had reached the door outside Kate's office.

'You walk fast for a woman,' he commented as he caught up with her. 'Wait, please,' he said as she put her hand on the door. 'Just one moment, Miss Avery.'

Blowing out a breath, she spun to face him. 'What do you want, my lord? Why are you here? And please do not insult my intelligence by repeating that story about your carriage—we both know there is no such thing as a down-side axle.'

She refused to meet his gaze straight on, but he didn't need to look into her eyes to know that she was deadly serious. And so, having no plan or strategy in place, he decided on the one thing he hadn't tried yet: the truth.

'Miss Avery, I would like to court you.'

'I beg your pardon?' She inhaled deeply. 'No, you're lying…this is a cruel joke.'

'It's not. And I'm not lying—well, I am. I don't want to court you. I want to marry you. And—'

The door slammed in his face.

Ever the optimist, he thought to himself, *It could have gone worse.* Besides, she hadn't said she *wouldn't* marry him. As far as he was concerned, as long as the word *no* did not leave her lips, he could continue his pursuit without breaking his promise to Sebastian.

Still, wooing Miss Avery was proving to be a more chal-
lenging task than he'd anticipated. And time was running
out. Even if they married at the end of the week, and conceived on their wedding night, it would take another nine
months for an heir to be born. There was scarce room for
error, and there would be no second chances. He would
have to find a way to woo her—and quickly.

I must intensify my efforts.

Yes, that was it. His gestures needed to be grander and
more opulent, to show her that he was being serious about
courting her.

Ash didn't believe in miracles but, considering what he
had accomplished in a single day, he could, in fact, categorise what he'd achieved as miraculous.

'Is everything set?' he asked Holmes as he looked
around the ballroom.

'Yes, my lord.'

His valet had worked all night, then travelled from London to help him put together his grand proposal for Miss
Avery. After his 'walk' with her yesterday, he'd sat down
and devised a plan, written down everything he required
and paid someone from the nearby village to rush the letter to his staff back in town. Sure enough, by noon, everything—and everyone—was in place.

He just needed to lure Miss Avery out of that damned
room.

Ash hadn't seen her since she'd slammed the door in his
face. She hadn't shown herself at dinner, and when he'd
enquired about her Lady Avery had said Violet was at the
dower house, as the Dowager was feeling under the weather
but didn't want to dine alone. Kate, on the other hand, had
looked ready to skewer him with the knife and fork in her

hand. Obviously she had heard about his plan to marry Miss Avery, and possibly his failed proposal.

Ash had spent the night with a chair propped against his door.

'All right, Holmes, wait here. As soon as she's inside—' he pointed to the main doors leading into the ballroom '—I want everyone to start right away.'

'Yes, my lord.'

'Excellent. I shall fetch Miss Avery now.'

Ash had barely stepped out of the ballroom when he saw Sebastian marching towards him.

'What in the world is going on, Ash?' Sebastian's dark eyebrows slashed downward. 'Eames says you have had the ballroom—*my* ballroom—locked up and forbidden any of my staff from entering this entire wing?'

'And a good day to you too,' Ash greeted him. 'Don't worry, I just need your ballroom for...oh, the next fifteen minutes or so. Then I'll be out of your hair.'

Sebastian blocked his way. 'Ash, Kate informs me that Miss Avery has told her that you proposed yesterday. You promised me you would leave her alone if she refused your suit.'

'But she didn't refuse it.'

He blocked Ash once more when he tried to sidestep him. 'Yes, she did, otherwise Lady Avery would be shouting from the rooftops with joy.'

'Miss Avery didn't say no. I didn't hear the word.'

'Ash, you need to stop the wooing.'

'I swear to you she didn't reject me. Yes, she slammed the door in my face, but until I hear her say *I don't want to marry you* then the wooing shall continue.'

'Ash, she doesn't want you. Accept it.'

Damn Sebastian. But, then again, perhaps his friend was

right. Miss Avery didn't want to marry him. There were dozens of girls who would say yes to his proposal in a heart-beat. He should leave now and stop pursuing Miss Avery.

But for some reason he just couldn't.

With a determined shrug, he feigned a step to the right, prompting the Duke to obstruct him, then quickly moved around Sebastian's left side to escape.

Sebastian let out a furious grunt when he realised he'd been fooled, but it was too late as Ash sprinted away.

'Besides,' he called back, 'the jugglers have already been paid!'

'Jugglers? What jugglers? Ash!'

Chapter Six

⁓⧼⧽⁓

Violet had re-read the formula exactly twenty-three times and she still couldn't process it. *L equals the length of the stroke in inches... D equals the diameter of the driving wheels in inches...* How could she focus when a single sentence continued to intrude into her thoughts?

'I want to marry you.'

Slamming the book closed, she knocked her forehead on the cover three times, then let out a groan.

It didn't make sense. Nothing made sense any more. But, then again, ever since she'd met the Marquess of Ashbrooke logic and her life had become incompatible.

I wish everything would go back to the way it was.

That, however, made even less sense. Time moved forward, not backwards. Things couldn't go back to the way they had been.

Pushing herself away from the book, Violet sat up straight. This was all a joke—because how could Ashbrooke change his mind so quickly? He hadn't been able to stand the sight of her all the way up to New Year's Eve and now he wanted to marry her? Was he ill in the mind? Or did he perhaps have a head injury? She recalled reading an article in one of her father's journals about men returning from the war with Napoleon who had suffered head trauma and whose personalities had completely changed. However, as far as she knew, the Marquess hadn't participated in any battles between New Year's Day and today.

A knock at the door shook her out of her thoughts. 'Who is it?'

No answer.

'Who is it?' she called, a little louder this time.

Violet drummed her fingers on top of the desk. Who could be knocking and why weren't they answering?

Rising to her feet, she cautiously crept towards the door. 'Who's out there?'

Still no answer.

Oh, it must be that new maid.

Yesterday, Violet had rung for a pot of tea. However, she'd been so caught up in her work that she'd failed to hear the knock on the door. The poor thing had been so painfully shy that she'd stood outside the door with the tray for thirty minutes, until Violet had got up to check that the kitchens had received her request.

Shrugging, she opened the door—but there was no one there.

She was about to close the door when she noticed a slip of paper on the floor. Glancing around, she bent down and picked it up, then unfolded it.

Come to the ballroom.

'The ballroom?' she said aloud.

Who would send her such a note? She flipped the paper over but found no other writing. Was it Kate?

The Duchess had been furious when Violet had told her about Ashbrooke's sudden proposal. 'You don't have to see him again,' Kate had promised, and had then made an excuse for her so she could stay in her rooms during dinner. When she hadn't found him at breakfast this morning, she'd breathed a sigh of relief. Kate had not appeared either, but the Duke had told her she was feeling ill and was still in bed.

Perhaps she had recovered and was up and about?

So Violet made her way to the ballroom.

She knocked before opening the door. 'Hello? Kate?' When no one answered, she waited a few seconds before turning the handle. 'Kate, are you in here?' she called as she entered.

The room was empty and silent, but there was something not quite right. For one thing, an enormous curtain had been drawn across the room, effectively halving the space and blocking out the light from the windows.

What on earth—

The curtain dropped to the floor, revealing a horde of people on the other side.

But they weren't just ordinary people.

A small orchestra began to play the overture to *The Marriage of Figaro*, and the blast of trumpets and drums and scurrying violins and flutes sent an unpleasant jolt of shock through her body.

Then groups of dancers filed in through the door, surrounding her. Their colourful bejewelled costumes bombarded her vision along with their frenzied, frantic movements.

Her palms began to sweat at the overwhelming display, but she somehow found the will to weave through the dancers and find a route of escape. However, as soon as she escaped that circle of hell something else exploded from one side, nearly jolting her out of her own skin.

Were those men blasting fire from their mouths?

Violet raised a hand to block out the blaze and prevent it from burning her eyes. All the sights and sounds were proving too much. Terror and panic overwhelmed her and her heart hammered in her chest. An acrid, burning sensation rose up her throat as her stomach turned, threatening to expel that morning's breakfast.

Slowly, she took deep breaths as she methodically touched her thumbs to each finger, counting from one to ten repeatedly. The harsh, abrasive sensations receded and her breathing evened. However, all her progress was lost as a horrid squawk blared into her ears.

Was that a—

Squawk! Squawk!

She could only stare as the gigantic bird—a peacock—spread its magnificent tail. But that only proved to be a momentary distraction as four jugglers began to descend towards her.

The noise and the spectacle crescendoed, but time seemed to stand still. Her body swayed as the ringing in her ears made it difficult to find her balance. Despite the cacophony, she heard a distinct male voice behind her. She managed to swing around.

'Miss Avery,' Ashbrooke began, reaching out to her. 'Will you do me the honour of becoming my wife?'

Violet opened her mouth, but nothing came out, and Ashbrooke's handsome face swam before her eyes as her vision darkened. Her chest constricted, making it difficult to breathe. Her attempt to inhale some air only seemed to make it worse.

'What the blazes is— Violet!'

Someone caught her as she toppled forward.

'Violet—dear God!' Kate cried. 'Violet, what's wrong? What do you need?'

'Need...to...leave...'

Without another word, the Duchess put an arm under her and hauled her out of the ballroom, away from the insanity of the Marquess of Ashbrooke's circus.

'What the blazes were you thinking, Ash?' Kate berated Ash once she'd found him hiding out in Sebastian's study.

'I wanted to give her a proposal she couldn't ignore and show her how serious I am,' he retorted.

'Well, she received your message—and now you need to leave.'

'But she didn't say no.'

Kate's nostrils flared as she sent him a death glare. 'That's because you nearly killed her, you imbecile. Not to mention you woke Henry from his nap with that commotion.'

'I'm sorry for waking my godson.' Ash cowered away. 'Is she...all right?'

His heart had dropped when he'd seen the abject terror on Miss Avery's face. It was at that moment he'd known he had made a terrible mistake.

'No thanks to you.'

'May I see her?'

'Absolutely not.'

Ash swallowed the lump in his throat. 'I'm sorry. I truly am.'

How had he been supposed to know his grand gesture would send Miss Avery for her smelling salts? She didn't seem the type to have a weak constitution. But he supposed the peacocks had been a bit much.

'Ash, there are about a hundred women back in London who would be willing to marry you. Why are you pursuing Violet when she clearly wants nothing to do with you?

Is it guilt? Because you think it's your fault no man will marry her? And now you're giving her a pity proposal?'

Ash hadn't even thought of that. It would have saved him the trouble of hiding his real reason for proposing to Miss Avery from Kate.

'That was hardly a pity proposal, Kate. I brought in fire eaters, for goodness' sake. Do you know how difficult it is to find them in the winter? Poor Holmes must have roamed half of London searching for them.'

'You thick-headed buffoon.' Kate threw her hands up in the air. 'She doesn't need your proposal. She doesn't need *you*.'

For some reason the words hit their mark like an arrow, right in the chest.

'My love,' said Sebastian, wrapping an arm around his wife's shoulders. 'Would you mind giving us some privacy? I'd like to speak with Ash alone.'

Kate crossed her arms under her chest and huffed. 'Fine. I'll check on Henry.'

While she accepted Sebastian's kiss on her temple, she glared at Ash before marching out.

'You idiot!' Sebastian bellowed. 'Give me one good reason why I shouldn't toss you out right now.'

'I haven't broken my promise, Sebastian. She still hasn't said no. Perhaps I went overboard and—'

'Overboard? You capsized the entire boat!' Sebastian rubbed a palm down his face. 'Have you thought about perhaps considering *her* wants? Finding out what she wants in a husband and in a marriage so you may appear more amenable to her?'

'Amenable to her? I'm rich and titled—what more could she want?'

Sebastian clicked his tongue. 'All your experience with

women and you haven't learned a thing. Ash, for once in your life, use the intelligence that I know you possess. If you can't figure out how to make her accept your proposal, then you don't deserve her. Have a think. I'm giving you one last chance, but after this I'm afraid I'm going to have to ask you to leave Miss Avery alone.'

And with that, he left.

Ash placed his hands on his hips and expelled a breath. It was obvious his usual tactics for pursuing a woman— dazzling them with his wit and charm—weren't working. Perhaps Kate was right. He should just give up.

'Never,' he said aloud.

He was the Marquess of Ashbrooke. Renowned rake and seducer of women. He was not admitting defeat so easily.

But how the hell could he figure out what Miss Avery wanted in a husband when he couldn't even get her to speak with him? And even if he did, it wasn't as if he could ask her outright.

He had to find a way to learn more about her.

An idea struck him.

'Ah!'

It was underhand and unethical—so it just might work.

Chapter Seven

Miss Avery had stayed abed the whole day and night after the proposal debacle, but the moment she was feeling well enough to leave her room Ash sprang into action. Thanks to a few well-placed bribes amongst the Highfield Park staff, he knew exactly where she and Kate were throughout the day. He saw his chance when a footman informed him that Miss Avery was scheduled to leave with the Duchess to visit the village. Knowing the two women would be gone for the day, he made his way to the east wing and let himself into Kate's office.

The Duchess would truly kill him if she found him there, so it was a good thing Ash had no plans for getting caught.

Ash crept inside, then made a quick assessment of the room. It looked as if it had been a ladies' sitting room at some point, with light pastel pink wallpaper, lace curtains, and cosy, plush furniture, but all the comfortable chairs had been pushed to one side. Instead a large oak desk and a drafting table dominated the middle of the room.

Curious, he circled around the table to the front, where various sheets of papers were stuck to the top. Leaning forward, he attempted to read what was on them, but there were no words—or at least not in English. There were numbers and symbols written in clear handwriting, seemingly

in some semblance of order that Ash could not decipher.
But what were they?

He was about to pluck one from the table for a closer
look when he heard the noisy squeak of the door handle
as it was turned.

Damn!

Panicked, he dived towards the curtains and managed to
hide behind them just as the doors flew open. He pressed
his body against the window, ignoring the cold draught fil-
tering through the cracks and through his thin shirt.

I should have worn my coat.

'It's a pity the poor road conditions forced us to turn
back,' Kate said. 'I was looking forward to showing you
the White Horse Inn Brewery.'

'And I was looking forward to seeing it,' Miss Avery
replied, then she shuddered. 'Brr... I am glad to be inside.
The cold is brutal today.'

Ash swallowed the panic building inside him as Miss
Avery walked towards him. She drew the drapes on the other
side to slide them closed, coming but mere inches from him.

She's going to find me. Then I'll be dead.

'There, that should keep out the draught.'

He relaxed once she'd walked away.

'At least we can finally finish our work,' she continued.
'I'm sorry for the delay, Kate. I promise I'll work on those
figures for you today.'

Work?

What kind of work was she talking about? Did it have
anything to do with those papers on the drafting table?

'Oh, pish-posh, you've only just recovered from your
fainting spell.' Kate paused. 'Are you sure you're well
enough to be up and about?'

'I told you. I'm fine. It's just something that...happens.

Too much noise or fast movements and colours around me seem to trigger these spells.'

Ash, you idiot.

He smacked himself on the head silently. Somehow he'd managed to find all the things that made her ill and put them together in one space. No wonder the poor girl had been sent to her sickbed.

'I've learned to cope with it over the years,' she continued. 'Small gatherings, parties, and even balls are not so bothersome, although I often need a day or two to recover from them, but I haven't had an episode like that since I was a child. The ballroom…it was just too much.'

Kate harrumphed. '"Too much" is the very definition of Ash— Oh, apologies. I shouldn't have mentioned his name.'

'It's all right, Kate.'

'I should have asked him to leave the moment he arrived. I knew he was lying, of course, but I swear I was as surprised as you when he came.'

'I believe you. And, really, he is the Duke's friend and this is his home. You couldn't have asked him to leave— not if your husband wanted him here.'

The Duchess huffed. 'Believe me, we are still having that conversation…'

'I did have something I wanted to tell you, Kate. I've decided to accept your offer.'

'Really? That's wonderful. Oh, we'll make so much progress now. But wait—is this because of Ash? Because of what he said and did?'

'No… I mean, yes.' She sighed. 'The truth is, I would never have attracted any suitor nor made any kind of match in the first place. Why would any man want to marry someone like me? Ashbrooke only verbalised what everyone else would have found out—that I'm bizarre. Too odd. Too broken.'

Indignation—and shame—rose in Ash at those words. Despite the fact that he hadn't mean to call her bizarre in a disparaging way, it was still his fault.

'Don't say that, Violet.'

'It's true, Kate. Oakwood Cottage and the library were lost the moment Papa died and it was left for me to save it through marriage. I've come to accept it. It's all right, really.'

Ash froze at the words.

So that's why she needs to marry.

Her father's death had left them destitute. She needed a rich husband to save them from poverty.

'No. No, it's not. Oakwood Cottage was your home and your papa's library was your solace. If anyone can understand what you are going through, it's me. Whenever I work with engines I feel like my grandfather is alive again and that he's here with me. And when I thought I was losing my freedom to work and my factory it was as if he was dying once more. For you to lose the one place that meant so much to you and to him—it must feel like you're losing your father all over again.'

A dead silence filled the air.

'But at least with your offer of a job Mama and I won't be penniless.'

'I'm so glad you've accepted. You truly are gifted with numbers. I've never seen anything quite like it. And with you as my chief mathematician I'll be able to shorten my timeline for creating new designs and increase efficiency at the factory. I have so many ideas for us to try.'

'I cannot wait. Now I only have to convince my mother. I fear she'll never agree to it.' Miss Avery let out another shiver. 'The fire's gone out.'

'I've instructed the maids not to enter this room unless one of us is around, so no one has come to stoke the fire. Why don't we go to the library for some tea? We can celebrate your new position. But let's stop by the nursery first. I should check on Henry.'

Ash held his breath, waiting until he heard the sound of the door clicking shut before he expelled it. Pushing the curtains aside, he stumbled out from his hiding place. A dizzying sensation threatened to overcome him, so he braced himself against the drafting table. Once the feeling passed, he lifted his head and focused on the neat writing on the paper.

Her handwriting.

This was all Miss Avery's work.

In an instant, he saw the symbols and numbers in a different light. Reaching out, he dragged a fingertip across a line of equations. The beauty and the wealth of knowledge in her mind was in these pages. He couldn't decipher any of it, but now he did understand her.

Miss Avery—Violet—had a logical mind for mathematics. And if Kate—who was quite intelligent herself—said that she was gifted, then Violet must truly be beyond brilliant.

Ash had once had an instructor at university like her—Professor Halston. He'd been a mad old bat, set in his ways, and had liked order and routine. Normally quiet and unassuming, he'd once thrown a book at a student who was tapping his pen on a table. In one instance a few students who'd hated him had chased him around with Roman candles; he'd been absent for an entire week.

Halston had been truly unlike any of his other professors. He had not succumbed to Ash's cajoling or flattery when he'd needed better marks or extra points in his exams.

No, Professor Halston's mind could only be changed with logic and reason.

So, that was how Ash would formulate his next and hopefully final proposal. This time, it wouldn't take him much time or effort to put it together. No, he didn't need pomp and ceremony for this one. He just needed to get Violet alone.

So he implored Sebastian to help him once again, promising that if she rejected him he would leave her alone.

Early the next day Ash headed to the orangery and waited by the fountain. Fishing out his pocket watch, he kept his eye on the time, as he knew Sebastian would be punctual. Sure enough, at eleven fifty-eight, he heard voices and footsteps coming towards them. Ash strained to hear the conversation.

'Such a marvel,' Lady Avery gasped. 'It's like summer in here.'

'There is a boiler underneath us that produces steam and filters it out through the vents,' Sebastian explained.

'I should like to see that,' Violet said.

'Perhaps Kate could show you some time.' The footsteps halted. 'Oh, dear.'

'Your Grace? What's wrong?'

'Lady Avery... I feel incredibly foolish.'

'Foolish?'

'Yes. My wife is with Henry as he's been crying all morning. She thinks he might be ill and has asked me to retrieve... Oh, dear, I can't remember it. Something to help soothe Henry. I was supposed to ask the kitchen to prepare it.'

'Oh, goodness.' Lady Avery's hand covered her chest. 'Did she ask for a poultice of some sort?'

'Yes—exactly. I should have known you'd understand.

You are a mother, after all.' Sebastian tsked. 'I feel so very terrible, not knowing about such things.'

'You are a man, Your Grace, you are not expected to know about these things.'

'Lady Avery, I don't suppose you are knowledgeable about poultices?'

'I… Well, I do recall one that I used for Violet when she was an infant.'

'Lady Avery, could I impose upon you…?'

'Not an imposition at all, Your Grace. It would be an honour. Come, let's go back to the kitchens. Violet, could you—'

'Surely we don't all need to go? I mean, kitchens are hot and dirty, and the staff will be skittish enough having me there with you. Miss Avery, didn't you say you wanted to see the fountains?'

'Yes, Your Grace.'

'They're just up ahead.'

'Your Grace, surely we can't leave Violet—'

'There's no one else here, Lady Avery. She will be fine.'

'Well…if you say so, Your Grace.'

Ash straightened up, smoothing his palms down his coat and trousers. His heart pummelled out an erratic rhythm, but he managed to calm it with deep breaths. A knot tightened in his gut as he spotted Violet coming around the corner. When their eyes met, she gasped.

'Miss Avery—'

'What are you doing here?' Her voice was strained and taut with tension, as if she were going to burst into tears at any moment.

'I just… I wanted to…'

'Stop.' She held up a hand. 'Just say it. Please.'

'You know why I'm here. I want to marry you.'

The colour drained from her face, and from the way her body tensed he could sense she was ready to flee.

'Please, Violet.' She didn't flinch at the use of her name. 'I promise—really promise this time—that if you say no I will never approach you again. But just hear me out.'

She eyed him, those stunning orbs boring right into him. 'All right, my lord.'

'Thank you.' He blew out a breath. 'First, is this place...? I mean, are you comfortable here?'

'I...' Confusion crossed her face. 'Yes.'

'It's not too bright? Does the steam from the vents bother you? If it wasn't so cold outside, I would take you somewhere peaceful.'

'It's fine, my lord.'

'Excellent.' He cleared his throat. 'Violet, I know you would probably prefer I get right to the point, so I shall tell you the truth. I know about your father's death and that you will soon be without a home.'

'How?'

Guilt poured through Ash, but he knew he had to tell the truth. 'Violet, I was spying on you.'

'What?'

'I overheard you speaking with Kate in her office... I was hiding behind the curtains.'

Her mouth formed a perfect O. 'You were hiding? Eavesdropping? Did you see anything in the office?'

'Enough. And I apologise. But I just wanted to know you. Understand you. Please forgive me.'

Her teeth chewed at her lip. 'I supposed you would have found out about my father.'

'Eventually.'

'And you are being honest with me—which I appreciate.'

'Good. So now you must marry me.'

'I beg your pardon? I must?'

'Yes.' He could see the confusion her face. 'You need me, so I can pay off your father's debts, and I need you, Violet.'

She frowned. 'I highly doubt that. I have nothing to give you.'

He chuckled. 'Actually, there is something you can give me.'

'And what is that?'

'An heir.'

Colour drained from her face. 'No—'

'Before you say no, please allow me to continue. Listen, and then you can say no.' His nerves felt frayed at the edges, but he soldiered on. 'A few days ago a solicitor came to my house…'

And he told her everything—the truth about the clause, the Canfields, and his need for a legitimate heir.

'So you see, you can help me fulfil the requirements of the clause before my next birthday.'

'I do not see why it must be me. Surely there are multitudes of women in London who would be more than willing to marry you and produce an heir.'

Why indeed?

But before he could come up with an answer, she spoke first.

'Are you proposing to me out of pity, my lord? Because you have ruined my chances of finding a match?'

'Yes,' he blurted out, hoping that was the right answer. 'I mean, yes, *partly*. And I'm only partly responsible for that horrid nickname, you know. I did not spread it amongst the Ton.'

'But you invented it. Why?'

'Because you are.'

'Bizarre?'

'A beauty.'

Her eyes grew wide and her lips parted.

Taking advantage of momentarily stunning her, he continued. 'There is nothing wrong with being different, Violet. I found you quite refreshing that first night we met. I had misinterpreted your intentions because of what your mother said, but I see now that you are not some scheming debutante. After learning more about you, I've come to the conclusion that you're a logical, reasonable woman. And our marrying makes sense.'

'And that's all you require of me? An heir, to be produced within the next year?'

'Yes. The only other stipulation I have is that you cannot fall in love with me.'

She scoffed. 'I hardly think that's possible.'

He ignored the knot in his chest. 'See? That makes you the perfect candidate. I don't have time for silly games and romance and sweet nothings. I need to secure my lands with an heir, and you need my funds to save your home and your papa's library.'

Her eyes lit up at the mention of her father.

'It makes perfect, logical sense.'

'There is a flaw in your argument, my lord.'

'What is it? And, please, do call me Ash.'

'Ash…' She said the name aloud slowly, experimentally, as if she were testing the way it sounded to her ears. 'There is a chance I could produce no heir at all and then we would both end up penniless.'

'True. But that could happen anyway. You currently have no suitors, and I have no time. There's no way to predict if my chances of begetting an heir would be higher with another woman, but the probability of saving your home increases if you marry me.'

'I—' Her mouth clamped shut. 'I could end up homeless, married to a man with no prospects.'

'Well, there's one more thing.'

'And what is that?'

'Once we do produce an heir, you'll be free to follow your own pursuits. I imagine your mother would never allow you to work with Kate at the factory—not unless you become completely destitute. As your husband, I'll give you my permission to do as you please, even if we don't secure the lands. In a year you'll be free of me, and of your mother.' He paused, allowing the information to sink in before he continued, 'What do you think?'

She stood there, not speaking, not moving for what seemed like a lifetime. 'My lord—Ash,' she began when she finally spoke, 'I appreciate your honesty and this logical solution to our problems. But there is one more thing you must know about me.'

'And what is that?'

'I should not... I cannot...' Colour bloomed in her cheeks. 'You will not want to marry me after I tell you.'

'You need to tell me, don't you, for me to assess that?'

Her gaze lowered. 'I'm afraid I cannot have marital relations with you. I'm a virgin, you see, and...'

'I expected as much. Violet, it's normal to fear intimate—'

'No, no.' Her arms stiffened at her sides. 'This isn't a virgin's fear. The fact of the matter is, I cannot stand being touched.'

'You can't? Why not? What do you mean?'

'Do you remember the other day? In the ballroom?'

How could he forget? 'Yes.'

'I was overwhelmed. By all the new sensations. Anything new and unknown drives me to panic—to fear. It was too much. Some days, the whole world is too much. I've learned to live with it, through practice and experience. I can cope with nearly all the sights and sounds bombarding me because I've had years of repetition to show me the variables and possible outcomes, so I can make the right decisions. It's not perfect, and sometimes I fail spectacularly—like when I blurt out random facts or my thoughts just come flying out of my mouth.'

She pressed her lips together.

'I've read about what the marital act requires and, frankly, the thought of being touched like that...everywhere... I cannot stand it. It makes me want to vomit. The fluids...the contact...the—'

'I understand. You don't have to elaborate further.'

'You see, that's the flaw in your logic. Rather, *I'm* the flaw. I'm too broken—'

'Stop.' He held up a hand. 'It doesn't have to be that way.'

'What do you mean? Can you fix me?'

Fix her? 'No, Violet. What I'm trying to say is that it's natural to fear sexual relations, especially when you've never experienced them.'

'Is it? Were you ever afraid?'

He strangled the laugh building in his throat. 'Anything new can be overwhelming. But what if it wasn't so new to you?'

She cocked her head. 'What do you mean?'

'You say you need time and practice and repetition to help you overcome your fears. What if you practised?'

'P-practised?' Her eyes widened. 'Is that possible?'

'Of course it's possible.'

'But with whom?'

Without hesitation, he said, 'With me, of course.'

* * *

Violet could only stare at the Marquess's—Ash's—handsome face as she processed his words. 'Practise with you?'

'Yes, who else?'

Her mind immediately focused on the details. 'And when would we begin?'

'Now is a good time.'

'What would this practice entail?'

He tapped a finger on his chin. 'Tell me, how did you train yourself to overcome your panic and fear in other overwhelming situations?'

She bit at her lip. 'My papa taught me some techniques. He was like me.'

'Ah-ha.' The sound of the snap of his fingers reverberated across the room, bouncing off the glass ceiling. 'If you brief me on these techniques, I may be able to adapt them for our practice.'

'So you could be like a teacher? The way Papa was with me?'

'Er…not exactly. I mean, your father…er…' Ash's complexion had turned an alarming shade of grey.

'Are you all right?'

'Um…yes. But let's not speak of your papa at this moment, as I doubt he would approve of my…er…techniques.'

'He's dead, Ash. He won't be here to disapprove.'

He let out a strangled sound. 'Still…in order for me to practise with you, I would prefer we don't mention him.'

'As you wish.'

Hopefully he wouldn't be acting this strangely throughout the practice session, she thought.

'First I must prepare my mind and anticipate all the possible outcomes of the situation, so as to reduce any chance of surprises catching me off-guard. Knowing things in advance allows me to anticipate all the variables and prepare.'

'So, no surprises?' He paused. 'If I tell you what I'm going to do, would that help?'

'Immensely.'

'Understood.' His firm lips pursed together. 'Violet, I'm going to move close to you. Very, very close.'

'Wait.' She processed the information and blew out a breath. 'All right.'

He crossed the distance between them with one step. This close, he towered over her, but she found it didn't bother her—not even the fact that there was only a small gap between them. Knowing he was going to do this had allowed her to prepare her mind and body.

'How are you feeling? Relaxed?'

'More like...unbothered.'

Though her mind was not protesting at his closeness, her body was reacting differently. An unusual tautness had built in her stomach, like a string being pulled. It only increased when she inhaled and received a whiff of something pleasant coming from... Ash?

Curious, she leaned her head forward and sniffed.

'Violet? Is something the matter?'

'Nothing. I mean...that smell.' She inhaled once more, just to be certain. 'Are you wearing a different cologne today?'

It was different from the one he'd had on the first night they'd met.

'I hope I don't smell like Mr Eldridge,' he joked.

He obviously remembered that story from the night they'd first met.

'Um...not at all.'

In fact, he smelled *good*.

Leaning forward, she took in another whiff.

Oh, Lord, it *was* good.

'I'm afraid I didn't have time to put any on as I was in a rush this morning. That's all me, I'm afraid.'

'Oh.'

Was that his natural scent?

'Is it all right?'

'Yes, it's fine.'

Wonderful, actually.

However, she had to restrain herself from continuing to sniff at him, lest he think she were a bloodhound.

'Please continue.'

'As you wish. Now, I am going to hold your hand.'

Her nerves frayed. 'Which hand?'

'Does it matter?'

She nodded.

'The left one. With my right.'

'A-all right.'

Violet closed her eyes and held her breath. Their gloved fingers made contact, then the slightest pressure wrapped around her left hand.

He let go.

'So?'

'It was not…unpleasant.'

It had been over much too soon for her taste.

'I see. Shall I go on?'

'Yes.'

He continued, telling her where he would touch her—her upper right arm, her left shoulder and her elbow—before actually making any contact. With each touch, Violet found she needed less and less time to prepare.

'How are you now?' he asked. 'Are you feeling uncomfortable? Is this too much? Should I stop?'

'No!' That sounded rather emphatic. 'Not at all.'

'All right.' He raked his hand through his golden hair, leaving it tousled. 'So, we've established that when it comes to touch informing you allows you to prepare. What's next?'

'Um…the next technique is exposure.'

'I beg your pardon?' he spluttered.

'Exposure to all the different variables makes them… well, not variable any longer.'

'Oh? So repeated touches should help?'

'Yes.'

'All right. Now, I'm going to touch your—'

'You needn't say it all over again,' she interrupted. 'I mean, you've already established that you're going to touch me, and where. Once you've said it, I don't need it to be repeated.'

'Oh, thank the Lord. Otherwise this would take a very, very long time. So…'

He gave her hand a tentative squeeze, then brushed against the same spots on her arm, shoulder and elbow. Violet did not tense with each one, nor did she find it repulsive. In fact, she was mildly disappointed that it was once again over so quickly.

'I trust my touch was not offensive?' he asked.

'Not at all.'

'May I touch you…more?' he asked, hesitant.

A curious sensation prickled the back of her knees. 'Oh, yes.'

'On other places?'

The idea that he wanted to keep touching her on other places on her body took a while longer for her to process, but eventually she bobbed her head up and down.

'Violet, I want… May I touch your cheek?

She drew in a breath. 'Yes.'

Raising his hand, he brushed a thumb across her cheek-bone.

Just as he was about to withdraw, Violet found herself reaching up to stop him. 'You may touch me for longer.'

The corner of his lip tugged up. 'If you say so.'

As his thumb continued its caress, the tingling behind her knees increased and spread up the backs of her thighs. She sighed and leaned into his hand, but when his finger strayed lower to touch her lips, she jolted.

'Apologies.' He pulled away. 'I should have... Violet, I'm sorry.'

Her eyes flew open. 'It's...it's all right. Apology accepted. Please, go on.'

'Are you sure?'

'Yes.'

Once again he caressed her cheek, adding more pressure. This time, his touch was most definitely pleasant. The fabric of his soft gloves was soothing, and the warmth of his skin seeped through. He had leaned closer too, so his tantalising scent tickled her nostrils.

'Violet?'

'Hmm...?'

'May I kiss you?'

The request sent a shock through her, and panic rose.

'Violet, are you all right? You seem to be breathing rather rapidly.'

'What?' She slowed her breath, taking deep, long gulps of air. 'No, breathing helps me. Steadies me.'

He didn't move...didn't even take his hand away. And as she took deep breaths she concentrated on the sensation of the fabric of his gloves and his scent.

'I'm sorry. That was a lot to ask.'

'No... I just... I've been learning to tolerate touch since I was a child. But I haven't... I've never—'

'Been kissed? On the lips?'

She shook her head. 'No.'

'No daring young boy from the village has ever tried?' he asked in a light tone.

'I never go out to the village.' It was far too noisy and crowded and smelly. 'I just stay at home.'

'Violet...my sheltered, shy Violet. I can almost picture you at home, surrounded by your books all day. You must look adorable?'

'Adorable?'

'Yes. Spending your days in your father's library, learning about mathematics.'

'And philosophy and nature and biology.' Truly, Papa's library was extensive, and she'd read nearly all the books twice. 'It is my favourite place. I've never felt so safe anywhere else.'

'Think of that place, then, when you're feeling overwhelmed.'

She pictured the library. The smell of paper and leather and tobacco. The feel of the rough paper and soft leather underneath her fingertips. Papa's soothing voice as he read aloud.

'There you go,' he whispered. 'All better?'

She realised her breathing had returned to normal. 'Yes.'

'Now may I kiss you? On the lips?'

'Yes.'

His head moved down towards her in slow motion, his eyes closing. Violet found herself doing the same. The touch of his lips was much lighter than she had expected. His mouth brushed against her for only the briefest moment before he pulled away.

'How was that?'

'F-fine.' Opening her eyes once more, she looked into his sapphire gaze. 'C-could you do that again?'

The request came out much too quickly, but she was unable to stop herself.

'Longer this time?'

'Really?'

'Yes, please.'

His mouth descended on hers, this time with more force. Firm lips pressed against hers, moving in a slow rhythm. It was pleasant, but it felt lacking. Deficient, even. So she pushed herself up on her tiptoes. This caused him to add more pressure to the kiss. And then he drew her bottom lip into his mouth. Something wet and warm stroked over her lip—his tongue. The sensation was new, but she didn't mind it. She whimpered from the sensation.

'I… My apologies.' He pulled away. 'I didn't mean to… It was too much.'

'No, not at all.'

'No? How was it for you?'

Violet struggled to describe it. Perhaps it was because she had never felt anything like it—not on a first touch. Her heart raced, her limbs were loose, and there was a fluttering in her stomach as if a hundred butterflies wanted to burst forth.

'We should stop,' he said. 'I should go— Mmph!'

The idea that he wanted to stop and leave her had caused panic to rise in Violet, and so she'd acted on impulse—lunging up at him and raking her fingers through the back of his hair to pull him down to her lips.

Their mouths met in a frenzied, hurried dance. His arms wound around her waist, but the touch didn't repel her, although she would have slid to the ground had it not been for the support.

Violet parted her lips, hoping he'd understand the invitation. He did, and he dipped his tongue between her lips, darting in quickly. When she moaned aloud and pulled his head closer he plunged in, rubbing his rough tongue against hers.

Lord, he smelled *and* tasted good.

And she wanted more.

Her fingertips raked his scalp. That elicited a throaty moan from him, bringing a strange thrill through her. She wanted to taste more of him, so she pushed her tongue into his mouth, mimicking his earlier movements. Her arms wound tighter around him, pressing her to him, and the sensation sent her to the edge. His hips brushed against hers and she felt a hardened bulge against her belly.

He abruptly pulled away.

'My lord—Ash, did I do something wrong?' Violet could not read his face...could not decipher the look he gave her.

Was it good?

Bad?

Was he angry?

His eyes nearly bulged out of their sockets and his face was flushed. 'Are you sure you've never been kissed before?'

'That was my first. Second, if you count the first one you gave me. Did I do anything wrong? Was it awful?'

'Awful?' A rich laugh escaped his mouth. 'Not at all, Violet. You didn't do anything wrong, and it certainly was not awful. I found myself...overwhelmed.' He adjusted the front of his coat. 'But I'm afraid this practice must cease.'

'Oh...' Disappointment filled her.

'For now.'

He touched her face again and Violet tried not to rub her cheek against his glove—and failed.

'We can continue later, though.'

'There's more to practise?' she asked, incredulous.

'Oh, so much more, Violet. If you are amenable.'

She was absolutely, positively amenable. 'I am. When?'

'How about tonight?' His voice lowered. 'In your room.'

It was a shocking thought. To have a man—Ash—in her room tonight.

But also intriguing.

'Is that too forward?' he asked, his jaw set. 'We don't have to anything you don't want to, but if you want me to come I promise to leave the moment you become uncomfortable. Just say the word.'

Warmth pooled in her chest. Had any man—anyone, really—ever been so thoughtful of her?

'All right. What time will you be there?'

His expression relaxed. 'Once everyone has gone to bed I will come to you.'

'I need a time. So I can prepare.'

'How about…eight minutes past eleven?'

'Eight minutes past eleven?' she repeated. 'Why not make it eleven o'clock or half-past eleven? Even a quarter past would have been preferable.'

The corner of his mouth quirked and she recognised that he was teasing. It was a triumphant feeling, to unlock a new facial expression. She quickly added it to her mental catalogue.

'You are jesting with me.'

'Only because you are so adorable.' He planted a kiss on her forehead, then stiffened. 'I forgot to tell you I was going to do that.'

'N-no, it's fine. As I said, once I've been exposed to a variable, it becomes no longer a variable.'

The touch of his lips to her forehead had been enjoyable, in fact, in a different way from his other kisses.

'I'll remember that.' He tapped a finger to his temple. 'You should return to the house. I shall follow along later, so no one suspects you were here with me.'

'Of course.' She'd forgotten that they were alone, unchaperoned. 'Good day, Ash.'

'Good day, Violet.'

Violet wasn't sure how she managed to get through the rest of the day. It was as if she was walking in a thick fog, and no information could penetrate the cloud surrounding her mind. Working on her equations was a futile exercise. Dinner was practically a muddle of confusion—especially with Ash just a few feet away from her, acting as if nothing had happened. And having him so near only built the tension inside her, stretching it taut, waiting to snap.

When she was finally in bed, and Gertrude had left her alone, Violet expected the tension would disappear. However, as she stared at the clock, it only grew with each passing minute.

Five minutes past eleven.

Six minutes past eleven.

Seven minutes past eleven.

Eight minutes past.

And nothing.

The second hand continued ticking. It was halfway across the clock face when she heard the door creak open and Ash slipped inside, wearing only a black robe while his feet were bare.

'You're thirty seconds late,' she stated.

'Apologies.' He closed the door behind her. 'Damned candle blew out. Had to grope my way here.'

Violet sat up, then swung her legs over the side of the bed. 'Next time, just say a quarter past eleven, then you'll be early.'

He grinned from ear to ear. 'If I had my way, the next time I find myself in your rooms will be on our wedding night.'

Her heart drummed madly at the thought, and that tingling behind her knees returned.

'Now, I'm going to come closer,' he announced, then strode over to her. 'Is this all right?'

'Yes,' she whispered. 'And I told you—you don't have to repeat telling me about anything that you've already done before.'

'You are referring to all the things we did in the orangery this afternoon?'

'Yes.'

'Did you like it, Violet?'

Dryness permeated her mouth. Unable to utter a word, she nodded.

'Which part?'

Her gaze lowered to the floor. 'All of it.'

'Would you like me to do it again?'

'Yes.'

'Good.'

A hand reached out to cup her chin and tip her head up. She flinched, making him draw his hand away.

'Violet…?'

'Your hand,' she said. 'You're not wearing gloves.'

'Oh, should I go and get them?' Panic filled his voice. 'I can—'

'No!' Her arms reached out to grab the lapels of his

robe. 'Oh…' Distracted, she rubbed her fingers over the soft, furry fabric. 'That's nice. Velvet?'

'It is.'

The smooth nap against her skin was soothing. 'Ash? Could you please continue?'

'Of course. I'm going to touch you now, Violet. With my bare hands.'

Once again he cupped her chin, their skin touching. This time she didn't mind it at all. In fact, she rather liked the feel of his warm fingers pressing on her.

'Can we do what we did this afternoon?'

His head swooped down to capture her mouth in a kiss. This time it was more urgent—demanding, even. She found herself sliding her hands up the lapels of his robe and then pushing her fingers into the nape of his neck—oh, the hair was so soft there! Unable to help herself, she wound the locks around her fingers and pulled.

'Violet…' he gasped against her mouth. 'You're going to be the death of me.'

Releasing his hair, she dropped her hands to her sides. 'What did I do wrong?'

'Nothing. I mean, it's all right. It felt good.'

'I made you feel good?'

'Yes, darling.' He nipped at her lips. 'It was very, very good. Now, shall we continue our practice?'

'That would be best. What is next?'

Ash paused. 'You said you know how the marital act is done?'

She nodded. 'In theory, yes. The…mechanical aspects. The man's member enters the woman's organ and expels its seed to fertilise her.' She frowned. 'Is there more to it?'

'There is so much more to the act of making love. There's touching.'

'Where?'

'Everywhere.'

Surprisingly, the thought didn't repel her. In fact, the most curious warmth pooled in her belly at his words.

'And it will feel good. I promise. May I show you?'

'All right.'

'Lie down on the bed.'

She did as he instructed, backing away until she reached the edge, then climbing in. The mattress dipped beneath her, indicating that he had joined her.

'Violet, I'm going to lift your night-rail.'

The fabric swept up her thighs, exposing her skin to the cool air. Ash pushed it all the way up, over her breasts.

'Open your eyes, Violet.'

She did—and found him looking down at her.

'You're so lovely, Violet. All of you. I'm going to kiss your breast. Your left breast.'

Her body tensed, and she almost protested, except once his warm mouth had wrapped around her left nipple she lost all thought. His tongue circled the hardened bud, lashing it with a wet, warm heat. Her body seemed to have a life of its own as she began to squirm under his touch.

Much to her disappointment, he released her. 'I'm going to kiss the other nipple, then I'm going to caress your thighs and touch you between your legs.'

And he switched his attention to her other breast, while his hand gently landed between her thighs. He teased her, fingers pressing and massaging the soft flesh there.

The sensation made her dizzy—in a good way. She thought that was the culmination of it all—until he reached her sex, his fingers sifting through the tuft of downy hair before seeking out the swollen petals of her most intimate part.

Her hips bucked at the touch. His fingers were working

her like magic. Then he found the swollen bud at the crest and centred his attention there, stroking it in a maddening rhythm that made her cry out in the most unladylike way.

Ash released her nipple. 'I'm going to kiss you here.' His finger pressed hard on her. 'I want to make you come, Violet,' he murmured. 'It should feel good, but if you feel overwhelmed, or uncomfortable, just say the word and I will stop.'

He moved lower, trailing kisses down her body before reaching between her legs. Nudging her thighs apart, he ran his tongue across the crease of her sex.

Her fingers reached for the sheets, curling around them, and her feet kicked out as Ash's mouth and tongue worked her to a frenzy. His movements switched from gentle and teasing to fast and feverish, bringing her to the edge. She writhed underneath his touch as her body exploded with pleasure, and when he pushed a finger inside her she didn't even mind that he hadn't warned her first.

She was too lost in ecstasy to care.

'Violet? How do you feel?'

'I...I...'

Lord, that had been... Well, the words in the English language to describe it had apparently not yet been invented.

'Was it good, at least?' He sat up, then moved away from between her thighs, curling up beside her.

She nodded. Once her heart had stopped racing and her limbs were relaxed, she asked, 'But what about the rest of it?'

'The act to conceive, you mean.'

'Yes. It will be painful?'

'I'm afraid so. But I will do my best to relieve your discomfort and it should only hurt the first time.'

She knew that. After all, if copulation caused agony all

the time, the world's population would have dwindled to nothing.

A soft kiss was pressed to her temple. 'What else can I do to ensure there are no more surprises?'

'May I see you?' She plucked up her courage. 'Touch you?'

His blond eyebrows drew together. 'You don't mind?'

'No, I don't mind it when I do the touching. So, please... may I touch you?'

'You have my permission to touch me.' Rolling onto his back, he untied his robe. 'Anywhere. And you may do anything to me.'

Violet sat up. Unsure what to do, she ran her hands over the lapels of his robe, then parted it, revealing the expanse of his chest. Tentatively, she pressed her palms on it, feeling the hard muscles covered in a soft mat of hair. She rather liked the feel of the soft and hard at the same time. Feeling bolder, she further parted his robe, exposing his naked torso to her gaze, then lower to—

'Oh.'

'Oh?' His head rose from where it rested on the pillow. 'What's wrong?'

'I...' She glanced down again at his stiff member, jutting out from the thick patch of hair between his legs. 'Are you sure that's going to fit?'

He stifled a laugh. 'I'm very sure.' Reaching out, he stroked her arm encouragingly. 'When you're aroused, and after your orgasm, your sex becomes wet.'

She pressed her thighs together, confirming what he said.

'That will help me ease into you. If not, I also have an oil we can use. It should make it hurt less.'

There was still some doubt in her mind, but he'd been honest with her so far, so she had to trust that he knew best.

'May I touch you? Th-there?'

His blue eyes darkened. 'As I said, you have my permission to touch me anywhere. In perpetuity.'

Violet hesitated, then squared her shoulders before extending her hand towards his abdomen. Her fingers brushed up and down his length tentatively, but it didn't really feel different from touching his arm or the rest of him. So she wrapped her hand around it.

Curious.

The hardness was definitely there, like steel, but the warm skin and flesh made it feel so alive.

She wondered what would happen if she stroked it.

Ash moaned as she moved her hand up and down. Her fingers gripped him tighter, moving in a steady rhythm. When she increased the speed, his hips bucked up to meet her hand.

'Yes… Violet… Don't stop.'

She switched her gaze back and forth from his hard shaft, which now glistened at the tip, to his face, which was twisting with an expression she could only guess was ecstasy. It was difficult to decide where to focus her attention, as both sights fascinated her.

'Violet…stop!'

Abruptly, she released him. 'Did I hurt you?'

'No, no, darling.' He heaved himself up, then reached for her hand and squeezed. 'It was marvellous. I just want more.'

'More?'

'Hmm… Will you let me try something else? Something new?'

'Are you going to complete the marital act?'

'No, but we will get as close to it without breaking your maidenhead.' He pushed her down on the bed so she lay on her back. 'Think of it as more practice to get you accustomed to the idea of lovemaking. Do you want to try it?'

She bit at her lip. It was intriguing, this proposition of his. 'Yes, I want to try.'

Placing his hands between her thighs, he spread them apart. 'I'm going to position myself between your legs, and then I'm going to get very close to you.'

Violet braced herself as his body pressed down on hers. She had prepared herself to hate it, but to her surprise she rather enjoyed the feeling of his weight on top of her. His arms snaked around her, which brought her even closer to him.

'Oh…' She pressed her face against his neck. His delicious scent was so much stronger coming from the skin behind his ear. 'You really smell so good.'

If a perfumier ever found a way to bottle that scent, she would buy out his entire stock.

'Now I'm going to move.' His hips stroked up and down slowly. 'Like this.'

'Mmm-hmm…'

She was still rubbing her nose on his neck, savouring his smell, so she didn't pay much attention to the sensation. However, when he shifted his hips, and his shaft rubbed right along her crease, the friction sent a jolt of pleasure up her spine.

'Ash!' Her hands gripped his shoulders.

He grunted and continued the motions, his warm, hard flesh stroking her, spreading her wetness around. Once in a while, his tip would connect with the bud atop her sex, sending the most delicious thrill through her.

His weight, his smell, their bodies sliding together, the sounds they were making—everything was new, and the sensations were overwhelming, yet she was much too distracted to panic. That pressure began to build within her again, and she orgasmed once more as Ash whispered encouraging words in her ear.

He continued his movements on top of her, rubbing himself against her until his body tensed and he let out a strangled cry. Wetness splashed against her belly, and then he slowed his movements before rolling over on his back, his breath coming in gasps.

'Ash…' she began a moment later. 'Did you…?'

'Yes. I had an orgasm as well.'

'Did it feel good?'

'Very much so.'

'Does this practice satisfy you?' he asked. 'Does it reassure you and help you overcome your fear of touch?'

'Yes. But only with you.' Frankly, the thought of doing that with anyone else made her stomach churn.

He grinned. 'And so now you have listened to my arguments, seen the logic of my reasoning, had your objections quelled and your fears allayed, Miss Violet Avery, will you do me the honour of being my wife?'

Truly, she couldn't argue with that proposal. And so she answered without hesitation. 'Yes, I will.'

'Excellent.' He breathed a sigh of relief. 'We will be married in three days.'

'Three days?' She sat up quickly. 'How? Isn't there a procedure we must follow? Banns to be read and such?'

'Indeed there is, but I secured a special licence before I left London.'

Before he'd left London?

'How did you accomplish the paperwork so quickly? And what clergyman would issue you a licence without the name of the bride?'

'I did know the name of my bride—yours.' He flashed her a grin. 'The licence already has our names on it.'

'Our names? You procured our marriage license before you came here to ask me to marry you? What if I had said no?'

'I had my doubts, yes, but I thought I had better be prepared, just in case.' He winked at her. 'But that's all moot now, since you've said yes.'

'But three days… Is that even enough time to arrange a wedding? What about dresses and breakfasts and bridesmaids?'

He paused. 'My apologies, Violet. I didn't consider your preferences.' He kissed her on the temple. 'I suppose we could wait another month. That would be enough time for you to have your trousseau made, plan the wedding, send out invitations—'

'Invitations?' She swallowed hard.

'Yes, for the guests. I suppose you and your mother will want a big affair? With one hundred guests in attendance, perhaps?'

The thought of standing in a room full of people with the focus on her had her palms dampening and her stomach turning.

'No, thank you. Let's get married here. With the Duke, Kate, the Dowager and Mama.'

'Whatever you want, darling. Tomorrow morning, I—*we* will speak with your mama, and then we will announce our engagement at breakfast. Will that be all right?'

It sounded quick and efficient—she liked it. 'Yes.'

'Excellent.' He gave her a quick kiss. 'Now, I should get back to my own rooms before anyone discovers me here.'

Ash left the bed, then hurriedly dressed, bidding her goodnight before he slipped out through the door.

As she lay in bed, all alone in the dark, one thought repeated in Violet's head.

She was going to be married.

To Ash.

Chapter Eight

'**M**arriage?'

Lady Avery's exclamation made Violet cower. Seeing her shrink back, Ash took her hand and squeezed. He was glad they'd asked her to meet them in the library before breakfast, without anyone else around.

'Yes, Lady Avery. I asked Violet to marry me yesterday and she said yes.'

She looked to Violet. 'Why didn't you tell me?'

'It just…happened.'

'My lord, you haven't courted her properly. There is a process to this…a way to do things.' She tsked. 'Think of her reputation.'

In his haste in attempting to secure Violet's hand in marriage Ash had forgotten a small, yet crucial part of the equation—Lady Avery's permission. She was still Violet's mother, after all. While she might not object to the marriage itself, she would certainly protest against its expeditiousness. He would have to convince her to allow him to marry Violet in three days.

But that was a simple matter for Ash. Charming ladies into doing what he wanted happened to be his speciality.

However, what explanation would a woman like Lady Avery believe?

Think, Ash, think!

An idea struck him.

'Lady Avery, please forgive me.' He mustered his most remorseful tone, even casting his gaze downward. 'I'm afraid I was struck by your daughter's beauty and wit from the first moment I saw her.'

The woman's eyes grew to the size of saucers. 'Are you saying you fell in love with her at first sight?'

He nodded vigorously. 'You see, all these years I have thought myself immune to Cupid's arrows. I've avoided his sights for many years. But alas!' Waving his hand dramatically, he pounded his chest with his fist. 'He found me. I was struck. In love.'

Silently, he sent a prayer to Professor Kingston, his deceased teacher of poetry and literature during his university days.

'Desperately so. I had to make Violet mine.'

'But you have had months to court her. You never even paid her a call.'

'This is my first time being in love, my lady.' He glanced over at Violet, who was now eyeing him suspiciously. He grinned at her. 'I resisted, like…er… Romeo and Juliet.'

'Didn't they die?' Lady Avery's gaze narrowed at him.

'Er…no… I mean, that must have been in a different version you read.' He cleared his throat. 'Anyway, for weeks I was sick with love…unable to eat, sleep, or do much else, really.'

When Violet rolled her eyes, he tugged at her hand.

'So you came here to propose?'

'Yes. I could not stand it any more. I saw her at the Spanish Ambassador's party and I knew I had to confess my feelings before they burst out of my chest. Yesterday morning I came upon her in the orangery and took my chance.

Confessed my love to her on my knees and asked her—no, *begged* her—to marry me.'

'You said yes, Violet? Without telling me?'

'We are telling you now, Mama. And I didn't say yes right away. I had to think about it, and I told him last night.'

'Last night? When?'

'This morning!' Violet blurted out. 'I mean I accepted this morning, which is why we wanted to speak to you.'

'Oh, I see.' Her face lit up, as it seemed to dawn on her what was happening. 'Of course you'll be wed. Violet, I can't believe it. You're going to be the Marchioness of Ash-brooke.'

Lady Avery lunged at her daughter and pulled her into an embrace. Ash could not help but cringe himself as he saw how uncomfortable Violet was with the touch.

'There is one more thing, Lady Avery.' Ash thought he might as well spring it on her now, while she was still giddy from the news. 'I would like to marry Violet in three days' time.'

'Three days? But my lord…that's not…you can't…' she spluttered, releasing Violet. 'Why so hasty, my lord? Surely there must be a proper engagement period, with enough time to prepare a grand wedding. Doesn't a wedding in springtime sound lovely?'

'Yes, but…uh…' He needed a good excuse. Could he tell her he was dying? Being shipped off to war? Prison?

'Mama, he's compromised me,' Violet stated flatly. 'He stole into my room after dinner and we were alone. All night. So, you see, we must marry right away.'

The colour bled from her mother's face—and then she fainted. Thankfully, Ash caught her before she landed on the floor.

'Violet.' He carried Lady Avery to a settee and gently lowered her on it. 'Why did you say that?'

Violet shrugged. 'You were flailing.'

'I was not flailing,' he said, miffed. 'I was thinking.'

'And flailing.' She placed her hands on her hips. 'This was more efficient.

And it was the truth. Mama could not object to an expeditious wedding now.

'Besides, we are running out of time, are we not? I've calculated exactly how many months we have left before the deadline, and as far as I know the gestation period for humans is still nine months.'

The corner of his mouth quirked up. 'Logical as ever.'

'What on earth is— *Ash*.' Despite her miniscule frame, Kate's stature seemed to fill the entire frame of the doorway as she glared at the Marquess. '*Now* what are you doing to poor Lady Avery?'

'I merely saved her from falling to the ground when she fainted.'

Kate raised a dark eyebrow. 'And why did she faint?'

Violet cleared her throat. 'Entirely my fault, I'm afraid. You see, Kate, I told her that the Marquess and I must be married in three days.'

'M-m-married?' The Duchess's face turned scarlet and her eyes widened.

'Yes. Ash has compromised me, and so we must be married.'

'You blackguard!'

Kate lunged for Ash, but Violet managed to put herself between them.

'Kate, please, there is no need for violence.'

She glanced back at the Marquess. 'My lord—Ash, could you please have a footman fetch Mama's maid to tend to her?'

'Of course.' Ash stood up and brushed some imaginary lint from his lapels.

The Duchess opened her mouth and then closed it quickly.

Relief poured through Violet. 'I shall explain everything once we are alone.'

Once Ash had left, and Lady Avery's maid had arrived with some smelling salts, Violet led Kate away to the office.

'All right, we are now alone.' Kate folded her arms over her chest. 'Speak.'

Violet didn't bother to mince words with her friend, so she laid out the entire truth about the clause and her agreement to help Ash produce an heir and save his estate.

'I knew he was hiding something,' the Duchess fumed. 'I thought he was proposing to you out of pity, because of that blasted nickname debacle. Of course he has ulterior motives.'

'As do I, Kate,' Violet reminded her. 'And we will benefit mutually from this marriage.'

If I can birth an heir.

'You must agree his argument makes logical sense.'

'Ash using logic…' She shook her head. 'Despite my objections, I must admire his tenacity. But still…he did not really seduce you or compromise you?'

'I…er…he compromised me, but not fully.'

Kate stared at her, slack-jawed. 'I beg your pardon?'

Violet frowned. Surely the Duchess was well versed in sexual relations? Or perhaps the Duke did not participate in anything other than the marital act.

'Kate, I regret to inform you that, as I have recently discovered, there's more to the marital act than the penetration of the man's—'

'I—I am well aware, thank you very much,' Kate spluttered, her face once more turning an alarming shade of red. 'So you and he were intimate, while still keeping your virginity?'

'Yes.'

Violet explained to Kate how Ash had helped her overcome her aversion to touch.

His touch, anyway.

'Oh, Lord.' Kate blew out a breath. 'Dear Violet, I am well aware that the…er…pleasures a man is able to give you can be…overwhelming. But now that you are not… er…under the spell of…uh…his touch, are you sure you still want to marry him?'

Violet nodded vigorously. 'Yes. It's the best chance I have of saving Oakwood Cottage and Papa's library. And even if we fail to produce an heir I would have the freedom to work for you. Don't you want that?'

'Of course I do. But not at your expense. There's so much more to marriage…' The Duchess clicked her tongue. 'What about love?'

'Oh, we have taken care of that.'

'You have?'

'Of course. I have promised I won't fall in love with him.'

'Promised— Violet, forgive me, but that is the most inane thing I've ever heard.'

'Inane? But it makes perfect logical sense. Love is not a prerequisite for marriage, is it? Most people marry to gain some benefit, and ours will be no different.'

Kate's lips twisted, and then she let out a resigned sigh. 'All right. If this is truly what you want, then I will stand by your side.'

'It is.'

'And if things go awry, you know I will be here as well.'

'Thank you. I appreciate that.'

Not that she thought things would go awry.

Well, they could. No plan was foolproof. And one could only predict an outcome, not guarantee it.

But, then again, there were no guarantees in life. Not even Papa had been able to guarantee that he would live long enough that they didn't have to be in this situation. Life, sadly, was not like mathematics, where there was only a wrong or a right answer. She could only choose the options that would give her the best outcome.

Sure enough, in three days' time, Ash and Violet were married.

'You're really wed,' Sebastian stated as he handed the groom a flute of champagne. 'I can't believe it.'

'Did you doubt me?' Ash scoffed.

The small ceremony had been held at the parish church in the village, with only Sebastian, Kate, the Dowager and Lady Avery in attendance. Afterwards, they'd headed back to Highfield Park, where a beautiful wedding breakfast had been set up in the orangery. Once they'd finished the meal, the footmen had arrived with cake and champagne.

'If I was a betting man...' Sebastian shook his head. 'Well, let's say I would have lost this one.'

Ash placed a hand over his heart. 'I'm hurt,' he said in a mocking tone. 'But it's all done.'

Finally, he'd secured his bride. How he wished he could see Alberta Canfield's face when she saw the announcement in the papers. Ash had made sure every newspaper and gossip rag in London received it.

'This is only the beginning, Ash,' Sebastian said. 'There is still the part where you have to produce an heir.'

'I know.'

He glanced over at Violet, who was listening with rapt

attention as the Dowager explained something about the orchids hanging from the pots overhead. That was his Violet—intense, focused.

His Violet.

His wife.

'And what about the financial side of things?' Sebastian asked, breaking into his thoughts. 'Any news on that? On Oakwood Cottage?'

'Yes, I received a letter from my man of business this morning.' Ash wanted to keep his end of the bargain, so he'd asked Mr Bevis to make enquiries regarding Sir Gregory Avery's accounts. 'The debt isn't substantial or unreasonable. Sir Gregory made a few bad investments and had to take out a mortgage to keep afloat. His scholarly work, book royalties and speaking engagements were enough to support the family and make payments on his debts. Unfortunately, he died suddenly.'

An ache filled Ash as he thought about what Violet had gone through when her father had died. When his own father had passed away, Ash hadn't had time to feel sad. He did, however, remember a profound sense of relief.

'And then what happened?' asked Sebastian.

'He left Lady Avery and Violet with very little. Mr Bevis says that currently they have enough funds to last at least until July, but after that the bank will take possession of the house. I asked him to look into the Avery finances further, to see if there were any other assets left to sell, so they can keep making payments until I secure my lands and pay off their mortgage.'

That was still a few months away, and Ash would deal with it when the time came. For now, he had other things to worry about—that was producing his heir, which might very well be conceived tonight.

His wedding night.

Ash had not touched or kissed Violet since the night she had accepted his proposal, but she—and her sweet, responsive body—had been on his mind the entire time.

This had not been part of his plan.

Well versed in sexual acts, Ash enjoyed women, loved sex, and had spent many a pleasurable night in the company of various lovers. There were few things he hadn't experienced before, and no act he hadn't tried at least once. He rarely bedded the same woman for more than a few weeks, as he fully enjoyed the buffet of available bed partners in London.

Yet, being with Violet…it had been indescribable. At first he had assumed it would be boring, having to tell her what he was about to do, and that it would take away the thrill of sex. However, he'd found it refreshing. Exciting in its own way. He'd marvelled at her reactions to his touch, at her little sighs and moans. She'd been so eager and responsive it had left him wanting more. He wanted to know all the secret places on her delectable body, and gain permission to touch all of her.

He gripped the champagne flute tighter.

Control yourself, Ash. You're not some eager young lad who's had his first taste of a woman.

When he'd first decided Violet would be the one to help him fulfil his duty, he'd thought he would bed her only once or twice. That was all that would be needed? He'd spent most of his life trying to prevent conception—surely it couldn't be that difficult to get a woman with child?

But now—

'Ash, are you all right?' Sebastian eyed him warily. 'You look deep in thought.'

Lifting his flute to his lips, Ash finished the champagne,

then gestured for the footman holding a bottle to refill his glass. 'Fine. I'm fine.'

She might very well conceive on their first try, he supposed. He might only need to bed her once. Maybe two times.

Yes, definitely. Two, maybe three times.

And once that was done he would never have to bed her again. As he'd promised her, they would go their separate ways. The child would be raised at Chatsworth Manor, and Violet could go and work for Kate at the factory. And he... Well, Ash supposed he would go back to whatever the hell he'd done before his life had been turned upside-down.

Violet's low, husky laugh caught his attention and his head snapped towards her. She was standing in the middle of the path with Kate, and a shaft of sunlight streamed down over her. She looked like an angel in her pearl-white gown.

As if she felt his eyes on her, she turned to face him, and smiled shyly when their eyes met. His gaze dropped low to her lips, moved down her long neck to the swells of her breasts, and he remembered how her nipples tasted.

Breaking away from her mesmerising stare, he finished the second glass of champagne in one gulp.

Chapter Nine

Ash could not remember the last time he'd been nervous entering a woman's room. A meeting with a new lover typically brought excitement and thrill, and had him relishing the thought of the pleasures that awaited him. But this was different. This was his wedding night, and Violet was his wife.

Ridiculous, he sneered silently. She would be no different from any woman he'd bedded. Tonight was about conceiving his heir and saving his lands.

'Come in,' came Violet's reply to his knock.

He slipped into the room, much as he had the last time he'd come. Violet sat on the edge of the bed, staring up at him. His breath caught at the sight of her, hair loose, sable waves tumbling down her back, eyes wide and luminous in the glow of the candlelight.

Two or three times, he reminded himself. *Four at most.*

'I hope I'm not late?'

He hoped his jest would mask the feelings bubbling underneath his relaxed facade.

'We didn't set a time, so that means you can't be late.'

Logical, lovely Violet. 'Ah, but if we did, I would have set it for three minutes past seven.'

Her face scrunched up. 'What is your fascination with imbalance? There is beauty in symmetry.'

'Really, now?' He crossed the room until he stood over her. 'Hmm... I see what you mean.' He cupped her chin with his thumb and forefinger, enjoying the fact that she didn't flinch or seem surprised by his touch. 'Your face is perfectly symmetrical. Even. One side is the precise mirror image of the other. But...' his thumb ran over the beauty mark over her lip '...this mars the symmetry of your face.'

Disappointment crossed her features. 'And makes me less beautiful?'

He shook his head, then leaned down to kiss the mark. 'No, Violet. I think it makes you even more beautiful. And unique. And tempting. I've been wanting to do that since I met you.'

She inhaled a rapid breath. 'You've already kissed me so many times.'

'But not on your beauty mark.'

He pressed his lips to it again, then shifted to capture her mouth. She opened up to him, arms winding around his neck, hands raking into his hair to pull him closer. Did she have any idea how much that affected him? Just thinking of her fingers pulling at his hair made him hard.

He drew away, wanting this whole thing to be done.

And yet, not.

You're doing this to save the estate.

Once Violet was with child he would never have to sleep with her again. Still, he wasn't a monster. Despite her eagerness Violet was still a virgin, and she would not fully comprehend what happened during the sexual act until she had experienced it for herself.

'Are you ready, Violet? Is there anything more I can do to prepare you?'

'Will we do the same things we did the other night?'

'Yes. And more.'

'The sexual act?'

'Yes. I will do my best to ensure you are comfortable and to reduce the pain.'

A vial of the oil he'd promised her was in the pocket of his robe.

'Then I'm ready.'

Taking a step back, he removed his robe and draped it over the headboard. Violet did the same with her silk robe.

'Wh-what are you wearing?' he rasped.

She grimaced. 'This?'

'Yes. *That.*'

The white silk chemise, held up by red ribbon straps, had a low neckline that showed off her breasts. The fabric skimmed over her torso and came down to the tops of her thighs, showing off a good three inches of skin before matching silk stockings covered the rest of her.

'My modiste said I needed to wear this tonight. That you would like it.'

'Very much.' His blood heated at the sight of her wrapped up so daintily in silk. 'But I'd like it better off. The chemise, at least.'

The stockings would stay on.

He pushed the ribbon straps to the sides, then pulled at the fabric, allowing it to fall at her feet.

'Violet, you're gorgeous.'

He'd thought he'd only dreamed about her sensuous body, but no, it was real. Every detail—her high, pert breasts, the soft pink nipples, the dip of her flat waist, the silky triangle between her legs—was real and just as he remembered.

And all mine.

Pushing her back to the bed, he climbed in with her, moving over her. 'You're so beautiful, Violet…'

He caressed her breasts, kissing the flesh around her nipples to tease her before he drew a bud in. She tasted so damned sweet he could feast on her the whole day.

'Ash…' she moaned, her hips wriggling underneath him. She probably wasn't even aware of it.

'Patience, darling.'

He shifted his attention to the right nipple, then used his fingers to gently pinch the other one. For a moment he feared she would object, since he hadn't told her what he was going to do, but she did not seem to notice.

Shifting his position, he moved lower, kissing her bare skin as he trailed down over her stomach and right down to her curls. He nosed at her, then licked up her crease, causing her hips to lift off the mattress.

He steadied her hips with his hands, then spread her wide so he could further access all her soft, pink, secret parts. His mouth pressed up to her and his tongue explored her petals, parting them so he could dip inside to taste her nectar.

Fingers raked into his scalp, sending a jolt of pleasure all the way to his erection. But he continued his feast, lapping at her sensitive flesh. Once she was sufficiently wet, he slipped a finger inside her.

Still much too tight.

Ash had never been with a virgin before—a fact he'd withheld from her lest she changed her mind. But he would do his best to ensure her comfort, even if he had to stop and try again another time. The thought of hurting her made him sick to his stomach.

He wiggled his finger, easing it gently in and out. She responded, pushing her hips against his hand, urging him to move faster. So he did, and as his fingers thrust more deeply into her he drew her swollen bud into his mouth and suckled hard. Her cries of pleasure turned more vocal and guttural as her body trembled with her impending release.

That's it, my Violet.

He guided her through her pleasure, allowing her to peak, before helping her settle back down. Her breath eventually evened out and she lay on the bed, eyes closed, skin covered in sweat, looking more lovely than ever.

'You did well,' he said, pressing his lips to her temple.

Her eyes fluttered open. 'Am I ready?'

'Only you can answer that, darling.' He kissed her gently. 'Physically, I believe you're ready.'

Yes, she was so wet, and more than ready to accept him. He just needed to get on with it. Spill his seed inside her and get her with child.

But she looked, oh, so lovely and tempting. He wanted to tease her more. Play with her. Make this night into something special so that once they parted she would never forget it.

And never forget him.

'Ash?'

'You're very ready, but…'

'But?'

'I do love seeing you climax. Will you let me touch you some more?'

Her pupils blew, the dark pools engulfing the light blue of her eyes. 'I would very much like that.'

'Excellent… Because there is so much more we can do and other ways I can bring you pleasure.'

In Violet's mind, it seemed they had already explored all possibilities of the pleasures of intimacy, save for the act of copulation itself.

'But how else can you pleasure me?'

'Do you trust me, Violet?'

'Yes,' she replied without hesitation.

'As I said, I love seeing you orgasm. And I think it would benefit you too, if you could see just how beautiful you look when you're at the peak of your pleasure.'

'See myself? How?'

He didn't answer her, but slid off the bed, then pulled her along to follow him to the dressing mirror in the corner of the room.

Oh.

'Ash, you can't…'

'You said that you trust me, did you not?' He positioned her so she was at the dead centre of the mirror, her naked body on full display.

Violet was familiar with her body, of course, but seeing herself so fully exposed was a shock to her system. She looked away.

'No, Violet. There's nothing to be ashamed of.' He brushed her hair aside, then nuzzled at her neck. 'Please look at yourself and see how beautiful you are.'

Turning her head back, she glanced at her reflection, swallowing audibly. 'I can't. It's shameful.'

'There is nothing wrong or shameful about the naked body,' he began. 'Look at the symmetry of your form, your curves, your limbs. Just looking at you makes me ache.'

She felt something hard brush against her buttocks.

'I want you so terribly. I want to be inside you. Do you understand what I mean?'

Her throat had gone as dry as a desert, so she bobbed her head instead of speaking.

'But for now I'm going to touch you. I'm going to make you come, and you're going to watch yourself. See what you look like and how you look when you're at the height of your release. Do not look away.'

His last words had a force behind them that sent a thrill through her. 'I won't.'

'Good girl.'

Unblinking, she watched as his hand spread across her stomach, then crept up to her right breast. His thumb and forefinger pinched her stiff nipple, making her gasp.

His hand froze. 'Did I hurt you?'

'No.' She leaned her body into his hand. 'It was good.'

He continued to tease her, rolling the nipple between his fingers, cupping her breasts with his warm palms as if testing their weight. His other hand reached up and mimicked the same motion on her left breast. She watched in fascination, looking at the symmetry of his hands and the way he manipulated her flesh. For some reason she did not understand, seeing him touch her added to the excitement building inside her.

He released the right breast, then lowered his hands between her thighs, cupping her sex and covering the entirety of it.

'Everything about you is beautiful, Violet.' The heel of his palm pressed against her. 'These past few nights I've been dreaming of what it would be like to be inside you.' A finger unsealed her crease and teased at her. 'You're still so wet...so slick and tight.' The digit dipped into her and she clenched around him. 'Violet, you're going to kill me.'

'Kill you? How?'

'With how hot and tight you are. Do you think you can take another one?'

Breathlessly, she nodded.

A second finger joined the first inside her. 'How do you feel?'

'Full…' It sounded terribly depraved, but it was the first word she could think of.

'When I am inside you, you will feel much fuller than this.'

Her eyes rolled back as he thrust his fingers inside, moving in and out of her. His mouth was attached to her neck, sucking at the soft skin there, sending a frisson of pleasure through her.

It was too much, and yet she didn't want him to stop. Her hips met each thrust of his hands, and that tension was once again building inside her.

Too much…

'Don't close your eyes.' He nipped at her neck. 'Look, Violet.'

Her gaze fixed on the reflection—her reflection, her body. Her hips were wantonly shoving against his hand, her mouth was open wide as she cried out, and her breasts were bouncing with the rhythm of her movements, her flesh all pink and flushed. Then she locked eyes with him, and instantly she recognised the look of ecstasy on his face. He truly was excited by watching her being pleasured.

'Ash!'

'Hold on to me. Let it happen.'

Reaching back, she gripped his shoulders as pleasure razed her body. He continued to whisper words of encouragement to her until the sensations ebbed away and her limbs turned limp.

'I have you… I have you.'

The floor disappeared from under her. Ash had picked her up and was now carrying her.

'You did so well, darling.' He kissed her as he slid onto the bed with her. 'Now you are ready.'

She wanted it to happen so badly. Needed it, lest her body expire from the craving he aroused in her.

'Please… Ash.'

He covered her body, just like the last time. 'Spread your legs…that's it.'

She held her breath, waiting, until she felt his blunt intrusion. It felt much larger than she remembered.

'Violet…darling…' His face was scrunched up as he continued. 'So…'

Violet tried to relax—truly she did.

But, Lord, the pain.

It was too much.

She closed her eyes tight, telling herself it was going to be all right. That the searing pain that increased with each push wouldn't increase. That it would be all over soon.

'Violet?'

She hadn't even noticed he'd stopped.

'You're hurting?'

If she said no, he might stop before they'd completed the act.

But if she said yes, he would continue.

'Darling, you're like a wound-up spring.' He slowly withdrew from her. 'Relax your limbs. Unclench your jaw. Open your eyes.'

Relief poured through her as the intrusion left her body.

'Violet, I have hurt you terribly.' A kiss landed on her forehead. 'Forgive me.'

'You didn't mean to,' she whispered. 'Please, just…just get it over with. I won't make a sound. I won't move. I promise.'

A dark look crossed his face. 'No, I shan't let you lie there in agony while I rut you like some animal. Wait one moment.'

Reaching over her head, he reached towards his robe.

'I should have done this in the first place, but I was much too carried away. Here…'

Gently, he rolled her to her side.

'Will you let me try making love to you one more time, Violet? We can stop and try again later, or tomorrow if it proves too painful for you.'

That would only prolong her torture. 'No, I want to try now.'

It was only the first time that it would hurt, he'd said. She would endure it for now.

'As you wish. But if it's too much, just say the word and I shall stop.'

She nodded.

Ash opened the vial and poured a few drops of oil onto his fingers, then spread it over her sex. It didn't feel like anything to Violet, but she did enjoy his gentle ministrations. Once he had finished he moved closer to her, so that his front was pressed to her back.

The contact of their skin was comforting, and her tense muscles loosened. His left hand cupped her left breast, teasing the nipple and massaging her. Then his lips clamped down on her neck, kissing her there, suckling and teasing the flesh. When his teeth nipped at her she gasped, the sensation sending a pleasurable jolt all the way to her lower belly.

His hand moved from her breast to her sex, massaging the flesh, pressing against her. His fingers expertly manipulated the swollen bud above her crease, coaxing a quick release that had her writhing back against him and her buttocks kneading against his organ.

A hand slipped under her left knee, lifting it up. 'Hold

your leg up for me...yes, that's it. Now, I'm going to enter you once more.'

She braced herself, waiting for the invasion. It pushed at her, slowly and the pain returned, though to a lesser degree.

'Is that better?'

'Somewhat.'

He pushed further, but stopped. 'Relax your body. You will adjust, I promise. We will go slow.' His fingers brushed at where they joined, then her bud, rubbing in slow circles. She moaned, moving her hips, allowing more of him inside her. When his mouth found her neck once more, she cried out as the bite of his teeth shot a bolt of pure ecstasy through her. His length slid in, and the pain was unbearable, but just for the briefest moment. Her mind was too busy processing the pleasure from his mouth and fingers to care.

'That's it. You did so well, Violet.' He nibbled at her neck.

'I...' Just as he'd said, she felt so much fuller than she'd expected.

'How are you feeling? Does it hurt still?'

'Somewhat. Wait.' There was a slight soreness there, but that lessened as each moment passed. They lay still for what seemed like the longest time before she spoke again. 'I think I'm all right now,' she whispered. 'Please, Ash. Make l-love to me.'

'I'm going to start moving, Violet. The friction will feel good for you.'

'And for you?'

'And for me. Very good.' He shifted his hips to pull back, then pushed in again. 'Did that hurt?'

'Surprisingly, no.'

'Excellent.' He repeated the motion, this time with more pressure, then again.

'Oh!' she cried out. 'That feels good.'

He thrust into her, again and again, building the tension inside her. Reaching back, she grasped at the back of his neck and pulled at his hair. This caused him to curse and increase his thrusts. His arm snaked around her, between her breasts, and grasped her shoulder, bringing her down as he moved upwards with ever increasing speed. Finally, she lost control of her body, and shattered into a million pieces as her orgasm ripped through her very being.

His movement slowed, then halted. She unclenched her fingers from his hair, then twisted her neck, so that she could look up at him, his handsome face scrunched up in concentration.

Reaching up, she brought his head down for a kiss. 'Thank you.'

He smiled against her mouth. 'You're welcome. But we aren't finished yet.'

She inhaled a quick breath when he left her, feeling oddly disappointed. But then he pushed her onto her back and climbed on top of her. Once again, the pressure of his body soothed her.

Nudging her knees apart, he began to enter her again, but this time it was only mildly uncomfortable, and once he was inside she found that she liked the sensation of fullness. When his pelvis came into contact with her swollen bud, the friction sent a delightful shiver through her. She repeated the motion, and both of them moaned aloud.

Ash braced his elbows on either side of her, his arms slipping under her before his mouth covered hers in a hungry kiss. Violet raked her fingers down the strong muscles of his back, gasping and crying into his mouth as he moved inside her, their bodies dancing in perfect rhythm as they both raced to the peak. She was just over that crest when he let out a deep, rough growl and he thrust into her one more time, convulsing as he flooded her with his seed. With one last grunt he collapsed against her, burying his face in her neck.

'No, don't go,' she pleaded, when he attempted to roll away from her.

'But I'm heavy.'

'I know,' she said with a sigh, tightening her arms around him. 'And I love it. You're like a heavy blanket. A really heavy one.' There was something about the weight and pressure of him that was soothing. 'Please? Just stay?'

'For a little bit.'

'All right.'

Violet relaxed under him, allowing his weight to settle over her. She remained there, blissful.

'May I move now?' he asked a few minutes later.

She supposed he couldn't remain there for ever. 'Yes.'

He shifted away. 'I can't be your blanket for the entire night. But I can offer you the next best thing.'

'And what is that?'

He spread an arm out. 'Come. Lie here with me.'

She stared at him, unsure what to do.

'It's like a hug,' he explained. 'But lying down. And we can do it the whole night.'

'We'll be hugging for the entire night?'

'Well, at least until I lose the feeling in my arm,' he said with a chuckle. 'Give it a try.'

That didn't seem necessary. Perhaps she should send him back to his own rooms. Married people didn't sleep in the same bed, did they?

However, seeing Ash lying on the bed with that lazy smile on his beautiful face made something in her chest flutter in the most pleasant way.

Shrugging, she lay down beside him, placing her head

on his arm, her back to his front. When his other arm came around her she finally understood. And while it wasn't the same as having him on top of her, this was just as good.

Everything about tonight had been good.

No, it hadn't just been good. It had been...marvellous.

Violet couldn't even recall why she'd thought being touched was repulsive.

Well, she still thought it was, but not Ash's touch.

His hands...his clever mouth...every part of him was wonderful. And the pleasure he gave her was nothing like she'd ever felt before.

Being with him in this way didn't seem repulsive to her, not the way it had been described in Papa's medical books. There had been perhaps a brief mention of pleasure, but the authors had glossed over it, or intimated that it was only men who experienced it.

But with Ash...except for the pain, everything had been exquisite.

Was she cured of her aversion to touch now? Would any other man make her feel this way?

The thought of being touched by another man, however, still made her stomach churn.

There was no need to think of such thoughts now, she thought with a yawn, and then she settled into his arms and closed her eyes.

When Violet awoke the next day, panic rose through her at the unfamiliar sensation of a warm body pressed behind her. But it quickly receded once memories from the night before flooded back.

She breathed a sigh of relief and relaxed against Ash.

Her husband.

They had remained entwined the entire night, their bodies touching.

And because it was Ash, she didn't mind at all.

'Awake already?'

The rough, raspy quality of his voice caught her off guard. But she found that she quite liked it.

'Is your arm asleep?'

'It's dead,' he said with a chuckle, then yawned. 'But do not fret. I have another one.'

'You're jesting.'

'I am.' He shifted her around so that she faced him, then lowered his head and kissed her. 'Good morning.'

'Good morning. Do you think…? Do you think we conceived last night?'

It was the question niggling at the back of her mind and she just couldn't stop herself from asking it.

The corners of his mouth turned up. 'We can't be certain. We must wait for your monthly flow. If it doesn't arrive, then you may be pregnant.'

'That's at least three weeks away,' she stated. 'Is there anything we can do to ensure our success?'

'Of course we can. We must continue our efforts until we can confirm you are with child,' he said in a most serious tone.

'Continue? How many times? For how long?'

'As many times as it takes. And for however long it takes.'

Chapter Ten

Ash had been so focused on his plan to woo Violet, and then the wedding, he hadn't thought much about what would happen after the ceremony. While Sebastian and Kate were happy to host them at Highfield Park, they couldn't stay there for ever. And so, two days after their wedding, Ash took Violet, along with Lady Avery, to his home in Hertfordshire, Chatsworth Manor.

'Oh, your home is beautiful, my lord,' Lady Avery exclaimed as they alighted from his carriage, which had stopped just outside the manor.

'Thank you, Lady Avery. It's been in my family since the First Marquess.'

Slowly, he glanced up at the house. The outside was made of yellow Bath stone and built in the Palladian style, as indicated by the portico. There was one main block, or *corps de logis*, which had three storeys and contained all the bedrooms and living areas. The two pavilions on either side each had two storeys, and consisted of the kitchens, the scullery, and servants's areas.

It was indeed, a very grand manor, part of his heritage.

Something real and solid he could be proud of.

Yet, a knot grew in his stomach as the memories flooded back into his mind, reminding him of why he didn't come here often.

Maybe it wasn't worth saving and he should just let the Canfields have it. Then perhaps the memories of the past would disappear.

'Ash, it's lovely. Thank you for bringing us here.'

He glanced down at Violet as she too, stood gawking up at the house. He couldn't help but drop his gaze to her belly, wondering if she was with child at this very moment.

For some reason the thought both thrilled him and filled him with dread.

Which was preposterous. The sooner they confirmed she was carrying his child, the better. Then they would be much closer to securing his lands and his wealth, as well as her Oakwood Cottage.

It would also mean he no longer needed to sleep with her.

'Come, let's go inside.'

Placing a hand on her lower back, he guided Violet towards the front door. The servants were lined up in a row to welcome them, with his butler and housekeeper at the head.

'Thank you, everyone, for welcoming us. May I present Violet, Marchioness of Ashbrooke, and her mother, Lady Avery.'

'Lady Ashbrooke. Lady Avery,' the butler greeted with a low bow. 'Welcome to Chatsworth Manor. My name is Bennet, I am the butler, and this—' he gestured to the white-haired woman in a black uniform '—is Mrs Hogsworth, the housekeeper.'

'My lady.' She bowed her head.

'How do you do?' Violet replied.

Bennet continued, 'Please, if there is anything you need, do not hesitate to ask.' The butler led them inside, into the richly appointed hall. 'Would Her Ladyship like a tour? Perhaps she'll want to go over the accounts with Mrs Hogsworth?'

Ash shook his head. 'I'm afraid we are tired from our long journey here, Bennet.'

'My sincere apologies, my lord, my lady. That can wait. All your rooms are ready, and Her Ladyship's and Lady Avery's things were unpacked by their maids when they arrived yesterday.'

'Thank you, Bennet. Could you kindly show Lady Avery to her room?'

'Of course. I've put her in the Queen Anne room, as you requested.'

'The Queen Anne room?' Lady Avery said.

'It's our best guest room, Lady Avery,' Ash said. 'The Second Marquess had Her Majesty's bedroom recreated there. It is said the chest of drawers inside belonged to her.'

It also happened to be at the other end of the manor— the farthest from the master bedchamber.

'I do hope you like it.'

'It sounds wonderful. Thank you, my lord.'

As Bennet led Ash's mother-in-law away, Violet took his hand and squeezed it. 'Thank you for inviting her to live with us, Ash.'

'Of course.'

Despite Violet's exasperation with her mother, he knew she was the one constant in her life, and with the upheavals coming her way his wife would need all the stability she could get. 'Now come along, we need to rest.'

She lifted a dark brow at him. 'Are we really resting?'

He grinned. 'You know me so well, wife.'

Taking her hand, he led her up the stairs and down the hall to the east wing of the manor where his bedchamber was located. Pushing the door open, he ushered her inside. The massive room was decorated in dark colours and woods, plush carpets and thick velvet drapes. A large bed stood in the middle, atop a dais.

Violet glanced around. 'And where is my bedchamber?'

'Your bedchamber?'

'The Marchioness's room,' she stated, glancing around. 'Bennet said Gertrude had already unpacked my things. Is there a doorway to connect with it from here?'

Ash paused. It hadn't occurred to him that Violet would want her own bedchamber.

Of course she does, idiot. That's how married people live.

'Is it through here?' Violet walked over to a door on the left side of the room. 'It's the only door here.'

Ash blinked.

The Marchioness's room.

His *mother's* room.

He swallowed hard, forcing the lump down his throat. 'Yes. That's it.'

Turning the knob, she pushed the door open. Once she'd disappeared through the door Ash gripped the doorjamb as a dizzying feeling came over him.

How could he have forgotten about that room? When his mother had left, Father had forbidden anyone from mentioning her ever again. Then he'd had all her things taken out and burned, and the room sealed. As far as he knew, no one went in there. It was as if the entire bedchamber hads simply disappeared, vanished into thin air.

Like his mother.

'Ash?' Violet's head poked through the door.

Pushing those intrusive thoughts aside, he said, 'Is—is the bedchamber to your liking?' He hoped she wouldn't ask him to go inside.

'Yes. Gertrude has arranged all my things.' She hesitated. 'I...I suppose I'm expected to sleep in there?'

'If that is your preference.' His stomach knotted. 'Is it?'

Slowly, she lifted her head. 'I have not... We have never slept apart since the wedding. It would feel much too...new to me. Do you think, just until I've acclimatised myself a little, that I could stay—'

'Yes.'

He closed the distance between them in a heartbeat before pulling her back inside his room and into his arms. The thought that she wanted to be with him—even though it was because of her aversion to novel experiences—made his heart leap out of his chest.

'You should sleep here with me. For now. Until you've acclimatised yourself.'

She melted against him. 'I'd like that very much.'

'Shall we finally leave the manor today, darling?' Ash asked as he rolled away from her, his body boneless from another intense lovemaking session.

'Perhaps once my soul has returned to my body,' Violet replied with a long, drawn-out breath. 'Not that you give me any time to recover.'

Ash propped himself on an elbow and smirked at her. 'Are you complaining, wife? You seemed to have thoroughly enjoyed yourself this morning. After all I made you climax three times.'

'No complaints,' she replied. 'None at all.'

It had been two days since they'd arrived at Chatsworth Manor, and most of the time had been spent in their bedchamber. Thankfully, nobody in the household—not the servants nor Lady Avery—had remarked on their preference for indoor activities.

Ash supposed that was to be expected from newly wedded couples, and he didn't want to disappoint anyone. Besides, he was taking his duties as Marquess of Ashbrooke seriously. Making an heir and securing his lands was serious work, and he was focused on the task.

Ash glanced out of the window. 'We could go for a short walk outside. We could go exploring.' It had been one of his favourite activities as a child. 'It doesn't seem too cold. We could bundle up, take a quick gander, then come back for tea?'

She rolled over onto her stomach, her pert, adorable buttocks on display for him. 'I don't really like the outside. But I suppose we will have to see other people at some point.'

'It's settled, then.' He slid out of bed and put his robe on. 'I'll ring for Gertrude and then I'll get ready.'

'All right,' Violet said, as she stretched like a cat in her naked glory, making his mouth water.

He almost changed his mind about leaving the bed.

One hour later, Ash had finished dressing and Violet emerged from her bedroom, bundled up in her coat, hat, scarf and gloves, and they headed out.

Truly, he didn't want to leave; he could stay in bed with Violet all day and all night. However, his body and his lungs craved fresh air, and he wanted Violet to see the gardens and the woods around the manor. Besides, he and Violet had made love so many times in the last two days it seemed impossible that she wasn't yet with child.

A strange dread swirled in his gut. His mind told him that he wanted—no, *needed* her to become pregnant as soon as possible. It was the only way he could stop the Canfields from taking the lands. Perhaps that was why— despite his own reservations—he'd brought her here. To remind himself of what he could lose. Not just the house and the lands, but the income and the well-being of his tenants and servants.

But despite all that a small, selfish part of him didn't want her to be pregnant yet—not when it meant he would no longer have any reason to be in her bed.

Ash brushed off those thoughts. This was why he'd married Violet, after all. To produce an heir. And once that goal was met they could start leading separate lives. He had promised her that, and he was eager to have things back the way they'd been before he'd met her.

'Brr…it's still cold,' Violet complained as they stepped out into the back gardens. 'I hate winter.'

Ash tipped his head back and breathed in the cool air. 'Really? Believe it or not, I love it, especially out here.' It had been too long since he'd last visited Chatsworth at this time of year. He mostly stayed in London, where amusements were plentiful for a bachelor like him. Well, a former bachelor anyway.

'You love winter? But why? It's so cold and wet and slushy.' She shuddered. 'The only thing I'm glad for is that it's a good excuse to stay inside with a cup of tea and a book.'

'Shouldn't winter be your favourite time of the year, then? Since you're excused from outdoor activities?'

She shrugged. 'I stay inside most of the year anyway. Nevertheless, I'm allowed to hate or love whatever season I choose.'

'So, you like spring, then?'

She made a face. 'Ugh…it makes me sneeze.'

'Summer?'

'Too hot and sticky.'

'Autumn?'

She shook her head. 'I don't like the crunchy leaves.'

Stopping, he turned to her. 'You don't like *any* season?'

'I told you. I stay inside most of the time.'

He laughed. 'Of course, my lovely logical Violet.' He took

her hand. 'Come, some fresh air will do you good. Then I promise we can go back inside.'

A lovely blush painted her cheeks. 'Back to our bed?'

Minx.

'Or perhaps I could show you the wonders of the library.'

'What kind of wonders? Do you have a rare book collection?'

'No, but there are other wonders. Like…' He proceeded to whisper to her what he planned to do to her against his grandfather's volumes of medieval writings.

The colour on her face heightened. 'I don't think Thomas Aquinas would approve of such things.'

'Aquinas is dead, darling. Although you may be right… Perhaps I should take you against Chaucer's works instead. He was quite the bawdy bard, that one.' He brushed a stray lock of hair off her cheek. 'Shall we continue?'

Chatsworth Manor had an extensive garden to the rear, though at this time of the year there wasn't much to see. In the spring, however, it was a magnificent sight, filled with blooming flowers and lush greenery.

'It's actually quite peaceful,' Violet remarked as they strolled down the main path leading away from the house. 'It seems like there's no one around for miles. We had a lot of neighbours, and Mama's relatives were always dropping by. It was hard to find peace and quiet.'

'Except in your papa's library.'

'Yes.' Her hand gripped his arm. 'Thank you, by the way. For checking into Papa's finances.'

The day after their wedding Ash had told her what he had found out about the debts and repayments.

'Of course.'

A look of strain crossed her face, and a wrinkle appeared between her eyebrows.

'Do not fret.' Leaning down, he pressed a kiss on the worry line. 'Come, let's keep walking.'

'But where shall we go?'

'Hmm…' He tapped a finger to his chin. 'Why don't you lead us? And no, we are not going back to the house, not yet.'

Her lips turned down into the most adorable pout. 'But I've never been here before, Ash. How do I know where to go?'

'You don't.'

'But—'

He held up a hand. 'I told you—we are exploring. That means going forth into the unknown.'

'You know I hate surprises.'

'This isn't a surprise, darling. It's just…something you don't yet know.'

'By definition, that is the nature of a surprise.'

'Yes.' He kissed her cold nose. 'But you know what isn't a surprise?' He threaded his fingers through hers. 'This. Me. I'm here. And I promise everything will be all right. Do you trust me?'

Her hand squeezed his. 'I do.'

'So, lead on, dauntless explorer.'

Ash wasn't quite sure why he urged her to expand her boundaries, but he had a feeling it would be good for her. In the last few days Violet had opened up so marvellously, exploring her sensual side. She was so eager and uninhibited, he thought, why couldn't she apply the same enthusiasm outside the bedroom?

She led him through the gardens, mostly staying on the paths. When they reached the last of the tiled walkways, she stopped.

'It's the end,' she declared.

'Is it?' Raising his booted foot, he stepped off the path.

He grinned at her, and to his surprise she followed suit.

He was quite happy to let her meander about, allowing her to set their route. They moved deeper into the forested area, but thankfully since the trees were bare it wasn't too dark.

As they proceeded, Ash couldn't put his finger on why this particular area looked familiar. There was something about the way the land rose uphill and the line of trees on the east side that he recognised, but for some reason he couldn't place where they were, exactly.

A shiver ran down his spine.

Silly.

Of course this place was familiar. He'd spent a lot of time here as a child. As he'd grown older, he'd spent more time in the schoolroom, and less and less time in the woods. Perhaps his memory of this place had faded from being away for so long.

'Look over there.' Violet pointed to something in the distance.

'What is it?'

'Water. I think it's a lake.' She dragged him down the hill. 'I want to take a closer look.'

'Lake? We don't have a lake. But we do have a—'

The pond.

He halted as a tightness wrapped around his throat like a garrotte. His stomach tied up in knots and sweat built on his brow.

'Ash? Come, let's go and see what it is.'

She tugged at his arm, but he couldn't move his feet, his boots seemingly stuck to the ground.

'What's wrong?' She cocked her head to one side.

He swallowed the lump in his throat. 'Nothing.'

'It's not nothing,' she retorted. 'Ash, I'm not a child or a

fool. Your complexion has turned grey and despite the chill in
the air you're sweating profusely. Is it because of that pond?'

He nodded. 'It was *the* pond.'

'*The* pond?'

'Where my father drowned.'

His guts churned. Fearing he might lose the contents of
his stomach, he pulled his hand away from her and spun
around.

The climb back up the hill was gruelling—and exactly
what he needed. With his lungs burning and calves aching,
he could ignore the dull pain in his chest. When he reached
the top, exhaustion took over, so he collapsed to his knees.

'Ash! Ash, please!' Violet scrambled to catch up with him
'I—I know I've made a terrible mistake, leading us here.
Please, forgive me.' Her voice trembled. 'Th-this is all my
fault. I'm sorry.'

'No, no, darling.' He pulled her into his embrace and
her arms wrapped around him. The soft body melting into
his soothed the ache in him. 'It's not your fault. You didn't
know. Hell, I didn't know either.'

It was as if his mind had erased this place from his
memory.

'I'd forgotten where we were.'

She inhaled as her arms tightened around him. 'I'm so
sorry for your loss.'

'It was a long time ago.'

'What happened? How did he drown? Why did no one
rescue him?'

'He died alone.'

'Alone? Why would he swim out here alone?'

'He wasn't swimming. He'd been drinking then stumbled out into the pond. They found his body floating in the
middle of the water.'

She stiffened in his arms. 'Was it an accident or did he take his own life?'

'I don't know, exactly. Could be both.' An acrid burn rose up in his throat. 'He drank a lot, even before…'

'Before what?'

'Before Mama left us.'

Violet whimpered, burrowed deeper into his arms and pressed her face to his neck.

Ash wasn't sure why he was telling her this, but it was as if a dam had broken inside him and he couldn't stop the flood of emotions from rushing out.

'When I was a child, I didn't see my parents very much, but when I did they were always arguing. Mama was a beauty, and many men sought her out, even though she was married. My father was a jealous man, despite the fact that he had just as many lovers as she did. There was this one night, when I was nine years old, my parents hosted a ball, and my mother invited her current lover, an Italian count, to spite Father.'

Violet tightened her embrace.

'Father was livid. He cornered the Count, there was a fight, and Father nearly killed him.'

Ash only knew this because his father had confessed it to him one night while in a drunken stupor.

'That was the final straw for Mama and she left us the next day. I never saw her again.'

He paused as the ache in his throat made it difficult to speak.

'My father hung on for another year, drinking himself into oblivion each day.'

His father had spent most of his days passed out or screaming and crying at anyone who dared to get close enough.

'Then one night he disappeared. He was missing for three days. One of the groundskeepers found in him the pond.'

Ash had never ventured out to the pond ever again.

Violet said nothing, nor did she ask any questions. She just held on to him tightly, never wavering, never letting go.

After what seemed like an eternity, Ash gently prised her arms off his body. 'I'm cold,' he said.

Brushing her hands on her thighs, she rose to her feet and offered him a hand. 'Then let's go home.'

Ash allowed her to lead him back, and by some miracle they made it without getting lost. But then again, this was Violet, so he had no doubt her keen mind would find a way to navigate them safely back.

'We were out much too long in the cold,' she explained to Bennet when they entered the manor. 'Please have some hot tea sent up.'

He followed her up the stairs to their bedchamber, where she proceeded to strip off all his damp, cold clothes. She pulled back the covers and nudged him to slip between them. There was a knock at the door, then a maid came in with a tray.

'By the bed, please. Thank you.' When the maid slipped out, she said to him, 'How about a cup, Ash?'

He shook his head. 'No, thank you.'

'Then what would you like?' She inched closer to him, placing a hand on his forehead. 'Do you need anything else?'

'Just you.' He snaked a hand around her wrist and pulled her down, melding his lips to hers.

Without a word, she crawled between the covers. Her clothes came off quickly, and he rolled her underneath him. Spreading her thighs he entered her in one stroke, filling her to the hilt. She cried out into his mouth, wrapping her legs around his waist.

Ash lost himself in her, fusing their bodies together tightly, bringing them both to the peak of ecstasy. Her cries and purrs were like sweet music to his ears, drowning out the haunted past. When she clasped him, he surged into her, flooding her with his seed.

Ash couldn't bring himself to let go of her.

Not yet, he pleaded to some unknown entity.

Violet was real. She was here. She was not a memory from the past that threatened to consume him until nothing was left.

Violet sighed, not saying a word, her arms still grappled around him. She wouldn't release him—she never did. She had told him that for some reason she found the weight of his body soothing. When he tried to move, she would always protest, begging for another minute. He usually indulged her until she fell asleep.

It was a mistake to come here. To bring her here.

He gently pulled her arms away and rolled off her. Thankfully, Violet didn't object. Instead she let out long sigh and moved onto her side. She let out a small yawn, but nothing else as she curled herself around a pillow.

Ash stared up at the ceiling, unable to move. He longed to curl up with Violet, but he could not bring himself to touch her again.

Being here…the memories…his parents…it was too much.

They had to leave.

Some time must have passed before Violet woke up, because the room was dark as pitch.

'Ash?'

'You're awake.'

'Mmm-hmm.'

Her hand reached for him, and upon finding him across the bed from her, she cuddled up to him. Pressing her nose to his chest, she breathed in his wonderful, unique scent. She could find him in the dark just by that amazing smell alone. Indeed, some days it was all she could think of.

Correction: *he* was all she could think of, all the time.

And that thought, which was illogical, scared her.

It had been less than a week since their wedding, and yet Violet had many questions in her mind.

Did Ash enjoy their lovemaking?

Was she doing the right things?

Was she pregnant yet?

How long would it take?

And how soon would Ash leave her bed once they confirmed it?

It was that last question that made her mind lock up and cease functioning.

'I was thinking of something.'

Ash's voice in the dark shook her out of her thoughts. 'And that is?'

'We should go on a honeymoon. There wasn't time to plan one, with the wedding and all, but it's only proper that as newlyweds, we should go abroad and travel. Would you like that?'

That idea had her mind—and limbs—locking up. Outside England everything would be new to her. It would be like the proposal debacle in the ballroom, only a thousand times worse.

But then she remembered his face as he'd told her about his father. The way his skin had turned pale at the sight of the pond. And how his lower lip had trembled as he'd struggled to breathe.

That expression had been marked—no, it had been burned—into her consciousness permanently.

The look of distress.

And she decided she never wanted to see that expression on his face ever again.

Moving deeper into his arms, she placed a kiss on his chest. 'Yes, Ash, I would like that.'

Chapter Eleven

When Ash had told her they were going to Paris, Violet had been overcome with panic.

She'd never been before—never been abroad at all—and the idea of going to a place where everything was unknown to her had made her want to run into a closet and hide.

However, she understood why he wanted to leave. He might not have said it aloud, but she knew. Just as Oakwood Cottage would always remind her of her Papa, staying at Chatsworth Manor brought back memories of his father.

And she didn't want him to suffer.

It didn't make logical sense. Their marriage was a mutually beneficial agreement. Whether he suffered or not should not be any of her concern. But seeing the look of distress on his face had her pushing logic—and her own fear—aside.

And so she would endure Paris for him.

On the day of their arrival, the concierge at the hotel had informed them that the owners, upon hearing they were on their honeymoon, had given them a gift—a special meal at the hotel's restaurant.

'Must we go?' Violet asked as they prepared to leave. 'Can't we eat in our suite?'

The very idea of dining in a crowded restaurant—her first time ever—sounded daunting.

'I'm sorry, darling, but it would be rude to refuse a gift. We won't be long, I promise.'

'All right.'

They headed downstairs to the restaurant, where the staff showed them to their 'best' table, which Violet hoped would be one tucked away in the corner, away from everyone and everything. To her horror, they were seated in the centre of the room, right in the middle of the din, with staff rushing about, the clinks and clanks of cutlery echoing off the domed ceiling, and too-loud conversations booming across the room.

'The chef has prepared a special menu just for you, and I shall serve the first course soon,' the waiter informed them in heavily accented English. He then poured them each a flute of champagne from the bottle inside an ice bucket by the table. 'But for now, enjoy your champagne.'

Violet sipped at her drink nervously, looking at Ash as he glanced around. He seemed to be enjoying himself, marvelling at the sights around them.

'Do you dine at restaurants frequently in London?' she asked.

'I do,' he said. 'Often I'm at my club, which does have a restaurant, or I go to the West End. Once in a while I'll even dip into a public house. I have an excellent cook at home, but I hate dining alone.'

Eating in a quiet room by herself sounded wonderful to Violet, especially now as the cacophony of sounds around them swelled.

'Hey, what are you two celebrating?'

Violet started as the lanky, bespectacled man at the table beside them turned in his chair to face them. The grating sound the feet of his chair from scraping on the wooden floor made her teeth hurt.

'We're on our honeymoon,' Ash replied, lifting his champagne flute.

'Honeymoon? Congratulations to you, then. Hey, guys!' He turned back to his companions. 'These two here are on their honeymoon!'

The rest of the group cheered, shouting and hooting as they offered their congratulations. The throb in Violet's temple pulsed.

'Thank you,' Ash said. 'Are you by any chance American?'

'We sure are.' The man extended his hand. 'Thornton Owens, from Boston, Massachusetts.' He then proceeded to introduce the rest of his group. 'This is Christopher Davies, that lovely young woman in the green dress is Julie Wright, and the stunning blonde over there is Sophie Watson.'

'I'm pleased to meet you,' said Ash. 'I am Devon St James, Marquess of Ashbrooke. This is my wife, Lady Ashbrooke. We're from London.'

'I was just there last year, Your Lordship,' Mr Davies shouted as he attempted to be heard over the hubbub. 'Nice city.'

'Great meeting you, my lord, Lady Ashbrooke.' Mr Owens lifted his glass to them. 'We should let you get on with your dinner.'

Violet breathed a sigh of relief once Mr Owens turned his chair back to his companions and their first course arrived. However, her reprieve was only temporary as every once in a while, Mr Owens would turn his chair again to ask Ash something about London or his opinion on trivial matters, like the weather or Parisian food. By the time they were on their dessert course, Mr Owens suggested they joined their tables together.

'You don't mind, do you, Violet?' Ash asked.

Mind? Of course she did. But how could she say no,

when Ash flashed her that handsome smile that made her lose all thought. 'N-no, I suppose it's all right.'

His smiled turned brighter as he stood up and helped Mr Owens push their tables together.

'Tell me,' Ash began, 'what is a group of Americans doing in Paris?'

'We've come here for inspiration.' Mr Owens waved around them. 'We're starving artists, seeking to create our masterpieces. I'm a writer, by the way.'

'What have you written? Can I purchase it in a bookshop?' Violet couldn't help but ask; she'd never met a real writer in the flesh. Was he a philosopher? Or perhaps a playwright? Or maybe he was a novelist?

'Nothing yet, Lady Ashbrooke,' he said. 'I'm still waiting to be inspired by Paris.'

'And how long have you been here?'

'Three years.'

'Oh.'

'I'm a dancer,' Miss Wright interjected. 'At the ballet.'

'I saw *Swan Lake* a few weeks ago,' Violet offered. 'Have you performed in that?'

Miss Wright inhaled from the cigarette between her fingers, then blew out a plume of smoke. 'It's not that kind of ballet, honey.'

As Violet choked on the harsh air, the rest of the table broke out into peals of laughter. She looked at her husband, confused, but he only said, 'I'll explain later, darling.'

'And I'm a painter,' Mr Davies announced proudly. 'And, yes, I've had my paintings exhibited, and that's all thanks to my muse, Sophie.' He nodded to the stunning blonde woman in the red dress.

'That means she don't work,' Miss Wright scoffed.

'You're just jealous,' Miss Watson retorted.

'Now ladies, put the claws away,' Mr Owens said. 'We have guests and we don't want to scare them away. My lord, you're a delight and so is your beautiful wife. It's great to meet you.'

'And you are a lively, interesting bunch. Isn't that right, Violet?'

She could only swallow a gulp and nod.

No one seemed to notice how uncomfortable she was— or no one cared. The spirited conversation continued with a lively and energetic dynamic that Ash seemed to enjoy. He had a clever comeback for every question or thought thrown his way, and he volleyed back with witty remarks of his own.

He fit in perfectly.

Violet, on the other hand, couldn't help but be reminded of the moral philosopher Sydney Smith, who had written about a square person trying to squeeze himself into a round hole.

She simply did not fit in.

'So, Devon,' Miss Watson began as she scooted closer to Ash. She had placed her chair on his left side once they had joined their tables together. 'What does being a marquess mean, aside from people having to call you "my lord".'

Violet's stomach knotted at the woman's audacious use of Ash's Christian name. Had she not been taught proper etiquette as a child? She also seemed to be missing key pieces of her gown, as her décolletage was thoroughly exposed whenever she leaned forward.

'It means I don't work either,' Ash joked.

Miss Watson threw her head back and laughed. 'Devon, you are utterly hilarious.'

Her hand landed on Ash's arm. The touch was brief, but Violet did not miss it.

It had been years since Violet had had a proper fit of anger, but at this moment she was coming very close. A white-hot fury rose inside her, and she grabbed a fork, her knuckles going white with her grip. The urge to stab the woman's hand grew with each passing moment.

A warm, firm hand landed on her arm—Ash. He was peering at her with an expression she hadn't yet catalogued, trying to catch her gaze. Ashamed of her violent thoughts, she couldn't bear to look him in the eye, but she did release her grip on the fork.

'Ladies, Gentlemen,' he announced in a calm tone. 'I'm afraid the hour is growing late. Lady Ashbrooke and I must retire.'

'Aw, you can't go.' Miss Watson pouted. 'We were just getting to know each other.'

Violet was sorely tempted to retrieve the fork.

'It's not even that late,' Mr Davies protested. 'We should go check out some restaurants on the Seine.'

'I'm afraid you will have to make do with your own company for the rest of the evening. Shall we, Violet? Goodnight, everyone.'

Gently, he tugged her to her feet.

'I'm sorry, darling,' he said once they were safely behind the doors of their suite. 'I should have realised that might have been too much for you.'

She still couldn't speak, as the vision of the American woman touching Ash permeated her mind. She wished she could wash it away like dirt on a window.

'Come. Let's get to bed.'

His voice was soft and soothing as he guided her towards their bedroom and then proceeded to make her forget about the terrible dinner and that horrid woman.

* * *

Despite the rough beginning, for the rest of their time, Violet thoroughly enjoyed Paris.

Yes, the city itself was a twisting, gloomy, maze of cramped streets and the buildings of all shapes and sizes and styles were all smashed together with no sense of rhyme or reason, and yet Violet thought it was quite charming once she got used to it.

Their hotel on the Seine, La Neuville de Paris, was a marvel, but it wasn't its grand facade or luxurious decor and furnishings that had impressed her. At first, the idea that they would be living and sleeping in a place where there were people all around, above and below them had made her skin crawl, but Ash had reserved the top corner suite just for them. It was quiet up there, and their suite of rooms was expansive, not to mention, the bed spacious and the sheets were made of the softest silk. They felt marvellous on her naked skin, especially when Ash made love to her on top of them.

Then there were the various activities and amusements, like museums, pleasure gardens, restaurants and cafés. Normally they would have set her nerves on edge, but Ash scheduled their daily jaunts for very early in the morning or in the late afternoon, so there were fewer people around. Sometimes, instead of dining out, they would sit in parks, tucked away in cosy corners on benches around the city, and eat from a basket full of goodies prepared by the hotel staff. Or they would have cold sandwiches, cheese and bottles of wine bought from local shops, as they sat wrapped in winter coats. In fact, he seemed to have a knack of finding quiet, serene places in the middle of this noisy, crowded city.

Of course, the rest of their time was spent in bed, and

Violet found she really didn't mind it at all. She had never known there could be so much more to lovemaking than the marital act itself, and she found she enjoyed most if not all of it. Her body was so attuned to Ash that he only had to send her one look—an expression she had catalogued as lust—and she practically vibrated with need when she recognised it. She craved him, obsessed over him, wanted to know all the ways to please him and record them in a mental list she could access at any time.

It was illogical, and no matter how many times she ran through the possibilities in her head, she couldn't find a good reason why she was so obsessed with him. The chaos made her head hurt whenever she tried to define it or find reason for it.

Surely this will pass.

Once she was with child, and had given birth to said child and heir, she could go back to an orderly life, one with a predictable routine. No more passionate encounters, surprises, or the unpredictable ball of chaos that was Ash.

In other words, no more Ash.

The idea hollowed a pit in her stomach.

Preposterous.

Yes, these emotions had to pass.

Once they were back in England, back to what was familiar, her obsession for him would wither away.

At the moment, however, she was still in France, lying in bed alone. It was their last day and it had been particularly busy, leaving her drained. All the sights and sounds had been too much, and she had begged Ash to take her back to the hotel and leave her be. So he'd left her alone in their bedroom, where she'd lain down for an hour.

Now she was finally feeling refreshed, she padded out

into the living area, where he was sitting in an armchair, feet up on the coffee table, reading a book.

'Ash?' she called.

He glanced up from behind the book, concern marring his handsome face. 'Are you feeling better, darling?'

She nodded, then walked over to him. He tugged at her hand and planted her on his lap. 'I was just feeling drained.'

'I was afraid you were sick, or that you were cross with me.' He looked like a young boy being scolded by mother.

'I'm fine.' She cupped his cheek. 'And I'm not cross with you. Sometimes when I'm overwhelmed and surrounded by too many people I need some time by myself. So please do not think that just because I do not want to be near you I'm angry with you.'

'I shall remember that.' His face relaxed. 'Do you feel refreshed enough to go on one last walk with me?'

'I would very much like that.'

After bundling up, they left the hotel and took their usual path along the Seine, in a quiet section away from the markets and cafés and the noise from the restoration work being done on the Notre-Dame cathedral.

'Have you enjoyed our honeymoon, darling?' Ash asked as they made their way along the serene waterside.

'Oh, yes. Very much so.'

'I'm glad.' His hand tightened around hers. 'What was your favourite part?'

A blush tinged her cheeks, making him throw his head back and laugh aloud.

'Aside from *that*.'

He winked at her, obviously guessing she'd been thinking of their time spent in bed.

'The churches,' she said. 'And the library.' They had been

a godsend, as they had been quiet and peaceful, an oasis in a messy, crowded and frenetic city.

The corner of his mouth tugged up. 'Of course you enjoyed those the most. What about your least favourite part?'

She thought about Miss Watson, but decided there was, indeed, something much worse than that odious woman.

'The stinky cheese.'

They continued their walk in silence, reaching the end of the path, then turned back. As they made their way to the hotel a flower seller stopped them, offering her wares, speaking in soft, rapid French.

Ash looked to Violet.

'She says you should buy some pretty flowers for your pretty wife.'

Violet had been their translator for most of their trip, as Ash could only manage a few words of French on his own.

The woman's head bobbed up and down then pushed her basket at him.

'How could I say no to a woman who obviously has good taste?' Winking at the woman, he produced a coin from his pocket and offered it to her.

She, in turn, handed him a bundle of pink camellias. '*Merci, monsieur.*'

'*Merci, madame,*' he replied. 'Well, I'm afraid I've exhausted all my French. I'm sure my tutors would be terribly proud of me.'

Violet said a few more words of thanks to the woman before she hurried off. 'Thank you,' she said when he handed her the flowers.

'You must have had excellent tutors when you were growing up,' he remarked. 'Being that this is your first time in France and yet you know so much of the language.'

'I didn't have any tutors,' she explained. 'I taught myself.'

'You taught yourself how to speak French?' His jaw looked as if it might become unhinged at any moment. 'How? And why?'

'I didn't exactly teach myself to speak French,' she began. 'I taught myself to *read* in French.'

Her pronunciation was horrible, if the number of times the people she'd spoken to had asked her to repeat things was any indication.

'Papa had a paper that I wanted to read, but it was in French. He was far too busy to read and translate for me, so I took it upon myself to obtain language books and teach myself.'

'And what was this paper?'

'It was written by a mathematician,' she stated. 'A female mathematician. Madame Lenoire. And the paper was the Mathematical Theory of Elastic Surfaces.'

'And it was worth it? Learning an entire language to read one paper?'

She crossed her arms over her chest. 'It won the Grand Prize at the Paris Academy of Sciences.'

He tsked. 'You truly love numbers, don't you?'

'What isn't there to love about mathematics? It is truth, because numbers cannot lie, and nor is it vague. Yes means yes and no means no. It's precise and concise. Mathematics can explain anything and everything. It is, at its core, the very universe itself.'

He seemed to ponder her words. 'I'd never thought of it that way before. My logical, lovely Violet.' Taking her hand once more, he tucked it into his arm. 'Let's enjoy our last evening in Paris.'

Thankfully that evening, Ash had once again arranged for dinner in their suite, consisting of Violet's favourite dishes she had tasted in Paris. They dined on crispy duck confit, rich beef cooked in red wine, and an assortment of sweet baked desserts. Violet was eating a delicious pastry in the shape of a cone when some of the sweet cream inside oozed out, spilling onto her fingers. Putting the pastry on a plate, she licked her fingers, then unexpectedly locked gazes with her husband. Instantly, she saw it—the look of lust on his face, plain as day. Heat pooled in her belly.

He cleared his throat, dismissing the lone waiter standing in the corner. Once they were alone, Ash leapt out of his seat, then dragged her to the settee, their mouths crushing together in a desperate kiss.

Ash clawed frantically at her clothes. 'Damn buttons.'

The ripping of fabric told Violet that he'd torn the back of her dress. Her skirt, petticoats and hoops thankfully easily came off and pooled around her feet. When his fingers came upon her corset, he let out a string of curses. Then, 'Wait.'

'Wait?'

Reaching over to the dining table, he grabbed something shiny—a knife.

'I'll buy you a new one,' he growled as he twisted her around.

The compression around her torso loosened as he cut through the strings, then ripped the offending corset from her body and tossed it aside along with the knife.

'You're beautiful.'

He pulled off her drawers, then whipped off her chemise, exposing her breasts to his hot gaze. Pushing her down on the settee, he covered her body then fixed his mouth over a nipple.

Violet threw her head back, enjoying the sensations of his wet tongue lashing at her nipple. He switched his attention to the other one, torturing it equally. When he made a motion to rise to take off his clothes, she stopped him.

'Violet?'

She rubbed her cheek against his wool coat. 'This feels nice. You feel nice.' The scratchy fabric abraded her nipples deliciously, and she spread her legs and wrapped them around his hips, the velvet of his trousers rubbing against the insides of her thighs. 'Is it possible…for you to keep your clothes on?'

Without another word, he reached down between them to unbutton his falls. 'I need you, Violet,' he groaned, then thrust into her in one stroke. 'Want you. Only you.'

Violet clung to him, the sensation of his clothes rubbing against her naked body brought her pleasure to new heights. She quickly orgasmed, shuddering violently beneath him as he continued to pummel into her. Once she was done, he slowed down to a stop.

'That was…amazing.' She buried her face in his neck to breathe in his scent. 'Did you…?'

'No, darling. But it's early and I'm not done with you yet.'

Rising to his feet, he slipped his clothes off, tossing them onto the floor along with her destroyed shirt and corset. 'Since we're trying new things, do you think you'd like to try something else?'

She was too mindless deny him. 'All right.'

'Excellent.' Taking her hand, he pulled her up to stand, then sat down on the settee. Reaching between his legs, he wrapped a hand around his member and stroked it up and down. 'I love looking at your naked body,' he groaned. 'Violet, do you want to make love to me?'

'Me? What do you mean?'

His gaze moved from her to his stiff shaft. 'I want you on

top of me, Violet. I want to watch you move and bounce and writhe as you take your pleasure. Can you do that for me?'

Violet hesitated, though the sight of him bare and naked before her excited her. 'I want to, but I don't know how.'

'I'll help you. Come.'

With his help, she straddled his lap, the tip of his erection brushing against her curls. 'Hold the tip…guide it into… ah yes, Violet.' His head rolled back.

Slowly, she sank down, taking him inside her inch by inch. The feeling was the same as when he was on top, but somehow it was different. When he filled her to the hilt, she braced herself on his shoulders. 'Now what?'

'Move, darling.'

'How?'

'Any way you want to.'

Violet paused, unsure what to do. Then she wiggled her hips. 'Does that feel good?'

'You feel good,' he said. 'But see if you can move more.'

Lifting her hips, she slid up his length, then pushed down. The friction sent a jolt of pleasure through her. 'Oh.'

'There.' His hands cupped her buttocks. 'Let me help you.'

He helped her set a slow, steady rhythm. Once she found her stride, he let go, allowing her to do the work. She set a slow pace, but eventually began to move faster and faster. Each downward stroke of her hips sent shocks of delight up her spine.

'Violet… Violet…' Ash gripped her buttocks, kneaded at her soft flesh.

Raking her fingers into his hair, she pulled his head back and brought her lips down for a kiss. He groaned into her mouth, his hips thrusting up to meet hers.

Violet shifted her knees, pushing forward. 'Oh!' Her

pleasure increased with each movement, building up inside her.

'Come, Violet,' he said through gritted teeth. 'Please. I need you to— Oh!'

She shuddered above him, her breasts bouncing as she rode him hard. He captured a nipple in his mouth, biting down just as her body exploded. He let out a throaty cry, his hips rocking erratically as he pulsed inside her. Her release wrung every ounce of pleasure from her body, leaving her limp as she collapsed against him.

'You were magnificent.' He crushed her against him. 'As I knew you would be.'

That had only the beginning, and for the rest of the evening Ash took his time with her, teased her, gave her endless pleasure, all the while telling her again and again that he wanted her.

Afterwards, as she lay in his arms, she slipped a hand down to her belly, as she had done every night since their wedding, wondering if there was a child inside her at that very moment.

Ash had said he wanted her—but perhaps only until she'd had his heir. What he really, truly wanted was his lands and his income. This was the reason they'd married after all.

And once she'd given birth to the future Marquess of Ashbrooke, she too would have what she wanted—Oakwood Cottage and Papa's library.

They would be back in England soon, and things would go back to normal.

That idea, however, caused a different thought to take root in her mind.

What was normal?

And what about after she gave birth? What would normal be like then?

Violet urged herself to think of Papa's library and Oak-wood Cottage. Of Papa and how he had been the only person in the world who'd loved and understood her. She would never have her father back, nor the same life she'd had before he'd passed away, but she would at the very least have the memory of him.

That was the 'normal' she should be thinking about. Of her routines, of curling up on a chair, surrounded by the warmth and reminder that her father had understood and loved her.

She closed her eyes and nestled deeper against Ash, allowing his scent to envelop her senses as she fell asleep.

Chapter Twelve

The smells and sights of London felt like a welcome balm to Ash. Everything here was familiar, the soul of the city so attuned to his own.

Paris had been much too frenzied and dizzying, even for him. He'd enjoyed the city, but their time there hadn't been real—it was like a pleasurable dream, but one he ultimately had to wake from. No, London was where he belonged.

'Thank you for agreeing to stay here,' he said to Violet as they pulled up at his townhouse.

'We had to come back sometime.'

On her lap, her fingers did that little dance where the thumbs touched her fingers one by one. Ash had noticed she did that whenever she was nervous or anxious.

'We'll visit Chatsworth Manor again one day, won't we?'

'Of course.'

Though the reason for leaving Chatsworth remained unspoken between them, it was obvious to Ash that Violet knew exactly why they had to leave. Besides, it wasn't as if they would never ever go back there.

Unless he lost the lands due to that damned clause.

But only time would tell, though if he remembered correctly, Violet had said she should have her monthly flow any day now, which would at least tell them if their efforts during the last month had been successful. If so, she would soon start growing large with his child, and eventually give birth to the heir who would save his legacy and her home.

That would also mean they would no longer need to share a bed.

That dreaded feeling pooled in his gut once more at the thought of never touching Violet again. Of never feeling her sweet body under his or hearing her cries of pleasure. Of possibly never seeing her.

Which was a ridiculous thought because that was their bargain. And he couldn't come up with any logical reason why they should continue sleeping together once she was pregnant.

In fact, Ash realised, after his thirty-first birthday, whether or not she gave birth to his heir, there would be no reason for him to be with Violet.

'Welcome, my lord.' Bennet greeted him as they entered the house. 'I hope you had a wonderful honeymoon.'

'We did, thank you.'

'My lord. Violet.' Lady Avery descended the stairs and headed straight for them. 'Welcome back.' When she opened her arms to embrace Violet, Ash stepped into them instead. 'Oh. Oh, my...'

'I've missed you, Lady Avery.' He released her, then gripped her shoulders to prevent her from reaching for Violet, who audibly sighed with relief. 'And, please, what is this "my lord" business? It's Ash. We are family now.'

Lady Avery looked positively giddy. 'Yes, my lor— Ash. And you must call me Mama.'

'I would be honoured.' He wrapped an arm around her shoulders. 'How about some tea in the parlour, Mama? Have you been enjoying London while we were away? Violet, why don't you go and refresh yourself for now, and join us when you can?'

Once he had finished his tea with Lady Avery, he crept upstairs to their bedchamber. The curtains had been drawn to keep out the sun, save for a sliver of light. Violet lay in bed, curled up on her side.

Her eyes opened the moment he walked in.

'Your mother does love to talk.'

Sitting beside her, he brushed a lock of hair from her forehead. He soaked in the image of her sleeping, saving it in his mind that when the time came they would no longer need to be together.

'I know. I have lived with her all my life.' Violet sat up. 'Thankfully, she will be leaving tomorrow to visit friends in Bath.' She rubbed at her eyes. 'Thank you for distracting my mother so I could have some time alone. She would have had a million questions about Paris, and I wasn't ready to be bombarded with them.'

'So I had to answer them all,' he said with a chuckle. 'Feeling better? I know the journey was long and difficult.'

'It was, but I'm glad to be back on English soil where most things are familiar.' She grimaced.

'Then why the frown?'

'Because we are also back in *London*.'

'Ah, you mean, society.' He clucked his tongue. 'There is nothing to worry about, darling. I'm certain the gossip about our hasty wedding has died down.'

Everyone in town would be guessing that their expeditious marriage was due to the fact that Violet had either been compromised or was already with child—which was precisely what he wanted the Canfields to think.

'No one will dare disparage you. You are now the Marchioness of Ashbrooke.'

Groaning, she fell back onto the pillows. 'That's precisely why I'm dreading being back. Being your marchioness means we must attend all sorts of events. Balls and soirees and dinners. I've already seen the pile of envelopes on Bennet's tray.'

'You poor girl.' Cupping her cheek, he kissed her temple. 'Do not worry about accepting every invitation.'

'But you still have to accept some, right?'

'I do.'

'And now we are married, so must I?'

'Unfortunately, yes.' He took her hand. 'But I promise I will do everything in my power to ensure you're comfortable wherever we go. Why don't we look at the invitations together and we can choose which ones to accept?'

Wide, luminous blue eyes looked up at him. 'All right.'

Ash wanted nothing more than to allay Violet's fears, so he did not accept any invitations for the next three days. They still came pouring in, of course, especially now word had spread that they had returned from their honeymoon.

Eventually though, they had to accept some of them, but he allowed her to choose which ones. After sifting through them, Violet chose the Houghton Ball, as Kate, Sebastian, and the Dowager would be there as well.

'Have I told you how ravishing you look, darling?' he said as they rode to the Earl of Houghton's home in Hanover Square. 'That blue gown suits you so well.'

'Not yet.' She was doing that exercise with her fingers. 'But since we left you have called me beautiful, stunning, and graceful.'

He chuckled. 'Only you would keep track.'

Once they arrived at the ball, Ash held Violet's hand tight. He'd noticed that adding pressure to his touch seemed to soothe her, so he was mindful to do it whenever she seemed fraught.

'The Marquess and Marchioness of Ashbrooke!' the butler announced as they arrived.

A hush fell over the crowd, followed by a low buzz as all eyes in the room fixed on them. Despite his grip, Ash felt Violet falter.

'Don't look at them,' he instructed. 'Not if it makes you ill at ease.'

'Where am I supposed to look?'

'Anywhere, as long as you are comfortable. Haven't you noticed that when haughty titled ladies are announced, they don't look anyone in the eye? That's because they don't think of anyone as their equal, and therefore believe they do not deserve a second glance.'

'I see.' She tilted her head. 'All right, I shall try it.'

Jutting her chin forward, Violet kept her gaze above most people's heads. They glided across the room and she seemed to him to be a queen among her subjects.

Spotting Sebastian and Kate, he guided her to them, and she visibly relaxed once in their company.

'You did well, darling,' he said, leaning down to whisper in her ear. 'I'm proud of you.'

Perhaps making a successful entrance had taken the pressure off Violet, for she was more at ease for the rest of the ball. Many of the guests clamoured for an introduction, and she was polite and gracious to all of them. However, as more and more people descended on them, he could see her patience was wearing thin.

'If you would excuse us?' he said to a group of ladies who had surrounded Violet. 'I would like to dance with my wife.'

He led her towards the dance floor, where they took their place as the waltz was announced.

'If you'd prefer to have some peace and quiet we could go out to the gardens instead,' he said. 'We can leave before the music starts.'

She shook her head. 'I actually don't mind dancing at all.'

'You don't? You actually like it?'

'I don't like the social aspect of it or having a stranger touch me.' She placed her hand on his shoulder while he took the other one in his. 'But everything about dancing is beautiful. The symmetry, the rotations, the repetition. Dancing uses all kinds of mathematics, like counting, shape-making, mapping, patterns, formations. No two dances are ever the same, but that's the beauty of it.'

The music began, and Ash whirled her across the floor.

She continued. 'All the dancers must stay in rhythm, counting the same pattern, so as not to bump into each other and stay in time with the music. And as you're leading the dance you're mapping out the size of the dance floor, so we don't go out of bounds, as well as—' Her lips clamped shut. 'I'm boring you, aren't I? I do tend to ramble on and on, my apologies.'

'You're not boring me, Violet.' He tamped down the urge to stop in the middle of the dance floor and kiss her. 'It's fascinating, what you're saying.' Only his lovely, logical Violet would equate something frivolous like dancing with mathematical concepts. 'I want to hear more. Please, do go on.'

And so she did, explaining further how mathematics and dance were closely related. Truly, it was perhaps the most enjoyable dance he'd ever had in his life, and he was almost sad when it came to an end.

Almost, but not really, because they'd stayed at the ball long enough.

Now he needed to be alone with his wife.

And the only reason for that, he reminded himself, was that she was not yet with child. There was still the danger of losing his lands and income. He had a duty to his name, title, and his servants and tenants to do what he could to save his legacy.

'Would you like to go home, Violet?' He lifted her hand to his lips and kissed the inside of her palm, not caring if anyone saw them.

Her lashes lowered and her cheeks pinkened. 'I would.'

One benefit of married life, Violet realised, was that it was much easier to establish routines. When she'd lived at Oakwood Cottage, she'd observed the same ones every day since the age of eight: upon waking, she washed, dressed, had breakfast. Whenever she entered her father's library she sat in her chair, placed her teacup on the table to her left, picked up whatever book she was reading with her right hand, and curled her feet underneath her. At night, she did the reverse of her morning routine. Dinner, undress, wash, then bed.

When she had been under the Dowager's sponsorship for her Season, it had been difficult to stay within the confines of a predictable routine. She'd constantly been dragged from country to Town, from early-morning dress fittings to afternoon tea, from balls to the ballet. Additionally, every day had been like a bombardment of information to process—where were they going? What would they do there? Who would they meet? What were they going to eat? It had been exhausting, to say the least, and she hadn't been able to count on any day being the same.

Now that her days were predictable, she gravitated towards those routines she craved. Her morning and evening routines were mostly the same as in Oakwood Cottage, save for the addition of her husband's presence during breakfast and dinner, as well as their making love at the beginning and ending of the day.

Her afternoon routine, on the other hand, was devoted to her work and duties as Marchioness of Ashbrooke. She had transformed the sitting room into her own office, where she worked on calculations for Kate, read through the latest scientific journals, sifted through invitations and letters, and met with either Bennet or Mrs Hogsworth to discuss any household concerns. Of course, Ash almost always introduced chaos to her day, coming in at all times and coaxing her to do something with him—usually in the bedroom. Although at other times he'd taken her to a museum, a sweet shop, and even Hyde Park one unusually warm afternoon.

Of course, now that she had found peace and serenity in the steady, predictable pattern of her daily life, she feared it would all come crashing to an end. And one day, in the middle of her morning routine, she saw the spot of red on her wash cloth.

No.

She checked once more and sure enough, blood had stained the white cloth like crimson ink.

'Gertrude!' she shouted. 'Gertrude, help!'

After helping her clean up and dress, the maid was dismissed, then Violet sat down on the bed, her hands gripping the edge of the mattress, the dull ache in her lower back like a portend of doom.

She was not pregnant.

What am I going to do?

Ash had left early today, as he had to attend to some business with his solicitor, so she would be alone at least until dinner time.

I should just go on with my day.

And she did just that—or at least she tried. She had taken too long to come downstairs, so her breakfast had gone cold. The eggs were congealed and the sausages tough as leather, so she pushed them away and headed to her office. But with her current state occupying her mind, she couldn't concentrate on the figures she was supposed to be working on for Kate's prototype test, and when Mrs Hogsworth came to discuss tonight's menu, she didn't even answer the door.

By the time she had to dress for dinner, Violet had turned into a disorderly mess.

Leaving her office, she rushed upstairs towards the master bedchamber, but stopped just outside the door.

Ash would be home any moment.

He can't see me like this.

But where would she hide?

Glancing over to her left, she found just the place.

The Marchioness's—*her*—bedchamber.

While all her clothes were neatly stored there, the only time she ever entered the room was to dress and undress, as she still slept in the master bedchamber with Ash. The covers and sheets on the bed remained untouched and perfectly stretched out over the mattress, as if they'd been preserved. Ash had never been in here either, preferring to wait for her in the other room, so it was the perfect hiding place.

Flinging the door open, she rushed inside, slammed the door shut, and locked it for good measure.

Then she waited, sitting at the edge of the bed, looking out of the window as the sun waned in the distance.

'Violet, are you in there?'

Ash.

'I've been going mad, looking for you. Bennet says no one has seen you for hours. What are you doing in there?'

'Go away.'

'Darling?' The knob jiggled. 'Did you lock yourself in there by accident?'

Flinging herself off the bed, she marched towards the door. 'I said, go away.'

'Violet, what's wrong? Are you sick? Hurt?'

Yes. And yes.

'Leave me alone.'

The jiggling of the knob intensified. 'Please, I'm worried about you. Tell me what's wrong.'

'No! I don't want to see you.'

'Don't want to see me—why not?' he asked, outraged.

'I just don't.'

'What have I done wrong, darling? Have I done or said something to offend you?'

She bit her lip, feeling her eyes well up with tears. Lord, he was going to be so disappointed in her.

'Please...' she hiccupped. 'Leave me alone, Ash. I don't want to see you.'

'Violet, open this door now!'

'Go away!'

'Violet!'

Bang-bang-bang.

The violent crack of his palm against the door made her jump back.

'I demand you open this door!' he shouted. 'Or I will break it down.'

'You wouldn't.'

There was a pause. 'No, I won't. But Bennet has the key, and I can easily retrieve it from him. It would take me all of five minutes to have this door opened. So I'm afraid that if your idea was to hide in there for all eternity, you might have to change your plans.'

His words sank in, and she conceded to his line of reasoning. Her plan to hide was irrational. She unlocked the door and took a step back. The knob turned and the hinges creaked with an ear-splitting noise that frayed her nerves.

Ash stood in the doorway, expression grave. 'What's the matter, Violet?'

Her lips parted, but no sound came out. Her thumbs began to touch her fingers in a rapid, frenzied movement. 'I have terrible news.'

'What is it?'

'I…I am… My monthly flow has arrived.' His expression remained impassive. 'So… I am currently indisposed, my lord.'

'I see.'

She spun away from him, not wanting him to see the tears ready to spill down her cheeks. 'I—I will sleep here for the week, u-until—' A gasp escaped her as strong, muscled arms wrapped around her.

She burst into tears.

'Violet, oh, Violet…' he soothed, kissing her temple and trailing his mouth down the side of her cheek. 'It's all right, darling. Shh…'

Bending down, he slipped an arm under her knees and lifted her up, then carried her all the way into the master bedchamber. He laid her down on top of the mattress with a gentleness that made her heart ache.

Then he turned and left.

Violet curled up on her side into a tight ball, as if doing so would protect her from the outside world. She had let Ash down. There would be no heir and he would lose everything. All because of her. The very thought made her sob harder into the pillows.

'Violet, please don't cry.'

Ash?

Turning to face the other way, she saw his shadowy figure in the doorway.

'You'll make yourself sick.' He carried a tray in his hands. 'I have tea for you,' he began as he strode inside. 'Also some sweets, biscuits, scones, lemon tea cakes that Gertrude says you crave at this time of the month, those chocolates from Paris that you like, and a poultice for your, er, condition.'

She sat up, marvelling at the heavily laden tray he set down on the bed next to her. 'A poultice?'

'Yes.' He scratched at his neck. 'I asked Mrs Hogsworth what women…who are indisposed need during this time to help them. I've heard that, well, it's not the most pleasant time, but having no experience in such matters, I sought out assistance. Gertrude helped as well, and Mrs Hogsworth made a poultice to place on your stomach to ease the pain.' He took a linen-wrapped pouch from the edge of the tray and offered it to her.

Leaning forward, she sniffed, then wrinkled her nose. 'Ugh, take it away. It smells horrible.'

He looked visibly relieved. 'Thank goodness. I was dreading having to smell it the entire night.'

'Entire night?' Did he mean to still sleep in here with her, even though she couldn't make love?

'It would have been dreadful. I am certain she put something ghastly in there, like chicken hearts or rat tails.' He shivered. 'Are the pains too much? Shall I have Bennet call for a doctor?'

'There's no need for a doctor,' she said. 'And no, the

pains aren't debilitating for me. But I do get a sore ache in my lower back for the first few days.'

'Ah, I see. We must keep you comfortable, then. Let's get you undressed. Can you stand? Or would you prefer to sit up?'

'You must call for Gertrude,' she instructed. 'She'll assist me.'

'Nonsense.' He waved a hand at her. 'I've been removing your clothing by myself for the last month, I think I can manage.'

Tugging at her hand, he helped her to her feet, then proceeded to remove her dress and all the outer layers of her clothing until she was down to her shift, drawers, and of course, the usual undergarments for her menses.

Once she'd settled back under the covers, he handed her a cup of tea. 'Are you hungry? I had forgotten it's dinner time. Shall I have a tray sent up?'

'I cannot have a full meal when I'm indisposed. But please do not miss out on your dinner because of me,' she urged.

'What, and have you gobble up all these treats without me?' he asked, seemingly offended. 'I've brought enough to feed an army.' Dragging a chair over from the corner of the room, he set it beside the bed. 'Hmmm...perhaps it's not so bad to be a woman, after all, if it means having an excuse to eat like a spoiled child once a month.'

A giggle escaped her mouth as he winked at her. 'It's usually only those tea cakes that I indulge in when I'm in this condition. You did not have to bring half of Cook's pantry up here.'

'Oh, really?' He plucked the box of chocolates from the tray. 'I can finish these off, then?'

She scowled at him. 'Not if you value your life.'

Chuckling, he took a piece of chocolate from the box, then leaned over to pop it into her mouth.

Together, they feasted on the treats while Ash entertained her, telling her amusing stories from his childhood and university days, as if his sole purpose in life was to make her laugh. When there was nothing but empty plates and crumbs on the tray, he left to take it—and the putrid poultice—outside, then came back to the bedchamber and proceeded to remove his clothing.

'Ash,' she began. 'I cannot...in my state...'

'What? Oh, no, darling, I just wish to be more comfortable for bed.' He discarded the rest of his clothes until the was down to his shirt and drawers. 'We don't have to do anything.'

'It's a bit early to sleep, don't you think?'

'Then why don't I read to you?'

As he climbed into bed he glanced at the book on her bedside table. Picking it up, he read the title aloud.

'*Algebra, with Arithmetic and Mensuration, from the Sanscrit of Brahmegupta and Bhascara.* Sounds riveting.'

Violet did not need to rifle through her catalogue of expressions to know he was being sarcastic.

'It is,' she replied, moving to his side so that she could lean against him and lay her head on his chest like a pillow. She sighed and breathed in his comforting scent. 'You can start at Chapter Twelve, page one hundred and fifteen, section two hundred and forty-nine to two hundred and fifty-one.'

He cocked an eyebrow at her, but said nothing as he rifled through the pages to the correct section. '"The last remainder, when the dividend and divisor..."'

Violet wasn't really paying attention to Ash—at least not to the words he was saying. No, she just loved hearing the sound of his voice, the low dips of his tone and the vibrations of his chest as he spoke. She didn't even mind when he tripped on the words in Sanskrit or skimmed over the tricky symbols and formulas. In fact, some of the sentences he read out weren't even coherent, but she didn't notice as his hand had found its way to her lower back, moving around in soothing circles, easing the ache away.

At some point, Ash's hand simply dropped to his side and when she glanced up, she saw that her husband was fast asleep. She reached over and put the book aside, then pulled the covers over them, then breathed out a sigh.

Ash had been so good to her these last weeks, which was why she was so afraid of disappointing him. He'd helped her so much while they were in Paris, and at the Houghton ball, making sure she was comfortable in all kinds of situations. She wanted to do the same for him, to be a good wife, a good marchioness, since she'd already failed in the one thing she was supposed to do.

And now he was saddled with a wife who abhorred meeting new people and attending loud parties.

It was obvious that from the few occasions they did go out, Ash was in his element when surrounded by people. He charmed others so effortlessly, but more than that, he just naturally drew them to him, like a sun in the centre of the universe, surrounded by planets.

He probably missed going out and socialising. He must find it boring to stay at home or go to the same few places with her. He was probably itching to attend raucous parties and stay out dancing until dawn, but held back because of her.

Maybe if she could find her place next to him, among those other planets, she could at least make him forgive her for not getting pregnant. She would try to fit in his world, to somehow change into a round peg. This was something she could do for him, seeing as he had been so considerate to her all this time.

I can do that for him, she thought as she snuggled deeper into his arms.

Chapter Thirteen

'Tell me, darling,' Ash said as he guided Violet to her seat. 'How does mathematics play into the world of opera?'

This evening they were attending a performance of Rossini's *Otello* at the opera. He had been surprised by her choice, as he knew that the loud music and crowds would certainly fray her nerves by the end of the evening.

But then again, he was astonished that she'd planned this outing at all and she had accepted a few other invitations too. In the past week they had gone to some ball or soiree nearly every night. The strain on her face at the end of the evening was evident, but she didn't complain or beg him to go home. No, she soldiered on, allowing herself to be surrounded by well-wishers and curious onlookers who wanted to see the new Marchioness of Ashbrooke. There had even been one evening when they hadn't gone home until dawn, and though she'd looked ready to fall over, she had nonetheless stayed by his side.

Violet sat down and smoothed her gloved hands down the skirts of her gown. 'Aside from the composition of music, the patterns, the structure, transpositions and inversions?'

'Oh, please, give me the more difficult answer,' he said, grinning at her.

The corner of her lips next to her beauty mark quirked up. 'You're jesting again.'

'Me?' He placed a hand over his heart, but when she scowled he took her hand and squeezed it. 'I was merely wondering if you truly wanted to be here. While it's quite nice that we have Sebastian's private box to ourselves tonight—' he gestured to the empty seats beside them '—I'm worried the music might be too much for you.'

'Not at all. I mean, I've only been to the opera once, and I quite liked it. Anything music-related—assuming the musicians are well trained—I enjoy.' She focused on her fingers where she fiddled with the lace edge of her gown. 'Papa loved music. He played the violin, was quite good at it. He could have been a professional if he hadn't gone into academics.'

'Really?'

She nodded, but kept her gaze cast downwards. 'He would play for me once in a while. I remember just watching him, listening to him, and the rest of the world seemed to disappear.'

"There is geometry in the humming of the strings, there is music in the spacing of the spheres.'

Her head snapped up to meet his eyes. 'Pythagoras.'

'You must be rubbing off on me,' he said with a wink. 'I'm very glad you're feeling much better now.'

The light drained from her face. 'As am I,' she replied flatly.

He cursed inwardly at his thoughtlessness. 'Violet, I—'

The lights dimmed before he could even finish his sentence, so he settled back as the orchestra began to play.

Ash hadn't meant to bring up her condition, but he was truly concerned for her. In the last week she'd seemed like her usual self, going through her routines, acting as she usually did. However once in a while, he would observe the brief flashes of melancholy on her face.

He hated seeing her like this, but then again, he couldn't sulk and give up. There was still time, his birthday was months away. Besides, just because she hadn't conceived this month, it didn't mean she wouldn't in the next.

And if he were truly honest, he was looking forward to continue trying with her.

'Violet, what's wrong?' he whispered.

The overture was barely halfway done and she was fidgeting in her seat.

'It's my glove.' She scratched at the back of her left hand. 'There's a loose seam.'

'Just ignore it. Mrs Hogsworth can mend it when we get back.'

'I can't.' Her fingers clawed at the fabric. 'Help me, please.'

'Fine.' Seizing her left hand, he began to pull at the fingers of the glove.

'Ash!' she hissed. 'What are you doing?'

'Helping you.' When he reached the little finger, he tugged the entire thing off.

'You can't do that— Oh.' She sighed when he rubbed her hand soothingly.

'There, is that better?'

'Yes, but you can't do that in public.'

'Do what?'

Her mouth parted as her eyelashes fluttered and a small moan escaped her lips. 'U-undress me.'

He leaned down and whispered in her ear. 'But it helped, didn't it? Are there any other parts of you that are itchy?'

Before he could say anything else, the opera chorus welcoming the conquering general Othello reminded them where they were.

Violet settled back into her seat and focused on the stage, pulling her hand away.

Ash fixed his attention on her ungloved hand, so dainty and perfect with its long, slim fingers and the soft skin of her palm. And what talented hands they were too; he recalled how they'd explored his body, wrapping around his—

He groaned, blocking the vision of her sweet hands on him. It had been over a week since he'd made love to her, but it felt much longer than that. He was like a man dying of thirst and hunger in the desert. He longed to touch her and to be inside her again.

Ash, you randy dog, she's unwell, he berated himself silently.

Still, he couldn't help himself. After a month of having Violet whenever he pleased, having to abstain was like torture. And now apparently his loins were so full that even the sight of her un-gloved hand was ready to undo him.

Which was, as he seemingly had to constantly remind himself, preposterous. He'd been with many women in the past and eventually he'd become bored with all of them.

Surely this obsession with Violet had to burn itself out eventually?

Determined to control himself, he straightened his shoulders and turned back to the stage, focusing his attention on Rodrigo and Iago as they plotted to bring down the titular main character. Everything was proceeding well enough, at least, until Desdemona made her entrance.

Who tonight, happened to be played by Alessandra Moretti, his former lover.

'Oh, hell.'

'Ash?' Violet's head snapped towards him. 'Are you all right?'

'Yes. Apologies, I was just…never mind.'

Shrugging, she turned back to the stage.

His affair with Alessandra Moretti seemed like a lifetime ago, though truly it had been only four or five years ago. She'd been a budding understudy back then, freshly arrived from Italy. As he was no opera enthusiast, he couldn't even remember how they'd been introduced—perhaps at a party held by some important foreign attaché, or a dinner hosted by some business magnate. But he did recall that she'd immediately set her sights on him—and he, of course, had been glad to be caught.

Their affair had lasted for weeks, but eventually he'd lost interest in her and ended things. Alessandra had been livid, proclaiming that she was in love with him, but a generous gift of jewellery had soothed her broken heart and he hadn't heard from her since.

Maybe she doesn't remember me, he thought.

However, at that moment Alessandra's head lifted towards Ash and their eyes met. She smiled at him before turning her attention to her scene partner.

Damn.

Ash sat through the rest of the opera, growing more and more impatient as the night drew on. Violet, thankfully, did not want to leave the box during the intermission, nor did she want to be crushed in the crowds as they filed out of the theatre when the opera had finished, so Ash suggested they wait inside until everyone was gone.

Once the theatre had emptied, he wrapped her cape around her, signalling that it was safe to leave. Before they could exit the box, however, the door opened and someone stepped in.

'Ash, I was told you haven't left— Oh.' Alessandra's full, pouting mouth rounded in a perfect O. 'I thought you were alone.'

The touch of a smirk on her face told Ash she had known very well that Violet was here. Alessandra had always been a vicious little thing. He wasn't surprised she'd made it up the ranks from understudy to lead soprano in such a short time.

'Good evening, Miss Moretti,' he greeted.

'Ash, I didn't know you knew the soprano,' Violet said. 'Hello. You were magnificent tonight. I truly enjoyed your performance. It was riveting.'

'And who is this, Ash?' Alessandra's eyes perused Violet from head to toe. 'Another one of the London beauties you run around with? How long will she stay with you?'

Ash was aware she knew damned well who Violet was, but Alessandra did enjoy toying with people's emotions, luring them into what they thought was a safe situation before striking like a viper. He would not allow her to hurt Violet.

'It's getting late. We should—'

'Ash, don't be rude,' Violet said. 'Please, introduce us.'

'Yes, please introduce us,' the soprano mocked as she mimicked Violet.

Ash looked at his wife incredulously. Alessandra's comments seemed to have completely gone over her head.

'Violet, this is Miss Alessandra Moretti. Miss Moretti, this is my wife Violet, Marchioness of Ashbrooke.'

'How do you do?' Violet said.

'How beautiful you are, my lady,' Alessandra said.

'So are you,' she replied. 'I liked your costume in Act One. It looked very uncomfortable, though. How do you manage to sing in it?'

Alessandra flashed him a look that seemed to say, *Is she joking?*

'We have some very talented seamstresses,' she said. 'And the costumes are not as tight as you may think, to allow me to breathe properly and hit the high notes.'

'Ah, yes, breath control is important for singers,' Violet remarked. 'Your lung capacity must indeed be superior.'

Alessandra laughed. 'Perhaps your husband can answer that. Ash, do you recall that time in the bathtub—'

'We really should be heading home.' Ash shot daggers at Alessandra.

'Oh, I do miss your home!' the soprano exclaimed. 'Does your cook still make those delicious crumpets? I love the way the butter melts over them when they're hot and gets into all the nooks and crannies.'

'Have you been a guest at the house?' Violet asked, and cocked her head to one side.

'Alessandra!' he warned. 'Don't—'

'Why, yes, my lady. Many, many times.' Her lips spread into a wide smile.

'Many times?' Violet's brows drew together. 'When?'

Alessandra's expression turned annoyed before she snapped, 'When he and I were lovers, of course. Are you bird-witted?'

The air was seemingly sucked out of the room and the tension grew thick. Violet blinked, then turned her head to look at Ash, a myriad of emotions visibly passing through her.

'Violet—'

She brushed past him and darted out through the door. He was about to run after her when Alessandra blocked his way.

'Ash,' she said in a low, sultry voice. 'I've missed you so much. I haven't forgotten about you even after all this time.'

'Go away, Alessandra!' he shouted, and he shoved her aside to dash out through the door.

He heard a faint string of Italian curses behind him, but he didn't care. He had to find Violet.

He ran down the corridor and spotted her just ahead, looking around, confused. 'Violet!'

She halted, then turned her head. Upon realising it was him, she scowled, then darted around the corner.

Oh, hell.

He pursued her, then spotted her going through a doorway at the end of the hallway. Following her, he realised the door led to the backstage area. It didn't take long to catch up with her, and as soon as he did, he hooked his arm into hers, then dragged her to the nearest room. Pushing her inside, he locked the door behind him.

Taking a deep breath, he turned around slowly. 'Violet…'

She stood there, her chest heaving deeply. 'You were lovers?'

'Yes.' He wouldn't lie to her. 'We were. It was a long time ago.'

'How long?'

'Four…maybe five years.'

'But not any more?'

'No, we parted ways after a few weeks.' He took a step towards her. 'Violet, I'm sorry.'

'Why?' Her eyebrows furrowed.

'You shouldn't have… I shouldn't have…' He raked his fingers through his hair. 'I didn't mean to hurt you.'

'You didn't,' she stated.

'But she did.' *Damn Alessandra.* 'She shouldn't have said that about you.'

'It's true, though,' she sniffed. 'I didn't understand what she was trying to say. Why won't people just state what they mean, instead of making insinuations and dropping hints? It's frustrating when I can't make sense of what people say. She's right. I am bird-witted—'

He quickly wrapped his arms around her. 'Don't say that.'

'But it's true,' she murmured against his chest. 'No matter what I do, or how hard I try, I can't read people. I wish I were smart and witty, like you, then it would make all this easier.'

He frowned. '"All this"?'

'Attending parties and balls. Socialising with your peers, meeting and making conversation with people, trying new things. I'm trying to be better for you.'

What the hell was she saying?

'You've been so wonderful to me these last weeks—making sure I'm comfortable, avoiding situations that could cause my anxiety to rise. You're probably bored to tears with me and miss going out to parties and soirees and being surrounded by people. I just want to be a good marchioness, since I have failed to conceive. I want to do this for you.'

'"Do this"? This is why you've been accepting so many invitations? As some kind of misguided attempt to placate me because you think you failed me?'

'It's true.'

Gripping her shoulders, he looked deep into her eyes. 'Violet, look at me, please?' When she lifted her gaze, he said, 'You have not failed.'

'The purpose of our marriage was for me to get pregnant, and that goal has not been met. That is the very definition of failure.'

He stifled a laugh. *My logical, lovely Violet.* 'It seems unfair to put the blame entirely on yourself when I'm half of the equation. One plus one equals two, correct?'

'I suppose.'

'We haven't failed—yet. We still have time. And many, many chances to try.' His hands slipped down to her waist. 'Darling, will you keep trying with me?'

Luminous blue eyes stared up at him. 'Yes.'

'Good.' Crushing her against him, he sealed his mouth over hers.

The tightness that had been building in his chest exploded, and his blood heated with desire. He hadn't kissed her in so long, only a few pecks here and there, and he'd forgotten how sweet she was. She opened up to him, tilting her head to one side so his tongue could fully invade her mouth, while her hands immediately dug into the nape of his neck to tug at his hair, making his desire spring to life.

A primitive sound erupted from his chest. His control, his reason and his wits dissipated as his hands slid down to her buttocks, then lifted her up.

'What are you doing?'

He planted her on the nearest surface he could reach—one of the dressing tables. 'Are you finished with your monthly flow?'

'Yes. Why— Ash!' she exclaimed when he lifted her skirts and slipped a hand underneath. 'You can't... Here? It's a public place. What if people hear us?'

'Who cares?' His fingers inched up her thighs. 'I've locked the door and everyone has gone home. And so what if they hear us?' Once he reached her sex, it didn't take him long to make her wet. 'Violet, I want you,' he whispered in her ear. 'I need you.'

'I need you too,' she whimpered, spreading her thighs. 'Please, Ash, come inside me.'

Needing no further invitation, he pushed her skirts up her thighs. He made quick work of his trousers, pushing them impatiently down his thighs. He surged into her, making her cry out. He drowned the sound by sealing his mouth over hers, their tongues tangling in a frenzied dance, feasting on each other as if they hadn't had a meal in days.

Lord, she was perfect, with her heat clasping around him so deliciously. He thrust rhythmically inside her, rough and wild, and she enjoyed every moment of it, urging him on by meeting his hips with every push. When her body began to shudder with her impending release he urged her on, riding it out with her until her glorious flesh gripped him tight. His release slammed into him like a wave, and he gritted his teeth as the force of it sent him into rapture.

Once his senses had returned, Ash withdrew from her and took a step back. Violet looked utterly delightful, her cheeks pink, hair mussed, panting hard. He pushed her skirts back down and helped her off the dressing table.

'Shall we go home?'

'Wait.' She wrinkled her nose at him. 'One plus one equals two?'

He burst out laughing. 'That was awful, wasn't it? I apologise for offending your sensibilities.' He kissed her square on the mouth. 'I shall leave the mathematical analogies to you from now on.'

'It is my speciality,' she replied.

'And when we reach home I'll show you *my* specialities,' he said, giving her a wink.

While Violet had seemingly forgiven him for the whole Alessandra debacle, Ash was still wrapped up in guilt. He'd had no idea that Violet blamed herself—and only herself—for failing to conceive. It was preposterous, of course. Not once had he ever thought she was solely to blame for their lack of success, nor did she have to compensate him by placing herself in unpleasant situations. While he did enjoy going to certain social events, it wasn't something that he needed in his life.

And so, the day after the opera, he sat down with her to sift through all their invitations and correspondence.

'Which shall we accept?' Violet asked as she eyed the stack of envelopes warily.

He shrugged. 'As long as we are present at the important events—weddings, funerals, parliamentary and royal functions and the like—you may turn down any or all of them.'

'Surely I can't decline all these invitations? You're the Marquess of Ashbrooke, you must accept them.'

'Says who?'

'The rules.'

'There are no written rules on accepting invitations.'

'Actually, there are,' she countered. 'Many of them.'

'Hang the rules, they're written by bored society matrons who have nothing better to do. Violet, I open only about half the invitations I receive and accept as few of them as possible.'

Mostly he went to events to socialise with other men or meet potential paramours—though perhaps he would keep that fact to himself.

'Musicales and teas bore me, and I can watch the symphony orchestra for better music and ring Bennet for a better brew. And don't even mention balls. I hardly ever go to balls—especially not in the midst of the Season, when the mamas are ready to fling their daughters at me.'

'Then what do you do to socialise?'

'Mostly I go to St James's with my friends.'

'Oh, to clubs like The Underworld?'

'Yes.'

There was also another type of establishment he frequented in St James, but he that was another thing he'd keep to himself.

'Anyway, Violet, as you are my wife, our socialising is

your responsibility now, and therefore I shall leave it entirely up to you to accept or decline these invitations on our behalf.'

Ash could not protect Violet from the Ton for ever, but he would do his utmost to make sure she never had to be in situations where she was anxious or uncomfortable or caught off guard.

Tonight, however, he was going to make an exception, because he'd been planning this particular outing ever since they'd arrived back from their honeymoon.

'I know you hate surprises, darling,' he said as they sat in his carriage on their way to their destination later that evening. 'But I hope you'll forgive me this once?'

Violet visibly paled. 'Oh, no.'

'I promise, it's a good surprise.'

'There is no such thing as a good surprise.'

He placed a hand over her hers. 'I aim to change your mind tonight. Ah,' he said as the carriage slowed. 'We're here.'

'And "here" is…?'

'Tut-tut, I told you it's a surprise.'

'I will see where we are once we leave this carriage, Ash,' she said wryly.

'Shall I blindfold you, then?' When she glared at him, he only chuckled. 'All right, come on.'

The carriage had driven into a wide driveway inside an enormous courtyard flanked by terraces on either side, with a bronze sculpture in the middle of what appeared to be King George III atop a pedestal and Neptune reclining on a platform below. They stood outside a large porticoed building with a large green dome on top.

'Welcome to Somerset House, home of the Royal Soci-

ety,' Ash announced as he helped her alight. 'We're attending a reception here tonight.'

Violet's eyes grew large. 'This is your surprise? Why
didn't you tell me?'

He blew out an exasperated breath. 'Because it's a surprise—and besides, this is not the real surprise.' He offered
his arm. 'My actual surprise is inside.'

When they entered the building, they were led into a
large exhibition room which was covered in oil paintings
from floor to ceiling, which was already filling up with
people.

'Who are all these people?' Violet asked. 'And what is
this reception for?'

Ash shrugged. 'I don't know.'

'You don't know?' Her voice pitched unnaturally high.
'Then why are we here? How did you get an invitation?'

'I didn't get an invitation. But someone else did.' He
nodded towards a group of people. One of them turned towards them, then smiled and strode over to them.

'Your Grace…' Violet curtseyed as the Dowager Duchess of Mabury approached them.

'Violet, it's been too long.' The Dowager looked at Ash
slyly. 'Keeping her to yourself, Ash?'

'Of course,' he replied smugly. 'Any man with eyes and a
brain would never let a woman like Violet out of his sight.'

'It is wonderful to see you, ma'am,' Violet continued. 'I
have missed our time together.'

'As have I, Violet.'

'Thank you for bringing me here tonight, Ash,' Violet
said warmly. 'You're right, there can be some good surprises.'

'You're welcome—but the Dowager isn't my surprise.'

She let out an impatient breath. 'Then what is it?'

Ash turned to the Dowager. 'Your Grace, is our guest here?'

'Yes, she's somewhere— Ah!' The Dowager waved at someone just behind Ash. 'There she is.'

Ash looked over his left shoulder and saw an older woman in a rust-coloured gown approach them.

'Madame Guilbert, *bonsoir*.' The Dowager accepted the woman's kisses on each cheek.

'*Bonsoir*, Your Grace, how lovely to see you after all this time,' Madame Guilbert greeted her in heavily accented English. 'I'm so glad you were able to attend.'

'I wouldn't miss it for the world, especially since you have come all the way to England. Now, these are the friends I was telling you about, who wanted to meet you.'

Madame Guilbert turned to them, '*Bonsoir*.'

'Ash, Violet…this is Madame Geneviève Guilbert. Madame Guilbert, this is Devon and Violet St James, Marquess and Marchioness of Ashbrooke.'

'How do you do, my lord, my lady?' Madame Guilbert greeted. '*Enchanté*.'

The Dowager continued. 'But perhaps you've heard of her work as Madame Lenoire?'

'*You* are Madame Lenoire?' Violet burst out.

Madame Guilbert's lips widened into a smile. '*Oui*.'

'Madame Lenoire…author of *The Mathematical Theory of Elastic Surfaces*?'

'*Oui*.'

Violet's eyes looked ready to pop out, and she inhaled a quick breath. 'Tell me how you derived your differential equation from your first paper? Why did you simplify your hypothesis when you made revisions? And can you explain—'

The Frenchwoman laughed. '*Pardon, madame.* My English it is…not so good.'

'*Je parle français, madame,*' Violet replied.

'Ah!' Madame Guilbert's face lit up, and then she began to speak in rapid French.

Violet listened intently, then responded with more questions.

'So, Ash,' the Dowager said, sidling up to him, moving away from the two women who were now deep in conversation. 'I can't quite believe I'm saying this, but marriage suits you.'

His eyes never left his wife's as he continued to watch her, enraptured by the way she spoke excitedly, her face lit up like a Yule log, her hands gesturing wildly in the air.

'You know, I think it does.'

Chapter Fourteen

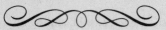

'What do you mean, you're not going to the ball?' Mama exclaimed.

Violet looked up from her tea, exasperated. Lady Avery had just arrived from Bath that morning and they were now sitting down to afternoon tea. She had asked Violet what she planned to wear to the Earl and Countess of Hereford's ball when Violet informed her she had not accepted their invitation.

Replacing her teacup on the saucer, she continued, 'I mean Ash and I will not be attending.'

Why did that need any further translation? How many other ways did she need to state it before Mama understood her?

'But it's the most prestigious ball of the Season. Mabury and the Duchess are attending, as well as Winford and his wife. You should come if only to see them. They are your friends, after all.'

'I can see Kate and Persephone any time at home,' she said. 'I don't want to go to the ball. Or any ball for that matter.'

And thank goodness she was now married and Mama would not be able to force her to go.

Mama tutted. 'Unfortunately, Violet, you'll have to show yourselves to society every now and then. It's expected.'

She shrugged. 'I haven't gone to any events, and I don't intend to.'

Her mother looked horrified. 'What do you mean?'

'Ash has given me free rein not to accept any invitations at all.'

'None at all?' Mama asked incredulously. 'You can't just never leave your home.'

'It's not never *ever*. We're still going to the important ones, like Henry's christening. But I don't plan to go to any balls or parties in the foreseeable future.'

'Oh, Violet.' Mama sighed. 'You are the wife of a peer, and though you may not realise it social connections can only be built when one is, well, *social*. These links and interconnections have to be maintained, not just for today, but for the future. Someday, your children might benefit from the relationships you cultivate now, ensuring they, too, are able to take their rightful place in society.'

Wait...*children*?

Her heart stopped at the thought.

Surely after she'd borne Ash's heir there would be no need for more children.

What about a spare?

She grimaced, the word tasting sour in her mouth. Though an only child herself, Violet thought it sounded crude and cruel to think of a second child as a 'spare', as if they existed as an extra cog for the machine, ready to be put in should the need arise.

'Violet? Are you listening to me?'

'Um...yes, Mama. I was just thinking...of the kitchen accounts.'

'Violet,' Mama pleaded. 'Think of your future. And your children's future.'

Violet let out a loud sigh. 'I'll think about it.'

'Thank you. It's in three days' time,' Mama said. 'You have plenty of time to respond.'

As they continued their tea, Violet couldn't help but ponder on her mother's words. They had buried themselves in her mind, and now she couldn't quite expel them.

Children.

When she'd first agreed to marry Ash and bear his heir the idea of a child had been an abstract concept for her. Something that didn't exist, a goal she had yet to achieve, like a mathematical formula that had yet to be completed.

But Mama's words had struck something in her, lighting up an area in her mind that reminded her that someday soon this 'abstract' being was going to be a real live person.

And fear seized her. True, abject terror at the thought that she would be a mother.

She would have to care for this being, nurture it, love it.

What if she couldn't do it?

What if she made a mistake and something bad happened?

Maybe Mama was right.

Her future child was going to be Marquess of Ashbrooke. Ash's son. He would probably grow up to be just like his father—handsome, bright, and social.

And, as his mother, she would have to do the right thing to secure her son's future.

So three days later she found herself on her husband's arm, being announced at the Earl and Countess of Hereford's ball.

'Are you sure you want to stay?' Ash asked as they strode inside.

'Yes, I'm sure.'

For as long as she could, anyway.

'Oh, there they are.'

She nodded to the other side of the room, where Kate and Persephone stood with their respective husbands. As they made their way to their friends Violet could not help but feel as if everyone if the room was watching them—which they probably were.

'Violet!' Kate exclaimed. 'Thank goodness you decided to come after all.'

'Hello, Kate, and welcome back. Persephone... Your Grace,' Violet said. 'How was the honeymoon?'

'Wonderful,' Persephone said. 'How about you? It's too bad our time in Paris did not correspond. We could have gone to see the sights together, dined at the same restaurants, seen the same shows...'

'It was a last-minute trip,' Violet explained. 'But, yes, Ash and I had a grand time. I'm glad you enjoyed your honeymoon too.'

The three couples continued to chat and socialise with each other, and once in a while were joined by acquaintances and friends. At one point Ash claimed Violet for a waltz, which she had to concede was one of the best things about attending balls. In Ash's arms, she didn't feel so uncomfortable or awkward.

When they returned to their friends, Violet noticed a man she had never seen before speaking with Winford. The Duke introduced him as Viscount Luton.

'How do you do, my lady?'

Luton was dark-haired, and Violet supposed he was handsome, though his portly belly and bloated skin did not do him any favours.

'And of course I know Ash. We used to run around in our university days with Mabury, spending many a night carousing in St James's.'

'Hello, Luton.'

Usually when Ash greeted an old friend he was bright and cheery, which was why it was difficult for Violet to ignore his chilly demeanour towards the Viscount.

Luton didn't seem to notice the cold reception. 'Ashbrooke, when I read that you'd married I thought someone was playing a prank on me. What happened to your vow to never get shackled?'

'Haven't you heard the saying that people can change?' Ash replied curtly.

'But there's also another saying—a tiger cannot change its spots.'

'Stripes,' Violet blurted out. 'A tiger cannot change its stripes. Tigers have stripes. You may be thinking of another proverb from Ancient Greece which states that a leopard cannot change its spots.'

The Viscount narrowed his eyes at her. 'Ah, your wife is as intelligent as she is beautiful.'

Violet's skin crawled under the Viscount's scrutiny.

'Aren't you going to thank me for the compliment, Lady Ashbrooke?'

'She doesn't have to do anything.' Ash's voice was deadly serious.

Luton laughed nervously and punched him in the shoulder. 'Good God, old chap, you really have changed. Maybe you're getting old.' He waggled an eyebrow. 'And you, my lady, should smile more. It will make you look even more beautiful.'

Winford cleared this throat. 'Luton, I think I see Lord Talbot over there by the refreshment table. Would you mind making me an introduction?'

'Not at all, it would be my pleasure, Your Grace. I'll see you later Ash, Lady Ashbrooke.'

As soon as the two men had left, Ash visibly relaxed.

'Violet, I need you to listen to me,' he said. 'And listen very carefully.'

'What is it?'

'Do not, under any circumstances, find yourself in the company of that man. And definitely not alone.'

'But I though he was your friend?'

Her husband's jaw hardened. 'Not all my friends are good people,' he said cryptically. 'Promise me?'

'I—all right.' She shrugged. Besides, she really could not see how she would ever be alone with that man.

Just as she always did in these situations, Violet found herself continuously drained as the evening wore on. By eleven o'clock she'd definitely had enough interaction and needed to go home.

'I'll have the carriage brought round,' Ash said, giving her hand a squeeze. 'But first I need to say our goodbyes to our host and hostess. I see Kate and Sebastian over there, talking to Lord Huntington. Wait with them and I'll come and fetch you when I'm done.'

'I will. Thank you.'

Violet made her way over to Kate, who introduced her to Lord Huntington. However, a headache had begun to throb away at her temple, making it difficult to remain in conversation.

Kate noticed right away.

'You poor dear, are you all right?' her friend asked. 'Do you need to sit down?'

'I'll be fine,' she assured her friend. 'We're heading home soon.'

'Where has Ash gone?'

'He's saying goodbye to our hosts.' Violet glanced around, trying to see if she could spot Ash. 'He should be here at any moment.'

Kate tsked. 'Knowing Ash, "saying goodbye" could take much longer for him than most people—not to mention if he sees an old acquaintance along the way, and he might stop and chat. I think you should go to the retiring room and wait there, so you can be somewhere quiet.'

Violet hesitated, but the thought of an empty, peaceful room was much too tempting at the moment. 'Then I shall find my way there. If you see Ash, please tell him to come and fetch me from there.'

'Of course.'

As she made her way across the room the ache in her temple grew, but thankfully she was nearing her destination. She was but a few feet away from the ladies' retiring room when a strong hand grasped at her arm.

'I beg your pardon. Let me go.' She tugged it away, but to no avail. 'I said let— Viscount Luton?' Her nose wrinkled. What is that smell?

'Lady Ashbrooke.' The Viscount's grip tightened. 'You must come with me.'

'I beg your pardon?' She sniffed. The Viscount smelled an awful lot like brandy.

'Ash has asked me to fetch you.'

She froze, unsure how to process the Viscount's words. Ash had told her never to be in Luton's company under any circumstances, but now he had sent him to fetch her?

The throb in her temple became a full pounding.

'Please, you must hurry,' said the Viscount.

'Hurry? Why?'

'Ash needs you. He's been hurt, you see.' There was a slight slur to his words that made him extended all the *S*s in his speech.

'Hurt?' Fear and anxiety spiked in her, and she forgot

all about her headache. 'How? Why? He was supposed to fetch the carriage.'

'Wheel ran over his leg.' Luton tugged at her arm. 'Come, let's go outside now.'

Before she could protest, he began to drag her away. All the noise, the smells, the lights and colours around her combined with the fear for Ash, made Violet's head swim.

Please be all right, she pleaded.

However, when the cool night air hit her face, she sobered and realised they were not out in the street where all the carriages were parked.

'Lord Luton, where are we?'

'Why, we're in the garden, my lady.'

'The what?'

'The garden,' he repeated, licking his lips. 'Surely you've heard of them? They're perfect for trysts.'

He advanced towards her menacingly and Violet took a step back. 'My lord—'

'My, but you're beautiful.' His eyes roamed over her, stopping at her chest. 'No wonder Ash couldn't help himself, even though he never beds virgins. Or married women, though it's ironic that he's tupping one now.' He chortled. 'Get it? Because you're married and he's screwing you?'

Lord, he was confusing. What was he trying to say?

'My lord, please. Where is my husband? I need to see him, especially if he's hurt.'

Luton chortled. 'And I thought you were intelligent. Ash is not here, nor is he hurt.'

'He's not? Then why did you say he was.'

'To get you alone, of course.'

'Wh-what for?'

'What else?' His eyes darkened. 'For our tryst.'

'I don't recall agreeing to such a thing,' she said, indignant.

He took another step towards her. 'Don't be such a prig, Lady Ashbrooke. You can't possibly be married to Ash and act like a prude.'

'I'm not being a prude. Now, please, I want to go back inside. I want to go home with Ash.'

'What? Ash won't mind. We share women all the time.'

Violet's stomach churned. 'My husband wouldn't give me away like a party favour.'

'I don't always need his permission. We have an understanding, he and I.'

Her heart dropped.

Stupid Violet.

Her eyes darted around, trying to find a way out. Luton, however, was two steps ahead as he lunged at her.

She screamed, but it was too late. His arms came around her, trapping her in his vice-like grip. A hand covered her mouth, muffling the rest of her shouts.

'Shut up, you stupid— Ow! You bit me!'

Violet used the chance and scrambled away from his grasp, lifting her skirts so she could free her legs to run back into the house. Before she could reach the door, she bumped into something heavy and solid.

'No! Let me go! I—'

'Violet, darling. It's me.'

Her heard stopped. 'Ash?' She lifted her head and found the face of her husband. Relief made her go limp. 'Oh, Ash, it's you,' she sobbed. 'Thank God.'

'Darling, what's the matter? And why are you out here? I was looking for you. Thank goodness one of the footmen said he saw you go out here. I— Luton?' His expression turned grave, and his body grew taut. 'What are you doing out here with my wife?'

'Ash,' Luton said in a casual tone. 'I was just getting some fresh air...as was your wife.'

'He dragged me out here against my will.' Violet straightened up and turned around to face the blackguard. 'He said you were hurt and that I had to come with him'

Luton's expression shifted. 'Oh, please, Lady Ashbrooke. You were the one who started it. Ash, she persuaded me to come out here. She said she needed some fresh air, and then tried to kiss me.'

'I did not!' she protested.

'Who are you going to believe, Ash?' Luton said. 'We've been friends since we were in short pants. How long have you known this woman? Besides, all these married women are alike. Once they're no longer virginal debutantes, they start itching for more. For variety.'

'He's lying, Ash. I would never go with him.'

Ash's jaw clenched and unclenched. 'Did he hurt you? Touch you? Kiss you?'

'No. I bit him before he could try anything.'

Ash's eyes blazed and he pulled Violet behind him. 'You put your hands on my wife, you drunken sod!'

'Don't be a stick-in-the-mud. We've always shared women. Why is she any different— Bloody hell!'

Ash lunged at Luton, knocking him to the ground. Violet screamed as her husband pinned Luton down by straddling his torso, then pulled back a fist before smashing it into the Viscount's face. He repeated it with his other hand.

Luton let out a sickening, gurgling sound. The sound of breaking flesh and bone sickened her stomach.

'Stop! Please, Ash you're going to kill him.'

But her husband was like a madman as he pounded

at Luton's face. She was frozen, unable to move an inch, watching helplessly.

'Violet? Ash was search— Bloody hell!'

Violet whirled around.

Winford!

The Duke sped towards the two men, then pulled Ash off Luton. Squatting down, he leaned over the Viscount. 'For God's sake, Ash, you've made minced meat out of his face.'

'He...touched... Violet...' Ash gasped.

Winford's expression turned grave. 'Violet, are you—'

'I'm fine.' Her feet unfroze and she hurried towards them. 'Oh, Ash...'

He looked a fright, with his hair tousled, his eyes wild, shirt ripped and hands all bloody. She leapt at him, wrapping her arms around his torso, and buried her face in his chest.

'Ash...'

'He's still breathing, thank heavens.' Winford rose to his feet. 'Hell, Ash.' He raked a hand through his hair. 'You should go home. There's a side gate through the garden, use that to get out to the front. I'll get Luton cleaned up and walking again so you don't swing from the gallows for murder.'

'It would be worth it,' Ash muttered.

Violet clung to him tighter. 'Don't say that. Please, Your Grace, do what you can.'

While she hated Luton, she didn't want Ash to go to jail.

Winford nudged Luton with a boot, making him moan in pain. 'I'll take care of him. And don't worry, I'll make sure he won't talk either. He owes The Underworld and a few other places heaps of money. He'll keep his mouth shut. There won't be any scandal.'

'Thank you, Your Grace.' She pressed her cheek to her husband's chest. 'Please, Ash, let's go home.'

* * *

Ash winced as he dipped his hand into the washbasin, staining the water red with the blood from his knuckles. The pain felt good, however, as it distracted him from the thoughts swimming around in his head.

Luton had touched Violet.

She could have been hurt.

He'd nearly killed a man.

I never should have left her alone.

They should have left the ball the moment he saw Luton.

Ash couldn't believe they'd used to be friends. Indeed, they'd known each other since their days at Eton, and then continued their friendship through university. He'd spent many an evening with him, taking in all the delights St James's had to offer. Over the years, however, Luton had drunk more and more, and often lost control, getting into fights that usually ended up with both parties being kicked out of whatever establishment they were in.

One night, about six years ago, Luton had convinced Ash to visit his favourite brothel. Luton had been three sheets to the wind, but the madam of that particular establishment hadn't seemed to care. Ash had been enjoying the company of a delightful French girl when he'd heard screams from next door—Luton's room. Rushing out, he'd stormed in and seen the lady he had purchased for the evening cowering in the corner, holding her hand over her bloody eye as Luton screamed at her. Disgusted, Ash had dragged Luton out and vowed never to associate with such company ever again.

A terrible feeling had come over him the moment he'd seen his old 'friend' at the ball. Not only had it brought back bad memories, he hadn't missed that lecherous look in Luton's eyes when he'd looked at Violet. It was true, in the old days they had shared women, but never in a million years would he ever share Violet with him—or anyone for that matter.

That liar.

How dare Luton accuse Violet of trying to seduce him? The thought that Violet could be unfaithful had never even crossed his mind. She was not that kind of woman.

Gritting his teeth, he dried his hands and began wrapping them in clean bandages.

'Ash?'

He swung around and saw Violet peeking through the doorway. He said nothing and went back to binding his wounds.

'Ash, I… Can we talk about what happened?'

The pain in her voice made him ache, but he didn't answer her.

'Please, I'm just so confused. I don't understand.' Her voice cracked. 'I swear I didn't want to go with him. He said you were hurt and— *Mmm*!'

Wrapping his arms around her, Ash seized her and then slanted his mouth against hers. He couldn't bear to listen to her any more, to relive what happened to her and remember that he'd failed to protect her.

He led her back to the bed, undressed her, then kissed her all over, making her come over and over again with his tongue and his mouth. When he finally did surge into her he held off, determined to give her more mindless pleasure before he sought his own release. It was only when she begged him to finish, saying that she couldn't go on, that he finally allowed himself to spill inside her.

Afterwards he held her in his arms tightly, refusing to let her go, and he fought sleep so that he could watch her. His logical, lovely Violet looked like a sleeping angel.

He'd made her promise not to fall in love with him.

Somehow, in his arrogance, he'd forgotten to make that same vow to her.

He loosened his hold around Violet as panic gripped him. Gently, so as not to wake her, he eased his wife's slumbering form off him. The urge to flee grew strong as his stomach turned to ice.

Ash had seen first-hand how love could turn disastrous. He'd sworn off it his whole life, refusing to be destroyed like his father. He'd seen what could happen when one loved another person so much that it consumed them.

I can't fall in love with her.

He shouldn't.

He wouldn't.

Chapter Fifteen

When she first awoke, panic rose through Violet as she felt the unfamiliar sensation of being alone in bed.

'Ash?' she called softly as she rose.

Glancing around her, she realised the bed and the room were completely empty. She sat there as the minutes ticked by, unsure what to do. Her routine was thrown off without her husband to make love to her first thing in the morning.

Maybe he was still hurt and had had to see a doctor?

Fear gripped her as she hopped off the bed, jumped into her robe and slippers, then dashed out of the room.

'Where is my husband?' she asked a footman in the main hall.

'Y-Your Ladyship?' The young man's eyes bulged and his gaze dipped up and down. 'H-he's in the dining room.'

She thanked him, then hurried to the dining room. 'Ash? Are you—' She stopped short when she saw her husband sitting calmly at the table, coffee cup in hand, folded newspaper in the other. 'You're having breakfast.'

'Yes, darling,' was his only reply.

'Without me?'

Ash placed his paper on the table. 'Have a seat. There's still plenty to eat.'

She padded inside and took her place to his left. A footman immediately filled her plate with eggs and toast and her cup with tea. She was about to start eating when Ash stood up.

'Mr Bevis is coming today and he should be arriving at any moment.' He leaned down and kissed her on the temple, then smiled at her. 'Have a good day, Violet.'

A deep sense of foreboding swamped her chest as she noticed something strange about Ash. More specifically, his face. Though his lips were pulled up in the gesture of a smile, there were no crinkles at the corners of his eyes.

His smile wasn't genuine.

She stared after him as he left.

Was he still furious about last night?

After they'd come home from that disastrous ball and he'd made love to her Violet had assumed everything was once again right between them. He'd believed her when she'd said it was Luton who'd lured her out to the garden and not the other way around. After all, he wouldn't have thrashed the Viscount within an inch of his life if he'd thought Violet had been the instigator.

She shook her head.

Perhaps I read his smile wrong.

Yes, that was it. There had been many, many times in the past where she'd been wrong about the meaning of facial expressions.

However, try as she might, Violet could not put her doubts aside. She thought about it all day long, obsessing over that one smile. When Ash had not emerged from his study, nor sought her out in the middle of the day, the fixation only worsened.

By dinner time, when she found herself dining alone, it had grown to a level that had her on edge. 'Lord Ashbrooke did not tell you where was going?' she asked Bennet as he served her first course.

'I'm afraid not, my lady. He only asked me to tell you not to wait for him to eat.'

Violet pushed the plate away from her. 'I'm not hungry, Bennet. I think I shall retire for the evening.'

After dressing for bed, Violet tried to read her book as she waited for Ash. But none of it made sense to her, so she gave up and put the book away. She lay there until the candle burned out, but Ash still hadn't returned.

Exhausted, she eventually fell asleep.

The sound of a creaking hinge woke her up. 'Ash!' she called as she bolted upright. 'Ash?'

'Sorry, darling,' he murmured in the dark.

'Where were you?'

'In my study.'

He'd been here the entire time.

'Why didn't you come to dinner?'

'Got caught up with some paperwork for the estate.'

The rustling of clothes told her he was undressing.

A lump formed in her throat. 'Ash, are you still angry about Lut—?'

'I'm so very tired, darling.' He slipped into bed and remained on his own side of the bed. 'Goodnight.'

Violet lay back down on the pillows and stared into darkness.

He was just busy, she told herself. *That's all.*

'I baptise you, Henry Alexander Wakefield, in the name of the Father, the Son, and the Holy Spirit…'

Violet stood among the gathered guests who had come to watch the future Duke of Mabury's christening. Her husband, who was godfather, was at the front, next to a tall blonde woman who held Henry in her arms as the vicar poured holy water over the baby's head.

Once the ceremony was over, everyone crowded around the parents, godparents, and Henry to offer their congratulations. Violet elected to stay in the rear, until the sea of guests had receded.

'Congratulations, Kate, Your Grace,' she said when she finally approached them. 'I'm so happy for you.'

'Thank you, Violet, Ash,' Kate said. 'I'm so glad you made it.'

'Well, I'm the godfather, aren't I?' Ash quipped. 'You couldn't very well get this done without me.'

'Only because you pestered me until I gave in,' Mabury said drolly.

'As he usually does,' the towering, burly Scotsman beside him laughed.

Kate had earlier introduced him as Cameron MacGregor, Earl of Balfour, who happened to be Persephone's brother. The tall woman who had been appointed as Henry's godmother was Maddie, his wife, an American who had first arrived in England with Kate when they'd come in search of husbands. The MacGregors had travelled all the way from Scotland, and were the reason Kate had waited so long to have Henry baptised. She had wanted Maddie to be there as godmother, but the Countess had also just given birth to her first child, a daughter named Isla, so she'd had to wait until both mother and baby were strong enough to make the long journey.

'I'm hungry,' Ash declared.

'Then let us head back to Mabury House, where Chef Pierre has prepared a special feast,' Kate said.

Ash placed a hand on Violet's lower back. 'Shall we, darling?'

Violet turned away, avoiding his gaze. 'All right.'

They made their way outside the church to where a line of carriages awaited. When the familiar red and black coach arrived, a footman helped Violet inside, then Ash joined her. She kept her hands folded on her lap, resisting the urge to touch her thumbs to her fingers, all the while keeping her head lowered. However, she couldn't help but steal a glance at Ash's handsome profile as he stared out of the window.

When he turned to meet her gaze, her heart jumped in her chest.

'Is there anything the matter, darling?'

'N-no.'

He nodded, then smiled at her.

Another fake smile.

The foreboding returned—or rather, it had never left. It was like a pressure in her chest that had been there for the past two days.

Violet had tried to convince herself that everything was fine and right between them. She'd made excuses for him— he was tired, or preoccupied with the business of the lands, or perhaps Winford hadn't been able to make the troubles with Luton go away and Ash was facing charges, so he was having to speak to lawyers and prosecutors.

But when Ash's real smiles failed to make an appearance she knew there was something very wrong. While she found it difficult to read other people's expressions, with Ash it had been so easy. And then there was the fact that he hadn't made love to her in two days. Aside from when she'd had her monthly flow, it was the longest time they hadn't been intimate.

Her thoughts spiralled as she obsessed over his behaviour. Had he changed his mind and now believed Luton instead?

Had he gone back to his opera singer?

Or perhaps he just didn't want her any more.

That had to be the reason. After all, theirs was a marriage of convenience. He was a worldly man, a rake before they'd married, and so it was only logical that at some point he would become bored with her in bed. Or perhaps he was tired of her odd ways.

Her mind fixated on that thought.

Ash was tired of her peculiarities, her need to stay within her routines, her aversion to noise, being overwhelmed by crowds, her obsession with numbers and mathematics.

He wanted someone who wasn't so bizarre.

So broken.

'We're here,' Ash announced as the carriage drew to a stop.

Mabury House was filled with guests and well-wishers, but the usual dread Violet experienced in such situations did not surface—there was no space in her mind to process it as the tension between her and Ash hung over her like a dark cloud.

Unable to bear it any longer, she broke away from him and hurried over to where Kate and the other women were fussing over Henry.

'He's so beautiful,' Maddie cooed. 'I think he has your nose.'

'And Mabury's eyes,' Persephone added.

'And hopefully both our minds—Violet, there you are.'

'H-hello,' she greeted. 'How is the little one?'

'Recovered,' Kate chuckled. 'From the way he was screaming when the vicar poured the water on him, you'd think he was being murdered.'

Maddie lifted the bundle in her arms. 'Isla was the same way.' She kissed the baby's forehead.

'Violet, would you like to hold Henry?' Kate asked.

'M-me?'

'Yes. You haven't had a chance yet.'

'I've never held a baby. What if I drop him?'

'You won't,' Maddie interjected. 'Go on.'

Without waiting for her agreement, Kate transferred the bundle into Violet's arms. 'There...support his neck... Ah, that's it. See? Easy, isn't it?'

Violet stared down at the bundle in her arms. 'He's so... tiny.'

It was a silly thing to say because everyone in the world started out as a baby. But seeing one up close made her realise how small and fragile infants were.

'It's good practice,' Maddie said.

'Practice for— Oh.' She meant for when she had a child. Or rather *if* she had one.

Kate, being the only one who knew the real reason she and Ash married, quickly changed the subject. 'Violet, I know you absolutely hate balls, but do you think you could attend Lord and Lady Waverly's ball? I haven't been to one in ages. I've been working from sunup to sundown getting the engine ready, and Henry's keeping me up at all hours.' She sighed. 'I love him, I truly do, and my work, but I'm going mad. I just want to be somewhere that's not the factory or the nursery, and it would be nice if I could have my friends there too.'

'I shall be there.' Maddie clapped her hands. 'I haven't danced in a long while either. It would be truly lovely to see all of you there.'

'I'll come, of course,' Persephone said.

'What do you say, Violet?' Kate asked.

Violet worried at her lip. 'I suppose it's not too late to accept.'

'Wonderful,' Kate clapped her hands together. 'I can't wait.'

'I— Oh.' Henry was whimpering as he kicked his little feet and Violet froze, unsure what to do. 'Kate...?'

'Oh, dear... Hand him over, Violet.'

'Let her, Kate,' Maddie urged.

Violet blinked. 'Let me what?'

'Soothe him,' she continued. 'Like this, see?'

The Countess rocked Isla back and forth, then patted her bottom.

Violet paused, then copied Maddie. Soon enough the child calmed and closed its eyes once more.

'You're a natural,' Maddie remarked.

Violet caressed Henry's little face, marvelling at the soft, plump cheeks. As she continued to soothe him the most curious feeling washed over her. Lifting her head, she saw Ash across the room, staring at her. He quickly turned away.

A pit grew in her stomach, and she glanced back down at the bundle in her arms.

From Ash's reaction, she knew he *had* tired of her, and her brokenness.

Not just the brokenness of her mind, but of her body and its failure to produce his heir.

Violet stole a glance at the other women, thinking about their interaction with their husbands. Though the three men could not be more different from each other, she'd observed a commonality among them: whenever they were around their wives, they all had the same expression on their faces.

She saw it each time Mabury entered a room, his eyes lighting up when the first thing he saw was Kate or Henry.

Or the way Winford's gaze never left Persephone, whether she was six inches or six yards away.

And even though she'd only met Balfour this morning,

she could not ignore the way his mouth turned up and the corners of his eyes crinkled when he grinned at his wife.

How she longed to see the same expression on Ash's face when he looked upon her.

Because she was certain that if she were to study her own features whenever Ash was around she would find herself with that same expression.

Chapter Sixteen

'Thank you, Holmes, that will be all.' Ash dismissed his valet with a wave. 'Tell Bennet I shall be downstairs soon.'

'Of course, my lord.' With a deep bow, the valet left.

Ash observed his reflection in the mirror, smoothing his hands down his lapels, checking his coat for lint or stray threads Holmes might have missed. His valet, of course, would have been deeply insulted if he'd seen Ash, but he would never reveal the real reason he'd stayed behind.

He was stalling.

'Coward,' his reflection said, before it flashed a scowl at him.

Spinning away from the mirror, he strode over to the door. However, he still made no motion to leave, not even reaching for the doorknob.

Hell, he *was* a coward. A coward for hiding from his wife.

He knocked his forehead against the door.

He'd told himself this was for the best—that he was avoiding her to prevent his feelings for her from further deepening. It was much too dangerous. Whether or not he produced an heir and saved his lands, they'd made plans to part ways afterwards. He'd known that from the beginning, but his arrogance had got the best of him.

Now his emotions were muddling him, making it difficult to make rational decisions. Luton had been the proof of that—he'd nearly committed murder out of jealousy.

With a deep breath, he pushed himself away from the door and stepped out of his room, then made his way downstairs. He couldn't stall any more. They were already meant to be on their way to the ball.

Still, there was a problem with the clause and his need for an heir. Making love to Violet only confused him, which was why he'd stayed away from her these past few days. He'd planned to wait it out until they could confirm that her flow had not arrived that month.

If he was lucky, Violet would already be pregnant.

She would be a radiant mother-to-be. He could already picture her belly swelling with his child. And she'd be a good mother. He'd seen her holding Henry the other day. Watching her holding that bundle in her arms had awoken something in him, a longing he'd never felt before.

He pushed the thought away. Besides, there was also the possibility that they'd failed to conceive this month. If so, then he would have to try again. Until then, he had to find a way to distance himself from her in the next few weeks, so he could perform his marital duty without getting caught up in her.

Losing his lands seemed almost worth it.

When he reached the top of the stairs he saw Violet already waiting in the hall below. His heart crashed into his chest at the sight of her, looking breathtakingly lovely in a light blue tulle gown. He imagined taking all the pins out of her hair and watching those sable curls tumble down her creamy shoulders. He would make quick work of her gown, so he could bare those luscious nipples to his gaze. He'd kiss that plump mouth and the beauty mark—

Her head turned when she realised he'd been watching her. Quickly, she averted her gaze.

Guilt knotted in his gut at the hurt on her face she couldn't hide. In the last few days, as he'd pulled away from her, Violet had withdrawn from him too. After their wedding he'd watched her bloom like a flower as she'd learned to control her anxiety and fear. Now she had regressed to the nervous girl she'd once been.

'My apologies for keeping you waiting,' he said.

'My lord, the carriage is ready,' Bennet announced with a clearing of his throat.

'Thank you.' He descended the steps, then offered Violet his arm. 'Shall we?'

She took it wordlessly.

The journey to the Waverly ball was deathly quiet and agonisingly long. Though Ash had averted his gaze from her, he knew Violet was fidgeting with her thumbs and fingers. They should have declined the invitation, but he knew the reason she wanted to go—Kate, Maddie and Persephone would be in attendance. Thankfully, that meant his three best friends would be there tonight. He found it ironic that when they'd each fallen in love with their wives he'd secretly scoffed at them for allowing themselves to be shackled to women because of something trivial like love. And now he—

No, he was not in love with his wife, and if he kept a close guard on his heart, he never would be.

Though the carriage ride seemed to take all of eternity, thanks to their tardiness they were able to drive quickly up to the front gate of Lord and Lady Waverly's fashionable townhouse in Belgrave Square. Once they were announced, they immediately found their friends.

'Ash, I thought you'd never come. Did you get into any

fist fights on the way here?' Cam remarked. 'Lady Ashbrooke, how lovely to see you again. And forgive my jest—I only meant most of it.'

'Thank you, my lord,' Violet murmured.

'Violet, Kate tells me you're a mathematician,' Maddie said excitedly. 'I can't believe the Dowager has found another one like us.'

The women naturally gravitated towards each other, and at one point left to go the necessary together, leaving the men to converse amongst themselves.

'I never thought I'd see the day,' Cam said, poking his elbow in Ash's side. 'The Marquess of Ashbrooke, finally caught in the bonds of matrimony.'

He sent Ransom and Sebastian a pointed look. 'You didn't tell him?'

'Tell me what?'

'It's your story to tell,' Sebastian said.

Cam scratched at his head. 'What story?'

Ash told him all about the Canfields and the clause.

'Goodness.' Cam sucked in a breath through his teeth. 'I'm sorry, Ash. Is there anything I can do to help?'

'If you know a way to travel through time, so I can go back and knock some sense into my great-grandfather, now would be the time to tell me.'

'Nay, but if you drown yourself in enough whisky you'll wake up three days later, and that's similar to travelling through time.'

'Ha-ha.'

'It's not too bad, though, is it?' Cam nodded at Violet, who was coming back towards them along with the other women. 'Your wife is a pretty lass. Can't ask for more if you're looking to produce an heir.'

'Oh, Cam, they have just announced the waltz.' Maddie grabbed her husband's hands. 'Will you—?'

'Aye.' His face lit up like the sun as his gaze fixed on his wife. 'Anythin' for you.'

Ash watched Violet's face as she stared at the dance floor. She looked so achingly beautiful, and the longing on her face was evident.

I shouldn't—

'Will you dance with me, Violet?'

Damn.

His wife started, and her luminous eyes grew large. 'I b-beg your pardon, my lord?'

'I would like to dance with my wife.' He held out a hand. 'Please?'

It seemed an eternity before she finally placed her hand in his.

He led her out to the dance floor, his heart quickening with each step. As they got into position he realised his mistake. The waltz was an intimate dance, one that had the dancers' bodies perilously close. This was perhaps the first time in the last few days that he'd been near enough to smell Violet's sweet lavender and powder scent. Desire heated his blood and flooded his brain.

The waltz began, and the couples on the dance floor twirled about. Ash couldn't help but remember the first time they'd waltzed, and how Violet had so eloquently described the melding of mathematics and dance. He observed the dancers around them, searching for what she had been talking about, trying to find the beauty and symmetry there.

But he failed—because the only thing he found was Violet.

His heart stopped for a moment.

Then the dance ended.

Violet curtseyed, then lifted her head. 'Thank you, Ash.'

It was too late.

He was already in love with her.

The tightness began in his chest, like a vice wrapping around his torso. Then the world spun around him. His vision blurred.

Not sure what else to do, he turned around and fled.

Ash didn't care where he was going, nor even which way he was headed. All he knew was that he needed to be somewhere the walls weren't closing in on him, somewhere he could breathe without this massive pain in his chest.

Wading through the crowds, he found himself in the main hall, outside the ballroom. He entered the first room he could reach. Slamming the door behind him, he braced himself on the nearest surface—a pianoforte, signalling he was in a music room. In any case, it didn't matter where he was. As long as he was far away from Violet, so he could think and breathe.

Was this what love felt like?

If so, he didn't want any part of it.

'Ash.'

'Who the—' He spun around and saw the shadowy figure in the doorway. 'Violet?'

No, it wasn't her.

'Ash,' Emma Bancroft repeated. 'How wonderful to see you again.'

'What are you doing here, Emma?' She was the last person he wanted to see right at this moment. 'Leave me alone.'

'I'm a guest here, just like you.'

As if she hadn't heard him—or hadn't wanted to—she advanced towards him. 'I hear you're married now. To *her*.'

'Emma—'

'I was so disappointed. Not only did you leave me before we had a chance to make things interesting, but for *her*. The odd Avery chit.'

'Watch what you're saying,' he growled.

She took a few more steps towards him. 'The way I see it, we're in the same boat, now that we're both married.'

'No, we are not,' he said vociferously. '*I* did not deceive anyone into thinking I wasn't married and try to start an affair with them.'

'Grow up, Ash. Don't you know married people have affairs all the time?'

Oh, did he ever.

She guffawed. 'But does it really matter now? Can't we forgive and forget?' She was now toe to toe with him. 'I heard you speaking with your friends in the ballroom.'

'Heard—you mean you eavesdropped?'

'You can call it whatever you like.' A finger tapped at his chest with each word. 'She's but a broodmare for you, so you can keep your inheritance. It doesn't matter to me either way—all peers have to sire an heir eventually. But why should you limit your services to a single mare? Surely a stud with an appetite like yours needs more?'

Ash blinked. It dawned on him that Emma had him trapped between herself and the pianoforte. But why shouldn't he indulge? Maybe this was the distraction he needed to free himself of his feelings for Violet.

She caught his hand and brushed her cheek on his palm. 'Oh, Ash. You know this is inevitable. Don't fight it.'

Maybe he shouldn't fight it. If he did this, perhaps he could forget about Violet, and fall out of love with her. So it wouldn't hurt so badly when she left him.

But Violet wouldn't leave me.

The thought came from nowhere. His first instinct was to block it out.

He leaned his head closer to Emma's.

Violet isn't Mama.

Ash froze.

Of course Violet wasn't his mother. How could he have even thought she could be like his mother? At least, not after all this time, after he'd learned more about her.

Logical, lovely Violet. The quiet girl who loved numbers, who had learned French to read a mathematics paper, and who spoke truthfully with both her mind and her heart.

His Violet.

And then a different thought came to him.

He wondered if he'd been worried about the wrong thing all this time. Perhaps he shouldn't have been concerned that Violet would turn out to be like his mother, that she would leave him. Rather, he should have been worried that he might turn into his father and drive her away.

His poor tortured father, who'd spent the last year of his life in agony, in love with a woman who would never fully love him back. He'd watched him suffer, day after day. The pain had dug into him like hooks, and he'd been unable to release himself from the torment.

When he'd died, the only thing Ash had felt was relief that his father was free.

Oh, Violet. You'd never let that happen to me.

'Ash?'

Starting, he pushed Emma away. 'Violet?'

His wife stood on the threshold, gaping at them.

This time it really was her.

Unfortunately for him.

'Violet—'

'Lady Ashbrooke.' Emma remained cool and calm. 'I'm sorry you had to see that. But you didn't really think you could keep him to yourself, did you?'

Ash brushed past her and strode over to Violet. He wanted to hold her, but feared she would flinch away from. Or break into a million pieces.

'This isn't what you think. We haven't—'

Plink. Plink. Plink.

Annoyed, Ash turned his head.

'Does this bring back memories, Lady Ashbrooke?' Emma had opened the lid of the pianoforte, her fingers resting on the ivory keys. 'What was it they called you? I bet Lady Katherine Pearson remembers. Ah, yes—how could we forget? The Bizarre Beauty.'

'Emma!' Ash could have wrung her neck. 'Don't you— Violet!'

She was gone.

I have to go after her.

'Ash!'

Arms wound around him tightly, preventing him from leaving.

'Emma, let go!' He prised her arms away from him, then twisted her around. 'I don't want you—get that through your thick head.'

'But we've just got rid of her. Let's continue what we started.'

She lunged at Ash, but he evaded her this time.

Ash bolted out through the door and headed back to the main foyer.

But Violet was nowhere to be found.

He was nine years old all over again, watching the door slam as Mama left.

He shook himself out of his daze. She was not his mama and he was not his father. The only reason Violet had left was because he was an idiot who'd let Emma Bancroft corner him against a pianoforte.

He would fix all this. Get on his knees. Beg Violet to forgive him and confess his love for her.

Now if only he could find her.

Violet had never run so fast in her life.

When she'd left the music room she'd turned in the direction of the ballroom, then changed her mind. She didn't care where she was going, only knew that she'd had to leave that room. If it were possible, she would fly away and leave London for ever. Since that was not possible, she settled for leaving by the front door.

She ran as fast as she could through the streets, past towering white stucco houses and terraces. Despite the empty streets and the mansions looming over her like phantoms, fear did not even enter her mind as her tumultuous emotions wrapped around her like an impenetrable wall.

Once her lungs started to burn with exertion, she halted. Pressing a hand to her breast, she heaved in great big gulps of air, trying to ease the pain in her chest. She was unsure of where she was exactly, but surely she was far away enough from that place.

But it was not far away enough from *him*.

Not even if she were to fly to the moon would it put enough distance between her and the Marquess of Ashbrooke.

When Ash had run away from her after the waltz, she'd felt like a rag doll being thrown about by an errant child. One moment he'd acted so distant, then the next he'd asked her for a waltz. She almost preferred the cold Ash to the one who'd danced with her before running away. At least she'd developed her own shield against the former.

She had stood there like an idiot, watching Ash flee. People had moved about her, whispering, pointing, but she hadn't been able to move. It had only been when someone had gently guided her off the dance floor that she'd realised she hadn't moved at all, even as the next set of dancers had assembled around her.

I shouldn't have gone after him.

Though her first instinct had been to be angry with him, she just hadn't been able to bring herself to ignore what she'd seen. She'd recognised what was happening to him, because she'd experienced it many times before. The look of panic on his face, his difficulty in breathing, loss of balance. She just hadn't wanted to let him go through that alone. He might be hurt or worse.

So she'd decided to look for him.

And she had found him.

Violet bit the back of her hand, refusing to cry. No matter how much it hurt, she wouldn't cry, not for that rake.

How could I be so stupid?

Of course he'd sought out other lovers. That was why he'd turned cold against her. He had grown tired of her. He wanted a new woman in his bed, someone exciting and experienced.

Someone not broken like her.

Ash had tried to fix her. Whether or not he knew it, that was what he'd been doing. Trying to get her used to his touch, finding quiet places for her, letting her avoid exhausting social events. He'd thought to repair her, so that she could someday be normal. Normal enough to be his heir's mother.

If she ever bore him a child.

'Violet! Violet!'

She spun towards the sound of the voice.

'Violet!' Ash waved his hand maniacally as he raced towards her.

No!

Picking up her skirts, she bolted away from him. She was a good distance ahead, so she thought she could get away, but it was a futile endeavour. Ash was much taller and stronger, and he eventually caught up with her.

'Wait!'

He ran ahead of her, blocking her way. She sidestepped him, but he only continued to obstruct her.

'We could keep running all night or you can stop and listen to what I have to say.'

'You have nothing to say that I want to hear, my lord,' she huffed. 'I might be stupid when it comes to social situations, but I do have eyes. Leave me alone and go back to your Mrs Bancroft.'

'She's not my Mrs Bancroft.'

'I caught you in an intimate embrace.' She would never forget the sight that had greeted her in the music room. 'I just want to be left alone. I don't want to be married to you any more.'

Turning away from him, she wrapped her arms around herself.

He spun her to face him. 'You seem to forget we have an agreement.'

'We can get an annulment. And there's still time for you to find another wife and produce an heir. Lady Helen or any other debutante would be happy to sign a betrothal contract even before the ink has dried on our annulment papers.'

'True, but unfortunately we would never get an annulment. No one would believe that a notorious rake like me would have left our marriage unconsummated. And it would take too long.'

'How about a divorce?'

Ash crossed his arms over his chest. 'Even longer.'

'Then I will run away to the continent or America.'

'Absolutely not.'

He doesn't want me to leave.

'It would take too long to get you declared dead.'

Oh.

'So you see, Violet, we have no other alternative.'

She sniffed. 'And I'm supposed to stay true to our marriage vows while you frolic with other women?'

What a fool she was. Had she honestly believed he would be faithful to her?

'Violet, I don't want her. She cornered me in there, and I'm afraid you caught us at the worst possible moment. Yes, I was tempted, but it's not what you think.'

'I'm not pea-brained, Ash. I know why you ran away from me after our dance and why you've been so cold to me.' Tears sprang at the corner of her eyes. 'I'm too odd, too broken. I can't even give you the one thing you need.'

'Do not speak like that.'

'It's true. I'm just a bizarre, broken woman who can't even act normally in a room full of people.'

'Violet, please—'

'You cannot fix me, Ash.' She lowered her head, afraid to look at his face. 'I know that's what you've been trying to do all these weeks, so I can be a proper marchioness.'

'Oh, for God's sake.' He placed his hands on her shoulders gently. 'Violet, look at me. Please?'

'No.'

'Violet. Look. At. Me. Or we shall stand here all night. Because I'm not letting you go until you do.'

Slowly, she lifted her head to meet his gaze—and his smile. Her heart gave a little flip-flop when she saw the crinkles at the corners of his eyes.

His real smile.

'You are absolutely right, Violet,' he began. 'I cannot fix you. I can't because there is nothing to fix. *You are not broken*. And I love you just as you are.'

Her heart stuttered. 'You...you can't.'

'Of course I can.' Cupping her chin, he brushed her thumb across her cheek. 'I love everything about you.'

'No, it's not possible. You and I...we don't make sense. You're you and I'm me.'

He chuckled. 'I wish I could find a way to explain it in a rational way, like the way you do when you speak of numbers. Mathematics can explain everything—but it can't explain why I love you. It can't tell me why you are the first thing I think of in the morning and the last before I fall asleep. There's no formula to calculate how much I love you or show me why the days seem longer when we are apart and time spent with you always seems so short. The real, universal truth I know is that you mean everything to me. Violet, please believe me when I say I love you.'

Violet could only stare at him for the longest time. She scrutinised every inch of his face in an attempt to catalogue the expression there. Had she seen it before? Perhaps, but maybe only in small doses. She recognised the longing in his eyes, as well as the hope behind them.

'Violet, please say something.'

'I can't.'

'Why not?'

'I don't know how to come up with a parallelism that could possibly be greater than what you just said. Anything I say would simply pale in comparison,'

His smile reached from ear to ear. 'Just tell me you love me.' A line appeared between his eyebrows. 'I mean, you *do* love me, don't you?'

'Of course I do.' She lunged at him, wrapping her arms

around him and slotting her lips against his for a long kiss. 'I love you, Ash,' she sighed against his mouth.

While she hadn't been able to name the emotion earlier, she was absolutely certain now.

'And I'm glad your analogies have improved.'

'I love you.'

He smiled—a real smile.

'Now, if you will let me, I would very much like to take you home and make love to you all night long.'

'Yes, please.'

After a lengthy, passionate lovemaking session that evening, they lay together in bed with Violet curled up against Ash's side.

'Ash?'

'Hmm…?' He opened one eye. 'What's the matter, darling?

She bit her lip. 'I have a question.'

'What is it?'

Disentangling herself from him, she sat up to face him. 'What if I don't get pregnant in time? Or at all?'

He shrugged. 'Well, what if you do?'

'But what if it's a girl?'

'But what if it's not?' he countered.

'But what if it is?'

'Confound it—'

With an impatient snort, he pulled her down once again to his side, cradling her in the crook of his arm as he stroked her back.

'Then I shall tell you the truth, darling. Our life will not be as we know it now. We will have to make our own way in the world. I won't have all the material things I'm used to, but I will have *everything* that matters.' He kissed her temple. 'I will have you, our lovely daughter or son, and other children I may be lucky enough to have with you. Unfortunately, the only thing you get is me, darling. But if you are satisfied with just me, I promise I will do everything I can to ensure your happiness. Does that answer your question?'

'Yes,' she said. 'But what—'

'Violet—'

'I was joking.' She kissed his shoulder. 'I love you, Ash.'

'And I love you, Violet.'

And that, perhaps, was the most incredible thing of all.

Epilogue

Hertfordshire,
1851

'Papa, tell us a story.'

'Once upon a time there was a very pretty and very smart girl.'

Nicholas Gregory St James, Viscount Gilmore, wrinkled his little nose. 'Ugh... Papa, why is this story about a girl?' He stuck out his tongue. 'I don't want to hear a story about a girl.'

'Why not?' cried Lady Charlotte Anne. 'Papa, girls can have their own stories, can't they?'

Ash looked from his son to his daughter. 'Of course they can, poppet.' He tapped her pert little nose. 'Girls can do anything, don't you know?'

'Like Mama?' she asked.

'Yes, just like Mama.'

Ash looked at his son. 'May I continue my story?'

Nicholas nodded. 'All right.'

He cleared his throat. 'Once upon a time, there was a very pretty and very smart girl. One day she was waiting for her carriage when a handsome prince came riding by. He saw the girl and instantly he fell in love with her.'

Nicholas made gagging sounds. 'Ugh...love and kissing.'

'Some day you may not mind kissing,' Ash told him.

'Papa, the story!' Charlotte tugged at his sleeve.

He cleared his throat. 'So, the handsome prince fell in love with her, and she with him, but unfortunately a witch came upon them and put a curse on the prince.'

Charlotte gasped. 'What curse?'

'She turned him into an ugly beast.'

'Then what happened, Papa?'

'Well…' He thought for a moment. 'The very pretty and very smart girl decided—because she was indeed very smart—that the ugly beast was still her handsome prince, no matter what he looked like, so she married him just as he was. The end.'

'What?' Nicholas exclaimed. 'That's it? But it's so short.'

'You didn't ask for a long story, did you, now, Nicholas?'

The boy let out an exasperated grunt, then fell back on the carpet. 'But I wanted dragons and fighting and soldiers.'

'Well, next time you should be more specific.' He chuckled, then lunged for the boy, tickling him until he was screaming and laughing in surrender.

'Papa, stop!'

Ash let him go. 'That'll teach you, you little munchkin.'

'I liked your story, Papa.' Charlotte climbed onto his lap and laid her head on his shoulder.

He kissed her head of golden curls. 'Thank you, poppet.'

'I like it too, but I think it has some inaccuracies.'

Ash's heart stuttered at the sound of the low, husky voice. He turned his head and saw his wife in the doorway of the nursery, leaning against the jamb.

'Inaccuracies?' he scoffed. 'What inaccuracies? I'll have you know my stories are based on real life.'

Violet padded over to them and sat down next to Nicholas, cradling him on her lap. 'Well, there was just one inaccuracy, really. The prince wasn't handsome.'

'He wasn't?'

Light blue eyes twinkled at him. 'No, he was *beautiful*.'

Before that fateful night he'd met Violet, if anyone had ever told Ash that he'd find himself happily married to the love of his life and have two wonderful children, he would have told them to go to the madhouse.

But here he was, living in marital bliss in the countryside, and he couldn't ask for more. He had everything he could want, a beautiful family, a big house, and a thriving estate.

And that last one was all thanks to Nicholas, who'd had the foresight to be born exactly one day before Ash's thirty-first birthday. About a year and a half later, he had been joined by his sister, Charlotte.

'What are you doing here, by the way?' Ash glanced at the clock. 'It's two o'clock. You should be working.'

Aside from being a partner at Mason & Wakefield Railway Works, Violet also pursued her own interests in academia. She was currently working on her third paper, and preparing to speak at the Paris Academy of Sciences next month.

'I know,' she said. 'But I missed you and the children.'

'But your routine—'

'Can be broken.' She grimaced. 'But only once in a while, on special occasions.'

'Ah, I see.' It was his birthday after all. 'Shall I call Nanny? So you and I can head up to our bedchamber?'

He flashed her a lecherous smile.

Violet leaned forward. 'She's already waiting outside. And I have something for you.'

'A gift?'

'A surprise.'

Ash licked his lips. 'All right, children, playtime is over. It's time for your nap.'

'But, Papa,' Nicholas whined.

'No buts—and you opened your presents yesterday, Nicholas.' He grinned at Violet as she helped him up. 'It's time to open mine.'

He swatted her on her behind, making her laugh, then followed her outside.

'Wait.' She placed a palm on his chest. 'Care to make this a little more interesting?'

'What do you have in mind, darling?'

She slipped her hand into her pocket and retrieved a long strip of cloth.

'A blindfold, Violet? Hmm... I like it.'

'Put it on, then,' she said, handing it to him.

Once he'd secured the blindfold, she took his arm and led him away. Ash tried to guess where they were going, but she seemed to be leading him in circles.

'Violet, where are you taking me?'

'I told you—it's a surprise.'

'You know, it's not fair that you can surprise me, but I can never surprise you,' he pouted.

'Oh, don't be a baby. You're worse than Charlotte.'

She stopped, then he heard a door creak and she gently pushed him forward.

'We're somewhere on the ground floor,' he guessed, since they hadn't climbed any stairs. 'Are we in a linen closet? Do you want to play master and chambermaid? Because I'd be very interested. You can pretend you're dusting the dresser and then I'll bend you over and—'

'Ash!' she warned.

'What—did you want to play the master instead?'

With an exasperated sigh, she whipped off the blindfold.

Ash blinked as his eyes adjusted to the light. 'What the—'

'Surprise! Happy Birthday Ash!'

When his vision cleared, Ash let out a gasp. There, inside the ballroom, all their friends and their families were gathered, laughing and clapping as they threw confetti at him.

'This is your surprise?' he asked Violet. 'A party?'

'Yes, you numbskull.'

'But where are the peacocks? The fire-eaters? The jugglers. What kind of party is this?'

Violet scowled at him.

'I'm jesting, darling. I love it.' He gave her a quick kiss on the lips. 'Thank you, Violet. And thank you, everybody,' he called out to the room.

'Yes, thank you, Violet,' Ransom said dryly. 'For stopping Ash before we—including all the children—heard any more of his depraved fantasies.'

'You loved it,' Ash said, then waggled his eyebrows at Persephone. 'Don't tell me you've never played master and chambermaid with him?'

Her eyes sparkled behind her spectacles, and she placed a hand over her protruding belly. 'I'll never tell.'

'And that means yes.' He winked at Ransom, who only glared at him. 'Thank you for coming. I know it's a lot to ask, with you being busy at The Underworld and the twins.' He glanced over to the two boys, who were running around playing tag with Nicholas.

'Anything for my best friend,' Ransom said.

'Hey, I thought *I* was your best friend.' Cam came up to him and enveloped him in a hug. 'Hey, old man, nice to see you. Happy birthday.'

'Cam, I can't believe you came all the way here for me. I'm utterly flattered.'

'I didn't come here for you. We're down here for Christmas, remember?' He jerked his thumb at Maddie, who was currently wrangling three little girls of varying ages while she balanced a one-year-old boy on her hip. 'Oops, I think Maddie needs me. Excuse me.'

Ash looked around, frowning. 'And where's—'

'Sorry we're late,' Kate called as she rushed over to them. She was still wearing her coat. 'That weather is brutal. Oh, no,' she clucked her tongue. 'We missed the surprise.'

Sebastian helped her off with her coat, then handed it, as well as his own, to Bennet. 'Sorry about that...the carriage took for ever.'

'Papa, we're going to play!' Henry announced as he scampered past them, his little brother and sister trailing behind.

'You know,' Ash said as he accepted a hug from Kate, 'you wouldn't have to take a carriage all the way here from London if there was a railway line. If only we knew somebody who owned a successful rail works company.'

Rail travel had boomed in England in the last seven years, and there seemed to be no stopping it. And at the forefront of that industry was Mason & Wakefield Railway Works. Kate's first locomotive engine, dubbed *The Ice Queen*, had been a smashing success and, thanks to her, goods and people were now moving around faster and farther all over England.

Kate rolled her eyes. 'You're one of our investors, Ash. Take it up at the board meeting next week.'

And thank goodness he had thought to invest the last of his money in Mason & Wakefield just before Nicholas had been born. Even though Violet had been pregnant, there had still been the chance she would give birth to a girl, so he'd decided to risk it all and invest in Kate's company. Violet had been worried, but since she'd already joined the

company he'd told her that he knew it was a smart investment—or rather, *she* was a smart investment. Even if Nicholas had been a girl and the Canfields had taken away the
lands around Chatsworth, it wouldn't have mattered, because Ash had become a very rich man.

'Well, now everyone's here,' he declared, 'where's the
cake?'

Everyone gathered around the table set up in the middle of the room, laden with goodies and a cake, singing as
Ash blew out the candles. After that, the festivities continued with more food and merrymaking, and because there
were nearly a dozen children in attendance, tears, fights,
and scraped knees.

'Are you all right, darling?' Ash placed an arm around
Violet. 'Is the noise too much?'

She shook her head. 'No, I'm still fine, but maybe I'll
go and lie down in an hour.'

He pressed a kiss to her temple. 'If you say so. But don't
feel you have to stay because it's my birthday. I already
have my wish. You don't have to suffer because of me.'

'I'm not,' she replied. 'Dare I ask what the wish was?'

'I can't tell you. You know that.'

She rolled her eyes. 'That doesn't make sense. How can
a wish not come true just on the basis of it being told.'

'My lovely, logical Violet.' He glanced at his children,
then back at her. 'You know what my wish is.'

'Jugglers?'

He burst out laughing. 'No, my love. Ah, here they come
now.'

Nicholas and Charlotte bounded over to them, holding
a wrapped present. 'Open it, Papa.'

Kneeling down, he unwrapped the gift. It was a miniature
portrait of the two of them. 'Thank you, I love it.'

'Mama helped,' Charlotte said. 'Can we go back and play now?'

'Yes, you may.'

Ash watched his children run off, then turned to his wife, who was watching the children intently. Her lips were pursed and her eyebrows were furrowed together.

It was a look he recognised.

'What expression of the children's are you cataloguing this time?' he asked.

'I'm not cataloguing, exactly.' She turned to him and cocked her head to one side. Then her lips curved into a smile. 'Ah, just as I thought.'

'And what is that?'

'I *have* seen that expression before.'

'On the children?'

'No.' She planted her hands on his chest. 'On you. I saw it for the first time seven years ago.'

'And what, pray tell, is that expression?'

'It's love.'

* * * * *

HISTORICAL

Your romantic escape to the past.

Available Next Month

Wed In Haste To The Duke Sarah Mallory
More Than A Match For The Earl Emily E K Murdoch

....

Miss Isobel And The Prince Catherine Tinley
Marriage Charade With The Heir Carol Arens

Keep reading for an excerpt of a new title
from the Historical series,
A WEDDING TO PROTECT HER FORTUNE
by Jenni Fletcher

Chapter One

Somerset, England, 1546

So this was Cariscombe Hall... Sir Bennet Thorne drew rein halfway along the narrow dirt road and considered the house before him. Meanwhile, the house, with its thick stone walls, squat corner towers and narrow arrow loops, seemed to consider him back.

It was old, probably a couple of centuries older than his own house, Draycote Manor, but built to last. Strong. Defensible. Uncomfortable. Unfashionable. A hulking grey relic of a past era buried deep in the forest like an outlaw trying to hide from the outside world. He was surprised that none of its previous owners had thought to tear the place down and replace it with something newer and grander, to add a few windows at least, though he had to admit the building had its own kind of charm. There was something indomitable and defiant about all of those turrets and buttresses, a resolute quality that appealed to him.

Strangely enough, he liked it.

Stranger still was the fact that this was the first time he'd ever seen the hall up close. Despite being born and raised on—then finally inheriting—a neighbouring estate, he knew almost as little about Cariscombe as he did the surface of the moon. Its recently deceased owner, Robert Flemming, had been a near recluse, friendly enough on the few occasions they'd met in town or at court, but always with a certain reserve. There had never been any entertainments or invitations to visit.

In that regard, nothing had changed. Ben wasn't visiting today either. He was only there as a favour, bearing a message he didn't understand, but that he ought to make haste and deliver. The sender had told him it was urgent, a matter of the utmost importance, even if it was hard to see why. Besides, he had his own home to get back to and he'd delayed that visit for long enough.

He set his jaw, about to ride on when a woman's voice floated out of thin air.

'Who are you?'

'What the—?' He swung round in his saddle, one hand reaching instinctively for his sword hilt, the other gripping his reins as his mare gave a startled whinny.

'Up here.' A pair of brown leather boots, swiftly followed by a faded and old-fashioned green kirtle, launched themselves out of one of the sycamore trees lining the side of the road, plummeting downwards through the foliage before landing neatly on the gravel in front of him.

Hastily, he removed his hand from his sword hilt, simultaneously impressed by the jump and annoyed at himself for having been caught off guard so completely. Whoever the woman was, she would have made an excellent spy. He hadn't noticed a single flicker of movement, nor heard so much as a twig snap, though she'd obviously been watching him the whole time he'd been staring at the house. Judging by the thick branch she was clutching in one hand, half hidden behind her skirts, she wasn't particularly pleased to see him there either. If the ferocity of her expression was anything to go by, she wouldn't have any qualms about clubbing him with it, if necessary.

'I asked you a question.' She jutted her chin out when he didn't immediately answer. 'Who are you?'

'Sir Bennet Thorne, at your service, lady.' He lifted his round-brimmed cap and bowed in the saddle, though he kept his eyes fixed on hers, too intrigued to look away. She had a distinctively feline appearance, with a pretty, heart-shaped face, accentuated by a widow's peak in the centre of her forehead. Her large hazel-green eyes were half obscured by the cloud of russet-red hair worn in loose disarray over her shoulders. Unwed then, though she was clearly of an age for marriage, eighteen or nineteen perhaps, despite the unladylike addition of several leaves and twigs in her hair.

'I've never heard of you.' Her tone suggested she didn't want to now either.

'I'm a friend.' He held his hands up, palms outward. 'I'm here to speak with Mistress Flemming.'

'Why? What do you want with my mother?'

'Mother?' He couldn't keep the surprise from his voice. 'You mean you're Annis?'

'Yes.' She nodded jerkily, as if she were unsure about the wisdom of admitting her identity. 'What of it?'

'You're not what I expected.'

'What did you expect?'

He lifted his shoulders, already regretting the comment. In truth, Annis Flemming was as much of a mystery as the house she lived in, for all that she was only five or six years younger than him and they'd grown up on neighbouring estates. He'd always been led to believe that she was sickly, far too sickly for guests. Her own father had told him so, and yet the fiery-looking woman standing before him now seemed perfectly, even robustly healthy. Capable of climbing trees and jumping out of them, in fact, but then some people grew out of childhood maladies. Perhaps she'd been a late bloomer or he'd simply misunderstood Robert Flemming's words. Only somehow, he didn't think so...

'Forgive me, lady. I spoke out of turn.' He gestured towards the south, deciding to change the subject before her scowl deepened any further. 'We're neighbours. I own Draycote Manor. I'm rarely there these days, but I knew your father a little. I was grieved to hear of his passing.'

'Thank you.' Her belligerent expression wavered, almost seeming to relent before hardening again. 'Is that all you came to say? Because if it is, I can share your condolences with my mother. There's no need for you to ride any further.'

Ben lifted an eyebrow, taken aback by her brusqueness. Robert Flemming had always been the epitome of civility and good manners. Clearly his daughter hadn't followed his example. Now that he knew who she was, however, he could see the physical resemblance. Her russet curls and the widow's peak ought to have given her identity away.

'That's not all.' He put his hat back on, deciding he'd tarried long enough, particularly in such hostile company. 'I also have a message for her.'

'From?'

'Another friend.'

'What friend?'

'One who prefers not to give their name.'

'I don't like mysteries.' Her eyes flashed and then narrowed. 'Give me the message and I'll pass it on.'

'Unfortunately, I promised to deliver it in person. I gave my word.' He dropped his gaze to her skirts. 'Stick or no stick.'

She stiffened, a crimson flush spreading up her neck and over her cheeks, bringing out the red in her hair until she almost seemed to glow like a beacon in front of him.

'A stick may be no match for a sword, but it could still hurt.' She brought the makeshift weapon out from behind her legs, her knuckles clenched tight around it.

Ben lifted an eyebrow, looking her up and down and then up again, faintly unnerved by her combative demeanour. Some degree of suspicion was natural, he could even admire her refusal to back down, but she struck him as overly defiant. What was she so afraid of?

'I'm not going to fight you, lady.'

'Then that gives me the advantage, don't you think?'

'Not if I ride around you.' He sighed as she immediately reached a hand out to grasp his bridle. 'All right, we'll do this your way. Give me some way to prove myself.'

'You say that you knew my father.' There was a note of challenge in her voice. 'Tell me something about him.'

'Very well. You look like him. You *don't* sound like him. He was a courtier, but he left court when he married your mother and retired here. As far as I know, he left home only a handful of times afterwards, usually when he was summoned by the King. How am I doing?'

'You could have learnt all of that from gossip. Tell me something personal.'

'Personal?' He rubbed a hand over his chin, admiring the tumble of russet curls over her shoulders as she tossed her head. Personal wasn't so easy. Robert Flemming hadn't exactly been a man for sharing confidences. Their few conversations had mostly been on subjects like the weather and livestock, although every so often a more intimate detail had crept in…

'Well?' She was already tapping her foot.

'I know!' He clicked his fingers triumphantly. 'I remember him telling me that you were born during a thunderstorm. It was a particularly wet year and nobody could travel. He said the roads were like rivers and there wasn't a single dry day until you were six months old. *And...*' he went on, warming to his theme '...for your eighth birthday, he had a chess set made from jet and amber. He said the two of you played every day.'

'Yes.' The suspicious light in her eyes dimmed, chased away by a sudden profound sadness. 'We did. Every evening until he died.' She dropped his bridle abruptly, twisting her face to one side. 'You can go. My mother's in the house, probably in the kitchens at this time of day.'

'Thank you.' He took up his reins again. 'May I escort you back there?'

'No.' Her voice was rough, as if she were struggling to speak at all.

'Well then...' He hesitated, reluctant to leave now that she looked and sounded so mournful. Apparently his talent for making women unhappy was stronger than ever. He'd spent barely five minutes with this one and already she seemed close to tears, which meant the kindest thing he could probably do was to leave her alone... 'It's been an honour to meet you at last, Annis Flemming.'

She made a dismissive sound and stepped aside, the branch still held tightly in her hand. She didn't wish him a good day.

Something was going to happen. Annis threw the stick aside and watched as the man dismounted and walked up to the intricately carved oak door of Cariscombe, though not before throwing one last look in her direction. Instinctively, she stepped sideways, concealing herself behind a tree. Men were trouble. That was what her mother had always taught her, although this one didn't seem like it. He'd said he was a friend and neighbour, but she'd never seen him before. She would have remembered. He was bigger and broader than any man she'd ever met, built like a bear with chestnut hair, a brooding expression and eyes so dark they were almost black. Definitely memorable. Most of the time, she gave little thought to her appearance, but something about him had made her acutely conscious of her tangled hair and ragged outdoor apparel.

Annoyingly, however, he'd been just as forthcoming as her mother, which was to say not at all, as if he were another part of the conspiracy of silence that hung over Cariscombe. It had been a month now since her father had collapsed suddenly one afternoon. She felt as though she'd been walking around in a fog the whole time, surrounded by dangers that everyone else could see, but that no one would talk about or explain, no matter how often or vociferously she asked. As if she were still a child in need of protection instead of an heiress who owned both the manor house and almost a hundred acres of land to the north.

Her mother was frightened, that much was obvious, and strange things had started to happen, too—first in the stables, where she'd noticed the grooms looking at her with half-hostile, half-fearful expressions, then in the house itself. A couple of days ago, the servants had started gathering in corners, whispering furtively together before leaving, usually at night and without any explanation, until only a handful remained. The last time she'd counted, there were only six people left in the hall altogether, herself and her mother included.

And now another strange thing was happening: this stranger's sudden arrival when visitors had always been so few and far between, bearing a message from a 'friend'. What friend?

She peered out from behind the tree, making sure it was safe to come out, before making her way along the dirt track that ran parallel to the road and through a gate into the apple and plum orchard at the side of the house. What had he called himself? Sir Bennet Thorne... If only she knew what his message was, but there was no point in trying to listen at doors. Margery, her mother's devoted attendant, would be standing guard as always, making sure that *she* was kept in ignorance.

Absently, she plucked a damson from a branch and sat down on the grass to suck out the juices. Perhaps she ought to have been more welcoming to Sir Bennet. If she'd been polite and flattered him then he might have given her a hint as to the contents of his message, but her nerves were strung too tight for good manners. And she wouldn't have known how to begin anyway. She hadn't met enough men in her life to know how to cajole them, and as for flirting... no doubt she would have made an even bigger fool of herself than she had by threatening to club him with a stick.

She winced at the memory and tossed the soggy damson stone aside, licking her fingers as she looked back at the hall. It was her home, the place where she'd woken every morning, eaten every meal, learnt every lesson, played every game and then gone to bed again for the past eighteen and a half years. She might have felt restless and frustrated there on occasion, wondering what lay beyond the village that marked the far edge of her travels, but she loved it, every archway and arrow slit and doorway. It was more than a house; it was her whole world, all that she needed. Until a month ago, she'd considered herself fortunate and happy.

Now, however, she was increasingly aware that her world, the one she'd always thought so safe and comfortable, was collapsing, beset by forces from outside. Her father's death had changed everything in ways she didn't understand but that seemed irreversible and inexorable. If she stared at the hall long and hard enough, she thought she might actually be able to see the turrets crumbling...

The sound of hoofbeats jolted her back to the present. Sir Bennet was already leaving, it seemed, mounting his horse, turning his back and riding away. Whatever his message had been, it hadn't taken long to deliver. What did that mean?

She pushed herself to her feet and gave her body a small shake, trying to rid herself of the dread that now plagued her every waking moment, but it was no use. The hollow, ominous feeling in her chest wouldn't be shaken away. Something was *definitely* going to happen. She could sense the tension in the air, as if an invisible rope was being slowly coiled and tightened, noose-like, around Cariscombe Hall and everyone inside. Unfortunately, she had no idea who was wielding the rope or what she could possibly do to stop it.

Worse than that, she had the horrible feeling that it was already too late.

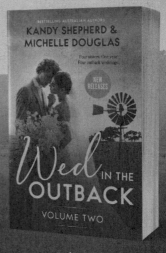

MILLS & BOON

Subscribe and fall in love with Mills & Boon series today!

You'll be among the first to read stories delivered to your door monthly and enjoy great savings.

WE SIMPLY LOVE ROMANCE